L/8/20

D1238767

BEAUTY AND THE MUSTACHE

KNITTING IN THE CITY #4

PENNY REID

Caped Publishing

Made in the United States of America

Second Edition: August 2014, June 2016

ISBN: 978-0-989281-09-6

DEDICATION

For Carl and Winnie
I love you in death as I loved you in life; to the stars and beyond, just
like always.

CHAPTER ONE

"There is no comfort anywhere for anyone who dreads to go home."

— LAURA INGALLS WILDER, LITTLE TOWN ON
THE PRAIRIE

*I*T WAS 6:14 A.M. and I was awake.

The engine revved for a third time—louder, longer, angrier.

I know an engine can't be angry, but this engine *sounded* angry. Specifically, it sounded angry with me. The engine must've been feeling pretty pissed in my general direction, because why else would it be waking me up after less than three hours of sleep?

But what the engine didn't know was that I was not afraid of its anger. I took crap from no engine, not anymore and especially not when the engine was under the control of one of my six brothers. Because now, I was a badass.

The only way one of them would be awake at 6:14 in the morning was if they'd never gone to sleep the night before.

Likely, they were either drunk or stoned or both.

Lovely. Just...lovely.

Good old boys revving their loud engines early in the morning was reason number thirty-three for why I never came home. I'd started making the list two days ago, when I'd decided that I had no choice but to fly to Tennessee.

Though I hadn't been home in eight years, my momma had visited me at college many times. Every year since I'd graduated four years ago with my BSN—a bachelor's degree in nursing—I'd taken her on a vacation with me, just the two of us.

But three days ago, she hadn't returned my call, nor had she picked up the phone when I'd called the next day. This was remarkable because she and I had spoken on the phone at the same time every day for the last eight years except for when we were together, of course. Our conversations didn't typically last very long, just a quick check-in to see if she needed anything, see how life was treating her. Sometimes she'd share gossip about people I'd grown up with, and sometimes I'd tell her about a new book I was reading.

Mostly, I think we just took comfort in the sound of each other's voices.

So after two days with no contact, I was worried. Finally, I resorted to calling Jethro, my oldest brother. He told me that Momma was in the hospital, and she was refusing to see or talk to anyone.

Therefore, I hopped a plane, intent on discovering the truth behind her mystery hospital visit. I was determined to take care of the woman who'd never failed to take care of me.

The car engine revved again. I growled, threw my covers off, and marched out my bedroom door. In my rush to rain a world of hurt on whoever was responsible for the early morning wakeup call, I slipped on the last three stairs leading to the first floor of my momma's house and cursed, almost falling flat on my ass. The resulting spike in adrenaline was rocket fuel to my irritation.

Gone was the girl from small-town Tennessee, mild mannered, sensitive, and ignorant youth that my brothers once knew. Before I left I'd just begun to fight back against their antics. Now I was a ninja of mind over matter. Whichever of my brothers was responsible for waking me up revving his hopped-up engine after I had endured a delayed, three-connection flight from Chicago to Tennessee was going to suffer.

Retribution. Revenge. Perhaps death. At the very least, someone was going to be the recipient of an epic titty-twister.

I flew out the front door and let the screen door slam behind me. I wasn't worried about waking anyone. If the inhabitants of the house could sleep through the ruckus coming from the garage then they could sleep through the banging of a porch door. Besides, the roosters were already holding a crowing contest.

Another thing I wasn't worried about was my state of undress. My family's property was situated on fifteen acres in the middle of Green Valley, otherwise known as podunk nowhere. It backed up to the Smoky Mountains National Park on the Tennessee side. If you didn't count all the cars on blocks, defunct trailers, old tires, rusted machine parts, and general trashy appearance of the grand old house and yard, it was actually a lovely spot.

Usually, my idiot brothers ran around half-dressed, so I paid no mind to the fact that I was in my pink tank top pajamas with matching sleep shorts. I was likely overdressed.

I avoided a pile of broken beer bottles on the path leading to the detached garage; really, it was more like a giant hanger. My mind told me that the structure was called a quonset hut and I told my mind to hush. I didn't care what it was called. I only cared that all of its inhabitants were soon going to be murdered by my hands. Then I would go back to sleep.

The sun was already up, which made the inside of the metal structure dark in contrast. Regardless, I could see the machine of my angst as I approached; it would have been impossible to miss.

Two male bodies leaned inside the open hood of an orange and white Charger. A third numbskull, currently hidden, was in the driver's seat revving the engine.

As was my custom, I was yelling before I'd made it to the garage. "I don't care which of you hillbilly, disease-infested, flea-bitten, catawampus-heads are in here making this ruckus, you better stop right this minute!"

Jethro turned as I approached and tugged his pants upward. As I suspected, I was overdressed. He wore nothing but his beard and a pair of stained jeans. Jethro's longish brown hair was askew and unkempt, like he'd just rolled out of bed, and his beard could do with a trim. But his brown eyes were warm and sharp as they surveyed me.

Billy, the second in our family, kept his back to me. I knew it was Billy because he had a tattoo on his left shoulder of a goat with the word *Billy* beneath it. He was likewise attired, which meant that his ass-crack was on full display for the sun in the sky and the small woodland animals in the forest.

Of my brothers, Billy and I look the most alike; we are almost replicas of my father. We both have dark brown hair that's almost black, blue eyes, and the same wide mouth with pillow lips, as my brother Duane used to say.

But where I was pale skinned and curvy, he was suntanned, muscled—presumably from manual labor—and tattooed.

"Well, hello gorgeous. When'd you get in? It must've been late." Jethro waved with grease stained hands, his white teeth a glaring contrast to his dark brown beard.

Billy called over his shoulder, "Why are you even up?" He sounded exasperated.

"Because you geniuses are out here testing decibel limits. I can't sleep through all the-"

Just then the engine revved again. The sound spiked, absorbing my words, and caused a new wave of aggravation.

"Argh! Which of you ugly idiots keeps doing that?" I guessed it was Cletus, the third oldest, behind the wheel. He was the sweetest, but also the least likely to comprehend the obvious.

I charged into the garage, nearly kicking over a quart of oil in my haste. I didn't care. I needed my sleep. I did not need an early morning of boys and their toys.

I began bellowing as soon as I crossed the threshold. "I swear to the god of moonshine, I am going to pinch your nipples straight off your chest!"

Without a second thought, I reached my hand in the open driver's side door of the charger and twisted the nipple within reach. I did this with relish, the gleefully vindictive kind, not the pickle kind. I also gripped the roof of the car with my other hand for leverage in case Cletus tried to push me away.

"Ow! What the…?"

A string of impressive expletives arose from the car. A large and powerful hand gripped mine and ripped it away from the male chest.

I gasped. This was for several reasons, not the least of which was that Cletus didn't know the equivalent word for *fuck* in Latin, nor did any of my brothers.

Therefore, this person whose nipple I'd just assaulted was most definitely not my brother Cletus.

A shot of adrenaline coursed down my spine, my eyes widened with shock, and I tried to unsuccessfully wrench my hand away. The fingers that held me were punishing; with one fluid motion the occupant stood from the driver's seat, twisted my arm behind my back, and brought my body flush against his.

He was breathing hard.

I was breathing harder.

I stared at him.

The occupant stared back.

Gray-blue eyes, almost silver, held mine in a vice grip of anger and surprise. I felt an electric bolt, like I'd been tazered in the stomach. Other than a very slight shadow of wonder, he wore an expression that would have made a thunderstorm proud.

As well, he was so ruggedly sexy I'm sure my mouth fell open to protest the unfairness of his existence. Luckily, no sound emerged. I was too busy oscillating between stunned, mortified, and turned on.

This man was definitely not one of my brothers.

First of all, this guy had a blond beard and a smattering of blond chest hair. All the Winston boys had dark brown beards except Duane and Beauford, who were twins. They were numbers five and six in the family and had ginger beards.

Also, this guy had a bronze tan. He was tan all over, like a grease stained surfer or a Viking marauder who spent all his time at sea shirtless.

And... what number was I on?

Oh yes. Third, he was the kind of expertly disheveled, ruggedly handsome that made me forget what number I was on.

He was massive. Like, six-foot-four huge. His chest and arms and stomach and shoulders were cut like a boulder; he felt stone hard.

The staring continued. I watched confusion war with fury as his glare devoured my face, lingered on my lips, and darted back to my eyes.

Unable to handle the intensity of his stare a moment longer, I blurted, "I'm so sorry!"

He blinked at me and shook his head once, quickly, as if I'd just appeared. He released my hand and stepped away as though touching me might burn him. "What the hell was that?"

I ripped my gaze from his and looked at his chest. It was a nice chest—a *very, very* nice chest—but his left nipple was red and angry. My nipple-wist marred the otherwise physical perfection of his chiseled torso. A small sound of dismay tumbled from my lips.

"Oh my God, I'm so sorry," I stammered, and I reached forward and petted the offended skin. "I never would have purpled your nurple if I'd known you weren't related to me. It's just that I was trying to sleep. Really, I should have known you weren't Cletus; he would have guessed my intentions a mile away and taken evasive maneuvers."

"Evasive maneuvers?"

I glanced up from where my fingers continued to caress his wounded nipple to his silver eyes, now a tad less thunderstormy, but a tad more cautiously.

I blinked at him, my breath seizing in my chest, and I completely lost my train of thought.

"What?"

The Viking's eyes looked directly into mine. After a short pause, he glanced down at his chest. I followed his glare to where my fingers were caressing his man-nipple. I flinched, yanked my hands away and balled them into fists between us.

"Sorry," I blurted again. "Sorry about twisting your nipple. Also sorry about petting it afterward. Furthermore, I'm sorry that I can't seem to stop talking...."

His eyes lowered to my feet then swept up my body in an unapologetic assessment, loitered on my bare calves and thighs for a minute, then dawdled on my chest.

"Who are you?" He asked my chest, sounding annoyed.

"Who am I?" I asked, because honestly—and I might lose my badass card for this—part of me had forgotten my name. Because he was the kind of ruggedly sexy that made me forget what number I was on and what my name was.

"Yeah, who are you?" His eyes finally met mine and he sounded even more annoyed. I could tell by his accent that he wasn't from Tennessee, though he had a distinct southern drawl. My brain told me it was Oklahoma or Texas.

"I...I'm Ashley Winston."

He sucked in a sharp breath, obviously surprised by my response. His frown was equal parts severe, confused, and angry from behind his unwieldy blond beard as he surveyed me.

Then he turned to Jethro. "You have a sister?"

The fact that the golden Viking had addressed my brother rather than me was a slap of sobriety, and I responded with mildly offended displeasure. "Yes they have a sister."

Jethro had followed me around the car when I charged into the quonset hut and he tipped his head in my direction. "Yep. That's Ash."

"I thought Ash was a boy." The handsome marauder said this like he was both shocked and upset, like he'd been misled, lured into our cluttered garage with trickery and deception.

"No. She's a girl." Billy bellowed from under the hood of the car.

The man's eyes swept up and down my body again, a flagrant scrutiny. He did not look pleased.

"Obviously." The blond stranger said, like he'd just tasted something sour.

In that moment, I finally figured out what kind of handsome he was. He was fiction-handsome. Romance novel handsome; but not the clean-cut (billionaire) alpha male or even the tattooed (billionaire) bad boy archetype.

He was the Scottish highlander, Viking conqueror, bodice-ripper historical romance kind of handsome; an unshaven, lion wrestling, mountain man recluse, toss you over his shoulder and plunder your goodies kind of handsome. He was both scary and swoony. I wanted to braid his beard. I also wanted to run away.

But his less than flattering expression was just the reality slap I needed to propel me out of my stupor. I finally saw beyond my initial stunned reaction to his rugged handsomeness, and my anger boiled over anew. I remembered that it was six-something in the morning, and this male specimen of fineness was the reason I was awake.

Handsome or not, it didn't matter. I decided he was a jackass.

I gave him my very best *you're not worth my time* glare even as I fought against a delayed blush of embarrassment. I wasn't sure if I was embarrassed because I'd just inflicted pain to his nipple then tried to pet it, or if I was flustered because he obviously found me repulsive.

Really, I'd ogled him. Then, amidst my ogling, he gave me the grossed-out stink-eye.

Suppressing these disturbing and uncomplimentary musings, I turned to Jethro. "Sorry about maiming your friend, but will you please tell him," I indicated the bearded stranger with a thumb over my shoulder, "to quit revving the engine at six fourteen in the morning, or else I'll remove this car's spark plug wires and lock you all out of the house."

Jethro sighed, but he was still smiling. Come to think on it, he was smiling a lot, which was not typical for him. "Come on, Ash. We need to be at work in two hours. Cut us a break."

I blinked at him and briefly considered that I might be dreaming. "You have a job?"

Jethro's smile dimmed, turned brittle. "Yes. I have a job, baby sister."

I felt the stern line of my mouth soften and the back of my neck heat with renewed embarrassment. I had been gone a long time, and I had no desire to insult or hurt anyone, least of all my brother. He'd never shown any outward concern for me growing up, but he was still my brother.

Billy poked his head around the hood of the car and glared at me. Even though I was younger than both of them, I'd been the only consistently responsible child of the seven Winston brood when we were growing up, and the only girl. My brothers had always seen me paradoxically as an authority figure and a doormat.

I imagined it was similar to how they viewed my mother.

I fought the jitteriness still plaguing me from the titty-twister tempest and took a calmer approach. "Look, my flight *just* got in at two this morning, and I've had less than three hours of sleep. I'm supposed to be at the hospital in Knoxville at eleven to find out what's going on with Momma." I sighed and put my hands on my hips. "I just need some sleep."

"Bethany is in the hospital?" This question came from the stranger. My back stiffened at his use of my mother's first name.

Billy walked to the side of the car and leaned against it. "When I came home two days ago, she'd left a note."

"What kind of note?" The Viking asked; I didn't want to notice but he had a delicious growly and authoritative quality to his voice.

Stupid growly commanding Texan Viking voice.

"She said she was sick and had to go to the hospital," Billy explained.

My throat tightened as my eyes moved to the cement floor of the garage. I suppressed the wave of worried panic. I reminded myself that I hadn't been home in a while, and maybe she was sick with the flu or just needed a vacation from the craziness that was living with my brothers. Maybe she was completely fine.

"I didn't know she was sick," the blond man said, coming to stand next to me, my shoulder at his bicep. In my peripheral vision, I noticed that he'd folded his arms across his sculpted chest, his right hand covering his left nipple.

"No one did," Billy said, looking straight at me. "Not even Ash," he added in a slightly sardonic tone.

"Why didn't you tell me? What exactly happened?" An unmistakable air of privilege and authority hung heavy around the stranger. "Start from the beginning," he demanded.

A gathering ache of frustration set up camp at the base of my neck. This man, this *unknown person*, sounded so entitled, as though he should be kept in the loop regarding what happened to my mother.

Maybe it was my lack of sleep; maybe it was the stress of not knowing what was going on with my mother; maybe it was because this man's sense of entitlement reminded me of every ivy-league ignoramus medical doctor I'd had to endure at my job in Chicago, but I had no patience for this behemoth at my shoulder despite his colossal handsomeness and the fact that I'd assaulted then molested his man-nipple.

I glared at his unkempt beard and longish blond hair, both of which annoyed me now, then shifted my stare to his silver eyes. "Why is this any of your business? And who the hell are you?"

Mr. Blond Beard considered me with impatience, as if I were gum on his shoe. I returned his malicious glower, as if he were gum in my hair.

I heard Jethro clear his throat, and I saw out of the corner of my eye that he gestured to the stranger with a greasy rag. "Ash, this is Drew Runous. He's my boss."

"Pleased to make your acquaintance, Miss Winston," he drawled, extending his hand in a show of ironic southern politeness, like older church ladies use when they say "bless your heart," and what they really mean is "you couldn't find your way out of a small shed with a map, lighted signs, and an escort."

But his face held no amount of pleasure. In fact, he looked positively aggravated by the audacity of my existence.

"Likewise, I'm sure." Ignoring his offered hand, I returned his ironic southern politeness with my own vitriol-laced volley.

When I'd left Tennessee eight years ago, Jethro's "job" was selling weed to vacationing teenagers then stealing their cars. I guessed that this self-important blond toolbox was likely in a similar trade.

I continued, "Your professional relationship with my brother notwithstanding, I'm certain even someone like you can recognize that this a personal family matter and is, quite frankly, none of your business."

Not waiting for his reaction, I turned back to Jethro. "Rev your engine all you like. I'm getting dressed and going to the hospital to see what I can find out."

I strolled out of the garage with my head held high and did my best to ignore the fact that I felt Drew's eyes—sure and hot as a brand—on my backside. This was accompanied by the unavoidable and spreading warmth in my chest associated with the awareness that a super-hot mountain of a man was watching me walk away.

I decided to overlook the knowledge that my hasty, arrogant dismissal of him was likely undermined by the fact that I was leaving in a snit while wearing nothing but my sleep shorts and pajama top. Also undermining my superiority was the fact that I'd just attacked his chest then fondled it. I'd even ogled him, and he'd responded with repulsion.

So…yeah, I didn't have much air in my sad little kite.

Once I was back in the house, the door behind me, I leaned against it and released a slow breath. My hands were fisted at my sides so I shook them out, flexing my fingers, and sent a silent prayer upward that whatever was going on with my momma was resolved sooner rather than later.

I climbed the stairs two at a time, holding the banister for balance, and crossed to the upstairs bathroom. I had no desire for any further interactions with Viking marauders, especially when the marauder was so good looking that it nearly eclipsed his entitled arrogance.

These were the thoughts in my head when I opened the bathroom door and, to my life-long horror, saw Beauford Winston—at least I think it was Beauford, though it could have been Duane, the other twin —standing at the edge of the tub. He was naked except for his ginger beard, a dirty magazine propped on the counter, and his hand wrapped around Beau Jr.

I screamed.

He screamed.

My hands flew to my face.

He cursed.

I heard a thud and I turned my back to him. I was now fully and mortifyingly awake.

"Shit, Ash. What the hell are you doing here?"

"Sorry, sorry, sorry—I should have knocked."

"Nah…" he huffed, "I should have locked the door. It's just that everyone knows Tuesday mornings are my time slot."

"Your slot? What do you mean your time slot?"

"It's my private time in the tub, you know, to get my rub on."

"Gah!" I shook my head and pressed my palms into my eyes.

"I can give you a copy of the schedule."

I heard the front door open and footsteps thundering through the house then up the stairs.

"Don't! Do *not* give me a schedule. I don't want to know. Just, can't you put a sock on the door or something?"

"That's what we used to do but then we kept losing socks. It's good to see you, Ash."

"Uh, you too…?" My hands fell away from my face and I moved to the doorway. "I'll just give you some privacy."

My escape was blocked by the worried visages of three shirtless, sweaty men—Jethro, Billy, and Drew Runous.

I closed my eyes and covered my face again; I seriously considered crawling into the cabinet under the bathroom sink, one of my favorite places to hide from my brothers' torture when I was a kid. I wondered if I would still fit.

"What the hell?" Jethro's winded exclamation met my ears, and I stifled a groan.

"Are you okay?" Billy asked. I felt a small, hesitant touch on my shoulder. "We heard screams."

I nodded. "Yes. Fine. I just need to learn to knock."

"Who screamed?" Drew demanded.

"I did," I said, inwardly grimacing.

"We heard two screams," Jethro contradicted. "Did you scream twice?"

"I didn't scream. I…I hollered." Beauford said.

"That wasn't a holler. That was a scream. You screamed like a woman." Billy said this like he was addressing a jury.

"Whatever, screamed, hollered, who cares. I should have locked the door." Beauford's easy-going tone made me feel a bit better. I didn't remember him being so nice. Then he said, "Oh, hey, Drew. Didn't see you there."

"Hey, Beau."

"What happened to your chest?" Beau asked.

I wished for the ability to disappear, especially when Drew responded, "Some woman couldn't keep her hands off me. What's going on in here?"

Beau didn't answer. The room was blanketed in a brief silence as, I was sure, understanding began to dawn.

Jethro was the one to break the awkward soundless comprehension. "Uh," He cleared his throat. "Tuesday mornings are Beau's time slot."

"I know that now," I peeked at them from between my fingers. "I'll just knock from now on."

"Do you want the schedule? We have a schedule." Billy's offer was paired with his thumb thrown over his shoulder, presumably pointing in the direction of where the schedule was kept.

"Nope, I'm good. I'll just knock."

The sound of barely suppressed laughter pulled my eyes to where entitled Drew stood in the hallway. His lips were compressed, rolled between his teeth, his big shoulders were shaking, and he stared at the floor like his life hung in the balance.

My mortification abruptly turned to irritation, then to fury.

Drew Runous and my brothers probably looked at me and saw the gullible little sister I used to be, not to mention the starry-eyed beauty queen I was in high school.

But I was now more than the accident of my genetics, more than the face and body I'd inherited from my parents, more than my back-woods Tennessee accent.

I wasn't that person anymore. I'd worked eight years to change and improve myself. I'd become someone new, someone stronger, armed with knowledge, fierce. I was someone who could hold her own in any situation, be it a discussion on post-modernism or Japanese art as an influence on Van Gogh; debating with an MD Harvard graduate when I disagreed on a course of treatment for one of my patients; or standing up to four bearded masturbators (obsessed with schedules, no less) in the upstairs bathroom of my momma's house.

In fact, I was *completely* different. I was a new person entirely.

"On second thought," I said, my hands dropping from my face, my spine straightening, "I will take that schedule."

Billy glanced over my shoulder to Beau then shot a look at Jethro. "Oh, okay. I'll get it for you."

"In fact," I crossed my arms over my chest and scowled at Drew the Amused Viking's persistent smile, "what days are free?"

Another stunned silence descended, and I noted with satisfaction that the marauder's grin fell as his eyes lifted to mine. They searched and burned. I knew, beyond a doubt, that he was imagining me in the bathroom naked, by myself, getting my rub on, as Beau put it. It was written all over his ruggedly handsome face.

Strangely enough, given our earlier encounter, he didn't look repulsed by the thought. Maybe he was just an equal-opportunity perv.

I refused to blush. I refused to appear even an ounce embarrassed.

Because he was staring at me—his gaze moving to my chest, then hips, then thighs—as though compelled to take mental notes. His eyes were hot and a little unfocused and, irritatingly enough, were making me feel hot and a little unfocused.

I couldn't conquer the thundering of my heart or the sudden twisting in my abdomen or the tingling awareness on the back of my neck. It was everything I could do to hide all the outward effects that his evocative, penetrating gaze elicited.

Instead, as Drew looked directly at me again, I slid my eyes over to Billy, who was staring at me like I was a three-headed possum.

"Uh, what?" Billy asked.

"Which days are free, on the schedule?"

Billy blinked at me and his voice cracked a little when he responded, "I think Sundays and Wednesdays, since Roscoe moved out. But you probably don't want Wednesdays."

"Why not?"

"Because that's usually when the new magazines show up in the mail."

I fought the urge to grimace. Instead, I nodded once and gave him a tightlipped smile. "Good. Put me down for Sundays. There's no postal service on Sundays."

Beau groaned, which he turned into an overly dramatic gagging sound. "Things I never needed to know about my sister."

With that, I strolled down the hallway to my room, pointedly *not* looking at the physical manifestation of every bodice-ripper hero I'd ever read. Like before, I felt the weight and heat of his gaze on my backside.

Once inside, door shut (and locked), I crossed to my bed and flopped down on my stomach. I willed the tingling and twisting heat that had taken up residence there to stop post haste.

I made three mental notes:

One: Always knock on every door, every room, every time. Drag my feet and bang pots and pans down the halls. This is not a house to be a ninja in.

Two: Never be alone with Drew Runous.

Three: Do everything in my power to leave before Sunday.

CHAPTER TWO

"The only true wisdom is in knowing you know nothing."

— SOCRATES

$\mathcal{T}$HE DRIVE FROM my momma's house to Knoxville took just under an hour. Lucidity was made possible by the triple-shot grande Americano I procured from Starbucks on my way out of town.

It's really true what people say about Starbucks. My hometown still didn't have a sit-down movie theater, an Italian restaurant, an OBGYN, or a Target, but they had a Starbucks. I guessed this was because Green Valley was located right next to the Great Smoky Mountains National Park. Our two main industries were lumber and tourism, and big-city tourists need their coffee.

When I made it to Knoxville, I stopped at a grocery store and picked up flowers and two get-well balloons with kittens on them. I knew based on several years of practical experience as a pediatric intensive care nurse in Chicago that unless my momma wanted to talk to me, getting near her or her doctors was going to be difficult. The flowers and balloons would give me credibility, but the kittens would get me in the door. Everyone loves kittens.

I parked the rental car in a visitor's spot and walked into the main entrance, flowers and balloons in hand. Once inside, I crossed to the information desk, I hoped it was being run by volunteers, who tend to be easily confused by pesky things like HIPAA (privacy laws).

"Hello, Joan." I said with a warm smile at the elderly woman behind the desk; her nametag was prominently placed, thank goodness. "I'm here to see my mother. I just flew in last night, and I'm not sure where I'm going."

She returned my smile. "What is her name, dear?"

"Bethany Winston. Admission date was two days ago, if that helps." My throat felt tight with anticipation.

Jethro, Billy, and the twins (Beauford and Duane) had all tried and failed to see her over the course of the last two days. They'd been told she didn't want to see any family and had restricted access to her records. This had struck me as a little odd, yet not out of the realm of possibility.

Tired though I was, I started forming a plan B, just in case I was denied information on my momma's location.

Plan C involved going floor to floor, room to room. Plan D involved dressing in scrubs and logging into the hospital electronic medical record. Plan E involved pulling the fire alarm.

Joan glanced up from her screen, her smile still friendly though not as wide. "You're her daughter?"

"That's right," I managed to say, nodding emphatically as I held my breath and hoped Plan A would be sufficient.

"Do you have ID?"

I nodded again, set the flowers on the counter along with the balloon weights, and dug around in my purse for my ID. I handed it to her and waited, searching her face for clues as to how successful I would be.

She glanced at my ID, then at the screen, then at my face, then at the screen, then at my ID, then at my face.

She handed the ID back to me. "Your mother's record has been flagged. There's a note that she's not to have any visitors other than you. I'm going to page her treating physician, but he may be a while."

I released the breath I'd been holding. "Okay, thanks. That's great. Can I go up?"

"Yes. She's on the fourth floor. You'll need to take those elevators." She pointed around the corner. "Check in at the nurses' station. They'll want to see your ID too."

I thanked her and placed my driver's license in my pocket with slightly trembling hands.

As I made my way to the elevator, I couldn't help but feel like everything was very, very wrong. I knew that it was a common practice to flag patients' records, especially to keep out unwanted family members or the media. My momma's decision to restrict access to her records struck an off chord.

My brothers lived with my mother. She took care of them. Even Jethro, the oldest, now thirty, still lived at home.

I briefly considered that she might be embarrassed. Perhaps she wanted to keep her diagnosis a secret because she didn't want to admit weakness in front of the six Winston boys. I didn't blame her. Winston men were famous for exploiting weakness.

I knew she loved them, but they drove her crazy. When I lived at home, they—as a group—had a tendency to freak out when faced with facts or reality, yet happily buried their heads in the sand otherwise. Until facts were spelled out, they were like unsuspecting hogs before Easter dinner—dirty and well fed.

I checked in at the nurses' station on the fourth floor and received a similar inspection. This time, however, when the nurse heard my last name, her smile fell and I read sympathy in her expression.

"She's in room 404, hon," she said, handing back my ID and glancing at the kitten balloons. Her voice was hesitant when she added, "Have you talked to the doctor yet?"

I shook my head, my trembling hands now shaking. "No. Not yet."

The nurse gave me a close-lipped smile. "Your momma's asleep right now. If you want to go sit with her 'til Dr. Gonzalez arrives, you can." Her tone was full of compassion.

"Can you tell me anything?" Without waiting for a reply, I added, "Why was she admitted?"

The nurse studied me for a minute but said nothing.

"I'm a pediatric nurse practitioner in Chicago," I said. "You can shoot straight with me."

Her smile returned. "I know, baby. Your mother told me all about you. But the doctor wants to speak with you first."

I stared at her for a moment—the compassion, the sympathy, the secrecy—and I knew.

This was textbook *modus operandi* for the terminally ill. Nurses never informed patients' families. It was always the doctor, and it was always done in person.

My eyes stung and I felt my chin wobble even as I bravely nodded. "Okay," I managed to croak, and I glanced at the ceiling, blinking. My head was overwhelmed and my heart was breaking, and I was still holding two *Get Well Soon* kitten balloons from the Piggly Wiggly.

"Aww, baby...." The nurse stood, walked around the counter, and wrapped her arms around me. "Baby, baby, baby...." Her soft body was a big pillow of warmth as she rubbed my back.

I sniffled, fighting the tears. *Not yet,* I thought, *not until I'm alone and can break something that makes a very gratifying smashing sound, like plates.*

"Come with me, Sunshine." She shifted so that her arm was wrapped around my shoulders. "I'll take you to your momma. You sit with her until the doctor comes, okay?"

I nodded numbly, allowing the older nurse to steer me to my mother's room. She opened the door and walked me to a seat by the bed. Sunlight streamed in through the open curtains, but it was still a hospital room. There was nothing remarkable about it other than the occupant.

I looked at my momma. Her eyes were closed. Her skin color was okay—not great, but not ashen—and she looked very thin, almost fragile. My mother had never been thin a day in her life. She'd been blessed with more boobs and hips than wits, and she had a lot of wits.

At five feet nine inches, I towered over her five-foot frame. Although I'd inherited her boobs and hips, my longer legs and torso distributed the wealth, whereas she'd always looked like a curvaceous, compact hourglass.

Her hair was streaked with gray. The last time I saw her she was still coloring it chestnut brown. My brain informed me that was two years ago.

My momma had always seemed young to me. She had Jethro at sixteen, Billy at seventeen, Cletus at eighteen, and me at twenty. The twins came two years later, and Roscoe—the youngest—arrived approximately four years after that. Seven children before she was twenty-seven, and six of them boys.

Now, thin and gray, she looked older than her forty-six years. She looked ancient, like all the stress and worry and hardship she'd shouldered raising a family of seven and handling my deadbeat father had finally caught up with her.

As instructed, I sat in the chair by her bed. The nurse reassured me once again that she would page the doctor, and then she left me alone with my momma.

I couldn't focus on anything. I don't know how long I sat looking around the room staring at nothing, unable to form a complete thought; maybe an hour, maybe more.

Images and sound bites from my childhood, of her care and love for me, of our daily telephone calls, lobbied for attention, and my mind felt slippery and confused.

My mother shifted, and my gaze was drawn to her as she opened her eyes. They fell on mine immediately.

"Ash…." she whispered. She gave me a weak smile. "Be a good darling and get me some ice cream. I'd give my eye teeth for some ice cream."

I watched her for a minute.

Ice cream—I could get her ice cream. That was something I could do. Because under no circumstances was I ready to talk about her death. Instead, I would go get her ice cream.

"Rocky road?" I asked quietly.

"If you can find it, though I'm not picky."

I nodded once and stood, moving to the door.

"Honey," she called after me. I turned and met her eyes, which were alight with amusement. "You can leave the flowers and balloons here. No need to take them with you."

I glanced from her to the balloons and flowers still clutched in my hands.

"Oh." I put them on the chair where I'd been sitting.

I'd almost made it to the door before she called me back again, "Ashley, one more thing. This is really important." The urgency I heard in her voice made my heart rate spike and my eyes sting.

I crossed to her immediately and covered her hand with mine. "Anything…you can tell me anything."

She gave me a weak smile, squeezed my hand with hers, and said, "This isn't something you need to worry about yet. But when the time comes you should use hemorrhoid cream to remove bags under the eyes."

DR. GONZALEZ FOUND me coming back from the cafeteria, my momma's rocky road ice cream clutched to my chest. He pulled me into a consultation room and broke the news I'd already guessed.

My mother was dying.

She had cervical cancer. It was stage four. It had metastasized everywhere. He gave her six weeks. Hospice had been called, and they were on their way.

She'd either ignored or confused the symptoms with menopause. He said she'd likely had symptoms for more than a year. I was not surprised that she'd disregarded her own pain. Her selflessness was her greatest strength and her most infuriating fault.

When I was sixteen, she'd walked around on a broken foot for two weeks. She finally went to the doctor when I handcuffed her to Billy's truck and drove her to the emergency room.

After the chat with Dr. Gonzalez, I delivered my momma's ice cream. Not long after that, the social worker for hospice arrived and spoke to us both. The entire experience was surreal.

My mother ate her ice cream and chimed in every once in a while with, "Now, I don't want anyone to go to any trouble on my account."

I could only stare at her. Words failed me. Thought and motor skills were also failing me.

It was decided that she would be released tomorrow and given transport back to the house. We would be assigned a day and a night nurse who would help us care for her over the next six weeks or so.

Six weeks.

I stayed for the rest of the day. We chatted about my job and her coworker friends at the library. She asked me to break the news first to her boss, Ms. Macintyre. Momma felt confident that Ms. Macintyre would know what to do about the rest of the staff.

I stumbled out of the hospital around 9:30 p.m. feeling exhausted and empty. My brain whispered to me as I walked to my car that the only thing I'd consumed that day was a triple-grande Americano at 7:00 a.m.

I wasn't hungry, though. I was the opposite of hungry, but neither full nor satiated.

I slipped into the driver's seat and stared unseeingly out the windshield, and was pulled from my trance by the sound of my cell phone ringing. I glanced at the caller ID. It was my friend Sandra, my *best* friend Sandra.

Relief and a tangible feeling I couldn't name seized my body, a pain so sharp that I gasped. It felt like the glass chamber that had surrounded me all day had finally shattered. I was suddenly breathing, and the air that filled my lungs hurt. The photo of Sandra's smiling face on my phone blurred, or rather my vision blurred because I was crying. I swiped my thumb across the screen and brought the phone to my ear.

"Hello?"

"Ashley! Thank God, you answered. Marie and I need you to settle a debate. Which is worse: not having enough yarn to finish a sweater or discovering that the yarn you used for the sweater was mislabeled as cashmere and is actually one hundred percent acrylic?"

My brain told me that it was Tuesday, which meant that back in

23

Chicago where I lived and worked and had a lovely life reading books and enjoying my friends, it was knitting group night. Sandra, a pediatric psychiatrist with a pervy heart of gold, was in my knitting group, as was Marie.

"Sandra...." My voice broke, and I rested my head against the steering wheel, tears falling messy and hot down my cheeks and neck and nose.

"Oh! Oh, my darling...." Sandra's voice emerged from the other end earnest and alarmed. "What's going on? Are you okay? What happened? Who made you cry? Do I need to kill someone? Tell me what to do."

I sniffled, squeezed my eyes shut against the new wave of tears. "It's my mother." I pressed my lips together in an effort to control my voice, then took a shaky breath and said, "She's dying."

"Your mother is dying?"

"They've called hospice. She has stage four cervical cancer. It's metastasized everywhere. She has six weeks...." I sobbed, almost dropping the phone and shaking my head against the new onslaught of tears.

The other end was quiet for a beat. "Okay...where are you? I can be there by tomorrow."

I shook my head. "No." I sniffed and wiped my hand under my nose then took a deep breath. "No, no. Don't do that. I just...I just needed to tell someone. I'm leaving the hospital now."

"Are you in Knoxville?"

"Sandra...." I covered my eyes with my hand and sighed. "You are not flying down here."

"Yes. I am flying down there."

"So am I!" I heard Elizabeth's voice from the other end. Elizabeth was also in my knitting group and was an emergency department physician. She worked with both Sandra and me at the hospital in Chicago.

Their threat to fly down to Tennessee sobered me, and I gathered a series of calming breaths before responding. "She's at the hospital in Knoxville. They're releasing her to home hospice tomorrow."

I related the rest of the facts surrounding my mother's sudden hospital admission, how she hadn't told anyone she was sick, how she'd ignored all the signs and symptoms until it was too late. Reciting the details calmed me. By the time I was finished, the tears had receded.

"Oh, honey." Sandra's impossibly kind and empathetic voice soothed me from the other end of the line.

"Tell her I found tickets," Elizabeth said in the background. "We can leave first thing tomorrow."

A disbelieving laugh tumbled from my lips. "You can't just drop everything and rush down here."

"Yes, we can. We'll see you tomorrow." I heard Sandra say, "I want the aisle seat." It was muffled, as if she'd covered the phone with her hand.

I heard a rustle and then Elizabeth's voice was in my ear. She'd obviously commandeered the phone from Sandra. "Honey, listen. Sandra and I will be there tomorrow. Just text Sandra your home address. Don't worry about anything. We'll stay in a hotel and help you get your mother settled. Where are you going now? Is anyone there with you? One of your brothers?"

"No. I'm on my way back to the house now to tell them the news."

Elizabeth *tsked* softly. "Oh, my dear friend, I wish we were already there. We would huddle hug and get drunk."

"Me too," I admitted, grateful that there were people in the world who loved me. I didn't have the strength to argue against their generous offer, so I simply said, "Thank you."

"No need for thanks. We'll see you soon."

I nodded, and my eyes watered again as I clicked off the call, but I blinked the wetness away. I needed to pull myself together. I needed to tell six boys that their momma was dying, and I had no idea how they were going to take the news.

After eight years with barely any contact, my brothers were basically strangers.

CHAPTER THREE

"Death is a vey dull, dreary affair, and my advice to you is to have nothing whatsoever to do with it."

— W. SOMERSET MAUGHAM

IMAGINED THAT this was what Snow White must've felt like when she woke up in the presence of the seven dwarves.

Seven hovering beards.

Seven sets of bewildered eyes.

Seven inquisitive expressions—partly suspicious, partly amused.

The fainting was my fault.

I drove home from the hospital in a daze. I walked to the front porch. Jethro came out of the house trailed by several others. I glanced over his shoulder. The world went black.

I should have known better. I was a nurse for hootenanny's sake! Two hours of sleep, no food, intense levels of stress; no wonder I passed out. I was lucky to have made it home without crashing my car. I'd never been in a position of forgetting to eat before.

Now I was laid out on the couch in my momma's house surrounded by a sea of beards. I heard the roosters in the back crowing up a fuss.

My brothers' expressions were varying degrees of anxious and curious. At last, my eyes settled on the measured, silvery blue stare of a stranger. My brain told me that this stranger's name was Drew Runous, that he was a pillaging Viking highlander laird, and that earlier in the day he'd mentally pictured me getting my rub on.

Drew was sitting next to where I lay on the couch, leaning over me, one arm braced to the side and his hand at my temple.

That's when the fuzzy-headedness began to retreat.

"What are you doing here?" I asked him groggily, placing my hand to my forehead as I tried to sit upright.

"Don't do that." He pushed my shoulders back to the couch. The hand at my temple moved to my wrist, his index and middle finger pressing against my pulse point. "You fainted. You need to take it slow."

"Listen to him, Ash. He's a doctor." I recognized the voice of my third brother. I turned to see sweet and anomalous Cletus just as he brushed a strand of hair from my face. He gazed at me with kind hazel eyes. "It's good to see you, baby sister."

I gave him a small smile. I hadn't seen him in eight years. An unexpected wave of nostalgia rushed over me. I ignored the tears stinging my eyes and responded, "You too, big brother."

"I'm not that kind of doctor," Drew said quietly, and my attention moved back to him.

"What?"

His stern face and gray-blue gaze focused on me. "I'm not a medical doctor."

I blinked at him and his bewitching eyes. "Okay...."

"But you said you was a doctor." Cletus glanced between him and Jethro.

"He is a doctor, just not that kind." Jethro placed his hand on Cletus's shoulder and spoke softly.

"What kind?" Cletus asked.

"He's a PhD. It's like being an expert in something. He doesn't do the people medical stuff."

"I know what a PhD is," Cletus mumbled.

"Fine, you know what a PhD is," Billy said to Cletus, but his stare was affixed to me. "What's wrong with you, Ash? Are you sick? Did you see Momma?"

I looked from Billy to Cletus to Jethro, and the events of the day —*Get Well Soon* balloons, the compassionate nurse at the hospital, rocky road ice cream, speaking with the social worker—crashed over me. I felt like I was being sucked into a vacuum cleaner. The world was eating me and screaming in my ears at the same time. I gasped, closed my eyes against the onslaught, and pressed my hand to my forehead.

"Crap..."

"What is it?" Jethro's voice was closer. "What happened at the hospital?"

I gathered a deep breath, held it within my lungs. When I was sure I wouldn't cry, I released it and opened my eyes. They found Drew's first. Inexplicably, maybe because he wasn't family and my dislike for him still lingered, I discovered that the words didn't strangle me as I spoke.

"I saw Momma," I said, "and I spoke to her doctor. She has cancer. It's real bad."

A stunned quiet fell over the room like fluttering snowflakes blanketing a field. It was a soft silence, reverent, and the air felt cold and hollow. I didn't see my brothers' reactions because my attention was still fixed on the stranger hovering above me.

Drew's hand on my wrist gripped tighter, and his eyes flared with some emotion I didn't have enough energy to decipher.

I ignored all this and continued to address him as though he were the only person in the room. "The doctor is sending her home tomorrow with hospice. He says she's got six weeks...or so."

"Six weeks....?" Jethro's voice broke through my self-imposed trance, and my attention flickered to him. He turned away and walked to the recliner at the end of the couch. He sat down heavily, his elbows on his knees, his head in his hands. "Six weeks."

I glanced at the other five Winston boys. They appeared to be equally shocked and dismayed, and my gaze snagged on my youngest brother, Roscoe. The last time I'd seen him in person he was twelve. He was now twenty.

"This doesn't make any sense," he said, glancing around the room as if it would give him answers. "How can she have cancer? She wasn't even sick."

I had no words to offer, so I stared at the ceiling making a mental list of all the things I needed to do before she arrived the next day.

"What can I do to help?" Drew's voice, now gentle and solicitous, pulled me out of my head and back to the scene of quiet chaos in the living room.

I shrugged and my vision blurred again with tears. They leaked from the corners of my eyes.

"Pray," I said, because it was the only thing anyone could do.

I recognized the frustration etched in his features; it betrayed the helplessness he so obviously felt. However, the last thing I expected him to do was lean forward, hold my cheeks in his palms, and place a soft, lingering kiss on my forehead while his unwieldy beard tickled my nose.

Therefore, when that was what Drew did, I was so astonished that I stopped crying.

He retreated, his hands still cupping my face, and his thumbs wiping away my tears. Drew threaded the fingers of one hand through the hair at my temple and brushed it away from my shoulders. Then, bringing his palm back to my cheek, he said softly, "I'll see you in the morning."

I stared at him bemused and not so far removed by the insanity of grief and low blood sugar to recognize that Drew was an odd possum. "Uh, okay."

Drew studied me, his gaze intent and as serious as a thundercloud. I watched him and imagined my expression mirrored that of a deer frozen in approaching headlights. His mouth hooked upward, though his eyes remained solemn.

"Ash is short for Ashley...." I guessed he was speaking to himself, because it emerged as though he were voicing a secret or a private joke.

So…still odd.

My hands moved to where he continued to frame my face, and I wrapped my fingers around his much larger ones. "That's right." I nodded as I held him. "Ash is short for Ashley. Is Drew short for Andrew?"

He blinked and looked startled. His hands stiffened, and he pulled them out of my grip, sitting straight for a short moment before standing. He was up, up, up, and away—tall like a tower or a great tree, or a mountain.

Drew was no longer looking at me. In fact, he was looking everywhere *but* at me. Through my perplexed misery-riddled daze, I thought he might have been a smidge discomfited by his forward behavior. As it was, given the day's events, his discomfiture and oddness made very little impact on my mental state.

I watched numbly as he picked up a leather-bound notebook from the coffee table and turned to Beauford; he whispered something in the twin's ear. Beau's eyes, rimmed with shock and emotion, met mine, and he nodded. Beau moved from Drew, motioned to Duane, and crossed to me.

"Okay, big sister, upsy daisy." Beau leaned down and gave me a wobbly smile. Before I could comprehend what he was about, he lifted me in his arms like I was a feather. "You need food and sleep. Drew is fixin' to cook you something good, and I'm carrying you to your room."

I opened my mouth to protest that I could walk, but Duane hushed me as he led the way upstairs. "Don't worry about nothing. We'll all be here when you wake up. You can boss us as much as you like in the morning."

Duane flipped on the light in my room and began straightening the bed, fluffing the pillow, and turning down the blanket. Beau set me on the floor next to the foot of the bed and wrapped me in his big arms.

"We missed you, Ash." His voice was watery, though I seriously doubted he would actually cry.

Duane joined us and hugged me from behind. "I'm sorry I put

maggots in your macaroni and cheese. I've wanted to tell you that for a long time."

Then Beau said, "And I'm sorry we used to hold you down and spit in your mouth."

"Ugh! Gross, Beau." I gagged a little. "I'd forgotten about that."

The memories stirred something in me. The severity of the twins' acts of torment was nothing in comparison to the frequency. They had launched volleys at me daily, hourly, whenever I was at home. I'd never thought of them as particularly lovable because my earliest memories involved their constant assaults.

I tried to reach out to my brothers while I was in college to form some kind of sisterly bond with them on a more grown-up level. In return, they showed up at my dorm room stoned, behaved like criminals, and hid buckets of freshly slaughtered pigs' feet in my friends' rooms. It took weeks for us to find them all.

I didn't know what to think about all that now. I *tsked* and laughed at the absurdity of the moment, the apology for things that happened years ago, yet it wasn't that absurd. Their wild behavior had kept us in limbo for eight years.

Too tired to talk, I lifted my arms to hug my brothers. We stood together for several moments then Beau and Duane pulled away. Beau held my gaze—his eyes still glassy—then he took a step back.

"You need anything, we're right next door."

"That's right, anything at all." Duane put his hand on Beau's shoulder. "But you might want to knock first."

He hadn't meant it as a joke. It was a sober warning meant to save me from embarrassment. Too late.

Beau closed his eyes, gave his head a subtle shake, and pushed Duane toward the door. "You're a dummy."

"What? What did I say?" Duane said, glancing between his twin and me.

"Just keep walking, dummy." Beau's eyes flickered to mine, apologetic and irritated, then he managed to guide his twin the rest of the way, closing the door behind them.

I went through the motions of putting on my pajamas and brushing my hair, thinking about not much, but what I thought about was on the spin cycle, and it was making me dizzy. So I sat on my bed and stared into the mirror.

I had bags under my eyes. In the morning, I would have to go hunting for hemorrhoid cream. Or I could just not care. I decided not to care.

I heard a knock followed by my door creaking open.

"Are you decent?" Jethro's voice sounded from the hallway.

"Yes. Come in."

He pushed his way into my room using his elbows because his hands were full. He held a plate in one hand with a grilled cheese and tomato sandwich on it, and a cup of tea in the other that smelled like lemon, peppermint, and bourbon.

"Food," he said, placing everything on the nightstand.

I glanced at the sandwich and tea, but made no response.

"Come on now, you need to eat." Jethro picked up the plate and sat next to me. "Doctor's orders."

My eyes flickered to my brother then to the perfectly grilled cheese sandwich. I took it. Took a bite. Chewed. Swallowed.

He passed me the tea. "Now drink."

I squinted at him. "This has bourbon in it."

"Yes, it does. Good, Tennessee bourbon, guaranteed to make the pain go away. Drink it."

Making the pain go away sounded pretty good, so I took a sip. It was warm, not hot, and tasted like bourbon and honey. I took a larger gulp then followed it with another bite of my sandwich.

"Thank you," I said; the warmth of the alcohol spread down my throat to my chest.

"Don't thank me. Thank Drew. He made all this."

I studied Jethro for another moment, took a bite of my sandwich. I debated whether I wanted to have this conversation at all, let alone now. In the end, I gave in to both curiosity and avoidance of heavier subjects.

"So...Drew. Who is this guy?"

"He's my boss."

"What does he do?"

"He's the federal game warden for this stretch of the park."

I frowned, not sure what a game warden was, so I asked. "What's that? Like a park ranger?" I followed this question with another large gulp of my tea-laced bourbon.

"Uh, no. He's not a park ranger. Game wardens are law enforcement officers. Most are employed by the state they work in. Drew is federal law enforcement. He was appointed to the Great Smokies by some big-wigs in Washington."

I watched Jethro as I bit, chewed, swallowed, repeat; I thought about this information. At least I tried to think about this information. The bourbon plus no sleep plus no food all day plus news of my mother's terminal diagnosis were all battling for dominance, Mad Max style, in my brain cage.

"Federal law enforcement." I shook my head hoping to clear it. "What does that mean in terms of a national park? And why was he appointed? And how come he's here? And how does he know Momma?"

Jethro nodded toward my tea and waited until I drank before responding. "Well, him being a game warden and a federal officer... what that means is that he's some kind of big shot, PhD guy sent down from Washington to keep the park safe. And I think he was appointed because he's an expert in endangered wildlife. He's here tonight because I asked him to stay just in case you had news when you got home from the hospital. And he met Momma at the library when he was appointed to his position at the park. They're friends."

I had trouble believing a few of his assertions. First, Drew "Mountain-of-a-Man" Runous did not strike me as a Dr. Runous unless his PhD was in lumberjacking or plundering or beard growing or headlining in sexy daydreams and dirty fantasies. Secondly, Dr. Runous's posture of entitlement this morning and odd possum behavior tonight made me question what kind of friends he was with Momma.

My eyes weren't cooperating; I couldn't keep them both open, so I peered at Jethro through my left eye. "What kind of *friends*?"

Even through one eye, I could see that Jethro was scowling at me.

"Nothing like that, Ash. Get your mind out of the gutter. He's one of us. He's like a son to her and a brother to all of us. For God's sake, he's a year younger than me. Plus he's not like that."

"Not like what?"

"He's…shy, I think. Quiet. He doesn't talk much, not even to me."

"He doesn't seem quiet to me, and he looks like he'd be a playboy, impregnating all the local girls with Viking babies."

"You have a wild imagination, sis. I think he's just the opposite. In fact, I'm not one to tell stories, but I think he might be celibate."

That got both my eyes open.

"We've all tried to hook him up, but he won't even go to the bar with us."

"Maybe he doesn't drink."

"No, he drinks. We've tossed back beer and whiskey from time to time. He just doesn't socialize much. And he's definitely not interested in Momma, so get that thought out of your head."

I shrugged. "Well, how am I supposed to know? He called her Bethany. And he's hanging around here, and he cooks, and he kissed my forehead, and his beard tickles, and…and he looks like a Viking."

Jethro frowned at me. "You're drunk. You need to eat more of that sandwich."

Instead, I sipped the bourbon and forced my eyes to focus on Jethro, who was looking blurrier by the minute. "What could Drew and Momma possibly have in common?"

"They talk about poetry, books, meaning of life stuff. He's always bringing her books. I think they like the same kind of stuff. He's got that PhD, and Momma, you know she always wanted to go to college."

I nodded because I did know. I did know that she always wanted to go to college.

But I was tempted to shake my head because I couldn't reconcile the image of Drew and Momma reading poetry together. This was partly because *I* used to read poetry with her. This was also partly because my first impression of Drew told me that he only read magazines related to guns, cars, naked ladies, and facial hair.

I finished half of the sandwich and washed it down with the rest of the tea.

"I need to sleep," I said, swaying a little.

"What about brushing your teeth?" This was an unexpected question coming from Jethro, not because he lacked appropriate dental care. In fact, he had lovely teeth. It was unexpected because it verged on nurturing.

My eyes were closed, and this time neither of them would be opening for several hours. "No…can't…must…sleep."

I fell backward against the pillow, already half passed out. I wasn't fully conscious when Jethro lifted my legs onto the bed, pulled back the covers, and tucked me in. But I did surface long enough to feel his kiss on my cheek, his hand squeezing my shoulder, and to hear him whisper something about sweet dreams before he flicked off the light and closed the door.

CHAPTER FOUR

"Woman's love involves injustice and blindness against everything that she does not love.... Woman is not yet capable of friendship: women are still cats and birds, or at best cows."

— FRIEDRICH NIETZSCHE

UANE DIDN'T LOCK the second floor bathroom door.

Therefore, upon waking, stumbling out of bed, tucking my toiletry bag under my arm, and shuffling to the bathroom, I had another lesson in the importance of knocking. The interaction also negated any need I might have had for caffeine to bring me fully awake.

He screamed.

I gasped then growled and grumbled as I marched out of the bathroom. "Is this all you boys do? Hide in the upstairs bathroom? Get a hobby for hootenanny's sake!"

I didn't bother to shut the door behind me. Instead, I raced down the steps to the first floor and used the bathroom under the stairs. When I was finished with my morning routine, I tucked my toiletries behind the sink and stared at my reflection in the mirror.

Really, I was fighting the urge to run back upstairs and read. I did this by giving myself a stern stink-eye.

Reading, for me, was like breathing. It was probably akin to masturbation for my brain. Getting off on the fantasy within the pages of a good novel felt necessary to my survival. If I wasn't asleep, knitting, or working, I was reading. This was for several reasons, all of them focused around the infinitely superior and enviable lives of fictional heroines to real-life people.

Take romance for instance. Fictional women in romance novels never get their period. They never have morning breath. They orgasm seventeen times a day. And they never seem to have jobs with bosses.

These clean, well-satisfied, perma-minty-breathed women have fulfilling careers as florists, bakery owners, hair stylists, or some other kind of adorable small business where they decorate all day. If they do have a boss, he's a cool guy (or gal) who's invested in the woman's love life. Or, he's a super hot billionaire trying to get in her pants.

My boss cares about two things: Am I on time? Are all my patients alive and well at the end of my shift?

And the men in romance novels are too good to be true; but I love it, and I love them. Enter stage right the independently wealthy venture capitalist suffering from the ennui of perfection until a plucky interior decorator enters stage left and shakes up his life and his heart with perky catch phrases and a cute nose that wrinkles when she sneezes.

I suck at decorating. The walls of my apartment are bare. I am allergic to most store-bought flowers. If I owned a bakery, I'd be broke and weigh seven hundred pounds, because I love cake.

I thought longingly of my eReader upstairs in my room. I hadn't read since the day before yesterday, and that was on the plane.

What I needed to do was face my brood of brothers and figure out next steps.

What I wanted to do was hide in my room with my latest novel and escape into a world without bearded, masturbating hillbillies, and a world where my beloved mother wasn't dying.

In the end, I surrendered to reality and made my way to the kitchen in search of coffee. I hoped at least one or two of them would be up. I hoped maybe I might persuade the others to have a family meeting sometime in the afternoon.

However, the scene that greeted me in the kitchen was surprising. Heck, it was downright baffling.

Roscoe, my youngest brother, was standing at our old gas stove making omelets. He was showered and dressed in jeans, a T-shirt, and tennis shoes, all of which appeared to be in good order. I hadn't really noticed much last night after my fainting spell, but now I saw that Roscoe wore his brown beard trimmed close to his face, the hair on his head cut short and stylish. In fact, it looked as if his hair had *product* in it.

Bizarre.

I rubbed my forehead, half wondering if I was still asleep. The entire picture in the kitchen was completely bizarre. My brothers were up at 7:30 a.m. They all appeared to be dressed for work—*work!*—and were interacting like mild mannered, well-adjusted, productive members of society. I was so confused.

Tangentially I noted that the roosters were at it again in the backyard, several of them crowing like the devil. I was beginning to get used to the sound; it was becoming the background music to the soundtrack of Tennessee.

Roscoe glanced over his shoulder and gave me a tight smile. It looked sad. "Hey, Ash. How you holding up? Want an omelet?"

I nodded, staring at him for another full ten seconds. "Yes. Yes, please. That would be great."

"You want toast too?" Cletus asked. "I can make you some toast." He was dressed in blue Dickies, which were worn but clean, and had a patch with his name sewn on the left pocket of his work jumpsuit.

"That would be great. Thanks, Cletus."

"She likes butter and strawberry jam, right Ash?" Billy, standing next to Cletus—wearing black suit, white shirt, and black tie—indicated to me with his coffee cup, his expression detached.

My eyebrows lifted at Billy's remembrance of my toast preferences as well as the fact that he was wearing a suit. "That's right."

Billy muttered something under his breath, just low enough for me not to hear.

"What was that?" I questioned him.

His blue eyes, same shape and color as mine, lifted and he gave me a cool glare. "I said you've been gone for eight years. It's a wonder we know anything about you."

I frowned at him, and was about to question him further when Jethro cut into the conversation.

"I heard a scream." He made this statement from the kitchen table. He was dressed in what appeared to be some kind of park ranger uniform. An open newspaper—a *newspaper?!*—was on the table in front of him along with a half-eaten omelet. "Was that scream from you or Duane?"

I sighed. "That was Duane." Then a thought occurred to me. "Today is Wednesday. I thought no one was assigned to Wednesday."

"Unassigned days are wild card days, first come, first serve deal. He's been up there since sunrise." Roscoe shook his head.

I rolled my eyes, wished I hadn't asked the question. "Anyway, I forgot to knock again. It was my fault."

"We should get a bell for your neck." Billy's blue eyes regarded me thoughtfully beneath dark brown eyebrows. He made this suggestion matter-of-factly, like it was a very reasonable, good idea. To him, it probably was.

Of the brothers, Billy was the most serious and stern. I could count on one hand all the times I'd heard him laugh while we were growing up. His cool attitude this morning notwithstanding, I also suspected he was the smartest in the traditional sense. Facts and figuring came easy to him, especially anything to do with machines.

"Might as well just change my name to Bessie while you're at it," I mumbled.

"'…women are still cats and birds, or at best cows.'"

This little gem came from the corner of the kitchen behind me, and was received by the rest of the room with a tangible stretch of silence. I frowned at the words—their implied meaning and their origin—and at the voice that spoke them.

As I suspected, when I turned I found Drew leaning against the counter, sipping coffee, and eying me over the rim of his cup with those silvery blues.

He was dressed in a uniform, the kind a very official, super important park ranger might wear. Unlike Jethro's, his had a lot more pockets, a badge, and a gun. A cowboy hat was at his elbow on the counter; he also wore cowboy boots. I noted with detachment that his beard and hair had undergone a transformation. His facial hair had been trimmed, though his blond beard was still impressive. The unkempt locks on his head had been brushed, pulled back, and fastened behind his neck.

I noted these things with a small degree of womanly interest. It was instinctual, incidental, the way a person would notice a Maserati racing down the street and think, *That's a nice car.*

His tidy, official-looking appearance—nay, his commanding appearance—did nothing to endear him to me, especially not after calling me a cow.

Therefore, I spoke my thoughts before I could catch myself. "Really? You're really going to quote Nietzsche to me? To *me*? Nietzsche? To the sole female in the room?" I motioned to the kitchen with a flailing, frustrated hand wave. "When I first wake up? Before I've had coffee? After finding one of my brothers mating with his hand upstairs for the *second* time in as many days, and *I'm* the cow?"

"Can't mate with hooves," Drew said, his delivery deadpan.

"And yet, many men prefer the company of sheep over their hands, or even women." I said this sweetly before I gave him my back and glared at Jethro. "I need to talk to you."

I tilted my head toward the family room and walked out of the kitchen, waiting for Jethro to follow. I didn't have to wait very long; but to my infinite aggravation, Dr. Drew Runous, PhD, trailed right behind my brother tucking his leather notebook into one of the side pockets of his cargo pants.

I scowled at him before looking at my oldest brother. I was careful to keep my voice even, sincere, and free of sarcasm when I said pointedly to Jethro, "Is it possible for us to have a conversation without your boss being present?"

Jethro rubbed the back of his neck and sighed. "The thing is, Ash, we've all been talking this morning, and it turns out...Momma appointed Drew here as her power of attorney."

"What?" My eyes bounced back and forth between them.

I was sure that I'd heard incorrectly. Maybe Jethro had said *MOMMA painted dew-hair as their flower of anatomy.* Honestly, that would have made more sense to me than the possibility that Drew held my mother's power of attorney.

"Ash, let me explain-"

"What did you say?"

Jethro swallowed thickly, met my stare, and repeated his pronouncement in a level tone. "Momma appointed Drew as her power of attorney."

Drew nodded once. He had the decency to stay silent and keep his face devoid of expression.

I sputtered for a minute. Then I consulted the ceiling. It was silent on the matter and, strangely, didn't seem to share my outrage.

At last I managed to speak. "Medical or financial?"

"Both." Jethro's mouth twisted to the side in a half smile, sheepish and bracing. "He holds her medical power of attorney, her financial power of attorney, and he's the executor of her will."

My mouth opened, but nothing emerged for seven seconds.

Then I laughed.

I laughed and laughed.

I laughed because I was frustrated and angry and sad and overwhelmed. I held my stomach and doubled over, my eyes blurring with tears of hilarity and misery and grief. Jethro guided me to the couch and sat next to me, his hand on my upper back.

Somewhere outside, the roosters crowed. I hated those damn roosters, always crowing, always making a fuss for no reason.

Drew opted to remain standing, his expression patient and sober.

"Ashley." Jethro's voice was tight and concerned.

"Just a minute," I managed to say when I'd caught my breath. I wiped my eyes and added, "I just need a minute."

It took several minutes. Maybe ten minutes during which I swung back and forth between the urge to erupt in absurd laughter and unleash a tide of mind-blowing anger.

After the initial red haze of fury began to recede, I tried to see past my frustration and hurt to the real issue. My mother was sick. She was dying, and likely would be gone in six weeks…or so. Things needed to happen. Arrangements needed to be made, and we needed to prepare.

This, none of this, was about me. It was about her, providing care and comfort to my momma in her final days with as much selflessness as she'd given me all my life. I rejected my instinct to take her decision to trust Dr. Nobody with her medical and financial wellbeing as an indication that she had no faith in me, her daughter.

I refused to be petty. I would waste no time on anger, and at the very least, I would do my best not to take this personally. She'd raised me better than that.

When I was quite finished, and at a complete loss as to what to say or how to proceed, I gathered a breath and released it on a big sigh.

"When did this happen?" I asked the room, not caring who answered.

"Three months ago," Drew responded, and he cleared his throat, his eyes flickering to Jethro's then back to mine.

I glanced between them. "Did you know she was sick?"

"No." Drew shook his head, his shoulders slumping. He appeared to be frustrated, and I believed him. "She didn't tell me she was sick. She just said she didn't want any of you to be burdened with making decisions down the road."

"Well…." I said, finding myself dangerously close to actual tears. I sucked in another calming breath and endeavored to keep my tone open-minded and free of derision, though I wanted to slap the beard right off his face.

"It would seem," I began, and then I stopped. I pressed my lips together, cleared my throat, and swallowed, taking a moment to steady my voice. "It would seem that you are the decider. So, Dr. Decider, please tell me what *I* can do to help *you*."

His eyes narrowed and searched mine. He seemed confused by my response. Obviously, it sure as heck wasn't what he'd been expecting me to say. Most likely, I guessed, he thought I was going to launch a full-scale attack with woman-hysterics, accusations, and manipulative maneuverings.

But that wasn't how I rolled. Prolonged irrationality wasn't in my wheelhouse. Recrimination was not my homeboy.

So we stared at each other.

I cleared my face of all expression and waited for direction. This was a ninja trait I'd perfected while interacting with egomaniac physicians. I clenched my teeth to keep from telling him what I thought he could do with his power of attorney, where he could shove it, and whether the sun shined in that particular locale.

Finally he spoke, "Your mother appointed me to this role because she didn't want any of you to have to think about end-of-life decisions. She did this to spare you, not to hurt you." It was obvious he was choosing his words carefully. His tone was reasonable, imploring, even gentle.

I nodded. He made sense, but it didn't make me feel any better.

I glanced around the room. "She's coming home today. What have you decided regarding her care?"

He grimaced, frowned, sighed. "I'm not trying to usurp your role, Ashley." He sounded frustrated.

I glared at him again, my jaw set. I spoke slowly so I wouldn't be tempted to scream. "And I'm not arguing with you. You have all the power in this situation. I just want to know what I can do to help."

Jethro finally spoke up, placing a hand on my knee. "I just found out, Ashley. I had no idea either. But I trust Drew. And Momma obviously trusted him. You know how she is, not wanting to burden anybody. Drives me crazy."

I gave my brother a small, conspiratorial smile. Jethro's confession softened my hard edges. I covered his hand with mine and squeezed. "No point in getting twisted up in things that don't matter. What matters is that Momma is coming home today."

I returned my gaze to Drew. "If you're waiting for me to freak out, that's what my little laughing fit was. I'm over it. It's done. Nothing I can do about this situation other than live through it. So, again, what have you all decided, and what can I do to help?"

Drew crossed his arms over his chest and glared down at me with skepticism. "We all talked a little this morning about how to handle the next few weeks, but…."

He paused when he saw my eyes widen. My blood pressure spiked, my vision turned red, yet I ignored my murderous impulses. I breathed in and out and listened with all outward appearance of calm.

"But your brothers said that you were likely the only one who had some rough idea of what to expect and how best to plan and proceed. This is assuming that you'll be staying in Tennessee."

I nodded, my acute hypertension gradually declining to near baseline levels. Drew was asking for my opinion. I didn't know if it was a token olive branch or if he'd just handed me an olive orchard. Regardless, it was a step in the right direction.

"Okay, well, I think we should put her in the den. It's downstairs, has a door, and is on the quiet side of the house. I can tell you that hospice will be providing two nurses, one to stay during the day, and one to stop in at night to monitor her condition. Regardless, I'm going to put a cot in the den and sleep in there with her."

Drew frowned. "You'll need sleep, good sleep. If you stay with your mother, your sleep is likely to be interrupted. How can you take care of her if you're exhausted during the day?"

I swallowed my sharp retort that where I slept was none of his business. "Someone *in the family* should stay with her all the time. I don't want her left alone."

"The nurse will check in on her."

"But the nurse isn't her family."

He narrowed his eyes at me then looked to my brother. "There are seven of you. You'll each take a one-night shift a week."

Before I could object, Jethro nodded and said, "We'll make a schedule."

I closed my eyes briefly and fought the urge to say, *You boys have a gift for making schedules.*

"So, you'll be staying for the duration?" Drew pressed me. "How is this going to affect your employment in Chicago?"

His question stunned me to the point that I was bereft of words. He sounded like a father asking his daughter to justify the soundness of her decisions. He almost sounded like he cared. It was unnerving; especially since my father was the least responsible and caring man I'd ever known and had never made a sound decision in his life.

An honest, guileless response—likely because I was so taken aback by the question—tumbled from my lips. "I'm part of a union. We have insurance that covers taking time to tend to critically ill family members. They have to hold my job for three months."

He considered this and nodded. "Of course there are other issues, like house upkeep, bill paying, groceries, incidentals, and the like." Drew stared at me for a moment—actually, he stared through me—and I could tell he was re-tallying and considering all that would have to be done. "You should return your rental car and drive your momma's car while you're here. And I'll give you access to her checking account for household expenses, but I'll take care of the monthly bills."

Drew's pragmatism surprised me. I hadn't thought of who would be paying the bills.

I nodded and stuttered, "That...that makes sense." Because it did make sense. In fact, I was grateful. I didn't particularly want to be the one having to think about paying bills and related logistics. I wanted to focus on Momma, on taking care of her and spending time with her.

"I also suggest we hire a house cleaner. Your brothers aren't up to the task, and you shouldn't be bothered with it."

I nodded again. "O-okay," I stammered, again surprised.

A long moment passed. At first, the atmosphere in the room grew lighter as Drew and I watched each other. But then his stare grew increasingly intense, sharp, heated. My neck began to itch. I didn't know him well enough to guess at what he was thinking, so I sat very still and waited, trying not to blush under his obvious scrutiny.

"Right." Jethro said, breaking the moment.

Drew blinked as if he were coming out of a daze and turned his focus to my brother.

"This plan sounds solid," Jethro said, and he put his arm around my shoulders and squeezed, then stood and nodded like everything was settled. "I'll tell the others how this is going to work. I can start putting together a schedule." He looked down at me and added, "Roscoe will be here with you all day; he can help you take your rental car back, and he'll be here when Momma arrives."

"Okay, sounds good." I stood as well, crossed my arms over my chest. Everything was happening so fast.

"I'm fixin' to put my coffee in a travel mug, then we can head out." Jethro gave Drew a nod and walked back to the kitchen.

I stared at the carpet and thought about the order of things to accomplish. Dress, eat, drive to town, drop off the rental car. I also needed to find out Elizabeth and Sandra's arrival time. Maybe I could pick them up at the airport.

I felt the heat of Drew's solid hand on my back just before he spoke. "I didn't peg you for the type to surrender so easily."

I looked up to find him standing a foot away. His gray-blue eyes ensnared mine and bored into me as though he was dually trying to figure me out and will me into submission. He'd said the words with a low intimacy that I felt in my knees and hips. The word *surrender* seemed to echo in the room and through my body.

The shift in the atmosphere was palpable, yet I found myself wondering if I were the only one who noticed. Was it a byproduct of my wonky, grief-induced vulnerability? Were my emotions susceptible to delusion? Was I imagining the galvanized tension between us?

I issued him a miniscule smile, hoping to convey irritation, while I tried to regain the abrupt loss of my body's ability to regulate its temperature. I was hot, flustered, ill prepared, and emotionally unequipped to interact with fictionally handsome men speaking to me in intimate tones and staring at me like I was cake.

And what the heck was wrong with me that I was even noticing Drew's tone of voice? Let alone his fictional handsomeness. My mother had just been given a terminal diagnosis for heaven's sake. I was wrong in the head.

I swallowed, finding strength in my self-recrimination. I leaned close and whispered, "Understand this, cowboy: I've surrendered *nothing*."

Inexplicably, he grinned. It was small and knowing and smugly sexy, and I found it intensely irritating. He quoted Nietzsche again, "'Perhaps truth is a woman who has grounds for not showing her grounds.'"

I stepped away, immediately finding relief from my muddled hormones by putting some distance between us. I held his gaze for a beat then walked backward to the stairs as I dismissively informed him of a real truth. "You can kiss my grits and my grounds, Nietzsche. And while you're at it, go jump in a lake."

"Which lake?"

I turned away and took the stairs two at a time, not liking that my palms had grown hot. "I don't care," I called out, "Preferably one with no water."

CHAPTER FIVE

"There is nothing I would not do for those who are really my friends. I have no notion of loving people by halves; it is not my nature."

— JANE AUSTEN, NORTHANGER ABBEY

OSCOE AND I drove into Knoxville to drop off the rental car. He took Momma's car and I took the rental. On the way back, we stopped by the hospital to check on Momma; she was asleep, so we met with the hospice social worker to arrange her transport home.

Roscoe held it together, which was the opposite of how Winston men usually dealt with stressful situations. Of course, this was based on previous experience, which was now eight years out of date.

I also held it together despite my ping-ponging emotions with Drew from earlier that morning and the bizarre, intimate moment that followed. But then, I usually held it together. My motto was *save your drama for your llama.*

I checked my cell phone on the way out of town, as I wasn't getting any reception at the house, and saw a text message from Elizabeth. Their plane was set to touch down at 4:15 p.m., but I needn't rush to pick them up because they would get a rental car. She finished the text with *we love you, girl*, and that made me smile.

The message helped, and knowing that Elizabeth and Sandra were coming gave me a sense of calm reassurance, even if it was only temporary. I felt like I was surrounded by strangers. These brothers who I *thought* I knew were turning out to be a mystery wrapped in an enigma, slathered in conundrum flavored cream cheese.

Since Roscoe and I only had each other as company for the hour drive home, I encouraged my youngest brother—who was now six-foot-two—to dish the dirt on the older ones.

Except, there was no dirt to dish.

"So, Jethro is a park ranger? How'd that happen?" I briefly wondered why my mother hadn't said anything about it. Even though she rarely spoke about my brothers during our daily phone calls, Jethro cleaning himself up and becoming a park ranger seemed like it would've been pretty big news.

"It's awesome, right?" Roscoe's smile was immediate and proud. "It's a pretty funny story. Jethro was…well, you know. He was stealing cars and partying, but he was smart about it. That boy was arrested so many times, but he was never charged. He was damn lucky."

"I remember. The day I left for college he was coming home from lockup." I could still recall wondering whether I should wait for him to get home or just head out without saying goodbye. I waited until supper, when Billy arrived and told me that Jethro was at the Dragon—one of three biker bars near this part of the parkway—drinking with his buddies and celebrating his criminal success.

Disgusted, I'd left right then.

"Well, Drew beat the shit out of Jethro when he caught him trying to steal his 1971 Aermacchi Harley-Davidson Turismo Veloce."

My mouth fell open, partly because an image of Drew straddling a classic Harley flashed through my mind and partly because the story was downright shocking.

I stared at Roscoe. "Did Drew press charges?"

"Nah. He told Jethro that he would pull some strings and get him a job as a park ranger if he promised to stop with the illegal bullshit."

"And he did?"

"Yep. Well, mostly. Jethro never was in very deep with the Iron Order, so he was able to extract himself pretty quickly."

The Iron Order was the biker club that controlled Green Valley and the surrounding counties. The Dragon Biker Bar was their hangout. At one point, I remembered Momma being afraid that Jethro would become one of them, but he never was much of a joiner.

Roscoe paused for a minute as he navigated a series of impressive switchbacks on the mountain road. In order to reach Knoxville, we needed to go up one of the mountains then down the other side.

When the turns were behind us, he picked up the story. "Jethro had to start at the bottom of the ladder and work up to the job he has now. He got his GED then went and got his AS degree, and finally, last year he got the job as a ranger. Now he and Drew work together all the time."

He then spent the next several minutes waxing poetic about Drew and Jethro. From the way Roscoe described it, they were preventing forest fires and protecting the endangered animals, and working toward every other kind of altruistic endeavor.

I detected a hint of envy in Roscoe's voice. It seemed that Drew had a number-one fan, and that fan was Roscoe Winston.

"That's great," I said in all sincerity. "That's really great." It was great. It was super great. And it probably meant the world to my mother. I couldn't believe she'd never said anything about it.

"Drew is...he's the man. He's really quiet. I think it's because he doesn't want to show other people up or make them feel like they're less than him. Did you know his father is a senator in Texas? He doesn't talk about it much, but he comes from money."

I thought about this information for a bit, marinated in it. Drew didn't seem all that quiet to me. In fact, he seemed downright chatty. Rather than contradict Roscoe's assertion regarding Drew's propensity toward reticence, I decided to keep my observations to myself.

"Roscoe, our grandparents had money too, but that doesn't make one person better than another." Our grandfather on our mother's side had been a politician and a very wealthy man.

"I know, but Drew has made all the difference. He helped Duane, Beauford, and Cletus with the paperwork for their auto shop, and he even helped them buy the place. He's part owner, but he doesn't see fit to interfere."

"Did you say *their* auto shop? They own the shop?"

Roscoe nodded and gave me a big grin, his blue eyes flickering to mine then back to the road, "Hell, yeah, it's theirs: Winston Brothers Auto Shop. Momma helps them with the books. It's doing real good. They have a hook-up on old, busted classic cars. They fix them then sell them in Nashville for big bucks to people in the music biz."

This revelation was surprising, but also freaking fantastic. I felt a surge of pride for the twins and my sweet brother Cletus. Good for them.

Annoyingly, I also felt a good deal of gratitude toward Drew. I decided to push those feelings to the side. If the shop was doing well, then Drew was well compensated for his investment.

"What about Billy? He was in a suit this morning. What's that about?"

"Oh, Billy's doing his thing at the mill. He's doing real good too, now that he no longer has to clean up messes."

"Clean up messes?"

"Well, you know he was always bailing Jethro out of jail and trying to keep the rest of us out of trouble—not that he needed to worry about me."

I thought back to my childhood recollections of Billy. Of my brothers, he was the most absent and withdrawn. Most men started working at the mill as soon as they reached seventeen. Billy started working there at sixteen. I was surprised he was still at home since he seemed to wish for escape even more than I did.

I also thought about his chilly reception of me earlier in the day and his comment about my being gone for eight years. I hadn't expected all my brothers to welcome me back with open arms. I was just a little surprised that Billy—who'd never seemed all that interested in me when we were kids—appeared to be the only one vexed by my long absence.

"What's Billy doing down there that he has to wear a suit?"

"He's got some fancy title, regional director of mill operations or something like that. He's been there forever, and you know how smart he is. He could have done anything; maybe even become a proper engineer if he'd wanted to."

Regional director of mill operations sounded very important. I wasn't exactly sure what that encompassed, but apparently, it meant that he needed to wear a suit to work every day. Which, on my father's side of the family, was like becoming the president of the United States.

I managed to get Roscoe to tell me about himself with some prodding. He tried to shrug off his accomplishments like they were no big deal. They were a big deal.

Roscoe was finishing his last year at the University of Tennessee, majoring in biology. I knew he was attending community college two years ago, as it was one of the few pieces of information my mother had shared about my brothers. However, I didn't know that he'd transferred to the state university sometime during the last eighteen months.

"That's so great, Roscoe. I'm...." I swallowed because I was going to say *I'm really proud of you,* but then stopped myself. I didn't feel like I had the right to say those words since I'd left him and the rest of my family nearly a decade ago. Instead, I finished the thought with, "I'm really happy for you. I'm happy for all of you. You're all doing so great."

"Yeah...." Roscoe nodded, glanced at me out of the corner of his eye, his tone teasing. "Now that you see we're not a bunch of skunks, maybe you'll come visit more often."

I blushed, embarrassed and ashamed of the years I'd been gone. Even though he was poking fun, his words hit a nerve.

I sighed, looked out the window. "Sure—if ya'll want me to."

"Of course we want you to. Don't be stupid."

"You could come visit me in Chicago. It's a pretty great city."

"Isn't it cold all the time? Sleet and snow and forty below zero wind chill and all that mess?"

"No, not all the time." I glanced at him and pressed my lips together to keep from smirking. "Just nine months out of the year."

Roscoe laughed and shook his head. "How do you stand it? Don't you miss four solid seasons? And the mountains, I can't wait to finish college and move back here. I don't think there's a more beautiful place on earth."

As if on cue, we passed a lookout turnoff with a particularly breathtaking view of the Smoky Mountains. They were ensconced in their typical blue mist and descended fold upon fold to a green tree-lined valley. I had to admit, it was beautiful country.

Instead of vocalizing this, I said, "Well, you haven't been many places on earth. You might change your mind once you go out there and check out what it has to offer."

"Nah." He shook his head and shocked the crud out of me by saying, "I spent a summer hiking all over Europe. Old buildings don't do much for me, but I can see why other people think they're pretty. I took a semester off school and did a road trip from New York to Los Angeles. We went the long way and saw the Redwood Forest, which is probably the second most beautiful place on earth. Then I flew to New Zealand. That's where the third most beautiful place on earth is, Doubtful Sound."

He paused for a minute because we'd come to a fork in the road and a stop sign.

I couldn't help my blurted question. "How did you afford all that?"

He looked at me, his mouth quirking to the side. "It wasn't all that expensive because I went with Drew, and he had to go for work. He had the option of going by car or flying to each location, so he picked the road trip and took me with him. He thought it would be good for me to see the country, see what's out there. He said I could go anywhere and be anything. I don't think I believed him until we went on that trip."

Roscoe and I stared at each other for a long moment until I blurted another question. "Why would he do that? Why would he do any of this—helping Jethro, the twins, Duane, you—what's in it for him?"

My brother narrowed his eyes at me, but a smile tugged at his lips.

"Family, I think." Then his eyes lost focus and he frowned. "It's not really my place to say."

"What does that mean?"

He shrugged, looked left and right for oncoming cars, and took the road to Green Valley. "It means just that. Drew's got his reasons, and I don't tell other people's stories."

WE MADE IT back to the house after 2:00 p.m. and immediately set to work rearranging the furniture in the den. We moved out a big wooden desk that had belonged to my maternal grandfather as well as several tables, the vintage sofa and matching chair, an old freestanding globe, and other various antique pieces. The majority of the items had been inherited by my mother from her parents, and she'd kept them all in pristine condition.

My momma came from money. She was an only child. The house we grew up in and all the land surrounding it had belonged to her parents. My grandfather died before I was born, but my grandmother died when I was ten—quite suddenly, from a stroke—and left the house and all her wealth to my mother.

This all happened two years after my parents separated. My grandmother also left trusts for each of us, which have been controlled by Momma, and which we can't access until our thirtieth birthdays. I didn't know how much money was in the trust, as I'd never given it much thought, but I did know that the money was why my father was always trying to re-insert himself into our lives.

We left two recliners in the room, all the bookshelves, and a side table. I was determined that one of us would be with her at all times, and the leather recliners were big and comfortable.

Once we were certain that the room would now accommodate her hospital bed, equipment, and the sleeping cot, we took a short break to have some lemonade and a sandwich. Well, I had lemonade. Roscoe had a beer.

Our timing was close to perfect; the transport arrived just after 4:30

p.m. Momma had slept through the entire trip. I knew she was likely on an impressive regimen of painkillers and sleeping aids. They were usually called quality of life meds, which really meant end of life meds.

Momma woke up just briefly when she was wheeled into the den. Her eyes were foggy and unfocused as she glanced around the room.

She asked, "Where are Mother's things? Daddy's desk?"

I leaned over her bed and held her hand. "We moved them out so we could keep you on the first floor but also give you some privacy."

She nodded then stared at me. "Ashley, I have to tell you something, and it's really important."

I squeezed her hand and braced myself. "I'm listening, Momma."

"The only thing that helps a baby through teething pain is bourbon on the gums." She then closed her eyes and was asleep again within seconds.

I stared at her for a long moment, replaying the words of wisdom in my head, and came to the conclusion that she must've been half-dreaming.

"Hi, I'm Marissa."

Still a little bewildered, I turned and blinked at the very pretty, twenty-something woman holding her hand out to me. She was in scrubs and comfy shoes, and was obviously a nurse. She wore her dark brown hair in long, small braids down her back, and her dark brown eyes were warm and compassionate.

I took her hand. "Hi. I'm Ashley, the daughter."

"Nice to meet you, Ashley. I'll be your mother's day nurse Monday through Thursday. I'll stop in during the day. George comes on Fridays, Saturdays, and Sundays. Tina and Joe will split the night shift."

I nodded. "Okay. Just so you know, I'm a nurse in Chicago—pediatric intensive care."

Her eyebrows lifted in surprised delight. "I'm from Chicago! I grew up on the south side. I just moved to Knoxville two months ago."

Roscoe cleared his throat from the place at my side where he'd suddenly appeared, drawing our attention to him.

"Hi. I'm Roscoe Winston. Pleasure to meet you, Marissa."

I lifted an eyebrow at the way he said her name and the way he held her eyes and the way he leaned forward with just a little too much swagger and southern charm.

She smiled at him like he was a cute puppy and accepted his hand for a shake. "Nice to meet you, Roscoe." She turned her attention back to me. "I'm going to get your mother settled and check her vitals."

"Sure. They should have taken her to the den. It's at the end of the hall."

Marissa gave me a warm smile then left to find the room where Momma would be staying.

Roscoe turned his head and watched her walk away. More precisely, he watched her bottom—in baggy scrubs no less—as she walked away.

"She's new in town. I wonder if I could show her around."

I elbowed him in the side and gave him my best disapproving scowl.

"Ow! What did I do?"

My voice was a harsh whisper. "You're flirting? With Momma's nurse?"

He didn't look at all repentant. "Yeah, sure. Why not?"

"Why not?" I couldn't believe him. "Why not?! Aren't you upset about Momma?"

Roscoe flinched and appeared to be a little hurt by my words, but he held his ground. "Of course I'm upset. Don't be stupid. But that right there is an exceptionally fine looking woman, and Momma being sick doesn't mean that I'm blind."

"Ugh! Men!" I shook my head and turned to leave.

Roscoe caught me by the arm and pulled me into the kitchen. "Now, hold your horses. Just you listen for a sec."

I pulled my elbow from his grip and crossed my arms over my chest, glaring at him.

He didn't appear to be affected by my disapproving glower. "Who is it going to hurt, me flirting with a pretty girl? Is Momma going to die faster?" I flinched, but he pressed on. "Is it going to increase her pain? Don't give me that look, Ashley Austen Winston. You would have us all dress in black and ring bells every fifteen minutes. I'm not going to feel bad for admiring someone pretty. You were always too serious for your own good."

What he really meant was that I was always too sensitive for my own good, and he was right. But I'd toughened up over the last eight years. I'd fallen in love twice, bludgeoned into it with all the bad sense of a girl with a user for a father, and come out the other side determined to learn from my mistakes.

I couldn't flirt and have it mean nothing, not like Roscoe could do. It was a defect in my personality.

My neck became hot and scratchy, and I felt tears gather behind my eyes.

He seemed to see or sense that I was close to crying because he pulled me forward and wrapped me in a hug. "Don't cry. I always hated it when you cried."

I sniffled and squeezed my eyes shut. "You did?"

"Yes. Who do you think left you bunches of wildflowers outside your door when Jethro or the twins pissed you off?"

My arms came around his torso and I rested my head against his shoulder. "That was you? I always thought that was Momma."

"No, dummy, that was me."

I sucked in an unsteady breath and hugged him tighter. "Thank you."

"You're welcome." He kissed my hair then pushed me back a foot so he could look into my eyes. "If you want to be miserable, there's nothing I can do to stop you. I'm miserable about losing her too, but I'm not going to spend the next few weeks wringing my hands. I'm going to enjoy the time she has left and live life like she always wanted us to do, and that includes getting my flirt on with the scoop of chocolate ice cream that just walked in the door."

I choked out a laugh and hit his shoulder. "Watch out, or I'll tell Marissa you just called her a scoop of chocolate ice cream."

He shrugged. "That's fine with me. While you're at it, find out what she thinks of vanilla."

I KNEW SANDRA and Elizabeth had arrived because I was awakened from my nap by a sound, and it wasn't one of those damn roosters for once. It was a very specific kind of sound. It was the sound of a man crying. And the sound woke me up.

I'd been dozing, curled up on the recliner in the den next to my momma's hospital bed. Judging by the light outside, it looked to be close to sunset. The day's events had left me all the various kinds of tired: physically, mentally, emotionally, and knitterly.

Knitterly tired is when you're too tired to knit. It's a depressing and desperate place to be.

I stretched, blinked the tired haze from my eyes, and glanced around the room. A male nurse—who I guessed was Joe —was sitting in the other recliner. It had been pushed back a distance from the bed. He seemed to be reading a newspaper in the dwindling light of the window. He was older, maybe in his fifties, and looked more like an orderly than a nurse. His head was bald, his neck was thick, his shoulders were wide, and he had a tattoo of a dragon on his forearm.

Then, to my astonishment, when I turned my head the other way, I found Drew sitting in a wooden chair pulled up next to mine.

I frowned at him.

He wasn't looking at me. He was looking at the book in his hands, which he was reading aloud. I wondered for a split second that his voice hadn't woken me, but then I realized why. As much as I wanted everything about him to be repugnant, his voice—especially while he read—was nice. It was soothing, yet as I listened, I discovered it was also well inflected. He enriched the text as he read.

This was terribly inconvenient, as I'd promised myself I would leave Tennessee with no admiration for Drew Runous.

"'Just that,' said the fox. 'To me, you are still nothing more than a little boy who is just like a hundred thousand other little boys. And I have no need of you. And you, on your part, have no need of me. To you I am nothing more than a fox like a hundred thousand other foxes.' Drew glanced up, his eyes immediately finding mine. They flickered over my face, taking in my sleepy appearance. Then, with no visible change in his expression, he returned his attention to the book. "'But if you tame me, then we shall need each other. To me, you will be unique in all the world. To you, I shall be unique in all the world.'"

He stopped reading, his eyes lingering on the page before he closed the book, though he held his place with a finger. I studied him unabashedly, likely because I was still half-asleep, and it didn't occur to me that staring at him was weird.

Drew's gaze lifted to where Momma lay asleep in the bed. His expression was warm and affectionate, and his voice gentle as he said, "Bethany, Ashley is awake."

I started, blinked at him, then looked at my mother just in time to see her open her eyes. She lifted her hand and gave me a little wave.

"Hi, Baby," she said with a smile. "Did we wake you up?"

"No. Something else did…I think." My voice was raspy from sleep.

Just then, the sound of a sob sprang into the room, and I remembered that men were crying someplace in the house. This, of course, reminded me that Sandra had arrived.

Momma laughed lightly, her grin growing as she looked at me. "I like your friends. Sandra is a hoot."

I returned her smile and reached for her hand. "How long have you been up?"

"Oh…a few hours I guess. We're good in here if you want to go say hi and visit. Your doctor friend, Elizabeth, made everyone ravioli. It was real good. She said her husband owns an Italian restaurant."

"Her mother-in-law owns the restaurant." I frowned because my mother knew all about Elizabeth. I'd told her all about how Elizabeth had grown up with Nico Moretti—now a famous comedian—and how they'd been married last year in Las Vegas.

"No matter who owns it, she knows how to make really fine Italian food."

"It was really good." This came from the nurse in the corner.

My attention shifted to him and I gave him a little wave. "Hi, you must be Joe. I'm Ashley."

He nodded, smiled. "Hey, Ashley. You're the nurse, right?"

"Yep. That's me."

"Let me know if you have any questions. I just checked your momma; she's doing real good." Joe's brown eyes shifted from mine to where my mother was sitting up. He gave her a warm smile.

"Thank you, I will." I said, considering this Joe who was a nurse with a tattoo of a dragon.

"You should go thank her for making dinner for your family," Momma said. "I know she wants to see you."

I nodded, distracted by Drew and the suspicion that my mother was losing her memory. Or rather, I suspected the pain medication was making her recollections fuzzy. I shifted to stand and noticed that a blanket had been placed over me.

I frowned at the blanket then at Drew.

It seemed everything was earning my frown of confusion.

"Go on, get." Momma prompted, squeezing my hand then letting it go.

Drew didn't move as I stood to depart, so I was forced to walk past him in the tight space made by our chairs, my bottom brushing his shoulder. Nor did he meet my eyes. Instead, he opened the book, which I recognized as *The Little Prince* by Antoine de Saint-Exupéry, and started again where he'd left off—with talk of taming and need.

I shook off the lingering Drew-disquiet, and my stomach rumbled as I walked. It was a reminder that food was needed in order to function, and thankfully, the smell of good food—garlic and fried onions—was wafting toward me. I followed the smell of Italian food and the sound of crying through the kitchen and into the dining room.

The scene that greeted me was not unlike something from a Dr. Phil episode.

Sandra had Cletus and the twins arranged in the family room—which was just off the dining room—and was holding some kind of impromptu counseling session. Her face was clear of expression, neither cool nor warm but rather accepting, open, and interested.

The loud sobbing, I realized almost immediately, was coming from Cletus. He was sitting in the chair closest to Sandra, and his face was buried in his hands. She was rubbing his back, but her attention was affixed to Beau, who also looked like he'd been crying at one point, but now he seemed to have his expressions of sorrow under control.

I didn't want to interrupt them. Sandra was an excellent psychiatrist, though she usually treated only pediatric patients. It was obvious that my brothers were receiving something from her that they needed, some kind of catharsis. This was her modus operandi.

A throat cleared behind me and caused me to jump. I turned and found Elizabeth standing at my shoulder, an affectionate and sympathetic smile on her face.

"Hey, girl," she said.

"Hey," I said.

Then she pulled me into a wrap-and-hold hug.

Elizabeth was shorter than me by about four inches, but she was also curvy and soft, and her hugs felt like being surrounded by a warm, beautiful cloud. Adding to this affect was the paleness of her skin, the golden blonde of her hair, and the ethereal blue of her irises. We gave and received comfort for a short moment before we were interrupted by Sandra's voice, which was closer than I'd expected.

"Ashley Winston."

Sandra was standing next to us, staring at me. She was smiling— from her big green eyes to her flaming red hair to her large white teeth —but it wasn't at all sympathetic. It was just a big, old, happy smile.

She launched herself at us, her arms coming around both Elizabeth and me, and kissed me on my cheek and then my chin.

"It is so good to smell your hair right now," Sandra said. Of course this made us both laugh, because who says that?

She squeezed us, causing Elizabeth to squeak. "Sandra...I... can't...breathe...."

"No matter." Sandra released her vice grip and reached for my hand. "Where is your room? We have some sharing to do."

I glanced over her shoulder at my brothers. Duane gave me a taut smile. *Bizarre.*

"Sandra, I don't want to cry. Please don't make me cry."

She shook her head, wrinkling her nose as though my request were silly. It was not silly. She had this superpower where people were absolutely *compelled* to spill their guts, myself included. She made burdens lighter, but she did this by forcing people to face truths, which usually resulted in crying.

I didn't want to face truths. I wanted to steal a few moments with my friends, saturate myself in the promise of my comfortable, contented life back in Chicago, and wrap my brain and heart in the bliss of distraction.

Truth was overrated and smelled like onions.

Bliss was underappreciated and smelled like chloroform.

"We don't have to talk about anything you don't want to talk about." She grumbled this statement and tugged on my hand. "Come on, where is your room? We brought you presents."

I hesitated only briefly.

"It's upstairs."

Sandra and Elizabeth followed me after a detour to the front door. I saw Elizabeth grab a duffle bag and Sandra a gift sack, purple tissue paper spilling out the top. Once inside my room, I sat on my bed and turned to face them.

Elizabeth took a seat on the bed, placed the duffle bag between us, and unzipped it. "We brought you some things—just some essentials and—and some other things."

Sandra hovered by the door. She was surveying the room, I could tell. Maybe she was making a mental tally of my dysfunctions based on the number of ceramic unicorn figurines on my bookshelf. (FYI, there were four of them.)

"You didn't have to bring me anything." I gave Elizabeth a reassuring smile. "I'm really fine."

"No, you're not. You're in shock, and you haven't yet processed the fact that your mother is dying." Sandra leveled me with a sensible, matter-of-fact gaze.

I braced myself for *the truths*.

Instead, she surprised me by sparing me. "But that's okay. You'll adjust. You'll figure it out. Or you won't. If you can't do it on your own, we'll help you figure it out. Either way you're covered."

My eyes lifted to the ceiling then lowered back to her; I was confused. "Then why did you instigate a therapy session with my brothers?"

She shrugged. "Because I don't know if they have an adequate support system in place to help them work through their grief, especially since your father...." Sandra paused when she saw my shoulders stiffen at the mention of my father.

When you have a despicable person as a parent, I truly believe you can't escape hating any part of yourself that resembles him or her. Whether it's a physical similarity, a talent, a propensity, or an inclination that you share, all commonalities are abhorrent to you.

I look like my father. I have his thick dark hair and bright blue eyes. I have my mother's nose, but I have my father's wide, full mouth and his height. I am his child, and I hate the man. I hate that I look like him.

My father is a gifted musician. Despite my love of singing and playing the piano as a child and teenager, as a young adult I rejected those creative outlets.

My father is a great dancer. I take pride in my corny dance moves.

My father is a talented con man and a charmer. I am honest to a fault and embrace the discord caused by my bluntly spoken opinions.

It's hard to find joy in gifts—or potential gifts—when they're tainted by association.

This is something that people with kind, well-meaning parents have difficulty grasping. It's not about self-pity and it's not self-loathing. It's a desperate desire to disassociate oneself from evil.

"Sorry," Sandra said, "I know you don't like to talk about him." Her tone was repentant, but she looked a tad frustrated as she gestured to the unzipped duffle bag. "Enough of this feelings stuff, look at your presents."

"Go on then." Elizabeth's mouth hooked to the side. "Dig in."

I opened the mouth of the bag wider and began pulling out items.

I found the pillow from my bed, candles, chocolate, tea, wine, more wine, my two favorite paperback romance novels, new yarn—and a vibrator.

"What...?" I looked at the vibrator; blinked at it, and I lifted my eyes to Sandra's. "What's this?"

"It's a vibrator. Haven't you ever seen a vibrator before?"

"Yes, Sandra, I've seen a vibrator before. Why in tarnation did you bring me a vibrator?"

"Well, isn't it obvious?"

"No."

"It'll help," she said simply.

I stared at her for a long moment then rolled my eyes. "It figures that you would bring me a vibrator. You are completely wack-a-doodle-doo."

"Wait a minute, if you must know, it was Janie's idea." She raised her hands in surrender like she wanted to keep me from launching into a tirade. Sandra was referring to our mutual friend and knitting group compatriot, Janie Sullivan. Janie was an Amazonian Princess-sized walking, talking version of Wikipedia. She was also completely oblivious to the obvious. This combination made her infuriatingly endearing.

"She read a study—which she shared with me—about how going through the death of a...of a parent is less stressful for people who are married or in a serious relationship, presumably because of the comfort they receive from their significant other. Part of that, Janie reasoned, and I agreed, is definitely orgasms. Also, I packed you condoms—lots of them, all different sizes. Believe me when I say that having the different sizes comes in really handy. No pun intended."

I sputtered for a few seconds then managed to finally say, "You're off your rocker, and Janie is nuts. You're both cracked nuts."

"I would have brought a life-sized cut-out of Charlie Hunnam, but this one," Sandra indicated to Elizabeth with her head, "thought it would be awkward."

I interjected, "Wack-a-doodle-doo!"

Just then, a rooster crowed in the yard, as though to echo my insult. We ignored it.

Elizabeth crossed her arms in a defensive stance. "It would be awkward. And, technically, it was larger than the allowable size for checked bags and carry-on luggage."

"I think they must make special accommodations for life-sized cut-outs. I mean, how else would you be able to cart them across the country? How do you think Darth Vader makes it to all those kids' birthday parties?"

"They're mailed…via the post office." Elizabeth's tone was droll and her expression flat. It was obvious that they'd argued this point prior to leaving Chicago.

"We didn't have time for the post office before we left."

"Please don't tell me you had a life-sized cut-out of Charlie Hunnam made." I already knew the answer.

"Okay. I won't tell you that we had a life-sized cut-out of Charlie Hunnam made. I also won't tell you that he is shirtless and currently waiting for you in your apartment. Thanks for giving me those spare keys, and you're welcome."

Before I could respond, we were interrupted by a knock on the door. Sandra promptly turned and opened it, then shuffled backward a few steps.

Drew hovered in the doorway, filling every inch of space with his giant frame. His eyes examined my room then ended their wandering when they landed on me. He looked tense.

"Is everything okay?" I asked then stood from the bed, ready to bolt down the stairs.

"Yes. She's resting. Duane and Beau are with her now."

"Oh." I relaxed a bit, breathed out a sigh. "Okay. Good."

He watched me for a beat, his eyes never wavering from mine, then said, "I'm about to head out."

"Okay." I nodded and glanced briefly at Sandra. She was looking between the two of us with narrowed eyes.

The room fell quiet. The silence became an odd, stiff thing. After a long moment where Drew walked the fine line between looking and staring, he shifted his attention to Elizabeth.

"Thank you for dinner. Everything was delicious."

"No problem." She waved away his praise then crossed to him and reached her hand out. He accepted it and they shook. "I'll see you tomorrow. It was nice meeting you."

"Tomorrow?" I asked them both. "What's tomorrow?"

Elizabeth walked back to me. "Drew and I are going to the hospital. I'd like to send your mom's records to Dr. Peterson."

"The oncologist?"

"Yeah, I talked to him about it before I left Chicago. Peterson is expecting the chart."

"Why is Drew going?"

"He holds the power of attorney…right? For the release of medical records?"

"Oh, yeah. Right." My neck itched, and I glanced at Drew. Again, he was looking at me, but this time it was a blatant stare. The intensity and vehemence in his expression caught me off guard.

"What?" I blurted, because I just couldn't take it. My eyes flickered between Sandra and Elizabeth for help. They were both looking at Drew with thoughtful expressions. "What's wrong?"

"Nothing." He said the word like we were fighting, like he was throwing it at me.

I frowned at his oddness and was about to question him further when Sandra stepped in front of me.

"Will we be seeing more of you?" she asked Drew. She crossed her arms over her chest and paused. I recognized her tone as one she used when conducting an interrogation, though her question was benign enough.

Drew's attention settled on Sandra, and he mimicked her guarded stance.

"Yes."

"So, Charlie…."

"The name is Drew."

Sandra ignored the correction. "How often will we be…*seeing* you?"

His eyes narrowed a fraction. "Daily."

"Reeeeally." Sandra lifted her chin. I could tell she was sizing him up. Heck, even Drew could tell she was sizing him up.

Neither spoke for a prolonged minute. Elizabeth and I glanced at each other, and I shrugged.

I was about to break the weird stink-eye stalemate with a suggestion that I walk Drew out—even though the thought made me strangely nervous—when Sandra said very gently, "Not all women are bad, you know. We're not all viperous bloodsuckers. There are some good ones...like Ashley. She's a good one. You might have noticed: the outside matches the inside."

My mouth fell slightly open, and I shifted back a step as Drew's eyes flickered to mine. They were such a steely cold blue that they nearly knocked me off my feet. His gaze was shuttered and hard, and his mouth was set in a firm, unhappy line.

"Good night," he said, and then he walked away, his steps audible as he descended the stairs.

CHAPTER SIX

"If we couldn't laugh, we would all go insane."

— ROBERT FROST

HE THREE OF us stood in place for several beats, and I knew without a doubt that my face held an expression of stunned bewilderment. I was still tired, and this day had started out on a bizarre note and was still circling the drain of strange. Maybe it was just everything happening all at once, but I couldn't quite wrap my mind around what had just occurred.

Therefore, I blurted, "I'm so confused."

"He is too." Sandra said this thoughtfully, still looking at the spot where Drew had been standing. "But not as confused as you are, because he's not blinded by grief."

"Sandra." Elizabeth shook her head. "Don't meddle. Ashley has enough going on."

I was sentient enough to detect an edge of warning in Elizabeth's tone. I glanced between them as the implication of their non-conversation hit me like a slow-moving river of molasses. "You can't...you can't possibly mean...?"

I didn't finish the thought because it was entirely ridiculous, like turning down fried pie at the state fair.

"Uh…yeah." Sandra shut the door and faced me. "I do mean that the good Dr. Runous is a smitten kitten. Or, maybe a better way to put it is a turned-on python." She frowned and her eyes moved to a position over my shoulder. "That's not a very good analogy either. I'm going to have to think on this."

"No, no, no. You are wrong. You are so, so wrong. He doesn't like me *at all*."

I'd been around plenty of good-looking guys in my life. I'd dated a few *I'm-too-sexy-for-this-pizza-place* narcissists. I knew better than to be attracted to the top one percent of good looking single men. The top one percent didn't believe in monogamy, or human decency, or manners, or—honestly—good sex. Sex was a stage and, after their curtain call, the show was over.

Drew was definitely in the top one percent. Therefore, I knew better. Furthermore, I was intensely aggravated with myself for noticing that Drew was in the top one percent. Additionally, why in tarnation was I thinking about sex?

"He may not like the fact that he likes you, but he does." This came from Elizabeth, her words reluctant and laced with an apology she verbalized as she continued. "I'm sorry, Ashley. But the guy is into you."

"By the way, what's in that little notebook he carries? The leather one with the Norse symbols on it?" Sandra asked us both, as if either of us would be in Drew's confidence and have any earthly idea.

"How should I know? I met him yesterday. We don't know each other. All of our interactions have been unsavory."

"But he looks at you like you are savory," Elizabeth said, "like he knows you, like he *knows you* knows you." After a brief pause, she added in a soft voice, "Like he's invested in you."

"You're misreading things."

"Both of us are misreading things?" Sandra snorted. "That's unlikely."

"No. You're wrong. He seems truly dedicated to my mother and my brothers. If you're seeing anything resembling warmth or affection it's because of them."

Neither of them looked convinced. It occurred to me that they probably weren't convinced because I wasn't convinced.

Sandra crossed to me. She gripped then squeezed my shoulders. "Look, all I know is, he came up here and looked at you like he knew you. Then he looked at you like he wanted to know you better. Then he looked at you like he was undressing you with his eyes. Then, most incriminating of all, he looked at you like he hated you."

"Yes. I noticed it too," Elizabeth chimed in. "He was basically staring at you the whole time. There was nothing subtle about it." She nodded her head for emphasis, though her expression was sympathetic.

I sputtered, floundered, and settled on saying, "You've got the last part right. He does hate me."

"Yes, he probably does." Sandra narrowed her eyes as she stepped back and surveyed me from head to toe. "I think he does hate you…in a way."

I stared at them because I could do nothing else. My brain was still slippery, overwhelmed. This was not a conversation I needed or wanted to have, especially not now.

My history with men was terrible.

My whole life—all twenty-six years of it—could be measured in the number of times I'd allowed myself to be conned by men, my father being the first. Then came my brothers (although their normalcy and kindness now had me all mixed up). Then came my best friend in high school, Jackson James. Then came every guy I'd dated in college and graduate school. They saw a nice piece of ass and a pretty face, and heard a southern accent and assumed it meant I was low class and uneducated.

I had a gift for attracting assholes and users, probably because every boy I knew growing up—and then every man I knew—eventually treated me like garbage. Now, working with big-ego, chauvinistic, ivy-league medical doctors was great. They served as a daily reminder of what real men were like and why my heart was safer with the fictional variety.

Plus, I wanted to believe that Sandra and Elizabeth were both wrong about Drew. I needed to believe they were wrong. But that was hard to do when I recalled the look of complete aggravation he'd given me in the quonset hut the day before, the Nietzsche quotes he'd intoned implying that I was a cow, and the fact that he was fictionally handsome.

Everyone knows that in real life, fictionally handsome men are vacuous vessels of Satan.

Add to all of this the fact that it didn't matter. How Drew felt about me was completely irrelevant. My hot and cold feelings about him were irrelevant.

My life was in Chicago, not Tennessee. I needed to keep my head down, live through the next four to six weeks (or so), soak up as much time as possible with Momma, then get back to my peaceful and unremarkable existence reading books and knitting.

Above all, I was going to avoid vacuous vessels of Satan.

"I can't deal with this right now," I said. "I can't even deal with the thought of it. My brain feels like it's covered in Crisco. Time is moving too fast and too slow. I have no desire to be liked or hated by Drew or anyone else."

"No desire?" Sandra prompted. "None whatsoever?"

"How can you ask me that?"

"Well, his parts fit with your parts. And he's here. And he's interested. And he's *extremely* easy on the eyes despite the fact that he never speaks. And you're both alive, so necrophilia isn't an issue."

"Do you really think I'm here on a man hunt?"

"No, of course not, and that's not what I meant. But you're allowed to notice a hot guy."

"Of course I've noticed! How could I not? He's like a Viking cowboy."

"Does he give you zings in your things?" Sandra asked this question using her best serious face.

I groaned. "Yes, if that means what I think it means, which means he's bad news. I have the uncanny ability to attract only users and assholes. It's like I've got a sign on me someplace that tells nice men to steer clear. If what you're saying about Drew is correct and he is attracted to me, then I guarantee you he's a jerk."

Sandra studied me with curious detachment, and I knew before she opened her mouth that she was no longer my friend Sandra; she was now Shrink Sandra.

"Why do you think you only attract users and assholes?"

"Because I do."

"You've never dated a nice man?"

"I did once—in high school. I dated a really nice boy named Jackson James—or at least he was nice to me until I admitted that I wasn't attracted to him. Then he made a big, public fuss, told everyone we'd slept together, and refused to talk to me again."

"And...?"

"After that, I promised myself I'd only date men I was attracted to, because I never wanted to hurt someone like that again. And since then, I've had my heart broken twice. The first time you know about— Grant, in college, the son of that big shot Wall Street tycoon."

"Sorry," Sandra said, her expression grim at the memory. "I'd forgotten about Grant."

"What happened with Grant?" Elizabeth looked between the two of us.

Sandra glanced at me and I shrugged my shoulders, indicating that I didn't care if she shared.

"He was an asshole. He was dating two other girls. But," Sandra added, turning to me, "he was a smooth asshole, wasn't he? There was no way of knowing what he was up to. And when you found out, you broke up with him."

This was all true. He was a really good liar. What I didn't tell Sandra was that when I broke up with him, he told me I was trash—I was a pretty face and a nice piece of ass, but all I'd ever be was back-woods, ignorant trash. He even said he would have been embarrassed to introduce me to his family, and that no man would want me once my looks faded.

It hurt my heart to think about it now, mostly because I was stupid enough to fall for him in the first place.

"And Sam wasn't your fault either." Sandra said this as *friend* Sandra. "He was just a flake."

Sam was my boyfriend for three months in graduate school, and I'd fallen hard. He was a musician who decided that he wasn't ready for a serious girlfriend; this was after we'd had sex, of course, and he'd told me he loved me. Six months after we broke up, he married a record executive's daughter.

"Do I want to know about Sam?" Elizabeth asked.

"No," Sandra said, and made a face like she'd just remembered what sour milk tasted like. Then she turned to me. "That's two guys, Ashley. That's hardly enough to make you swear off men."

"No, that's three guys if you count my childhood friend Jackson. If you count my father, then that's four guys who have broken my heart. If you count my brothers, then we're up to ten."

Sandra pressed her lips together and stared at me. "Drew is smokin' hot, got a head full of brains, doesn't bother much with chit-chat, and will be coming by *daily.*"

"But he's also pushy and entitled, and he rubs me the wrong way."

Elizabeth muttered under her breath, "If you let him, I think he'll gladly rub you the right way."

I stared at her, my eyeballs bugging out of my head. Then I flopped back on the bed, covered my face with my hands, and groaned. "Are we really talking about this? With my mother downstairs, sick and... she's not going to get better."

Sandra sighed. "Yes, and we're sorry." I felt the bed depress at my side. Sandra lay next to me and threw her arm and leg over my body, hugging me. "You're really vulnerable right now. It's natural to want and actually crave physical comfort. Drew would likely *love* to provide you with physical comfort. The thing is, there's an intensity about this guy that makes me worry for you. I just wanted to see if you returned his interest."

"Well I don't. I'm not interested in Drew."

Elizabeth chimed in. "You have a lot going on."

"Exactly." I felt Sandra nod next to my shoulder then squeeze me. "You're a sensitive soul. You read poetry for fun! You're a romantic. I don't want you leaving Tennessee with two broken hearts."

I shook my head, opened my eyes, and faced Sandra. She looked worried.

"I've learned my lesson, Sandra. I know better than to trust men. I'll just ignore him."

She gave me a little smile. "I doubt he's going to be easy to ignore. He strikes me as the stubborn type."

"He is stubborn, but he won't make a move. Even if what you're saying is true—which it isn't—he won't push me. My brothers trust him. And, more importantly, Momma trusts him."

"Honey, I hope you're right." She cupped my cheek, her smile wary and small. "But you should know, my dearest, that you don't need to be pushed in order to fall."

"TELL US MORE about Ashley as a little girl," Elizabeth said eagerly, her eyes darting to mine then back to Momma's. "Was she a rough-and–tumble kind of girl, or was she decked out in pink chiffon?"

It was Sandra and Elizabeth's last day, and we were all sitting in the den. Momma's weekday hospice nurse, Marissa, had also stopped by to train the weekend nurse, Tina. However, Marissa had stayed after Tina left and Joe had arrived for his shift, explaining that it was her day off and she wasn't in any rush to leave.

So, we all sat around Momma's bed chatting and drinking mint iced tea. It was nice to share my friends with Momma and vice versa, like two parts of my heart coming together. Additionally, their presence was comforting in general; this was especially true after Elizabeth heard back from our oncologist friend in Chicago. In his expert opinion, nothing could be done for my mother other than make her last weeks comfortable.

My mom sighed at Elizabeth's question, a happy smile on her face, and her eyes lost a bit of focus as she recalled what I was like in my growing-up years. "She was a bit of both, really. She loved to run wild with her brothers—when they weren't being big meanies." She paused and winked at me, then continued. "But she also liked to get dressed up in my clothes and shoes. One time I found her with lipstick all over her face." She chuckled briefly, the smile lingering behind her eyes.

I shook my head and grinned at the memory. "I was five and thought makeup consisted of only lipstick, meaning in order to put makeup on I just needed to put lipstick everywhere and it would magically do what it needed to do."

Sandra leaned in close to my mom and said, "That's how she puts on makeup now, too." Her tone was conspiratorial and her expression serious. "We're all too polite to correct her. It's very awkward when we go to the circus; everyone thinks she works there."

Marissa and Elizabeth laughed.

"Sandra, I've known you three days, and I can't imagine politeness stops you from saying anything." My mother grinned and winked at my friend.

Sandra sighed. "It's true. What is this politeness of which you speak?"

Momma laughed but then her breath hitched, and she winced and closed her eyes.

The mood in the room changed instantly. My hands balled into fists. Both Marissa and I stood and crossed to the bed as Joe handed Momma the remote that controlled the morphine pump. "Bethany, you shouldn't be afraid to use the medication," he said to her, his tone warm and kind. "It's meant to help."

Momma nodded and pressed the button once. "I know." Her voice was gravelly, unsteady. "I think maybe I'm just tired."

Elizabeth and Sandra exchanged looks then stood and began clearing dishes.

"Oh, girls, don't go yet," Momma protested.

"Don't think you can get rid of us," Sandra said over her shoulder, pausing just inside the door to the den. "We'll be back. We're just going to steal your daughter for a bit while we make dinner, but after that, we're coming in to do those tequila shots."

"You better rest up, Bethany," Marissa said, giving my mother a teasing look, referring to Sandra when she added, "Texas girls mean business."

Momma's medicine was already kicking in when we left. Marissa offered to stay behind just in case she woke up so I could help Sandra and Elizabeth with dinner.

We'd made it just three steps down the hall when we were stopped by Roscoe. He gave us all a warm smile. I noted that he had a vase of wildflowers in his hands. Often, over the last several days, I had mused that Roscoe reminded me of a puppy—eager to please and hungry for affection.

"Hey! Is Momma still up?" he asked.

"Uh, kind of," I said. "She's just resting now."

His face fell just slightly and he sighed. "Ah, well. I'll just poke my head in and leave these by her bed, maybe sit with her for a while."

"What's going on?" Billy appeared at the end of the hall and walked toward us.

He looked like he'd just come home from work. Apparently, he worked all the time, because today was Saturday, and he'd already put in some long hours during the workweek, coming home after 7:00 p.m. every day.

Sandra stepped forward and threw her thumb over her shoulder. "Go on in, Roscoe. Marissa is in there already; you could keep her company." The subtle shift in Sandra's tone had me looking at her with suspicion.

Roscoe's eyes brightened. "Really?"

Billy scowled. "What's she doing here? I thought she only worked during the week."

"She was training the weekend nurse," Elizabeth said, shimmying past my brothers on her way to the kitchen. "We've invited her to stay for dinner."

Billy grumbled something then turned, and walked down the hall toward the living room, but Roscoe stood a little straighter, his eyes moving to the den.

"Go on in, handsome," Sandra said, giving him a little grin.

He nodded once then walked past us to the door, tapping lightly before entering.

I watched Billy walk away, feeling a wistful sense of regret. He made me feel a bit like a usurper, like I was down here playing a role. Or maybe his frosty attitude toward me magnified my own feelings on the subject.

I caught Sandra eyeing me up and down, so I returned her assessing stare.

"What?" I said.

"What?" she retorted.

I narrowed my eyes further as we walked into the kitchen. "Want to tell me what's going on?"

Elizabeth was already bustling about the kitchen, pulling out pots and pans and vegetables.

"Oh, nothing," Sandra said breezily, and I noticed she was rinsing the glasses with more vigor than necessary. "By the way, did you see that you have a summer garden in the backyard?" she continued. "I asked your mother about it this morning during our one-on-one Sandra-and-Bethany coffee time. She planted the seeds a few weeks ago, but forgot about it. You have tomato plants, squash, lettuce, and green beans coming up."

"Okay...."

"Where's the good Dr. Runous? He's been scarce these last few days." Sandra's topic change gave me whiplash, and I blinked in confusion, trying to keep up.

"I...don't know."

"You probably scared him away." Elizabeth's eyes flickered to Sandra's and her voice was low. It sounded like a warning.

I'd definitely noticed Drew's absence. I'd seen him twice over the last three days and only in passing when he, Jethro, Billy, and Roscoe returned from some sort of exercise. They'd all walked in, hot and sweaty, both times. Drew had stopped to talk with Momma for a bit, but then he'd disappeared, and I'd been left with the image of a hot and sweaty Drew imprinted on my brain.

I didn't like that I'd noticed how very, very nice Drew looked after a period of heavy exertion. Therefore, I redoubled my efforts to push him from my mind. I wasn't in Tennessee to ogle Drew-flavored eye-candy. I was here to take care of my mother. Besides, more and more—as he seemed to be going out of his way to avoid me—I got the impression that he had mixed feelings toward me as well.

Sandra nodded to confirm Elizabeth's warning. "You also have eight roosters," she said, back on the topic of random farm observations.

I blinked, startled by the number, and—again—the new subject. "Eight? What do we need eight roosters for?"

"I don't know. Bethany said she was planning on butchering all of them but one, but never got around to it. You really only need one rooster to keep the hens in line, and the hens are strictly for laying eggs. Can you imagine how frustrating it must be for all those roosters, hanging around, crowing up a storm, picking fights with each other? I'm surprised one of them hasn't flown the coop. That's why there's that constant ruckus outside. You need to eat some of those cocks before you end up with a rooster situation."

I blinked at her with a deadpan expression, refusing to take the bait.

With lightning speed, Sandra once again changed the subject. "Oh, and I like your hospice nurse, Marissa. She's totally sassy. Your brothers are already fighting for her affections. I wish I could stick around and see who ends up on top...." Sandra paused and lifted her eyebrow for emphasis, "... of Marissa."

"Could you be any more gauche?" Elizabeth shook her head.

Sandra snorted, wiped her hands, and crossed to Elizabeth. "Don't pretend like you're shocked. You're a pervy perv too. And you're wondering the same thing. My money is on Billy."

"Billy? He barely acknowledges her." Sandra paused. "No, I'm thinking Roscoe. He's very charming, and he looks like he knows how to wield his axe."

"Oh, my God, they're my brothers! Ugh." A bubble of laughter escaped me and I shook my head, trying to keep my expression stern. I recognized what they were doing. They were trying to distract me from my grief and worry by being silly and gross. It was working.

"Everyone in this house needs some sexual healing. Marissa said she had sisters. I wonder how many she has. If you still don't want to get on Drew, maybe she's got a brother you could ride." Sandra winked at me.

"Just stop, please stop. I already walked in on the twins using their healing hands. No matter how much bleach I drink, I'll never be able to completely cleanse my mind or forget the horror of that sight."

"Wait, did you say twins?" Sandra paused, glancing over my shoulder as her mind worked. She refocused her gaze on me. "Were they using healing hands on each other? Together?"

"Sandra! That's disgusting!" Elizabeth smacked her on the shoulder.

"What? Men get to fantasize about ménage à trois with twin sisters, but I'm a sicko because my spank naughty list includes twin leprechauns?"

I gagged instinctively, covering my mouth with my hand, but I also laughed. Through my fingers I mumbled, "It's like there's a party going on in my mouth, and everyone is throwing up."

"That's right, Ashley. My mind just went there." Sandra said this loudly, her head doing a weird little jazzy pivot. "My mind went to the *double the ginger, double the fun.*"

"Inappropriate Shrink Sandra is inappropriate!" Elizabeth wagged her finger at Sandra, but she was giggling.

"Seriously, stop." I shook my head, holding my stomach—laughing and grossed out and close to tears of hilarity. "Please!"

Sandra crossed to stand behind Elizabeth and did a little hip pump dance; she wagged her eyebrows at me. "You know I like my sushi like I like my men...." She paused for dramatic effect then added, "...With two slices of ginger."

"You are such a freak." I lost it in a fit of giggles.

Elizabeth was laughing so hard she had to hold the kitchen counter for balance. Between loud bursts of chortling, she managed to say, "I like...my men...like I like...my meat...." She struggled for breath as she wiped tears from the corners of her eyes.

Sandra, now laughing so hard that she was completely silent, gasped out, "How's that?"

"Hot with a red…with a red…with a…."

"Don't say it!" Sandra waved her hands in the air and burst out laughing even harder this time.

Elizabeth couldn't finish for several seconds because she literally could not speak, her eyes shut tight as she laughed with abandon.

Then she blurted, "Hot with a juicy red center!"

"AGH!" I shook my head and covered my ears.

As luck would have it, Duane and Beau chose that moment to walk into the kitchen.

"AGH!" I yelled again, horrified but unable to control the laughter that convulsed my body.

My twin brothers looked at each other then at the three of us like we were aliens.

I don't think I could have stopped laughing if my life depended on it, especially when Duane asked, his features completely befuddled, "So, uh…what's for dinner?"

Then, because Sandra was Sandra, she shouted, "Steak and sushi!"

Sandra let out a loud guffaw and smacked her thigh.

Elizabeth held her stomach and shook her head, gasping for air.

My jaw hurt and my sides ached, and I had to bury my head in my arms, because every time I looked at either of them I ended up laughing all over again.

Despite the ridiculousness of the moment, I wondered in some dark place in the back of my mind how I would survive when my friends left me tomorrow. Who would I lean on? How would I cope with watching my mother slip away daily until nothing was left of her?

There was nothing funny about what was coming next, but without the laughter, I was afraid I would go insane.

CHAPTER SEVEN

"May you live every day of your life."

— JONATHAN SWIFT

*M*OMMA WAS THE hospice patient who cried wisdom-wolf.

"Ashley, where are you, honey? I've got something really important to tell you."

I was sitting in the recliner by her bed, knee deep in my third reading of *Catch 22*. I'd just given her a bath a half hour ago and helped her dress. She was weak and sleepy from the effort. The strain in her tone surprised me because I thought she was asleep.

I immediately set the book aside and reached for her hand. "I'm right here. What is it, Momma?"

"Come closer." She squeezed my fingers, so I stood from the chair and leaned over the bed so she could see me better.

"Ashley, you need to know, of all the things you wear, your expression is the most important." Momma said this with fevered earnestness. I gave her a gentle smile and she continued, her eyes losing focus. "And deodorant...always wear deodorant...and clean underwear."

This had become a usual occurrence. Over the last week and a half since she'd come home, my mother would get this look of urgency in her eyes and tell me to come close, insisting that she had some grave, important bit of wisdom to pass on. And when I leaned in close, it was always something peculiar, random, or mundane.

It didn't matter who else was in the room. Her coworker friends from the library stopped by for a visit, during which my momma urgently told me, "The angleworms aren't anxious for the fish to bite."

Her minister dropped in to check on the family, and Momma wouldn't let go of my hand until she'd said, "You'll lose your grip if you put too much spit on your hands."

One time she said, "When your kids tell you they have tummy aches, ask them if they've pooped yet. It's usually just constipation."

Another time it was, "Happiness and rheumatism keep getting bigger if you tell people about them."

And another, "Fear don't count if you really want something."

I couldn't figure out if she was pulling my leg with this stuff or if she was serious, so I decided to tell her corny jokes. Stuff like:

"How does the ocean say hello to the shore... it gives it a little wave."

"How can you tell the sun doesn't feel good... it's not so hot."

I needed to hear her laugh. When she laughed, it felt like it was okay for me to laugh—and I needed to laugh.

This time, however, I didn't tell her a joke, because her eyes were hazy and unfocused.

I nodded, reached my hand up to her cheek, and brushed a few hairs from her temple. "I will remember to wear a pleasant expression as well as deodorant and clean underwear at all times. I promise."

"Also, baby, you need to stop hovering. When was the last time you left this room?"

I shushed her. "I'm here to take care of you and spend time with you. This is where I want to be."

She grimaced and squeezed her eyes shut, her breathing short and rattled. I blinked away the stinging moisture in my eyes as I watched her struggle through the wave of pain. Her fingers gripped mine like a lifeline.

I studied her morphine drip and found it full. This was distressing, as Marissa had replaced the bag several hours ago.

"Momma, if you're in pain, you need to use your button." I kept my voice low and temperate.

She shook her head. "It makes me feel groggy. I don't want to sleep…not yet."

I inhaled a shaky breath and gritted my teeth. She moaned. It was a horrible sound and made me feel completely helpless. Movement at the door caught my attention. I looked up to find Duane and Beau hovering in the doorway.

Their eyes were wide as their gazes moved from Momma to me then back again.

"What's wrong? What can we do?" Beau stepped forward and placed his hand on my mother's forehead.

"She's in a lot of pain," I explained, and then I looked at Duane. "Will you get her some ice chips?"

Duane hesitated for a moment then disappeared. I decided that I would move a cooler into the room for her ice chips, just in case she needed them and I was by myself.

"What about the medicine?" Beau was all restrained energy, his expression mirroring the helplessness I felt.

"She…." I was going to explain that she wasn't pressing the button for the morphine pump, but instead I swallowed. It felt wrong talking about her like she wasn't in the room. I squeezed my mother's hand. "Momma, will you please take your medicine? Press the button."

She shook her head, her face pale, her mouth a tight line.

Moments like this made me wish desperately for the advice and comfort of my friends. Saying goodbye to Sandra and Elizabeth had been really difficult.

They'd stayed for three days. While Sandra and Elizabeth were here, I'd gratefully allowed Sandra to become the emotional center of the household while I retreated into the safety and comfort of my eReader and novels. She'd stayed up late, talking to one or more of the boys—or, rather, men—helping them work through and come to terms with the painful reality of losing their mother.

She'd also helped me, as had Elizabeth, by encouraging me to go on walks, help with dinner, take a shower…brush my teeth.

It was now a week after their departure, and I couldn't remember the last time I'd bathed. It was definitely on a day that started with a T. I couldn't bring myself to leave the den. I couldn't stand the thought of Momma needing me and me not being there.

Beau's eyes were somewhat wild as they moved over her face then down the length of the bed. His attention focused on the corded white remote with the red button on the end, the button my mother refused to press.

Beau picked it up and pushed the button several times. Then he looked up at me, his expression a strange mixture of defiant and apologetic.

I sighed and closed my eyes, grateful that he'd done it, because I hadn't been ready to take the choice away from her.

"Is everything okay?"

I opened my eyes to find Jethro and Cletus walking into the room. Duane was behind them holding a cup filled with ice chips.

Jethro stood next to Beau and frowned at the remote in his hand then he looked at me. "What happened?"

I shrugged. When I finally spoke, my voice was shaky and my chin was wobbling, but I didn't cry. "Momma wouldn't press the button."

My mother's tight expression was easing, her jaw unclenching, and her grip on me was growing slack.

Jethro nodded, looking grave. "Ash, why don't you take a break?"

I shook my head, my eyes on Momma. "I'm fine. I was just reading a book."

"Ash…."

Something about Jethro's tone, the way he said my name, made me look up. His eyes bored into mine, but they were compassionate. "Go take a shower."

I swallowed my automatic decline and nodded, gently laying my mother's limp hand on the bed. Jethro's grave expression, the set of his jaw, the hardness in his brown eyes told me I wasn't going to refuse his "suggestion."

Mindlessly, I went upstairs and quickly did as instructed. But I was really just going through the motions. Nothing about it felt cleansing or necessary. My heart was still downstairs, twisted up and bruised and refusing pain medication.

After drying off and changing into mostly clean yoga pants and a black T-shirt that didn't smell, I descended the stairs, intent on getting back to the den and my now permanent spot in the recliner by Momma's bed. I was going through my mental checklist: How much had she eaten today? How much had she slept?

I turned the corner to the den and caught the tail end of a hushed conversation. The hallway was clogged with six Winston boys and one Drew Runous.

"...Like I said, don't worry about it, Billy. You all have enough on your mind without having to think about the bills." Drew's voice was infinitely calm, yet he also sounded uncomfortable.

"You're paying them yourself." Billy's voice was a tad frustrated. "That's not right, Drew."

"I'll reimburse myself later."

"No you won't. You'll just pay for everything." I peeked around the doorframe and saw that Billy didn't look upset; in fact, he looked grateful and good-naturedly irritated. "I called the bank and checked the schedule. I know you've already covered the car payment and the electric bill for this month and next."

Drew sighed. "I don't want to argue about this, Billy."

Billy laughed lightly. "Are we arguing?"

"Hey, Ash," Jethro said.

My eyes flickered to my oldest brother, who was frowning as he held my gaze. In fact, the lot of them were all frowning and standing a little straighter and stiffer. Drew, however, wasn't looking at me at all; his attention was affixed to the wall behind Billy's head.

Sandra and Elizabeth's worries about Drew had proved to be completely unfounded. He hadn't made any advances of any sort, nor had he subjected me to any further Nietzsche quotes. We hadn't even engaged in any stink-eye stalemates.

Although, to be fair, it's hard to stare at someone who isn't there or who won't make eye contact. Drew visited Momma, but he seemed to have a talent for only coming by when I was elsewhere or asleep. For my part, I was noticing him less and less, even when he showed up hot and sweaty after a workout.

"Hi." I gave them a tight-lipped smile and a little wave. "What's going on?"

"Are you hungry?" This question came from Cletus. "Cause Drew brought food."

I gave sweet Cletus a smile and shook my head. "Thanks, but I'm not hungry."

"You didn't eat breakfast," Billy said. He was scowling at me.

I thought about this, realized he was right.

Not eating breakfast was very atypical behavior for me. I'd never, ever, ever, ever been the girl who skipped meals. In fact, I liked to plan my workdays and vacations around food. I was a foodie through and through. I didn't mind more junk in the trunk (or up front) if it meant cookies every day. But over the last week, nothing had tasted good.

"Okay...." I hesitated, glanced at the door to the den.

Surprising me, Drew came over to where I was standing in the doorway and placed his hands on my waist like he wasn't going to let me pass. He captured my gaze with his; then his attention flickered between my eyes and my mouth as he said quietly, "She's asleep, Sugar. You need a break. Come eat something."

His closeness, his warm hands on my body, the way he was looking at me with his steely eyes, the softness of his tone when he called me Sugar—it all pushed at some part of me that had been dormant for days. I elbowed the awakening sensations aside, wanting to focus on my mother.

"What if she wakes up?" I challenged. "I don't want her to be alone."

"I'll sit with Momma," Beau said sheepishly. His expression told me he felt some guilt for forcing pain meds on her. I wanted to tell him

I was glad he'd done it. As soon as the thought entered my head, I felt guilty.

"I'll sit with her too," Roscoe volunteered.

Jethro stepped forward and tugged on my elbow, pulling me out of Drew's hold, which tightened before he let me go. "Come on, Ash," my brother pleaded. "It's fried chicken and mashed potatoes. Maybe you could call your friend Sandra and have a chat."

I let Jethro lead me into the kitchen, and the entire Winston brood —plus Drew, minus Beau and Roscoe—followed.

"I can't, actually. My phone doesn't get reception out here, there's no house phone, and there's no Internet, so I can't use Skype." I said this flatly, without recrimination.

"Why don't you use Momma's cell?"

"I can't find it. It wasn't with her things when she came back from the hospital." The situation was not easily fixable so I'd decided to do nothing about it. None of the houses in Green Valley had Internet unless they had a satellite dish. There was no point in asking for a satellite hookup since I wasn't staying very long.

"You can use my phone," Jethro offered. "Or Billy's, or any of them."

I shrugged. "Nah. That's all right." I didn't really have the energy to think about it.

"You haven't talked to your friends all week?" Duane moved to the cabinet and grabbed a stack of plates. "That don't seem right. Don't y'all see each other every week?"

I nodded. "Sometimes I meet them for lunch at the hospital during the week. But, yeah, Tuesday is the day we all get together. We meet up and knit and crochet, and of course we talk."

"Tomorrow is Tuesday." Cletus placed a pile of forks and knives on the counter. "You're going to miss your time if we can't get you on the Internet."

"Don't worry about it." I glanced around the kitchen, not feeling particularly invested in the conversation. My eyes landed on Drew and found him standing off to one side, removed from everyone else, looking at his cell phone as if he were reading a text. For some random reason, I wondered who his cell phone company was.

"Hey, Ash, Momma's talking about someone named Jackson." Roscoe said this from the doorway. "Do you know who she means? She keeps asking if you're out with Jackson."

"Is she awake?" I moved toward the doorway, but Roscoe blocked my path.

"No, Ash. You need to eat. She's not really awake, just talking in her sleep, I think."

"She's not talking about Jack *Jackson* James, is she—that little twerp who followed you around?" Billy asked this as he put napkins at the place settings on the table.

"He wasn't a twerp. He was my best friend." I crossed my arms over my chest, but felt only a slight twinge of defensiveness.

Jackson and I had been best friends all through school partly because I'd never been very good at making friends with other girls. He and I just got along so well because we were both oddball social outcasts. In my experience growing up in small Hicksville nowhere Tennessee, little girls were mean, adolescent girls were cruel, and teenage girls were ruthless—but that was probably true everywhere.

Plus, Jackson James was the sweetest, kindest, most amazing boy in the entire world...until the end of our senior year when he dumped me.

I was stunned when that happened. I wasn't in love with Jackson— not in the passionate or romantic way that books and movies tell you is real—but I had come to rely on him. He'd been my first everything: my first kiss, my first boyfriend, my first *first*. And when he dumped me just before college, he cut off all communication. I was so devastated over the loss of my best friend that it felt like I'd lost a part of myself.

Over the years, the feeling of loss had dwindled to a slight ache, mostly related to nostalgia. I'd come to view him as another example —in a long line of examples—of why men were as trustworthy and reliable as tampons made of sand.

"Oh, please." Duane rolled his eyes. "Jackson James is an asshole.

I still don't know why you gave him the time of day. You could have had any guy in a hundred-mile radius, and you didn't give anyone a second look except that dipshit—and he was a scrawny little bastard. Didn't he play something stupid like the clarinet or something?"

I gritted my teeth. "It was the oboe, and he was really good." For some bizarre reason my gaze searched out Drew's and found him watching me. When our eyes met, he didn't look away. Therefore, I did.

Jethro grumbled as he placed the utensils around the table. "Real men play instruments with strings, like a guitar or a bass."

"Or the drums. Those got no strings," added Cletus.

"He just wanted to get in your pants," Duane said and shook his head, obviously having worked himself into a temper of disgust for my childhood best friend.

"Duane Faulkner Winston." Jethro's voice held a hint of warning. "Quit being ugly. That was disrespectful. Apologize to Ash."

Momma had given each of us her favorite authors' surnames as our middle names. Mine was fine, Ashley Austen Winston for Jane Austen. But I felt a little sorry for Billy, because his full name was William Shakespeare Winston.

Duane placed his hand on my shoulder. "I'm sorry, Ash. I didn't say it to be mean. It's just that everyone in town wanted to get in your pants, and that guy was the worst. It's rough having a beauty queen as a sister."

"Lots of guys to beat up," Billy mumbled under his breath as he finished placing the napkins.

I frowned at Billy and could feel my neck heat with embarrassment, but I addressed Duane's apology. "It's okay. I know you weren't trying to be mean. But Jackson really was my friend. I knew him when we were kids."

"You mean you felt sorry for him," Duane insisted. "He was a reject. You were the only one who was nice to him."

I closed my eyes and rubbed my forehead, feeling abruptly tired. "I think I'm going to go lay down."

"But you haven't eaten," Cletus argued from behind me.

"I'm sorry...I'm just not very hungry." I was already walking toward the hallway that led back to the den.

When silence followed, I thought I was home free. But then I felt a hand catch my wrist and pull me down the hall in the opposite direction of the den.

"I said...."

"I heard you." Drew's voice was like tempered steel, his eyes silver and flashing, and he had rendered me momentarily speechless. His presence was overwhelming. Despite my various states of exhaustion, I couldn't resist checking out his well-formed backside as he led me through the family room, out the front door, and onto the porch.

Once there, he let me go, but he stood between the door and me, his arms crossed over his chest, his face grim. Then, he stalked toward me.

I blinked at him, at the door, at the brightness of the early evening sunlight. My brain told me it had been more than a week since I'd been outside. When my brain also told me that I needed to pull myself together by voluntarily taking showers, eating three meals a day, and finding a way to keep in regular contact with my friends in Chicago— basically, to rejoin the land of the living—I told my brain to hush.

Drew was glaring at me, each of his steps bringing us closer, and his jaw was set. I mimicked his stance, though I backed up as he advanced. I'm sure the effect was pathetic. I was tired. I lacked the physical and mental energy to argue with anyone.

However, it seemed that my body did not lack the energy required to become hot and flustered at finding myself suddenly alone with Drew.

"You're sleeping on the cot in the den every night, aren't you?" His words sounded accusatory, and his jaw ticked.

I scrunched my nose at him, taking another step away. "Yes. I am."

"I told you that you and your brothers would take shifts. I don't want you sleeping in there every night. You need to take better care of yourself." His tone was straddling the line between angry and agitated. He stalked closer.

I shrugged, my back hitting the porch post. I couldn't retreat further.

"Fine," I said.

I'd learned, growing up, that if I said *fine*, people usually left me alone because they thought they'd won. Then, I ignored their wishes and did whatever I wanted to do. This approach also worked well with physicians when they got a bee in their boxers.

I could sit tight, say *fine*, wait for the narcissists to tire themselves out, then go back to my business; or I could try to fight back. Fighting back never worked. It was like trying to hold back a bursting levy with duct tape and a plucky can-do attitude. Better just to let the tide wash over you and ride out the egomaniac storm.

Drew was now two feet away. "You say *fine*, but I know you're going to go back in there and sleep on that cot again tonight."

I gave him my stone face. This wasn't any of his business. I wasn't his business. What I did or didn't do wasn't his business. But for some reason, my brothers and my momma had invited the entitled Dr. Runous into their lives and given him the reins.

I could do nothing about that, but I didn't have to like it.

Brow furrowed, mouth stern, eyes piercing, Drew stepped closer. I was forced to tilt my head backward to maintain eye contact, and my silly heart began to pound out a staccato rhythm.

Whether I liked it or not, whether it was convenient or not, Drew's proximity affected me. I was awake to him now, fully aware. I might have been barely going through the motions and neglecting my personal hygiene; nevertheless, he was an irritating reminder that I was very much a woman, and my body responded to silver-eyed, fictionally handsome men—especially when this man seemed to make it his mission to look after my momma and brothers.

"Ash, Sugar, you need to take better care of yourself." His voice dipped, deepened, and became soft and coaxing. He lifted his hand and pushed the hair behind my neck, his hand lingering for a beat. The back of his fingers brushed against my shoulder down to my elbow, making me fight against a shiver.

Then, abruptly, he snatched his hand back as if he hadn't realized what he was doing.

"Don't call me Sugar, I'm not your Sugar." I said this dumbly and without energy, my neck hot and itchy. I had the strangest, most insane desire to press and/or rub myself against him. He was so ludicrously manly and gorgeous and swoony.

"You can't hide the sweetness, Ashley. It's not something to be ashamed of."

"I'm not sweet." This emerged somewhat breathlessly.

"Yes. Yes you are. You are working yourself to ragged taking care of your momma. You're so sweet you're giving me a stomach ache and cavities." He said the words as though he were both impressed and aggravated, and he said them suddenly, as if he hadn't planned to speak them out loud.

He was looking at me with the same intensity he'd employed that night in my room when Sandra was sizing him up. He was looking at me like I *was* sugar, like I was cake covered in frosting, and he couldn't decide whether he wanted to bite me or lick me first.

I held my breath as I watched him, wondering what he was going to do, wondering if I would stop him. His eyes grew unfocused as he gazed at my lips, our heads inching closer.

The sound of voices from inside the house broke the spell, and Drew stiffened. His gaze moved over my face like he was surprised to see me there. Drew must've disliked what he found because his scowl intensified and his eyes narrowed into slits. Then, abruptly, he turned away.

His tone was clipped and low as he said, "Infuriating woman."

With that, he disappeared into the house, his exit punctuated by a slam of the screen door.

I released the breath I'd been holding and would have staggered if I hadn't been leaning against the porch post. I decided to wait a minute to give my body time to simmer down before I went back into the house. I definitely needed to simmer down. Drew had my heart beating a million miles a minute; he made my chest hot and my belly disconcertingly—yet deliciously—achy.

After several deep breaths, I took a few steps toward the house only to be greeted by Cletus poking his head around the screen door followed by two plates of fried chicken, mashed potatoes, and green beans.

"Hey, baby sister, I have food for you." Cletus's warm hazel eyes and affectionate words softened my heart more than a little. He gave me an imploring smile, and his tone was imploring as he said, "Come eat with me on the swing. I'll tell you about my auto shop."

Just like that, faced with sweet Cletus, I surrendered.

I inhaled then released a steadying breath, my hands falling to my sides. "Sure, Cletus…that sounds nice." I took my plate and sat on one end of the swing.

CHAPTER EIGHT

"Something will have gone out of us as a people if we ever let the remaining wilderness be destroyed.... We simply need that wild country available to us, even if we never do more than drive to its edge and look in."

— WALLACE STEGNER, THE SOUND OF
MOUNTAIN WATER

"WHEN WAS THE last time you went outside?"

"What?" I said, squinting as I glanced from my backlit eReader to my brother Billy. I had a gray spot in my vision from staring at a bright screen in a dark room for too long.

He glanced at Marissa. Even with the lingering gray rectangle clouding my vision, I saw them exchange a *look*. Her lips pressed together, her eyebrows raised meaningfully, her eyes slightly narrowed.

Marissa the traitor.

Billy's eyes widened, then he looked at me and growled. "That's it. Get up."

He didn't wait for me to move. He walked around my mother's

hospital bed where she lay asleep, and he pulled me from the recliner by my elbow and steered me out of the room.

Billy didn't stop until we were at the bottom of the stairs, and he only stopped then because I tugged my arm out of his grip.

"Wait a minute!" I spluttered, "Would you just hold your horses?"

His expression was impatient and irritated. "What?"

I frowned. He looked tired. His suit was wrinkled, and his beard was askew. "Are you okay? Did something happen?"

"I'm fine, Ash. Except for the fact that my momma's down the hall dying and my sister, after disappearing for eight years, has returned home just to become a ghost. Other than that, everything is just fine."

I flinched, partly because the family room was brighter than the den; but mostly because his words scalded the marshmallow wall I'd been trying to build around myself.

I had dropped all of the balls I should have been juggling—specifically, the care and feeding of myself and my family—in favor of spending every spare minute with my momma. She'd even remarked on it, joked that I was hovering, commented that I'd become so pale I was translucent. She called me a glowing white angel sent to take her to heaven.

A week had passed since my strange interaction with Drew on the porch. Since then I'd been pointedly avoiding him and everyone else. Whenever he came into the den to visit Momma, the air seemed to shift. I always ignored it and him by burying my face in a book. Seeing him and being near him made me feel off-kilter.

Something in my expression must've made Billy regret his last statement, because his eyes softened a fraction, and he *tsked*.

But then he growled with exasperation and said, "You need to snap out of it—out of this. You can't sit inside all day. Plus, you're not eating, you don't speak to us, and you don't even acknowledge when we're in the same room with you."

"I don't?"

"No, you don't. Since your friends left, I think I've heard you say three words that weren't spoken to Momma or to one of the nurses *about* Momma."

He was right. When Momma was awake, we talked, I fed her, I bathed and dressed her, or I read to her. Every day, however, she continued to dispense random bits of perplexing wisdom.

When Momma was asleep, Marissa tried to draw me into conversation.

But mostly I slept, made mental lists regarding Momma's eating and sleeping habits, or I read. If I remembered, I ate.

Until this moment, my brothers had let me be.

But I sensed that they were waiting for me to step up and demonstrate strength of character and leadership. I didn't want to, and I honestly felt like I couldn't. I wasn't a leader—but I wasn't a follower either.

I'd reverted to my childhood default; in Tennessee, I was an overly sensitive loner.

Now, as the truth of Billy's words sank in, my gaze dropped to the floor and I shifted my weight. I saw that my feet were bare and a little dirty. Then I noticed that I was in yoga pants. I wondered when I'd last changed my underwear.

Gross.

"This is it," Billy said. "This is your come-to-Jesus moment, care of your big brother. You're going to go upstairs," he pointed up the stairs. "You're going to take a shower, because you stink. Then you're going to put on clean clothes and come back down here. I have an errand for you to run, and you're not allowed to come back to the house until supper."

I stared at him, opened my mouth to object, but realized I had no idea what time it was. "Wait, what time is it?"

"It's almost noon."

"Why are you home? Shouldn't you be at work?"

"I came home during lunch because I was worried about you."

I flinched, startled. Billy was worried about me. One side of my marshmallow wall melted into goo.

"Get on upstairs or I will strip you naked and force you under that shower myself. No need to knock; nobody is on the schedule for today."

I nodded, my chin wobbling, my eyes filling with tears.

"And stop being so pitiful." He said this harshly, right before he pulled me into a hug-and-hold.

♥ ♥ ♥

I WAS SHOVED out of the house, but only after Billy supervised me doing my hair and putting on my makeup. He also picked out my clothes.

He justified all of this overbearing behavior by saying, "We are all worried about you."

For some reason, this worked. I was discovering that my brothers' concern for me was my kryptonite. Maybe I'd run away from them and Tennessee eight years ago out of an instinctual need for self-preservation and a desire to become someone else. They—as a group or individually—could effortlessly wrap me around their index, ring, or pinky finger.

Or maybe I was just feeling markedly overwhelmed, tired, and hungry, and was currently in a state of high suggestibility. Getting dressed, putting on makeup, and doing my hair all felt like going through the motions. I lacked the energy to care.

Whichever the case—dressed in jeans that were now a little baggy, a Mumford and Sons concert T-shirt, and converse sneakers—I was sent on my way. I was soon on the road to the backwoods ranger station; my mission was to give Jethro his provisions backpack.

I mostly knew where I was going. The twists and turns of the mountain road, along with the energy and focus required to navigate them, proved a great distraction. I was almost disappointed when I pulled into the makeshift parking lot for the small outpost cabin.

Billy had explained that this particular ranger station was a one-room cabin set on a hill. You parked at the base of the hill then walked a tenth of a mile (up the hill) to the cabin.

It was a beautiful day, and I briefly wondered what month it was. I decided, counting back two weeks, that it must be the middle of September. The air was still August hot and the ground was slippery from a morning rainstorm. I had to navigate the incline slowly, paying special attention to avoid the particularly muddy areas.

Halfway up the hill I felt the ground tremble in the same way it does when a galloping horse approaches. I stopped and surveyed the clearing.

Then I heard it.

Something was crashing through the forest. And it was large enough to make the earth vibrate. Before I could tell my feet to run, I saw it.

It was a black bear—quite possibly the largest black bear in the Great Smoky Mountains National Forest—and it was running right for me.

I gasped, horrified, even as I quickly calculated my chances of reaching the ranger station before the bear reached me. Those chances were a big, fat zero.

I did the only thing I could think of and what all children growing up at the edge of the wilderness are instructed to do if cornered by a bear in the woods.

I fell to the ground and played dead.

The muddy, wet ground seeped through my jeans and T-shirt. I tried to breathe and lay limp, but I couldn't. I held my breath, my body taut with the anticipation of becoming a bear snack.

As a rule, black bears don't eat people; not even the big, four hundred pound male bears like this one. They're typically shy and only venture out at dawn and dusk. Usually they're hanging out in trees, taking naps, and munching on berries.

So it made no sense for this creature to be running out of the forest at 2:00 p.m. on a Tuesday. He was plowing toward me like I was the last ripe berry bush of the season or a basket of fish.

I felt him thundering toward me as I played dead.

As I played dead....

What are you doing?! Some part of me demanded. *Get up get up get up get up!*

I opened my eyes, stared at the ground. A little voice that was growing louder with each ground tremble commanded that I face the end of my story rather than hide from it and *play dead.* Hadn't I done that enough? How much of my life was going to be about escape?

In a flash I remembered an article I'd read about a hiker who scared off a grizzly bear by standing tall and holding his jacket over his head; in essence it made him appear just as big as the grizzly.

Obviously driven insane by the pathetic notion of dying while playing dead, I jumped to my feet, grabbed the bottom of my shirt, and pulled it up and over my head as I faced the bear. It was close now; I could hear the labored breathing of the beast. I forced myself to open my eyes, and did so just in time to see it veer slightly off its original course. I tensed as it galloped less than two feet from where I stood like a mental patient with my shirt over my head.

That's right. The bear ran past me like I wasn't even there.

La-di-da, if you please.

And it kept on running, all the way to the other side of the clearing and into the wilderness beyond. I strained my ears, still holding my breath, and listened to the sounds of it crashing through the forest as the reverberations beneath my feet receded.

I twisted and looked over my shoulder, staring at the spot where it had disappeared into the woods.

"Oh my God!" I shrieked, looking to the left and right, followed by a startled, disbelieving, very hysterical laugh. "Oh my God, I just did that." My legs gave way and I fell down, my bare back—save for the scrap of my bra strap—hitting the muddy ground with full force, and I breathed in the smell of the earth.

I didn't care that I was caked in dirt and mud and grass stains. Nor did I care that my hair was damp and my body was sweatacular and sticky from adrenaline.

I was just happy to be alive with all of my appendages in place and not a scratch on me.

Then, I heard another noise, and I froze. It was a snarl. In comparison to the thunderous bear, it was a subtle sound. But the snarl caused a new wave of cold fear to twist in my stomach before crawling up my spine, because I recognized what the sound meant.

Slowly, I sat up and realized that the bear wasn't running *toward* anything. The bear was running *away* from the rabid raccoon currently eyeing me with madness.

I screamed and jumped to my feet just as the tiny raccoon, its mouth foaming, sprinted out of the forest and into the clearing.

"Raccoon! Rabid raccoon!!" I yelled, running uphill to the ranger station. "RACCOON!!!"

The moment was both terrifying and preposterous. I hadn't run from the four-hundred-pound black bear, but I was running from a rabid, smaller-than-average raccoon.

I hollered, "COOOOON!!!" but then grimaced, the hyper-civilized part of my brain shaking its head in severe judgment for using that word in any context.

I found I was gripping Jethro's backpack of provisions in one hand and my shirt in the other; so I ripped open the bag and started throwing anything I could find at the rodent—my shirt, Jethro's thermos, water filter, a bag of walnuts, underwear—all the while screaming, "RACCOON!!"

The little devil would not be deterred. It just kept coming and snarling and foaming. I tripped on something and fell, my arms bracing against stones, my teeth banging together with a jarring click, causing me to accidentally bite my tongue.

The iron taste of blood filled my mouth as my hands searched for something, anything to hold off the raccoon. I found a rock and threw it at the varmint, then another, and another.

In desperation, I screamed, "HELP ME! BEAR! BEAR!!"— deciding that the word *bear* would break through to anyone within earshot in a way that *raccoon* might not.

I clipped the little beast with heavy stone, confusing the animal for a few precious seconds, and launched to my feet. My hands were scraped; my arms scratched, bruised, and muddy; my jeans soaked through, but I launched myself up the rest of the hill, sprinting until I was sure my chest would explode.

When I was thirty feet from the cabin, I glanced over my shoulder and found the raccoon a mere five feet away. Reacting on instinct, I roared, turned, planted my left foot on the ground, and administered a swift goalie kick to the small raccoon in a way that would have made my high school soccer coach proud.

The raccoon sailed thirty or so feet down the hill then rolled another few feet. Apparently, it didn't require much recovery time, because it immediately started back up the hill in mad pursuit.

I heard the door to the ranger station open behind me. I turned and began sprinting to the safety of the cabin, paying no heed to Drew's bewildered and stunned expression.

"Ash? What the…?"

Without explaining or thinking, I reached for Drew's gun, withdrew it, flicked off the safety, turned, aimed, and shot the raccoon.

I'd like to say that it only took one shot, but that would be a lie. I emptied the entire magazine and pressed the trigger several more times after all the bullets were spent. Some of the shots missed, some didn't.

Take-home message:

Rabid Raccoon: zero.

Ashley Winston: still alive and rabies free.

I stood, gun in hand, breathing hard, staring at the ground in the distance for an indeterminate period. Adrenaline waned, my heart slowed, and my body began to shake.

"Ash…?"

The sound of Drew saying my name startled me, and I jumped. Before I could make any other movements, his arm wrapped around my middle, strong and solid, and brought my back against his chest. His free hand reached for the gun. Gently, he took it, holstered it, and shuffled us backward.

I noted that he kicked the door closed with his booted foot and moved us farther into the cabin. Unexpectedly, my knees failed me and I sagged. Also unexpectedly, Drew swung me into his arms and carried me to a faded red and white checked couch. Even more unexpectedly, instead of placing me on the couch, he sat and cradled me on his lap.

I didn't cry. I wasn't going to cry. After a long time of sitting on Drew's lap, I became aware that he was stroking my now wild hair and rubbing my mud-crusted, jean-clad thigh. I realized that I'd just faced a black bear with my eyes open and my arms stretched over my head. I replayed the rabid raccoon near-attack over and over in my mind, starting with the snarl and ending with eight gunshots.

Reality finally soaked in. I was wet, shirtless, scraped, bruised, muddied, and cold. But I was alive.

I stirred. Drew's movements stilled. I shifted. He leaned his head away and peered down at me, his bright gray eyes wide and searching.

"Hi, Drew," I said. The tremors had passed, and I wasn't shaking anymore, but my voice was weaker than I would have liked.

"Hi, Ash." His voice was deep, strong, and quietly commanding. "You want to tell me what happened?"

I blinked up at him, gathered a deep breath, opened my mouth to respond, and in burst Jethro through the front door of the cabin.

"What the hell is going on? The radio is going crazy with reports of a giant bear on the rampage and gunshots in this location. When I pulled up I found these…" Jethro held up his underwear, my shirt, his backpack, and a bag of walnuts, "…all over the side of the hill along with dead raccoon bits sticking to my shit like confetti, and…Ashley?"

Jethro glanced from Drew to me then back again. He seemed to be taking in my appearance: the scratches and fresh bruises on my arms, the dirt on my face, and the lack of shirt covering my torso.

His demeanor grew at once ominous and severe; he changed so abruptly that I flinched. His eyes were like glinting daggers as they settled to where Drew's hand rested on my thigh.

His dark eyes lifted to Drew's and held his with a menacing glare. "You want to tell me what you think you're doing to my baby sister?"

CHAPTER NINE

"Because sometimes people who seem good end up being not as good as you might have hoped."

— JONATHAN SAFRAN FOER, EXTREMELY LOUD
AND INCREDIBLY CLOSE

HE FIRST TIME I told the story of the bear-scare rabid-raccoon attack, I did it in a rush so that my oldest brother wouldn't murder Drew.

As soon as Jethro had calmed down enough to listen, Drew took off his shirt and handed it to me.

"There's a sink in the back and soap. Go wash those scrapes and, please... put this on." He said, his eyes averted to the floor. He didn't look at me again until I'd returned from the sink, my cuts and scrapes washed, the dark gray T-shirt covering me to just above the knees of my muddy jeans.

The second time I told the story, it took forever. Questions were asked ad nauseam about the size of the bear, which direction it went, where the raccoon came from—they wanted to know the *precise* location—when I'd lost my shirt, what happened to Jethro's provision bag, and how I'd cut and bruised my arms.

Drew crouched next to me the whole time, rubbing my back at intervals or stroking my hair. Instinctively I leaned against him, accepting his warmth and comfort; both felt wonderful, like being submerged in a warm bath. Jethro's face paled when I came to the part about the rabid raccoon; he gave me tight smiles that betrayed how helplessly frustrated he felt with the situation.

I was just finishing with this second recitation when more people arrived. Three additional rangers and two state game wardens showed up, not knocking as they entered.

Drew stood and Jethro made quick introductions; three of them seemed to know me or recognize me, presumably because I'd spent the first eighteen years of my life nearby. I didn't really look at the men or catch their names. I did note that they all had beards; just like two weeks ago, I was in a room with seven bearded men.

A little bubble of laughter escaped my throat before I could catch it; it wasn't loud, but it did make me look a bit unhinged. I glanced at the table, tried to focus on the sturdiness of it, the solid weight of the wood. I rubbed my forehead and found that my hands were still shaking; not as badly as before, but the tremors were definitely there.

Then, I was asked to narrate the story once more. When I related the bit about the raccoon, all the newcomers had similar reactions to Jethro's: wonder and horror.

Of course adding to this kerfuffle was the fact that Drew was shirtless. I tried to limit my noticing, but I still noticed. How could I not? I don't care how unnerved a woman is, she notices when a man has a chest and back and arms and stomach like Drew's.

My reaction to his physical perfection was *especially* heightened since I was still amped up on adrenaline. If we'd been alone, he might have been in danger of a different kind of bear attack from Ashley the bear. And he was being attacked.

By me.

I tried not to dwell on the fact that life and death situations apparently made me a horny toad.

Instead, I focused on the fact that I felt alive—really felt it—and it was good to be alive. It was good to feel.

Jethro hovered at my side, his hand on my shoulder during my recitation. My eyes kept flickering to Drew's, checking to see if he was watching me or if it was safe to steal a glance at his bare torso. Of course, it was never safe. He paced the room, but his eyes never moved from my face, his expression focused. I did, however, catch his gaze watching my mouth as I spoke, and sometimes lingering on my neck.

This didn't help my horny toadness.

When I got to the part where I took off my shirt and faced down the bear, Jethro shook his head and Drew mumbled, "I can't believe you did that."

When I finished, the menfolk began to talk among themselves, leaving me to stare dazedly about the room. Once again, my attention focused on the oak tabletop.

I caught the gist of their discussion. They were arguing—well, not really arguing at first—about making me recite the tale one more time. Jethro maintained that I'd been through enough, that they could retell it if needed.

The other five wanted to hear my version again. One of the men proposed that they voice record the story, then have me take them outside to diagram it all out.

Voices were lifting, and I continued to stare at the sturdy table. I'd never noticed the intricate pattern of a wood grain before. The marks were enigmatic and fascinating.

Then Drew was kneeling next to me. His warm hand was on the back of my neck sending little spikes of heat down my spine. His fingers were in my hair. He gently squeezed, bringing my attention to him.

As usual, his eyes were somber and ardent, but now they seemed more blue and silver and vibrant than I remembered. I noted that he had the beginnings of crow's feet around his eyes; I was distracted by the striking and bold shape of his eyebrows.

"Ash...."

"Yes?" He had a freckle just below his right eye, and it was very attractive…and distracting.

"Sugar, are you okay?"

"Yes." I sighed. Usually I wouldn't put up with being called *Sugar*; yet when Drew said it, especially like that—all soft, concerned, rumbly, and shirtless—it made me want to taste him.

Whoa…where is this coming from? What is wrong with me?

"What's wrong with her?" This came from one of the other men. "She high or something?"

"No, asshole," Drew snapped, but his eyes remained on mine. "She's in shock, and she's got a lot of adrenaline in her system."

I was aware of the room plunging into stunned silence. Somewhere in the back of my mind, I remembered that Drew was infamous for his lack of verbosity. I imagined his outburst was quite a shock.

Drew's striking and bold eyebrows came together and he frowned, studying my face, one hand in my hair, the other holding mine. "When is the last time you ate?"

I shrugged.

"We need to get some food in you. It's a wonder you're still upright."

"Thanks for catching me," I said dumbly, gazing into his eyes like a lovesick teenager. I didn't care. He was so epically handsome, and he was being so nice, and his hands felt so good, and he was so strong and sturdy, and did I mention epically handsome? And shirtless?

I was vaguely aware of another person walking into the cabin and the men shifting, shuffling their feet, and making room for the newcomer.

"Sugar, I'd be honored to catch you anytime you'd like to fall."

I opened my mouth to respond but was distracted from Drew's vivid eyes and attractive freckle by the sound of my name coming from a familiar voice.

"Ashley? Ashley Winston?"

I turned and blinked at my name, my eyebrows high on my forehead. Standing on the other side of the table was a man, and this man looked remarkably familiar. His hair was blond and cut short, his eyes were brown, he was approximately my age, and he was roughly six feet tall. The man was in a blue police uniform, which fit him very, very well. He had no beard covering his square jaw. At present, all his white teeth were on display in a wide smile.

"Ashley? It's me, Jackson." He indicated himself with both his hands.

I frowned at the name from my past and allowed my eyes to dart over him again.

I knew the name Jackson exceedingly well because Jackson was the name of my high school boyfriend and best friend growing up. But the Jackson I knew was short and scrawny, Anderson Cooper pale, played the oboe in the high school band, and had a severe acne problem.

He was not a muscular, six-foot police officer with a golden tan, a sandy beard, and a manly-man voice.

"Ashley, it's Jackson." His grin became lopsided and boyish. "Don't tell me I've changed that much."

I flinched when I finally recognized him because he *had* changed that much, but his smile was exactly the same.

"Oh my dear Lord!" I blurted then shot to my feet, letting go of Drew's hand. "Jackson James?"

Jackson came around the table, nodding the whole time. "Girl, what the hell happened to you? You look like you just fought off a black bear."

"You have no idea." A laugh tumbled from my lips as he folded me into his arms, giving me a big hug.

Jackson withdrew but continued to hold my hands in his. "I heard a little of it on the radio when it was called in." Jackson's eyes flickered over my shoulder to where Drew stood behind me, then they came back to rest on my face. "I heard about your momma. I'm so sorry."

I flinched again, this time because I'd completely forgotten about what was going on with my momma. I'd been entirely wrapped up in surviving; then, when it was over and I was safe, I couldn't seem to focus on anything tangible except Drew's impossibly handsome facial features, the warmth of his hands, the deep steadiness of his voice, and his shirtlessness.

"I'm so sorry," Jackson repeated, squeezing my hand. "I wondered if you would be in town. I'm just sorry it had to take a bear attack for us to run into each other."

"I'm surprised you decided to come all the way out here." This comment came from Jethro, who was suddenly at my side. My brother's proximity forced Jackson to drop my hands and take a step backward. "Isn't this a little out of your jurisdiction, Jack?"

"Yes, to be honest. Yes it is." Jackson's eyes flickered between mine and Jethro's, his expression open and guileless. "But the report made it sound like there was an exchange of gunfire. And when I heard Ashley's name…."

I felt a hand on my hip and a chest at my back. I deduced it was Drew's when he whispered, "Let me take you to get you cleaned up," his breath warm on my neck.

Unthinkingly, as if it was the most natural thing in the world, I leaned back against him. He slipped his arm around my waist and turned slightly to address the room.

"That's enough," Drew said. "She's done. You all need to leave."

I wasn't surprised when no one argued this time, given the tone of his voice. Even if he didn't have several inches on every man in the room, Drew's commanding presence and aura of perpetual in-charge-ness would have been enough. I surmised that when Drew Runous put his foot down about a matter, nobody was quick to contradict.

Bearded men were grabbing their hats and muttering to each other, their shoes scuffing on the wooden floor as they departed. I didn't miss that Jackson's eyes were focused on Drew's arm around my waist before they lifted to mine.

"I'll stop by the house this week so we can catch up." He gave me a friendly smile. "You're a very lucky young lady, Ashley Winston."

I blinked at him, but couldn't find the words to respond that luck had nothing to do with my survival. Me being a badass, however, might have been involved; also, Drew's gun. Jackson didn't seem to mind my silence because he gave me a wink and left without saying anything further.

Drew turned to Jethro and said over my head, "I'll take her with me; you've got that trip to prep for."

Jethro squeezed my shoulder. "Thanks." My big brother then gave me a kiss on the forehead. "I'm so glad you're okay."

I nodded and Jethro gave me an affectionate smile; he then crossed to the other rangers and gathered what he needed for his trip.

Drew turned me toward him, but I watched Jethro's back as he left the cabin. When I was alone with a shirtless Drew, I lifted my eyes to his.

As usual, he was watching me, but his gaze was devoid of the weird, intense heat that he'd employed the first few days of our acquaintance. He seemed to be regarding me with measured yet detached interest.

"You have a history with Jack?"

I nodded. "He was my high school boyfriend."

Drew frowned. "I thought you were smarter than that."

A spike of irritation shot up my spine and I stepped away from him, the day's events and lingering adrenaline fueling my blunt response. "Not that I need to explain myself to you, but growing up, Jackson James was the only person other than my momma who didn't see me as an ignorant, disposable piece of ass. He saw more in me than what I looked like. At least, I thought he did. But the years have given me wisdom. I've learned that no amount of good intentions or education on my part are going to change people's first impressions of me, or seeing what they want to see. I might be able to debate the merits of Gestalt theory with acuity and confidence, but that doesn't make a lick of difference if the other person isn't even listening. So I guess you could say that I am smarter than that *now*."

Drew's eyes sparked hot and fierce as I spoke, but I got the impression the ferocity wasn't directed at me. When I finished, he was once again glaring at me with his trademark heated intensity, but it was subdued and hesitant like he was trying to rein himself in. Several long moments passed, our bodies swaying toward each other. I felt like I was being pulled toward him, I was dizzy with it.

Or maybe it was just low blood sugar.

I broke the silence, no longer able to tolerate the electrified tension between us. "I can drive myself, you know. I did drive here earlier. Momma's car is down the hill."

Drew frowned, his eyes moving over my body, assessing me. "When's the last time you ate?"

I stared at him and rewound the day. When I came up empty, I rewound yesterday. I swallowed and said, "I had a bagel."

"When?"

"For breakfast."

"When?"

I pressed my lips together and scowled. "Yesterday."

He watched me for a beat, but before he could issue his retort, I yielded. "Fine. You have a good point. I shouldn't be driving when I'm exhausted and lightheaded from hunger. Point made and conceded. Moving on...."

I rocked on my feet, feeling slightly dizzy, and I had to take a step back and hold on to the table to steady myself. Drew wrapped his arm around my back to keep me upright.

"I'm carrying you," he growled, though he didn't sound put out. Mostly he sounded determined.

"Don't be stupid," I said and pushed him away. "I can walk."

"Ash...." My name was a whisper close to my ear. "Let me help you."

"I don't need your help."

"You needed it earlier."

"I didn't need you. I just needed your gun."

From the corner of my eye, I saw Drew close his eyes slowly, his mouth pressing into a stiff line. I couldn't tell if he was upset or trying to keep himself from blurting *that's what she said.*

At length he cleared his throat and lifted me into his arms. I thought about pitching a fit but decided against it. Really, I only had enough energy for an eye roll.

"I'm carrying you down the hill."

"Fine."

"Then I'm driving."

"Whatever."

"After that you're going to eat."

"Okay."

"Then you'll sleep."

"Sounds great."

Drew glared down at me in his arms and mumbled, "'Ah, women. They make the highs higher and the lows more frequent.'"

Good Lord, I must've been half-unhinged, because that Nietzsche quote made me laugh.

CHAPTER TEN

"The person, be it gentleman or lady, who has not pleasure in a good novel, must be intolerably stupid."

— JANE AUSTEN

REW GAVE ME a protein bar when we reached his truck. He motioned to it with his hand and his chin, indicating that I should eat it. I surmised we were now past the point where he felt it necessary to issue verbal commands. Mere gestures had become completely acceptable.

The only time Drew spoke to me during the drive was when I reached for the brown leather-bound notebook in the center console of the truck.

"Don't touch that." He snatched it away from me and placed it in the driver's side door pocket.

I held my hands up, gripping the empty protein bar wrapper in one fist. "Fine. I wasn't going to read it. I was just moving it so I could put the wrapper in the cup holder. What is it, anyway, your diary?"

His grip on the steering wheel tightened, and he appeared to be tremendously intent on the road even though he could probably drive these switchbacks blindfolded.

Abruptly he ground out, "It's field notes. Don't touch it again."

We didn't speak again during the drive, and soon I was lulled to sleep by the ups and downs and twists and turns of the mountain road.

I woke up on a couch that I didn't recognize in a very dim, unfamiliar room. I must have slept a long time because I could see the moon through a series of windows that spanned an entire wall. The moon cast everything in a pale, silvery light that reminded me of Drew's eyes...and that thought made me feel warm and discombobulated. Therefore, I pushed it away.

Then I noticed that I wasn't wearing my jeans.

I twisted my neck to get a better look at my surroundings. The other three walls were lined with bookcases, which, if my eyes could be believed, were stuffed with books to the point of overflowing. Other than the shelves, the room was outfitted with the brown leather couch I was laying on, a large wooden side table, two big leather club chairs, and a thick wooden coffee table. An acoustic guitar rested on a stand in the far corner.

I decided I liked the room. It felt like a real place, a place where I could knit and read, or lay in the moonlight and watch shooting stars as I gazed out the wall of windows.

I was covered with a sheet, which I tugged to the side, blinking as I sat upright and listening for a sign as to where I was and what I should do next. I heard a noise and spotted light from under a door I'd initially failed to notice. Feeling like the door was the obvious choice, I gained my feet and walked to it.

Once opened, I followed the sounds of dishes and pots, which also happened to be the source of the light. Tiptoeing around the corner, I found Drew at a gas stove stirring a steaming pot of something that smelled delicious before tasting it and adding salt.

He asked without looking up. "How are you feeling?"

I leaned against the doorframe. "Thirsty and...confused."

Drew's eyes flickered to mine, his brows drawn together. "Let me get you some water."

I watched him as he moved around the kitchen, grabbing me a glass and filling it with tap water. He was wearing dark blue jeans that fit him quite nicely, low around his hips, accentuated by a thick brown leather belt. Regrettably, he wasn't shirtless; he had on a white T-shirt that also fit him quite nicely. He walked toward me holding out the cup of water.

I accepted it with thanks and downed its contents, fresh and pure as a mountain stream, and felt instantly better. He stood in front of me, his hands resting on his hips. I felt his eyes moving over my body, which was still shrouded in his giant (and now dirty) T-shirt.

His belt buckle was rather big; the entire thing was the word SAVAGE. He was also barefoot, and I noticed that he had nice feet.

"Do you want more?" He asked as his eyes moved from my feet to my neck then to the purple bruises on my arms.

"No, thank you." I licked my lips and glanced around the room.

"Feeling better?"

"Yes, thank you." My eyes were consuming the sight of his kitchen. It was perfect. The counters were thick butcher block; his sink was oversized porcelain. The cabinets were painted a slate gray, almost blue, and the walls were pale yellow. It was uncluttered and charming and spacious. It looked like it should have been part of a movie set.

"I love your house." I said this without knowing I was going to say it.

Drew took the glass from my hand, our fingers brushing. The contact startled me and brought my attention back to him. His hand loitered, covering mine for several seconds as our gazes clashed.

He cleared his throat before responding. "Thank you. It's a good spot."

"A good spot?"

"Yeah. We're on Bandit Lake." He tipped his head toward the window above the sink where nothing was visible except an inky night sky.

"Whoa…really?"

He nodded. I noted his expression was one of hesitant pride. He should be proud; owning a place on Bandit Lake was more difficult than convincing a pig to take a shower. The houses were deeded to families and couldn't be sold. If the owners wanted to leave, they had to sell to the federal government because the land was part of the national park.

Each house sat on several acres and surrounded an exceptionally pristine lake at the summit of the mountain just ten miles from the parkway.

The lake used to be a gold mine in the nineteenth and early twentieth centuries. It was eventually abandoned, and the gaping hole was filled with water. The lake allowed only trolling motors—so no gasoline engines—and had no runoff from fertilizers or other chemicals. It was on the top of the world and was one of the cleanest lakes in the United States. It was also very well stocked with fish.

How he'd managed to nab the house likely made for a fascinating story.

"We're facing west. The sunsets are momentous."

I quirked a smile at his use of the word *momentous* to describe a sunset.

"I'll have to check it out sometime..." I said, and with these words I remembered where I was and who I was with and why I was confused by both. "Hey, so, why are we here?"

Drew stared at me for a beat and seemed to struggle—like he was restraining himself—before he turned back to the stove.

"What you do you mean?" His attention was once again focused on his pot of steaming something.

"I mean, why didn't you take me home?"

"I stopped by your house. Cletus packed a bag for you; it's in the bathroom."

"Why didn't you just leave me there?"

Drew sighed. "Because someone needs to take care of you, and your brothers have their hands full right now with your momma."

This logic made no sense at all.

"I can take care of me," I said, pointing out the obvious.

His gaze lifted from the pot where he'd just added a pinch of mystery spice, and pinned me where I stood. His expression was unreadable and unnerving. I felt like he'd decided something about me since we'd last exchanged words. He was much cooler and more reserved now. The light in his eyes had dimmed considerably.

Finally, he said, "I know." Then he looked back at the pot.

"You do?" I asked the room, making no attempt to hide my confusion. "Then why am I here?"

This elicited a sigh. "Because you need to eat, and I need to eat, and I have soup and bread and pie."

"You have soup and bread and pie?"

He nodded, still studying the pot.

I sniffed the air, realizing that the room smelled like chicken soup, fresh bread, and mystery pie of the dessert variety. My stomach noticed too, because it rumbled. Suddenly I was starving. Soup and bread and pie sounded really, really good.

"What kind of pie?" I stepped farther into the kitchen and searched the counter for pie.

"Pecan pie."

I shrugged to hide my pleasure. I loved pecan pie. So did my momma. Suddenly, I felt guilty for having pecan pie. Maybe I could bring her back a piece. Maybe she could have a bite.

"Your stuff is already in the bathroom. Go take a shower. Then we can eat." Drew basically dismissed me by turning from the steaming pot and busying himself with the dishes. I stared at his back for a few seconds and noted that his hair was damp. He must've already showered.

I glanced at my hands. They were dirty and scraped. In fact, I was dirty all over. I hadn't really noticed.

On autopilot, I shuffled out of the kitchen and down the hall. I had made it ten steps when I heard his voice call out, "It's the third door on the left."

With these instructions, I found the bathroom easily. He was right. Cletus had packed me a bag. It contained exactly two pairs of underwear and three sets of tank top pajamas. Unfortunately, he'd neglected to include anything else, like appropriate clothes, a bra, or toiletries.

I leaned out the bathroom door and hollered to Drew, "Can I use your soap?"

There was a brief moment of silence before he called back, "Yeah, sure. Use whatever you need."

I surveyed the shower-tub combo, found soap and shampoo. I also found his razor by the sink and shaving cream. For no good reason other than the satisfaction I would get by dulling his razor, I decided to shave my legs. Besides, what did he need a razor for? Didn't Vikings manscape using knives?

I snooped around the cabinet looking for conditioner. I was pretty sure he used conditioner. His blond hair was long and wavy and lustrous. It looked soft to the touch....

These thoughts made me mentally facepalm, because I shouldn't be thinking about Drew's lustrous locks when I was about to get naked in his house. In fact, I made a mental note to *never* think about Drew's lustrous locks.

I was about to shut the cabinet when several bottles of dark brown glass caught my eye. I picked one up and read the label.

"Ketamine...." I whispered to the bathroom. I glanced up at the mirror and saw that my eyes were large and wide. Ketamine was a controlled substance and was used as an anesthetic. The fact that he had multiple glass bottles of it stocked in his bathroom cabinet only served to solidify his image in my mind's eye as a marauding man of mystery.

I wasn't exactly made anxious by the discovery; more like creeped out and uneasy. Not helping matters, an owl chose that exact moment to hoot. It gave me a shiver and an intense sensation of hootiedoom.

I fought another shiver, telling my overactive imagination to hush, and abandoned my search for conditioner.

Stripping naked, I jumped into the shower. I soaped and rinsed twice. I washed my hair twice. Then I shaved my legs. When I was finished, the faucet was running cold. I had used all the hot water.

It felt good to be clean.

I frowned at this thought because my shower earlier in the day hadn't felt nearly as cleansing or necessary. Even though, one could argue, I was dirtier this morning after a showerless week than I had been after a rabid raccoon attack.

I dressed in my pajamas—similar to the ones Drew had seen me in when we'd first met and I'd twisted his nipple—and made my way back to the kitchen using his comb to brush my hair. Drew was just placing bowls of hot soup on the table. I noted that two slices of home-made bread were also at each place.

"Where do you keep your utensils?" I walked to the drawer closest to the dishwasher and opened it, searching for spoons.

"On the end, top drawer...."

Something about the way he said *drawer* made me stop and look up. He was frowning at me.

"What are you wearing?"

I glanced down at myself then back at him. "My pajamas."

"Are you staying the night?" His voice was tight.

I shrugged, growing irritated, my neck heating. "How am I supposed to know? I didn't know I was going to be eating here either. This is all Cletus packed. It's a bag full of pajamas and no bras."

He did that slow-eye-closing thing again and his chin dropped to his chest. When he spoke next, he spoke to the floor. "Would you feel more comfortable in one of my T-shirts?"

I studied him for a beat, a bit taken aback by his reaction to me in my PJs. I noted the tension in his shoulders, the way his hands were balled into fists. Sandra's words of warning echoed in my head while I tried to bat them away with facts.

Fact One: His perpetual grumpy face whenever I was around.

Fact Two: If he were interested in me, then why had he disappeared and avoided eye contact for the last two weeks?

Fact Three: Fiction-handsome meant vessel of Satan.

I knew I wasn't making any sense. I had no idea in that moment what I thought—about Sandra's prediction or anything else—other than food smelled really, really good for the first time in almost three weeks, and I was going to eat it and like it. I'd just flashed a bear Mardi Gras style and fought off a rabid raccoon. I was starving.

Drew might be attracted to me. As well, he might find me crass, trashy, repugnant, and annoying—a nice piece of ass, a pretty face, with a low class accent. His propensity to avoid looking at me could mean either of those things, especially since we were about to eat.

Because I found the former theory (attracted to me) inconvenient and outside the realm of my comfortable reality, I decided to embrace the latter (annoyed by me) instead.

I rationalized it this way: better to be oblivious to a flirtation than mistake kindness for flirting. One made you clueless; the other made you pathetic.

And none of this mattered, because he lived in Tennessee and I lived in Chicago, and nary the twain shall meet.

Therefore, I asked, "Would you feel more comfortable if I were wearing one of your T-shirts?"

His eyes lifted to mine, his mouth a firm line. He looked both bothered and hot...or maybe hot and bothered. I couldn't tell which. Drew nodded.

"Fine." I crossed my arms over my chest and glanced at the stove, feeling tremendously self-conscious. "Go get me a T-shirt. I'll grab the spoons."

♥ ♥ ♥

I WORE ONE of his clean T-shirts—extra-large, black—and again I was swimming in it.

We ate in silence until Drew volunteered—after my second helping of chicken soup—that we weren't eating chicken soup. It was pheasant soup, not to be confused with peasant soup, which is what I thought he'd said at first.

This conjured images of Drew the Viking chopping up serfs for dinner.

"Many of the local hunters like to leave gifts of game for the rangers and wardens."

"Well, either way—peasant or pheasant—it tastes like chicken. My patients bring me gifts too. Things like gift cards...and viruses."

Finally, Drew cracked a smile, his eyes losing some of their wariness. I was relieved that my comment seemed to break the weird tension that had plagued the evening since I'd walked into the kitchen wearing my pajamas. Eating in shared silence usually gave me heartburn.

He surprised me by asking, "So, you like poetry?"

I paused, my spoon halfway between the bowl and my mouth. I didn't know Drew well enough to know why he'd asked the question or where we were going with it, so I decided to say, "Yes, I like poetry."

He nodded, stuffed a piece of bread in his mouth.

"Do you?" I prompted, trying to encourage discussion. "Like poetry, that is. Do you like poetry?"

He didn't answer right away, opting instead to chew slowly and drink his beer. At length he responded with a dodgy, "Yeah." Then silence.

I waited for him to continue, since—after all—he'd been the one to broach the subject. But he didn't. He just looked at his food like it was the most interesting thing in the room. Maybe to him it was.

Tired of the silence, I said a little too loudly, "Well, that's good. Look at all the things we have in common, Drew! Poetry and...T-shirts." His eyes flickered to mine then back to his soup. If I was reading the sparkle in them correctly, he was amused.

Amusement was preferable to soundless stoicism, so I carried on. "We even use the same soap—at least today we did. I bet we even use the same brand of razor. So tell me more about yourself."

"What do you want to know?" He said this without looking up.

"Anything I guess. Where are you from?"

"Texas."

"And where did you go to school?"

"Texas A & M for undergrad; Baylor for postgrad." Drew stood, grabbed my empty bowl, and put it in his. He stacked all the dinner dishes into a tidy pile and carried them to the sink.

"Any hobbies?" I called after him.

He grabbed two new plates from the cupboard. Like before, I watched him walk around his kitchen. His movements were graceful and unhurried, paradoxically lazy and efficient. It struck me that so many things about Drew were contradictory.

Earlier today, he'd stroked my hair, called me sugar, rubbed my back; then, a few minutes ago, he'd glared at me with heated irritation when I walked in wearing pajamas. The last few weeks he'd been avoiding me, not making eye contact; then today, he covered me with a blanket while I slept. When he yelled at me for spending too much time in the den, and he sent Cletus out with fried chicken and potatoes.

He held my mother's power of attorney and was the executor of her will, but he paid our house bills out of his own pocket. I couldn't figure him out.

Drew returned to the table carrying two dessert plates, a knife, two forks, and the pie.

Once settled in his seat, he cut into a lovely pecan pie, one of my favorites, my absolute favorite being lemon meringue pie made by my mother.

At last he responded, though I was so focused on the pie that I almost forgot I'd asked a question.

"I like to cook…and read."

Finally, something!

"Me too." I accepted the generous slice of pie and immediately took a bite. It was really, really good. I pointed to him with my fork and said, "Well, I like to eat, which is like cooking. This is good pie. I do like to read. See, that's another thing we have in common—pie and books. So, what are you reading now?"

"Nikola Tesla's biography."

"I haven't read that. What about fiction? What's the last good novel you read?" I ate two more bites of pie.

His subtle smile flattened and his eyes finally lifted to mine and held. "I don't like fiction."

I blinked at him, and I'm sure my eyebrows were doing an interpretive dance of what was going on inside my brain. "You don't like fiction?"

"No. Never cared for it."

"Any fiction?" I chewed on a pecan as I considered him. "You've

126

never enjoyed any fiction? How come you're always reading fiction to my mom?"

He shrugged. "Because she likes it."

"What about movies?"

"I'm not really interested."

I gathered a slow, deep breath and studied his face. This explained a lot about him, why he was so joyless. A perfect vessel for Satan. Also, I'd finished my pie. So my expression of disappointment was two-fold.

"Do you like fiction?" he asked.

I nodded vigorously. "Oh, yes. I love novels. I love getting lost in someone else's story, thinking about life from their perspective, living their experiences."

"Why don't you live your own experiences?"

I wrinkled my nose at this question. "Why would I do that when I can be a hundred different people a year? Live a hundred different lives. Love a hundred times without worrying about danger or risk. And all from the comfort of my reading chair."

Drew's frown was severe and, unlike the other times he'd recited Nietzsche, he sounded a fair bit impassioned as he quoted, "'There is not enough love and goodness in the world to permit giving any of it away to imaginary beings.'"

I stared at him, his serious face, and his serious silvery eyes.

Drew was an odd possum.

"Okay," I said, twisting my mouth to the side. "Well, I guess we've found something we don't have in common. And for the record, I dislike Nietzsche."

"You're changing the subject."

"Maybe."

"Why? Does it make you uncomfortable when someone challenges you?"

I could feel my blood pressure rising, mostly because Drew looked as though he was enjoying himself, my pie was all gone, and he hadn't yet touched his own.

Who makes a pecan pie then ignores his own slice? And this was a truly remarkable pie. I'd scarfed mine down and was hoping for another piece. I hated that he had such a firm grasp on his self-control.

I didn't respond right away, and maybe I waited too long, because he said, "Perhaps if you spent more time with real people instead of fictional people, honest discussions wouldn't be so uncomfortable for you."

"I spend plenty of time with real people. You've met my friends Sandra and Elizabeth. Do you think I spend Tuesday nights with them discussing the weather? And I have a lot more friends besides."

"Is that where you would be now if you were in Chicago?"

This thought depressed me. I was missing my friends. "Yes. Today's Tuesday, isn't it? I'd be with my knitting group right about now...."

"So you like living in the city?"

"Yes."

"Why?"

I shrugged, searching for the words, and coming up a little thin on reasons. I liked my knitting group. I liked that people didn't know me, didn't automatically expect me to be Darrell Winston's trashy daughter. I liked that I'd been able to reinvent myself. I liked that I was respected at my job. I liked my independence.

Finally, I settled on, "I like my friends. And I like the culture."

His gaze narrowed as he quoted, "In individuals, insanity is rare; but in groups, parties, nations and epochs, it is the rule."

I glared at him and *tsked*. "Did you just call my knitting group insane, Nietzsche? That's not nice, especially after Elizabeth made you that delicious ravioli."

He shook his head. "No, I don't know your knitting group well enough to label them as insane. But I am calling clustered society insane. Don't you find conformism and adhering to arbitrary societal norms suffocating?"

"I find small minds suffocating, yes. But there are just as many small minds in the backwoods of Tennessee as in the bustling metropolis of Chicago."

He scoffed. "Except in the backwoods of Tennessee you don't have to answer to them; you don't even have to speak to them."

"Unless they kidnap you and make you eat peasant soup and pie."

His grin was immediate, and it looked like it took him by surprise, because he quickly tried to cover it by clearing his throat. "You don't have pie with your knitting group?"

"Not pie that tastes this good, but I still miss them."

"Instead you're here with me, having a great time, and not at all uncomfortable." He was still fighting his grin.

I couldn't believe anyone would ever call Drew shy or reserved. He wasn't shy. He was a bear, and he was pawing at me.

"I'm not uncomfortable," I snapped, but that was a lie. I was uncomfortable. And I was hot. And I was getting angry. "Maybe I just don't like bossy, presumptuous, mule-headed men who take forever to eat their pie."

His smile was wide and immediate. "So, what *is* your type?"

"I don't really have a type."

"Everyone has a type."

"Fine, what's yours?"

"Small, petite, blonde, big boobs." He made a curving motion in front of his chest with his hands, presumably to emphasize the *bigness* of the boobs, or to demonstrate that he might—in fact—be a big boob. His beard twitched, but his eyes were sober. I couldn't tell if he was serious or if he was being purposefully irritating.

Because here's the thing, when a girl asks a guy what his type is, she wants at least one of her physical characteristics to be a match. Otherwise, she's just been told he considers her repulsive.

Behold the logic of the female brain!

Alas, I am five foot nine; therefore, not small and petite. I have very brown hair and not big boobs, at least, not as big as Drew seemed to prefer.

I nodded slowly, fought against the urge to tally up his physical characteristics and claim swoony allegiance to his outward opposite. Under normal circumstances, I was politely honest to a fault, because that's how my momma raised me. Drew wreaked havoc on normal, and now I was tempted to irritate him in return.

I sucked in a large, silent breath, and forced myself to elbow past the petty desire. Maybe it was just a sign of my exhaustion.

I ultimately answered with honesty. "Fine. You want to know my type?"

He half nodded, half shrugged, but his eyes were bright and betrayed his interest. "Sure."

"Okay." I crossed my arms over my chest. "My type has a romantic soul. He'll make my brain and my heart fight over who gets him first. He does what's right, even when it's not easy—actually, *especially* when it's not easy. He knows the value of discipline, education, honor, and restraint. And his strength of character is the only thing that outweighs the strength of his love for me."

Drew's eyes flickered across my face as I spoke. The earlier sobriety in his gaze sharpened; otherwise, he held perfectly still.

I readied myself to be mocked. But it didn't come.

Several seconds passed during which we regarded each other like two wary statues. The air grew thick and my neck itched; it felt like a pressing weight on my shoulders. But the heaviness was weighted with a meaning I was likely too tired and aggravated to process.

When I could take no more of his steady silent stare, I added, "That's my type. You know, fictional."

I didn't miss his wince or the way his shoulders bunched at my use of the word fictional, which he found so offensive. I surmised *fictional* was his least favorite f-word. In response, I gave him a rueful smile.

"Fictional," he said in a flat, emotionless tone.

I nodded. "That's right. Fictional."

"You think no man exists who has honor?"

"You tell me, Nietzsche."

He wrinkled his nose as though my words gave him a bad taste in his mouth. "Nietzsche wasn't opposed to honor. He wanted people to challenge established societal norms that suffocate individuality and freedom."

I shook my head, annoyed that I was now forced to quote Nietzsche. "Okay, you give me no option, Drew. Here's Nietzsche, and I quote: 'To strive for honor means to make oneself superior and wish that that also be publicly evident. If the first is lacking and the second nevertheless desired, one speaks of vanity. If the latter is lacking and not missed, one speaks of pride.' Nietzsche equated honor with pride and vanity."

Drew stared at me, his eyes filled with wonder. "How did you...?"

"Of course *you're* surprised. You think women are cows." While he was distracted, I picked up my fork and nabbed a large bite of his pecan pie. It was good pie, and if he wasn't going to eat it then I would.

Just for fun, I said, "Moo."

At length Drew released a long-suffering sigh that ended with a laugh. He shook his head, staring at me like I was a fascinating new species. I liked how his white teeth were framed by his lips and beard when he grinned. I hated that I noticed.

"Your ability to quote Nietzsche verbatim is incredibly annoying," he finally admitted.

"Is it?" I lifted my eyebrow and stole another bite of his pie, pausing before I stuffed my face to say, "Or is it fantastic?"

"It's fantastic..." he mumbled, his eyes lowering to my mouth, "... and sexy."

I was startled by the admission, and I choked on Drew's pie. My eyes wide, I reached for my glass of water and chugged three gulps before setting the glass back to the table and regarding him.

I didn't actually believe my ears, so I struggled for a moment before my mouth formed its question. "What?"

"What?" He snapped, lifted a single eyebrow in challenge.

"What did you just say?"

"You heard me." Once again, his voice was deep, steady, and intimate—his eyes watchful and intent.

The top of my head felt hot, as did my chest, and my neck was on fire. I couldn't believe he'd said that. I just...I couldn't fathom it. It was way, way down on the list of things I'd expected Drew to say to me, ever, probably because I was in denial.

I could feel my shocked stare turn into a livid glare, and my jaw ached because I was clenching it so hard.

Pretty face, nice piece of ass, low class accent. That's what I was.

Drew—fictionally handsome vessel of Satan—had just really, really pissed me off. I was bruised and cut and drowning in grief. I didn't need to hear that I was sexy, *especially* not from him; not from the guy who held my mother's power of attorney and couldn't seem to make up his mind whether he despised me or liked me.

Because, the terrible truth was, I thought he was sexy too.

I thought he was off-the-charts sexy with his cooking and reading and brooding and shirtlessness and breathing—which meant he was a user and an asshole. And it would be completely troublesome for us to be attracted to each other. It would be epically problematic. The potential for disastrous heartbreak was momentous.

My mother was dying. *Dying.* I'd just stood up to a bear and murdered a rabid raccoon. Then I'd been dragged back here, made to take a shower with his wonderful-smelling soap, wear his shirt, eat his delicious dinner, and engage in a battle of wits.

I was surrounded by Drew, assaulted on all sides.

I didn't want this. I wanted none of it. I wanted my mother to be healthy. I wanted Chicago and books. I wanted comfort and contentment and predictability. I wanted my knitting group and Tuesday night shenanigans.

Maybe one day I'd find a nice normal man—an accountant or an actuary—who tinkered with clocks. I'd be up front about the arrangement so there'd be no hurt feelings, and he'd be content with companionship in lieu of passion.

Or maybe I'd just have my friends and myself, and that would be great. I could deal with that. I was fine with that. That was my life now, and I was happy.

What I didn't need or want was a bossy PhD game warden from Texas with sexy brains and sexy eyes and sexy everything. Because my heart was now smarter than he was sexy, it warned me that Drew would be my biggest mistake yet. I didn't have the strength to recover from the death of my mother and another man making me feel like trash.

"Why would you say that?" My voice was a bit shrill, and I had a hard time keeping the volume low enough to be considered indoors appropriate.

"Because it's true."

I shook my head, slowly at first, then faster. "You are such an ass."

I stood from the table, scraping my chair against the floor, but then I hesitated. He'd made dinner and cleared the dinner plates. Good manners dictated that I needed to clear the dessert plates and do the dishes.

Instead of leaving indignantly like I wanted to do, I surprised us both by pointing to his barely-touched pie and demanding, "Are you finished with that?"

"Why? Do you want my pie?" He asked this as though he was offering me more than pie, and the softness of his tone caught me off guard.

I sputtered for a few seconds then said, "No. I don't. I don't want your stupid delicious pie."

I grabbed my plate and fork and the dish of remaining pecan pie and its cover. I marched to the kitchen, chucked my plate in the sink, covered the pie plate, and found a home for it in the refrigerator.

Then, my fury a cloak of impervious distraction, I crossed to the sink and began doing the dishes.

I'd finished our bowls, dessert plates, and utensils, and was about to go back to the table for the glasses when Drew reached around me and turned off the faucet.

"Sugar, stop doing the dishes."

"Fine. They're all done anyway." I turned away from him and reached for the dry towel on the counter. "I want to go home. Will you please call one of my brothers to take me home?"

"Ash...."

"Listen, Drew." I faced him, my heart pounding in my chest, and I summoned every bit of ingrained politeness I had. "Thank you for dinner. Thank you for the shower and your soap and your shirt. Thank you for driving me here and for carrying me down the hill. Now will you please call one of my brothers to take me home?"

His eyes seemed to be searching mine. His expression was guarded, but I perceived flashes of dejection and misery there.

"I'll take you home," he said quietly.

I glared at him, debating whether it would be better to ride in his truck back to Momma's, or if waiting at his house until one of my brothers showed up was preferable.

"Fine." I turned on my heel and walked at a decidedly normal pace to his bathroom. I gathered my bag and the dirty clothes, pausing for a moment when I saw Drew's dark gray shirt in the mix. There was nothing for it. I would have to wash it along with the black one I was wearing.

Then, I would give them back to him the next time he was at our house because I wanted nothing from Drew Runous.

CHAPTER ELEVEN

"Why is it," he said, one time, at the subway entrance, "I feel I've known you so many years?"

"Because I like you," she said, "and I don't want anything from you."

— RAY BRADBURY, FAHRENHEIT 451

THE NEXT MORNING I awoke to the sound of voices. Actually, just one voice.

It was Drew's.

This was surprising because we had not parted on friendly terms when he'd dropped me off the night before.

The drive home was silent. I jumped out of his truck as soon as he slowed enough for it to be safe. I heard him curse just before I shut the passenger door. He had walked me to the porch despite my chilly disregard of him, and I'd slammed the front door in his face.

Presently it sounded like he was reading aloud. His voice was low, even, soft, and very, very near. I opened my eyes and glanced around the den from beneath my half-closed lids. He was sitting with his back to me in a wooden chair, and my mother was turned slightly toward him.

The first thing I noticed was that he was wearing his exercise clothes. His back was damp with sweat. The second thing I noticed was the passage he was reading. It was one of my favorites from Elizabeth Gaskell's very romantic novel *North and South* in which Mr. Thornton—dashing and desirable, yet scorned by the uppity Ms. Hale—makes his proposal. Miss Hale believes, quite pridefully and wrongly, that he makes the offer of marriage only because he is honor bound to do so. Therefore, Miss Hale rejects the dreamy Mr. Thornton.

"'I do not want to be relieved from any obligation,' said he, goaded by her calm manner. 'Fancied, or not fancied—I question not myself to know which—I choose to believe that I owe my very life to you—ay—smile, and think it an exaggeration if you will. I believe it, because it adds a value to that life to think—oh, Miss Hale!' continued he, lowering his voice to such a tender intensity of passion that she shivered and trembled before him...."

Stupid Miss Hale.

Why are heroines in romantic novels—despite their cleanliness and enviable lifestyles—so unlikeable? It's like they've been hit with a vanilla ninny stick, devoid of personality and blind to the gift before them. They're doomed to wander in ignorance until the last thirty pages of the book. By then I'm usually actively rooting against a happy ending because the fantastical fictional men deserve better.

This is true for ninety-eight percent of romance novels, with notable exceptions being Jane Austen's heroines Elizabeth Bennett and Anne Elliot.

In real life, it's the other way around.

Men are so clueless, self-centered, and undeserving, each a bland replica of the other. They're motivated by sex, sports, hunting, cars, and food. If they can't screw it, cheer for it, shoot it, drive it, or consume it, then it might as well be a diva cup or a maxi pad.

I closed my eyes and concentrated on the sound of his voice because despite my mixed and uncategorized feelings about him, Drew was coming to the best part.

"She did not speak; she did not move. The tears of wounded pride fell hot and fast. He waited awhile, longing for her to say something, even a taunt, to which he might reply. But she was silent. He took up his hat. 'One word more. You look as if you thought it tainted you to be...to be....'" Drew stumbled over the passage then paused.

I opened my eyes in time to see his shoulders rise and fall with a deep breath. When he continued, his voice was more subdued, almost sad. "'You look as if you thought it tainted you to be loved by me. You cannot avoid it. Nay, I, if I would, cannot cleanse you from it. But I would not, if I could. I have never loved any woman before: my life has been too busy, my thoughts too much absorbed with other things. Now I love, and will love. But do not be afraid of too much expression on my part....'"

He stopped reading, and I got the impression in the stretching silence that he would not continue.

My eyes were drawn to movement on the bed where my mother lay. She lifted her hand and set it on his knee. I saw that her eyes were still closed as though she slept, and I strained to hear the words she spoke.

"You read very well, Andrew. Very nice." Her words were slurred, and this made my eyes sting. Her words had been slurred and slow for the past few days, a byproduct of the morphine.

"Thank you, Bethany." He covered her hand with his, and I frowned at the familiarity of the gesture.

"Where have you been?" she asked.

I could see his hesitation; it was a tangible thing, a struggle. At last, he said, "I know I haven't been around much." My heart twisted a little when I heard the compassion in his voice. "How are you feeling?"

"Oh, not so bad. How're you?"

"I'm...well."

"How long have you been here?"

"About a half-hour."

I frowned at the entire exchange. My mother didn't seem at all surprised that Drew—Andrew as she called him—had taken it upon himself to read her awake after entering the house and positioning himself in the room she shared with her daughter.

Something was amiss. Rather, I was missing something.

"Is Ashley awake?" Momma asked.

I quickly closed my eyes, endeavored for complete motionless, and heard his chair creak as he shifted his weight.

After a few beats he said, "I don't think so. She hasn't moved since I came in."

The chair creaked again, presumably when he turned back to my mother.

There was a trace of amusement in her voice when she next spoke. "And what do you think of my Ashley?"

I stopped breathing, all my muscles tensed, and I became absorbed in my own stillness. He didn't respond right away, but his chair creaked again.

I tried to imagine his expression. If our previous encounters were any indication, his face was likely screwed up in distaste.

"I've known you for three years. In all that time you failed to mention that Ash was short for Ashley." His tone held a mild accusation.

"I didn't, did I?" Momma sounded pleased with herself. "Does the fact that she's my daughter and not my son make her any less remarkable? Is she less worthy of your friendship because she is a woman?"

"Hard to miss that's she's a woman, now that I've seen her."

At this Momma barked a subdued laugh. "Yes…yes, she is a woman. I'm afraid she's not much of a girl, though. She's been a woman more than half her life. Like you, she grew up fast."

Drew remained silent, and I heard my mom say, "Oh, you can speak freely. If she's asleep, no amount of us talking is going to wake her up. She's a solid sleeper, always has been."

"Not that solid. The first time I had the pleasure of meeting her, I'd just unknowingly woken her up."

"Ah, yes. Jethro told me about that. She gave you a nipple squeeze?"

Drew grumbled something and Momma laughed. "You're not starting any engines now, so tell me—what do you think of Ash?"

I felt him falter, then he surprised the voodoo out of me by saying, "She is... remarkable...and beautiful."

Pretty face, nice piece of ass.

I ground my teeth together.

"Yes. She is. She is tremendously beautiful, like her daddy is beautiful. Billy has it too, and Roscoe to an extent. I know you don't like it when I talk about Darrell—Ashley hates him the same as you—but she's got the look of him, whether she wants it or not."

"If that's the case, I think I understand a bit better now how Christine could fall for Darrell so hard after knowing him for such a short time." He said this very softly like he was talking to himself.

What the what?

"Do you now?" Momma asked. I recognized the tone she used. She'd use it on me when she felt I'd discovered something obvious, or when she wanted to encourage me in a particular direction.

"Yes. I do," Drew said. "And it's not very convenient either."

My mother snorted. "Lord, getting stupid for someone never is convenient. Your sister fell for Darrell, same as me, same as the others. You got stupid for that gold digger you told me about. She had the long game and played you for years before making her move. You must've been *real* stupid for her. Nothing makes smart people more stupid than beauty."

I heard the smile in Drew's voice when he responded. "Being stupid is not an experience I'd like to repeat."

Momma was silent for a long moment. "Now, you know better than that. You know you're not the only person to get burned in the history of humanity. If you don't want to repeat that experience, then don't repeat it. This time, get stupid for more than beauty. Get stupid for worth, with someone like my Ash."

What the WHAT?

Is this how Drew knew my family? Because his sister Christine had been conned by my father? And when had Christine fallen for my father's line? And where was Christine? And when did Drew meet my mother and my brothers? And who was this gold digger? And why was Momma talking to Drew like he was her most trusted friend?

I had mixed feelings about overhearing this conversation. The angel on my shoulder wanted to put an end to it; the devil on my other shoulder wanted to keep on listening. I knew so little about Drew. Asking my brothers about him was pointless unless I wanted to know how good of a shot he was or what kind of car he drove.

Despite my good intentions, the devil won.

Drew sighed. "Bethany...."

She cut him off. "No, you listen. I'm not proposing anything. I'm just using Ashley as an example. She's got so much worth. She's price-less, and she's beautiful. You said it yourself. Though she does her best to hide it, I think. Some people reject their God-given gifts because society makes them feel ashamed when they shine."

"Why did you lie to me?" He didn't sound angry. He sounded curi-ous. "Why pretend like Ash was a man?"

"I didn't lie...not exactly. I just...didn't correct your assump-tions. I liked talking about her to someone who knew what her courage meant, what it meant for her to escape on her own, to want something better, to work for it and succeed. You admired her when I let you think she was a man; I don't see why that should change now."

"It hasn't." He said this begrudgingly. Even I could hear the resent-ment in his voice.

"How inconvenient for you." She said this on a laugh. "Must be hard for a guy like you to admire a woman for her brains and goodness before you get a chance to disregard her because of her gender and beauty."

"That's not true." His voice had a hard edge to it. "I admire plenty of women. I admire you."

"And you think of me as a replacement for the mother you never had, and for the sister you lost." I couldn't believe how she was speaking to him. I couldn't believe that he let her. "I know you, Andrew. I know your family treated you despicably. You don't want to get hurt. I understand that—maybe I understand better than most people do. But not all good-looking women are gold-digging opportunists."

"I know that."

"You know what I think? I think you like her."

Drew made a funny sound: not a rejection of her statement, but not a confirmation either.

She continued, "You do! You like her. You admit she's lovely. You admit you admire her. Admit you like my Ash."

"I'm not admitting anything."

"Why not?"

"Because you're her mother, not my sister."

"So?"

"So, other than her goodness, sweetness, gracefulness, and wit, what I like about Ashley Winston shouldn't be discussed with Ashley Winston's mother."

If I hadn't already been as still as I statue, his words, so earnestly spoken, would have stunned me. Did he really see these things in me? Or was he just being kind to my mother?

"Oh, this sounds good. Now I *really* want to know," Momma said.

"Trust me, you don't."

"Are you falling for my Ashley?" Momma *tsked*. "What did she do, outsmart you?"

"Something like that."

It took all my stillness superpowers not to sit up in the bed and yell, *WHAT the WHAT?* My brain was overflowing with new and confusing information.

"How'd we get on this subject?" He sounded truly mystified and a little annoyed.

"I'm trying to make you see reason before I depart this earth and leave you bereft of motherly wisdom. And I'm trying to do the same for all my chickens...."

"Speaking of which, I want to ask you a question."

"Go for it."

"Did you know, when you made me your power of attorney—and everything else—did you know that you were...." He paused, and I assumed it was because he had no intention of saying it out loud, but he surprised me when he asked, "Did you know that you were terminally ill?"

She didn't hesitate in her response. "Yes. I knew."

Drew release what sounded like a tortured sigh, and they both sat quiet for several minutes. I thought about stretching, waking up for show, but I didn't. I had too many new pieces of information swimming around in my brain. I needed a second to catch up.

Momma then said out of nowhere, "She was in the Miss Tennessee competition, you know. She was only eighteen at the time, came in second."

I hated this fact about myself, hated that I'd done it—not because I was patently opposed to beauty contests per se. I was just so shy and reserved at the time, but I was also desperate for a way out of Tennessee, out of this small town with its one sawmill, one library, one high school.

Momma had money, yes. But she also had seven kids. Her parents were wealthy, but supporting a family without knowing how to invest her savings had eaten away at her nest egg. I didn't ask her, and she hadn't offered.

Thinking back, it was the memory of desperation that I hated, not the contest.

"Really?" He drawled. "That explains a lot."

My mother gave a small chuckle. "No. It really doesn't. Not at all, really. Can you imagine what it was like for her in a houseful of boys? And not just any boys; Winston boys and their friends."

"Brothers and sisters don't always get along; nothing unusual about that."

"True, but they were all just like their daddy growing up, wild with their own freedom, caring not two licks about anybody but their own selves. Yet Ash...as I've told you, she was quiet, curious, sensitive. Like you, she wrote poetry. Lord have mercy, the pranks they used to play on her—they never stopped. They never stopped tormenting, and pushing, and using, not until she left. Then they realized that some hurts can't be undone, and selfishness drives people away. But it was too late."

"You never told me what they did."

"Oh… let's see…."

I decided that my mother had said quite enough. I didn't need Drew hearing about how my brother Jethro had frequently tried to use dates with me as a trade with his football buddies for whatever he wanted from them. Jethro always said I was doing him a favor, but it felt suspiciously like I was being pimped out, especially when one of his eighteen-year-old friends insisted that I—a mere fifteen-year-old—was expected to put out.

Of course, another great example was the twins' preferred method of demonstrating their affection for me by rubbing their dirty underwear on my head—skid marks and all—or holding me down and spitting in my mouth.

But then, boys will be boys, as my daddy liked to say. I had to give my father credit because, in the end, he was right. Boys will be boys. And that's why I knew better than to open my heart to one.

I shifted my limbs restlessly under the covers and stretched my arms over my head. As I'd hoped, their conversation came to a halt. Fluttering my eyelashes as if coming fully awake, I turned my neck and glanced blandly around the room. I let my eyes move to my mother first, then to where Drew sat twisted in the chair facing me.

"Oh," I said when my gaze met his, my voice husky with sleep. "What's going on? Is everything okay?"

His eyes ensnared mine, held me immobilized. Back was the weird intensity and heat, but now I saw it for what it was—reluctant desire.

What I'd suspected last night after he called me sexy was confirmed this morning while eavesdropping; Drew liked me—or, at least the way I looked—a whole heck of a lot. And that's probably why he acted like Mr. Itchy Britches whenever I was around.

I knew exactly how he felt. Finding him handsome definitely gave me sand in my cracks. Everything about being attracted to him was inconvenient: wrong place, wrong time, wrong person.

But after sleeping on my hissy fit the night before, I decided what we needed to do was grow beyond this pattern we'd fallen into of snapping at each other, lapsing into a confusing and heated moment, then avoiding contact for days. We needed to move past the irritation of our mutual attraction and into a nice, safe, placid familial space.

The jury was still out on the rest of his intentions and life experience told me to be wary of handsome men wielding compliments. If we could reach a compromise where his intentions were made innocuous by defined roles, then maybe we could relax around each other.

Momma's slow speech cut through the thick silence. "Everything is fine. Andrew and I were just talking about how beautiful you are."

I smiled inwardly at my mother and her cheeky antics then let my eyes slide back to Drew. He also wore a smile; it was small and patient.

"Well, don't let me stop you," I said, swinging my legs over the side of the cot and reaching for my bathrobe. "Please, continue speaking of my beauty."

My mother laughed lightly then sighed. "When does Marissa get here? I promised her a recipe yesterday."

"Which one?"

"Mother's biscuits."

I nodded, knowing the recipe. "If you want me to, I'll transcribe it for you."

"No. Just get me the card and I can do it. I'd like to use my hands for something useful."

I caught Drew's eye and indicated with my head that he should follow me. His eyebrows lifted in what I guessed was surprise. Nevertheless, he stood, left *North and South* on the wooden chair where he'd been sitting, and turned to my mother.

"I've got to get going. But I'll be back tonight."

"That's fine, dear," she slurred, giving him a hazy smile.

Drew exited the room first, giving me a quizzical look.

"I'll be right back, Momma. I'm going to brush my teeth."

"Please do. For heavens' sake, I didn't want to say anything, but you've been looking rough the last few weeks. Maybe go get a facial and a hairstyle. While you're at it, get your nails done." She laughed lightly and winked at me. "Take your time, dear. I'm fixin' to take a little cat nap."

I crossed to her bed and gave her a kiss on the forehead. Her eyes were already closed. When I left the room, I closed the door behind me.

Drew was waiting for me in the hall, his arms crossed over his chest, his expression both solemn and curious.

We both started speaking at the same time.

"Can we just...."

"I need to tell you...."

He sighed and closed his eyes. I glanced at the ceiling.

"Please, you go first," I said, fiddling with the tie of my robe.

He gave me a measured look, but he relented. "I thought I saw an Indiana Bat in your backyard last week while I was here. It's an endangered species in this part of the forest. Since your property backs up to the park, it's not unheard of to have sightings from time to time."

"Okay." This news and conversation topic took me completely by surprise. I thought he was going to fuss at me for my poor behavior. Instead, he was discussing game warden business. "What does that mean?"

"It means the fiber-optic cable that's buried in your front yard, which is being used by the county, has been hooked up to the house. We're going to put cameras facing the park off the back porch, hoping to catch one of the Indiana Bats."

I nodded and shrugged. "That's fine."

"It also means you'll have free Internet access—really fast Internet access. I installed a router this morning." He pulled a piece of paper out of his pocket and handed it to me. "Here's the login and password for the wireless. You can choose your own, of course."

I stared at him, my mouth falling open by inches. My mind might be moving like a river of molasses these days, but I caught his drift and then some. He'd had Internet connected to the house. I could now call my friends in Chicago. I could now Skype with them on Tuesdays.

My eyes stung, and a rush of gratefulness swelled in my chest. Drew held my gaze, his own cautious and watchful.

"Thank you," I blurted. "Thank you so, so much." Instinct told me to hug him, but something about his glare told me that hugging him would be a mistake.

In the end, I squeezed his bicep. "Thank you," I repeated, my eyes going to where my hand rested on his bare arm. Four jagged white lines caught my attention and I frowned, speaking before I thought better of it.

"What on earth…? What happened to your arm?" I stepped closer, inspecting the scars.

"Ah, that was a bear." He said this matter-of-factly, like everyone has a bear scar.

My eyes lifted to his, and I'm sure my face betrayed my incredulousness. "A bear? You got these from a bear?"

He nodded.

"What? When? How?" My attention went back to the scars. They were ugly, like the bear had tried to take his arm off.

"I go trail running in the morning. Sometimes one or more of your brothers come; sometimes I'm alone. Sometimes there are bears on the trails." He shrugged like everyone goes on runs with bears. "Usually they leave me alone."

"How long is the trail?"

"Anywhere from six to twelve miles."

"And this time the bear…what—he wanted to take your arm and beat you with it?"

He grinned down at me. "No, Sugar, and it was a she bear. A momma bear can get testy if you come between her and her cubs."

"How did you get away?"

"I carry a tranquilizer gun strapped to my back when I run. I shot it, but it took a swipe at me before it went down."

"Oh, my God." I shook my head. "You are a lunatic. If you had a Viking name it would be Drew the Thrill-Seeker or Drew Never-A-Dull-Moment."

His grin dimmed to a small, perplexed smile like he didn't know whether or not my poking fun was mean spirited.

I frowned at the confusion casting a shadow over his features. "What's wrong? What'd I say?"

He shook his head, studying me as though trying to determine my intentions. "Nothing."

But it was something. I'd inadvertently said something to diminish the brightness in his eyes. I decided to let it go for now and let my hand drop. "Anyway...again, thank you."

"No need for thanks." He cleared his throat. "What did you want to tell me?"

"Oh, yeah." I'd almost forgotten. The gift of Internet connectivity and the bear attack story had driven all thoughts from my mind. I tucked the piece of paper that held the wireless password into the pocket of my robe.

Preparing myself for the conversation to come, I planted my feet and took a deep breath, determined to move us out of our perpetual loop of snarkiness. "Drew, I want to apologize for calling you an ass last night. That was very rude, especially after you fed me dinner and pie. I hope you will accept my apology."

Drew's jaw ticked, his mouth a flat straight line, but his eyes were vibrant and vivid quicksilver, traveling over my face. I had to wait several seconds before he gave me a stiff nod.

"Good." I sighed my relief and eyeballed him. "Good...." I repeated, not knowing what else to say. I was trying to gauge his mood, and wondered if now would be a good time to broach the subject of a cease-fire. I'd known him three weeks, but after eavesdropping on that conversation between him and my mother, I realized I barely knew him at all.

Ultimately I decided sooner was better than later, and I plowed ahead without thinking too carefully about my words. I didn't want them to seem rehearsed or forced.

"So, you appear to have a very positive relationship with my momma and my brothers, wouldn't you agree?"

His gaze sharpened and he licked his lips before responding. "Yes. I'd like to think so."

"Almost familial, it seems. Like, Roscoe told me about the road trip you two went on. That seems like something brothers might do together. And the way you helped out Jethro and the other boys with their auto shop, and how you seem to care a great deal for Momma, almost like she was your own."

Drew held very still, watching me but saying nothing. Since he didn't appear to be inclined to confirm nor deny my statements, I pressed forward.

"Do you have a sister?"

He flinched, blinking several times before releasing a slow breath. "I...." He swallowed and looked at the wall behind my head then back at me. "I had a sister."

I frowned at this. "Had a sister?" The words slipped out of me and betrayed my surprise. I'd expected him to say, *Yes, I have a sister. Her name is Christine.*

"Yes. She died." He added in a rush, "She committed suicide when I was ten."

"Oh!" My hand lifted of its own accord and affixed itself to his arm again, squeezing him. I shifted a half step forward. "I'm so sorry. That must've been really terrible. I'm so sorry."

"Why do you ask?" His voice was gravelly and tense, as if the memory was a fresh wound. Her death seemed to affect him with the same force twenty years later.

"Uh, I was going to suggest that, since you seem to think of my brothers as your brothers and you care a great deal for Momma, that maybe you and I could find some common ground too. Maybe you could think of me as a...as a sister."

Drew stared at me, the sadness in his eyes morphing into incredulous confusion then finally settling on bewildered amusement.

"You want me to think of you like my sister?"

"Not like *your* sister. I'm not looking to replace anybody; rather, as another sister—a new sister." I gave him a hopeful smile.

I was suddenly very aware of how small and intimate a space the hallway was as Drew's eyes traveled down my body and back up again. His were smoldering.

He surprised me by taking two steps forward, which caused me to step back and bump into the wall. He was crowding my space, yet the only place we touched was where my hand still rested on his arm just above the elbow.

"Ashley...." he whispered.

"Yes?" I breathed, my heart in my throat, my body hot all over.

"You are very beautiful."

"I...I am?"

"You know you are, because you're also very smart, and you're sweet, and you're kind. And there's not a man alive—that's not married or related to you—that wishes he were your brother."

Drew lifted his hands and I thought for a moment he was going to snatch them away, liked he'd done before. Instead he cupped my face, his thumbs caressing the line of my jaw. "I'm sorry," he said, the words escaping on a slow rumbly sigh. He shook his head slowly. "But I'm never going to be able to think of you as a sister."

My stomach flipped.

"How about a cousin?"

He shook his head again, his lips forming a hint of a smile.

"A niece?"

His smile stretched then flattened, and his head lowered a fraction toward mine, our mouths three inches apart. "None of my feelings for you are familial. I'm sorry if that upsets you, but I'm not good at playing make-believe, lying, or pretending—as you might have noticed."

"Oh...." I breathed, my knees weak.

"Here's the thing, Sugar," Drew's tucked a few strands of hair behind my ears, his fingertips brushing against the sensitive area of my neck. They lingered for several seconds causing a shiver to race down my spine. "You tell me what you need, and I'll give it to you."

His eyes were soft and searching, and he somehow managed to say this without making it sound lewd or suggestive. Rather, it sounded like a plea to let him help, like the thing he wanted most in the world was to see to my needs—whatever those needs might be.

"But what about you?" My voice was hushed. "What do you need?"

Drew's mouth hooked to the side but his eyes held no smile. "I don't need anything, not from you."

I flinched, because—whether he meant to or not—his words felt like a slap. I let my hand drop from his arm and I glanced around the hallway.

"Oh, okay," I said, nodding and feeling the hot confusion that accompanies rejection. At least he was honest.

He must've detected my desire to escape because he grabbed both of my hands and held them hostage between his. "Ashley, that's not— what you're thinking—that's not what I meant. You have a lot on your mind; you're barely taking care of yourself. You're not eating."

I nodded, still not looking at him, my throat working without swallowing. My mouth felt dry, and I needed water.

He pressed on. "I'm not asking anything of you other than to let me help. I have no expectations. I know your life isn't…it isn't here. You have a job and friends in Chicago. You need someone to help you get through this, through the next weeks, because things are going to get worse."

I blinked away sudden moisture from my eyes and was finally able to manage a swallow before I said, "So, you won't help by being a brother to me?"

"Hell, no."

I allowed myself to glance at him and was nearly overcome by the passion and sincerity in his eyes. I had to look away to regain my composure. I nodded, accepting that he meant what he said, because he wasn't good at playing make-believe.

I cleared my throat. "Then what about a friend? Could you be my friend?"

He didn't answer for a long time, so long in fact that I thought I might have upset him. I lifted my eyes to his, hoping to gauge his reaction. He didn't look angry or upset, but his eyes were sad. They were momentously sad. The melancholy hit me in my chest and made it difficult to draw a breath for three beats of my heart.

"Of course," he said, nodding and taking a step back, dropping my hands gently, giving me space. "I would be honored to be your friend —if that's what you need."

"Thank you." My chin wobbled, but I reined in the tears. "It's what I need."

Apparently, I was quite talented at playing pretend.

CHAPTER TWELVE

"To be yourself in a world that is constantly trying to make you something else is the greatest accomplishment."

— RALPH WALDO EMERSON

Y MOTHER PUT her foot down—figuratively—and ordered me out of the house the Friday after the raccoon attack.

She said I was hovering. She was right. I was hovering, but I was actually doing a lot better overall.

I'd changed. I felt different. I *was* different.

As cliché as it sounds, the day of the bear chase and raccoon attack had changed me. It was like turning on a switch. One minute I'd been content playing dead, waiting to become a bear snack; the next I felt anxious and restless with unspent energy.

I was still taking care of my momma, watchful when visitors arrived to make sure they weren't overtaxing her; spending every one of her waking moments with her and a lot of her sleeping moments too.

But now I was eating, talking to my brothers, voluntarily showering, and wearing clean clothes.

So, you know, behaving like a sane person.

The problem was, now that I had restless energy, I was making her restless. I think I was driving her a little nuts. She needed a break from me.

"Cheer up, gorgeous." Duane slipped his arm around my shoulders and gave me a squeeze. We were sitting in the back seat of Billy's car; Duane and Beau were sitting on either side of me. "Cletus is real good at the banjo."

"I didn't even know you played the banjo." I said this to Cletus who was sitting in the front seat.

"It's true. I play the banjo," Cletus said, clutching his banjo case.

"He started after you left, I guess." Beau scratched the back of his neck. "And the jam session is good fun. They serve barbeque as well as various and sundry salads."

I glanced at Beau from the corner of my eye. "*Various* and *sundry* salads?"

"Yeah, various and sundry—you know, all kinds, like macaroni, potato, macaroni and potato, fruit salad, coleslaw...." He nodded, and I saw his eyes widen before they flickered to Duane then back to me.

"I like the coleslaw," Duane added.

I smiled at them. My twin brothers were seriously adorable.

"So, tell me about it. Where is this place? What can I expect?"

"You can expect me to play the banjo, that's for sure. You can count on it." Cletus didn't turn as he said this; but his tone was emphatic like he was making me a sacred promise.

"People come from all over every Friday night. I reckon about fifty musicians show up, all types, all ages," Beau explained.

"Fifty? And they all play together?"

"No." Duane shook his head. "There's five or six rooms. You can walk from one room to the next and listen to whichever group you want. The musicians can move around too. If they want to change things up, they just walk to a different room."

"Each room usually plays a different type of music." Beau indicated his chin toward the front seat. "Cletus likes to stick with bluegrass, but one room usually has blues and another country and another folk."

"Where is this place? Is it a concert hall?"

"No, no, nothing fancy. It's the Green Valley Community Center, you know, the one down the block from Big Ben's Dulcimer Shop. When we were kids it was abandoned, I think, but it used to be a school. They serve food in the old cafeteria, and the music is played in the classrooms."

"They put a mish-mash of theater seats, church pews, and desk chairs in each of the classrooms so people can sit and listen to the music. All the musicians play on one end of each room, and the chairs face the musicians."

"You can visit all five rooms if you get tired of listening to Cletus the banjo wiz."

"How do they know what to play?" I asked the car, not really understanding the concept of a jam session. When I was a singer and played the piano, I had recitals, but I always used sheet music. "Will someone provide the music, or do you have to bring your own?"

Billy chuckled, finally speaking, "No, Ash. It's not like that. Someone starts, and the others join in. You don't know what you're going to play when you show up; you just play in the same key as everyone else and try to keep up. If you happen to know the song, then you can play along. Sometimes you get a solo, sometimes you're the melody, and sometimes you just play chords—whatever works for the group."

"Cool." I nodded, mostly comprehending the idea. I figured it would all make a lot more sense once I saw it.

"Sometimes Billy sings," Duane volunteered, "but not often."

"Yeah, but he will if Drew is there." Beau shifted in his seat, and he sounded a tad excited.

"Drew will be there?" I croaked; my chest expanded then tightened as a jolt of panic shot through me.

"I hope so." Beau grinned at me.

I tried to grin back.

I still spent every night in the den on the cot next to Momma, but of the last three mornings, I'd awoken to find Drew reading to her, or the two of them speaking in hushed voices.

During his conversation with Momma—the one I overheard—he said he liked my goodness, sweetness, gracefulness, and wit. Then, later, he told me to my face that I was beautiful, smart, sweet, and kind. I thought about this more than I should, and it made me feel direction-less and agitated. I never eavesdropped again. I was confused enough without hearing more of Drew's opinions.

In the mornings, I gave myself a few minutes to study him. If he was around the house during the day, I often caught myself staring at him. When he joined us for dinner in the evenings, I stole glances in his direction, especially during the rare times when he was engaged in conversation with someone or laughing, or any other time I was certain that his attention was directed elsewhere.

But Roscoe and Jethro had been right; he didn't talk much. Mostly he listened, observed, studied.

However, during those rare moments when he wasn't observing, I observed him. His movements were agile, and he walked with an artless, sensual cowboy swagger. I was sure he had no idea that the way he walked was at all sensual, but it was.

His voice was lilting and soothing. He was epically dreamy and tremendously gorgeous. But much more than that, his compassion and care for my mother, his patience with my brothers, and his open generosity for all of us would have made me swoon if I'd been the swooning type.

"If Drew is there, maybe you guys can sing together, like last time." Beau said this to Billy, leaning forward and tapping his shoulder.

"We'll see." Billy shrugged noncommittally and pulled into the community center, cutting the engine as soon as we were parked.

I glanced around the lot; there were a fair number of cars, and more were filling the empty spots. Just about 6:00 p.m., and it looked like the place already had a good crowd.

The building was definitely an old school, though it looked very small from the outside. The red brick and old white trim looked as if it had recently been restored. I quickly surmised that the inside consisted of one large room—the cafeteria—and two hallways. The first, the longer of the two, looked like it contained classrooms; the other looked like it held two or three offices.

Billy led the way, placing thirty dollars in a donations bucket at the entrance. Two older men sat at the table and stood when Billy walked in.

"Mr. Winston. Good to see you, sir."

Billy shook their hands with deference. "Mr. McClure, Mr. Payton, you know my brothers. I don't know if you remember my sister Ashley."

Their eyes moved to me and warm smiles lit their faces. Mr. McClure offered his hand to me first. I recognized him as the fire chief; he'd visited my elementary school when I was eight.

"My goodness, you grew up to be right pretty," he said, whistling and giving me a wink.

I glanced down at my dress, the first dress I'd worn since I'd been in Tennessee, and smoothed my hand over the light blue woven cotton. I liked the simple eyelet pattern, the square neck and the capped sleeves as well as the fit through the waist. It ended with a flared skirt that reached just below my knees.

It was by no means immodest. Therefore, I felt the whistling was a bit forward.

Mr. Payton, who must've been no less than eighty, had an exceptionally cheeky grin as he said, "Where have they been hiding you?"

"In Chicago," Billy said flatly.

Cletus stepped forward, and I was thankful for his interruption. "Mr. Payton, I must ask, how is your Ford?"

"Oh, she's running like new. You did a fine job."

Cletus gave him a little head nod, a pleased smile on his face.

"Speaking of cars, Duane, while you're here, would you mind taking a look at my air conditioner? It just aint cool enough, and I checked the fluid." Mr. McClure stood and motioned for Duane to follow, which he did readily.

"Save me some coleslaw," he called over his shoulder, giving us a cheerful wave. "This might take a while."

❤ ❤ ❤

DUANE ACTUALLY RETURNED within fifteen minutes, though his hands were dirty with grease. He'd identified the issue for Mr. McClure and arranged for the older man to bring his car by the shop.

Cletus chose a room playing bluegrass and stunned me speechless when, during the first song, he launched into an aggressive and impressive banjo solo. The group played a cover of Mumford and Son's "Beneath My Feet," and it was completely awesome.

The four of us stayed together for the first hour or so, listening to Cletus play his banjo. For my part, it was a wholly surreal experience to sit among my brothers, chitchatting at intervals, and just enjoying their company.

Billy excused himself after the first hour to go grab some food, and Duane went with him. Cletus's group was about to take a short break. I heard music filtering in from one of the other classrooms, and I turned toward the hallway, straining to hear what kind of songs the other groups were playing.

"Go on. Go check out some of the other rooms." Beau nudged me with his elbow. "We'll come find you when Cletus is finished, or just meet us back here."

I gave my brother a small smile, which he returned, and I felt an odd sense of wonder and gratefulness that I was lucky enough to be related to these genuinely remarkable, adorable men.

I slipped out of my seat as quietly as I could and walked to the hall, deciding I would just poke my head into each of the rooms for a song or two then head back to Cletus's group. This plan worked out perfectly for the first three rooms; they played blues, folk, and country respectively.

However, when I reached the fourth room, the final room, all thoughts of staying for just one song fled my mind.

Drew was there.

He was positioned toward the front of the group, sitting in profile, but all the way against the left wall. He was strumming an acoustic guitar, playing the chord progression along with two other guitars, a bass fiddle, and a violin as two banjos dueled for dominance.

I quickly searched for and found a seat at the back of the room, at the very end, closest to the door. The piece was entirely instrumental, but they played together as though they'd been practicing for years. Three of the musicians looked to be in their seventies or eighties, two men and one woman. One of the banjo players was no more than sixteen, but he was downright incredible. The other two musicians looked to be Drew's age or a little older.

The song came to a close and the audience clapped and cheered, showing their appreciation for the excellent music. I smiled as I watched Drew because he didn't seem to notice the audience at all. He looked like he'd be happy to play all day regardless of whether anyone —other than the musicians—was there to listen.

The bass fiddle called out a key—F major, I think—and played the chord progression, leading the others into the theme. Once again, they were off. This time I recognized it as "I Am a Man of Constant Sorrow," a song made popular by the Coen Brothers' film *O Brother, Where Art Thou?*

My delight was only increased further when Drew and the kid on the banjo began to sing the lyrics in perfect harmony. Then, I nearly fainted when Drew's face broke out in a huge grin, and he and the banjo prodigy exchanged a meaningful glance like they were sharing a private joke.

He was so relaxed and completely at ease singing about constant sorrow with a giant smile on his face. I wanted to laugh, not because the scene was funny, but because I was so pleasantly surprised. He appeared to be so happy, and his happiness was infectious. Also, he had a truly remarkable singing voice; a clear, velvety baritone that I felt in my bones.

I watched and listened, wholly entranced. After he sang of meeting us on God's golden shore, the song was over. I was bereft amidst the applause. This perfect moment, listening to Drew sing and play with such talent and obvious enjoyment, felt like a sudden and miraculous gift.

And then it was over.

The group moved on, and I was stuck. The other banjo player called out the key of G, playing the tonic. Drew fell into the accompaniment with both banjos, the other two guitars, and the violin, providing the chord progression while the bass fiddle lead with the melody of "The Highwaymen."

I stared at him for a stretch, still hearing the echoes of his previous performance and feeling melancholy that it was over.

"That Drew Runous has a nice voice," a woman in the row just in front of mine whispered loudly to her friend, snaring my attention. The two women appeared to be about Momma's age or a little older. Both ladies looked vaguely familiar—like hometown folks that I'd forgotten about—and I couldn't help but overhear their conversation.

"Yes he does, and he's a might good looking, too," the other woman said, an indulgent smile on her face. "My Jennifer is sweet on him since he helped with her car troubles when she was stalled on Moth Run, down by the Winston place."

"I didn't know they were an item."

"Oh, no, they're not, but Jennifer wishes they were. She can't get him to talk; only ever got one-word answers, though she's been up to the ranger station any number of times with muffins and the like. And you know he's never in town—well, hardly ever. I can't get more than three words out of him myself. She finally gave up." Jennifer's mother sighed.

"He is shy, that's true. Maybe she should be more up front about her interest. She's a beauty."

"Oh, she did that." The second woman chuckled a little and leaned closer to her friend like she was going to tell a scandalous story. I also leaned forward, irrationally invested in what was about to be spoken. I even went so far as to fiddle with my shoe to disguise my intent.

"Jennifer went down to the Cades Cove station knowing he'd be there. She brought her banana cake—you know, the one she won first prize for at the fair the last few years?"

"Everyone knows about that banana cake. What happened?"

"Well, she wore that yellow dress that her daddy doesn't like, and what do you think she did? She sidled right up to Drew, wrapped her arms around his neck, and kissed him."

The first woman pulled away, her expression shocked with disbelief. "Oh, my dear Lord," she loud whispered. "What did he do?"

The mother sighed. "He let her down gently, but he was a real gentleman about it."

"When was this?"

"Oh, I don't know. At the beginning of the summer, I guess. But you know he's been in town for years and aint never been attached to any girl that I'm aware of."

The two women shared a knowing look, as though Drew not being attached to a woman for several years automatically meant he was either suffering from some fatal illness, or he was gay.

I straightened in my seat and affixed my eyes to the front of the room when one of the ladies glanced over her shoulder. Fighting a guilty blush, I made the mistake of looking at Drew just as he turned his head, sweeping the crowd.

Our eyes met, and he did a double take. His mouth parted slightly, his eyes widened just a hint. Then he smiled.

Despite my red cheeks, I smiled back and gave him a little wave. I kept my eyes glued to the front of the room even when I felt the two ladies turn and peer at me.

I sat as still as a statue, and thought about making a quick escape, but Drew kept glancing my way through the remainder of the melody, a hint of a smile on his face, his eyes anchoring me to my chair.

When the song came to its conclusion and the bass fiddle announced that they would be taking a half hour break, I knew I couldn't cut and run. I didn't want to leave.

He set his guitar down behind him, resting it against the wall of the musicians' space. The crowd filtered out of the room. In order to avoid being caught in the swell by the door, I moved further in, walking to the far wall so Drew would have a clearer path if he chose to come talk.

His eyes never leaving my face, Drew navigated the theater seats, wooden chairs, pews, and stools, making his way to me.

I noted that several people moved to talk to him, but he put them off, gently saying, "Excuse me," or "I'll be right back." My heart rate increased as he neared, as did the size of his smile, and I felt a tad bit out of breath.

I didn't realize I was smiling until I spoke. "Hi, Drew."

Not breaking stride, Drew backed me up against the wall, his hands gripping my waist, his mouth unexpectedly meeting mine for a soft, sweet, caressing kiss.

I'm not going to lie. I kissed him back. But it was a confusing kiss for several reasons.

First, it gave me zings in my things, as Sandra would say. Maybe it was the beard; more likely, it was the man attached to the beard.

Second, it didn't feel like a friend kiss despite the fact that it was over in less than five seconds. But it didn't exactly feel like it was planned to be something more. In fact, I don't think he'd planned to kiss me at all. It was a truly spontaneous kiss.

Third, his kiss made me feel like I'd been filled up with a bolt of lightning; my restless energy increased tenfold the moment our lips touched.

I felt distinctly dazed as I gazed up at him.

"Hi, Ash." His eyes danced over my face. He looked happy, at least happier than I'd ever seen him. "It's great to see you."

I smiled up at him. "You saw me this morning."

"But you weren't wearing this dress."

Still dazed and finding no response for his statement, I said dumbly, "Cletus plays the banjo."

"Yes, sugar. I know that." His grin intensified as he removed his hands from my body and stepped back two steps. I almost followed him to stay in his orbit, but I managed to put a mental leash on my instinctual desire to do so.

"Did you enjoy the music?" His eyes were cheerful.

"Oh yes...you all were just great. You especially were fantastic. I loved watching your fingers move—you have great fingers. They're very long and really know how to move."

A small, amused frown creased his brow, and as the words spilled out of my mouth, his grin became massive. He glanced at the floor, stuffed his hands in his pockets, and lifted his blue-gray eyes to mine. "Well...thank you, Ash. I'll keep your admiration for my fingers in mind for future reference."

My neck started to itch as we stared at each other, likely because my brain slowly caught up with the conversation. It rewound what had just emerged from my mouth, and heated embarrassment swirled upward from my chest to my cheeks.

"I...I mean," I stammered, and I could feel the smile fall from my face as mortified understanding of what I'd actually said took the place of my kiss-daze.

"I know what you meant." He said this quietly, in a way that was meant to ease my embarrassment.

I cleared my throat and glanced at the floor then back to him. "Well, you also have an amazing singing voice."

His grin became a little self-conscious, but no less sincere or warm. "Thank you. That's nice of you to say."

"I mean it." I nodded vigorously, wanting him to understand that I was being honest. "I don't hand out false compliments because that only serves to diminish their value. I'm telling you, Drew Runous, you have an amazing singing voice. You should be singing all the time. You should live your life singing all your words—starting now."

He laughed. His eyes reminded me of shining silver bells on Christmas, merry and bright. "All right, I believe you. Thank you."

"Your Viking name should definitely be Drew the Singing Marauder, or I still like Drew Never-A-Dull-Moment."

He lifted a single eyebrow as he responded, "Nah, most people would call me Drew the Boring," his tone was flat and dry.

I snorted. "What people? Alligator wrestlers? Somali pirates?"

He shrugged and spoke plainly without bitterness or malice, like he was explaining a universal truth. "Normal people want to go to bars, parties, hook up; socialize, be seen. Money, power, influence...." He took a deep breath before adding, "I'm not like that."

"What are you like?" I asked before I realized that I'd spoken.

His single eyebrow lifted again at my bold question, and a hint of a smile tugged at the corner of his mouth. When he answered me, his voice held a suggestion of Texas swagger and charm, catching me off guard. "Sugar, I think you know what I'm like."

I couldn't stop the pinpricks of awareness dotting the skin of my arms, neck, and chest; nevertheless, I tried to flatten my grin. "Tell me anyway."

He just shook his head at me like I was a little strange. The truth was, I just wanted to hear him talk, and he so rarely spoke about himself.

"Okay...how many people our age debate philosophy? Read poetry? Learn about invasive species and the effect they have on sensitive ecosystems? Or how about moving to the middle of nowhere and just being? Just simply living?"

I got the impression that Drew was referring to someone in particular; maybe that gold digger my mother had mentioned. As well, I felt like he was giving me a rare glimpse into Drew—who he was, why he was always poking me with the Nietzsche stick—and I admired what I saw.

"Very few," I responded honestly. "And those who do usually end up being attacked by bears."

Drew laughed like I'd caught him off guard, and the sound was contagious. Soon we were laughing together. As the laughter receded, we watched each other for a stretch, during which I nearly lost myself in his silvery eyes.

I was thinking about living in the middle of nowhere with Drew, reading poetry, debating philosophy, and learning how to just be. I didn't think that sounded boring at all. If I added in my knitting group and books, it sounded like paradise—especially if he were shirtless.

Or naked.

When that image shot through my mind, I blushed scarlet and

looked away, pretending to be extremely interesting in the crowd milling about.

"It's good to see you like this," I finally said when I was brave enough to look into his eyes again.

"Like what?" He stepped forward, smiling down at me, and I lifted my chin to meet his eyes.

"I've known you going on a month. Usually you're...."

"I'm what?"

"Honestly, you're persnickety and intense, but..." I gripped his arm to stay any potential retreat, "...you're never boring."

We shared a smile and a gaze. It was one of those incredibly rare *I like who you are and I want to know you better* moments in life; when you look at another person and know that they're feeling a similar degree of affection and esteem for you too, and excitement at the possibility of a deeper acquaintance.

It's a spark—understanding the person as an individual and valuing him or her as such. It's the tantalizing potential and promise for more —more time, more shared experiences, more moments of intimacy.

It's a moment of perfect singularity, and it is completely different from mutual attraction because it's never based on physical factors, and it's not related to gender. I'd only ever experienced this phenomenon with female friends, the giddy excitement of finding a person who I genuinely wanted to know better.

But this time, with Drew, it felt more profound and a lot scarier.

CHAPTER THIRTEEN

"You talk when you cease to be at peace with your thoughts."

— KHALIL GIBRAN

"I'M GLAD YOU almost died."

I stopped, frowned, and turned to look at my brother Jethro over my shoulder.

"What did you say?"

His brown eyes stared back at me, his expression thoughtful and distracted.

"I said I'm glad you almost died." He smiled a crooked smile and crouched next to the water's edge. He picked up a flat, smooth stone and turned it over in his palm.

My eyebrows arched and I opened my mouth to respond, but then couldn't think of anything to say. Eleven days had passed since my waltz with the raccoon, and eight days had passed since the episode with Drew at the Friday night jam session. Both felt momentous, but for different reasons.

One made me feel more alive and more aware of my surroundings.

The other made me feel muddled and scared and more aware of my surroundings (especially if those surroundings included Drew).

Instead of responding to Jethro's disturbing statement, a sound escaped the back of my throat, similar to an *Uhhhhhh*.

Seeing or sensing my confusion, Jethro waved his hands through the air, still holding the stone, and shook his head. "No, no, no—you don't understand, Ash. You've changed. We were worried about you. You've changed since the thing with the raccoon; it's like you're finally awake."

"Oh," I said, immediately understanding what he meant, because he was right.

My relationships with my brothers were becoming a real thing. I credited the raccoon attack for waking me up, but I also recognized that two other important factors had improved interactions:

1) I now used the downstairs bathroom exclusively; I'd surrendered to the fact that the upstairs bathroom was an ophthalmic hazard as well as dangerous for my blood pressure and mental wellbeing.

2) I made loud noises everywhere I went outside of the den, downstairs hallway, and kitchen. This consisted of banging pots and pans, singing "Old MacDonald Had a Farm" at maximum volume, and—if I was in a particularly goofy mood—shouting, "Ready or not, here I come!" If I announced my presence, the chances of walking in on a scheduled or unscheduled sausage-packing session decreased exponentially.

The summer heat was becoming autumn temperate. I took walks, sometimes more than once a day. I enjoyed the woods and all the beauty of the surrounding wilderness. I removed my shoes and waded into the stream behind our house, which was where I was now, out with Jethro, hopping from stone to stone in the stream.

It was Saturday and his day off; he was spending it with me. We'd spent most of the day in the den with Momma, then later in the kitchen making turkey potpie. I made the crust; he made the filling.

But for the last hour or so, we'd been quietly exploring the wilderness of our childhood, reliving old memories, visiting old haunts.

"Hey, so...." Jethro paused, his attention on the stone in his hand. "I ran into Jack again the other day. He asked about you."

"Jack?"

"Yeah, you know, Jackson James, the dumbass that broke your heart in high school."

I wrinkled my nose then snorted. "He might have broken my heart, but it's not the way you think."

"I remember, Ashley. You were pretty torn up about it. No one knows why."

"First of all, I wasn't in love with him; I didn't like him that way." I wiggled my toes and shuffled a few steps forward, aggravating the floor of the stream and causing a little sand cloud to float over my feet.

"Then why were you his girlfriend?"

I shrugged and glanced up at my brother. "Because he was nice to me, and everyone else was an asshole."

He opened his mouth to respond then closed it. His eyebrows danced around a little on his forehead before he finally said something. "Well, you shocked the hell out of everyone when you chose him. And then he shocked the hell out of everyone when he dumped you."

I sighed at the memory and twisted my lips to the side. I'd broken things off with Jackson—romantically—during our last week of high school. I'd explained to him that I didn't see a future for us as boyfriend/girlfriend, but I'd desperately wanted to remain friends. I guess I misjudged his feelings because he told the whole school that he'd dumped me, which basically meant that the whole town knew within days.

Then he wrote me a letter telling me that he never wanted to see me or speak to me again.

Looking back on it now, it felt silly and ridiculous—high school, dumping, letters, rumors, *drama!* I no longer cared about who dumped who. I cared about losing my best friend.

"Hey! Where are you guys?" The sound of Billy's voice calling through the woods pulled both our gazes in the direction of feet crunching on fallen leaves.

"Over here." Jethro called back then turned to me, rolling his eyes.

"Billy is the smartest guy I know, smarter than Drew even, but he doesn't know shit about tracking in the woods."

I smirked in response, my black skirt gathered in my hands as I stepped down from the stone and into the cool water. The stream was up to my knees and rushed past with purpose. Therefore my skirt—which fell to mid-calf when I wasn't trying to keep it from getting wet—bared my legs to my thighs.

"I heard that," came a stern response.

I stiffened and my head shot up, because the stern response was Drew's voice, not Billy's.

Drew and Billy finally emerged and, upon catching sight of their approaching forms, I turned away and walked further into the water. I felt confused and flustered. My heart was beating like it wanted to escape, and my neck was hot and itchy. I didn't know where to look.

This was now my body and brain's response to Drew, especially after our hallway conversation and our very disorienting maybe-friend-kiss.

Since our conversation at the jam session, Drew and I hadn't talked much, not about anything of substance. But he no longer felt like an enemy or an entitled usurper.

He didn't feel much like a friend either.

I continued to study him in the mornings. And in the afternoon if he was around. And in the evenings if he stayed for dinner.

All this watching and no speaking or touching had yielded a whole lot of mixed-up emotions.

Yet, somehow, watching him from afar felt a lot more natural than interacting with him up close. Maybe this was because on some level Drew felt like a fictional character, too good to be true, too perfect to be real. This nagged at me. I felt like I was missing something obvious, or maybe I hadn't yet asked the right question to determine his ulterior motives.

Yes, I was a creeper, but I didn't care. Drew brought these compulsions out in me, so he could just suffer through my leering and take it like a man.

Or a girl. Because, if there's one thing a girl grows up learning how to do, it's suffering through leering.

"Jethro, I need the keys to the Chevy," Billy, always one to get down to business, hollered at us through the trees. He did this even though he was close enough to be heard if he'd employed a normal voice.

Growing up, Billy always seemed perplexed by the forest. He'd talk louder than necessary, do stupid stuff like throw rocks at beehives, and try to walk on stepping stones with his shoes on. It's like the woods made him dumb.

"Butter on biscuits, Billy! I told you I hung the keys up in the kitchen."

If I hadn't been so disconcerted by Drew's presence, I *definitely* would have given Jethro shit for saying *butter on biscuits* as a means to express his frustration. We'd all been raised with the notion that *butter on biscuits* was just as bad as the f-bomb.

I heard the footsteps retreat along with the sound of Jethro and Billy's irritated voices and mild insults.

Jethro: "They're right there on the hook, how could you miss them?"

Billy: "They're not on the hook. I'm not blind. I can see your ugly face, can't I?"

Jethro: "I don't know, can you? You couldn't find a tree in these woods."

Billy: "I can too. See? That's a tree." I heard him smack it for emphasis.

Jethro: "That's not a tree, dummy. That's a bush. I'll give you five dollars if you can find a leaf."

I pressed my lips together and laughed to myself. Their bickering was nearly constant. They reminded me a bit of the roosters in our backyard, crowing at each other just for the sake of crowing.

I hiked my skirt higher and crossed to the other side of the riverbank. The bottom of the stream was sandy in some spots, rocky in others. I walked slowly, enjoying the feel of the cool water coursing between my legs and the quiet sounds of the forest.

I should have felt peaceful and at ease, but I didn't. The hairs on the back of my neck prickled and a shiver raced down my spine. Instinctively, I glanced around and over my shoulder, finding the source of my disquiet.

Drew stood in Jethro's abandoned spot. His thumbs were hooked in his belt loops, his white T-shirt was tucked into the waist of his blue cargo pants, and he was wearing the thick brown belt with the large buckle that spelled SAVAGE.

And he was watching me. His face was neutral except a whisper of a smile curving his lips and lighting his eyes.

My gaze widened, surprised to find him on the other side of the bank. My steps faltered and stopped. We stared at each other silently, and the song of a nearby bird filled the air.

When the bird finished its solo, Drew lifted his chin—this had the effect of hooding his gaze—and said, "Good to see you out of the house again."

I gave him a tight smile. "And not being chased by a rabid raccoon, right?"

"Right." His grin widened and he nodded once. "So, you call your girls yet?"

My tight smile became soft and sincere. "Yes. Yes I have. Thank you again for that."

I knew he was referring to my knitting group back in Chicago. The first thing I'd done after logging on to the Internet was send off several emails to my friends, letting them know how things stood, how I was, and apologizing for not contacting them earlier.

Since then I'd Skyped once with my friends Janie and Fiona, once with Elizabeth, twice with my friends Marie and Kat, and two times with Sandra and her husband Alex (who I also considered a close friend). Alex shared my passion for novels and, therefore, we were frequently arguing the merits of one author or another. He'd just finished re-reading one of my favorites, *Lonesome Dove*, and was eager to debate the virtues of a happy ending versus a true-to-life ending.

He preferred a happy ending. I preferred a true-to-life ending. We argued about this often.

"No need to keep saying thank you." Drew shrugged, his eyes serious. "Whatever you need."

I felt suddenly shy and we fell silent again. I looked away, though I was sure he was still watching me. I let myself steal a glance at him from the corner of my eye and found I was right. In fact, his eyes were on my legs; specifically, where my skirt was hiked up to my thighs.

My bizarre burst of shyness was joined by an abrupt dose of self-consciousness.

Not helping matters, Drew picked that moment to say, "'My friend must be a bird, because she flies...'"

I stilled, aware of the sound my heart was making between my ears, and swallowed the rising sensation of delicious disquiet down, down, down.

Of course, I recognized the words he'd just said as the beginning of a poem. But the original Emily Dickenson poem was about a *he,* not a *she;* as in, *My friend must be a bird, because he flies.* It was a love poem, and it stirred something in my stomach and chest. The forest felt close and overwhelming, like I was being wrapped in a blanket of tree trunks and leaves.

Yet I managed to clear my throat and recite the next line: "'Mortal, my friend must be, because he dies'."

I could hear the smile in Drew's voice when he continued, "'Barbs has she, like a bee. Ah, curious friend...'"

I lifted my eyes and held his. We finished the poem together, saying in unison, "'Thou puzzlest me'."

Drew's smile was immense. I returned it because I was randomly powerless against the sight of him. He was bathed in the afternoon sunlight filtering through the trees and casting him in a golden glow. So, basically, he was dazzling.

After a long moment, looking at him made my chest hurt, so I moved my attention elsewhere and said, "What? No Nietzsche quotes today?"

"How about this one: 'Stupidity in a woman is unfeminine'."

I smiled at the water and nodded. "That's a good one. I can't stand the guy. But I admit that's a good quote."

"What's not to like? His well-constructed arguments against the insanity of group think and forced societal mediocrity? Or is it his magnificent mustache you can't stand?"

My eyebrows lifted, though I kept my attention affixed to the water's surface. "Nietzsche didn't have a mustache."

"Yes he did."

"No, that wasn't a mustache. That was the pelt of a moderately sized woodland animal and a lifestyle choice."

Drew's laughter filled the air, danced around my head, and landed softly on my ears. I was gratified to hear it, a deep belly laugh that— paired with his behavior the night of the jam session—further contradicted my earlier estimation of him as joyless. His laughter receded, leaving me with rosy cheeks, flushed with pleasure, and a wide grin claiming my mouth.

Since I was on a roll, I added, "I like this one too: 'Every deep thinker is more afraid of being understood than of being misunderstood'."

I glanced at Drew and regretted it. The force of his gaze nearly knocked me over. I frowned at his expression and tore my eyes away. I decided to vehemently occupy myself by studying the pebbles on the bed of the translucent stream, separating the orange rocks from the others with my toes.

But my feet halted their movements when I heard him recite several lines of poetry:

"Fire burns blue and hot.
Its fair light blinds me not.
Smell of smoke is satisfying, tastes nourishing to my tongue.
I think fire ageless, never old, and yet no longer young.
Morning coals are cool; daylight leaves me blind.
I love the fire most because of what it leaves behind."

My frown deepened because I didn't recognize the poem. I dared to give him a curious glance. His returning gaze felt heavy somehow, demanding and fierce in a way I couldn't immediately grasp; or maybe I wasn't ready to understand.

Regardless, I asked the question that was on my mind. "I don't recognize that one. Who wrote it?"

Drew removed his thumbs from his belt loops and stuffed his hands in his pockets. His gaze still unnerving in its intensity, he shrugged and said, "I wrote it."

My mouth dropped open slightly in surprise, and I blinked at his admission. "You wrote it?"

He nodded.

"You write poetry?"

He nodded again, glanced at the toes of his boots, then at back me.

I thought about the poem, or at least the lines I could remember. If I'd known he was going to recite one of his own, I would have told him to hold that thought so I could write it down, pick it apart later, and memorize it. I never, in one million years, would have guessed that Drew was a poet.

It seemed he had a gift for shocking the butter off my biscuits.

In what felt like a sudden departure, but what might have been after several minutes of me staring at him completely dumbfounded, Drew tossed his thumb over his shoulder and said, "I need to head out. I'll see you later."

With that, he turned to leave.

My heart did a weird clenching thing in my chest and my feet moved toward him without me telling them to do so. When I realized that I was basically chasing after him, dredging my legs like heavy weights to the edge of the stream, I instructed my body to cease and desist the pursuit.

But before I could stop my mouth, I blurted a question at his retreating back. "What does the fire leave behind? Destruction? Death?"

Drew didn't respond until he was almost out of sight. Then he turned and, walking backward for a few steps, he called out, "Ash—the fire leaves ash."

CHAPTER FOURTEEN

"He had never known such gallantry as the gallantry of Scarlett O'Hara going forth to conquer the world in her mother's velvet curtains and the tail feathers of a rooster."

— MARGARET MITCHELL, GONE WITH THE WIND

IVE WEEKS AFTER I arrived in Tennessee I ran out of jokes.

On the Monday that I ran out of jokes, Billy, Joe, and Marissa were sitting with Momma while she dozed, Marissa having decided to stay for supper after her shift ended. I was in the kitchen cleaning up the dinner dishes with Cletus and Jethro, lost in my thoughts while drying pots and pans.

I was thinking about Drew and wondering where he was. He hadn't come to the house for supper. He'd been MIA since our poetry recitation in the woods. I wondered obliquely if the rain, which had been falling non-stop for the last two days, was responsible for his absence.

Cutting through my musings, I heard my mother's voice calling my name, and my hands stilled just as Billy appeared in the doorway.

"Ash, Ash—come quick. Momma says she has something to tell

you." He paused just long enough to wave me forward then dashed back down the hall.

I set the pot down and barely registered the sound as it fell to the floor behind me. I was already jogging out of the kitchen and down the hallway to the den.

Momma's eyes were open, and she looked completely lucid. I tucked this vision of her away, took a snapshot with my mind—because it occurred to me that this might be her last lucid moment.

"Hey, Momma. I'm here." I reached my hand out and she gripped it immediately.

"Ashley." Her eyes were wide, and the usual urgency was present. Abruptly, I worried that she would say something profound instead of her usual random bits of wisdom.

I was terrified that this time, she would say something real and necessary and earth shattering, and it would mean the end of her.

But my fears were assuaged when she said, "Ashley, the roosters. We have too many roosters. I told your friend Sandra about it while she was here. You need to butcher them, all but one, or else it'll cause problems for the hens, and they won't lay as many eggs. Roosters need a purpose. If you don't give a rooster a purpose, they make trouble."

I gave her a small smile and nod, the knot of fear in my chest easing. "Okay, I'll do that. Tomorrow I'll butcher the roosters."

She nodded, relaxed back to her pillows, and sighed. "Good. That's good. Maybe you can make some fried chicken. Also, I think I promised Julianne at the library a bird. Do you mind?"

I shook my head. "I'll call her this week."

"Thank you," she said intently, her eyes moving between mine. Then she waited, watching me like she expected me to say something else.

I stiffened when I realized she was waiting for me to tell her a joke, and my throat tightened when my mind went blank. The dash into the den, my worry when I found her so lucid and awake, the fear that seized me when I thought she was going to finally share something actually urgent had pushed all the jokes from my mind.

My heart rate doubled as her eyes moved over my face, her expectant smile slipping.

"Why did the rooster go to KFC?" Billy, standing at my shoulder, blurted this question.

I glanced at him and, to my surprise, found that all my brothers were also in the room. Billy's eyes flickered to mine then back to my mother as he stated the punchline. "Because he wanted to see a chicken strip."

We fell silent for half a second, then my momma wrinkled her nose and shook her head. But she was also laughing. "William, that is a terrible joke."

"I've got one," Roscoe volunteered. He was standing on the other side of the bed holding my mother's hand. "Why did the rooster cross the road?"

"Why, Roscoe?" Her face split with a grin.

"Because he needed to cock-a-doodle-do something."

Light laughter lit up the room and Duane snorted, "That's the dumbest joke I've ever heard."

"Then you tell one," Roscoe challenged, narrowing his eyes good-naturedly at his brother.

"Fine, I will. And it will be awesome. It'll blow all the rest of your sad chicken jokes out of the water."

"We're waiting." Beau pushed Duane's shoulder.

"Any day now." Jethro called from where he stood by Momma's feet, his arms crossed over his chest.

"Okay, prepare yourselves." Duane looked at me, then Momma, and cleared his throat theatrically. "Why did the rooster cross the road, roll in the mud, and cross the road again?"

His red eyebrows were arched over his blue eyes as he glanced around the room with cocky—no pun intended—dramatic hyperbole and waited.

"No one is going to take a guess?"

"Just tell us the punchline and stop egg-zaggerating," Beau said and winked at Momma.

"That would be most egg-cellent," Momma said, managing to return Beau's wink.

"Fine," Duane said, finally giving us the punchline. "It was because he was a dirty double crosser."

Most of my brothers groaned and I chuckled.

Cletus, however, frowned and shook his head. "I don't get it."

This went on for a while, the boys telling terrible chicken jokes while my momma laughed and bantered. I didn't say anything. I didn't want to miss a single second. I tried to remember every laugh, every word, every smile. I was taking a video with my mind, filling myself with the memory, greedily clinging to the feeling of being surrounded by my family and sharing this happy moment.

With every joke, my heart lifted then dropped when the laughter dissipated. I worried it would be the last.

Sometime later, when the last joke did come, and we all looked around—at my momma who was asleep and at each other—a crushing sense of finality swept over me. The seven of us sat quietly in a stillness that felt like a punctuation mark.

It may not have been the end of the story, but it was definitely the end of a chapter.

THAT NIGHT I couldn't sleep. I tossed and turned on my cot, unable to get comfortable. The rainstorm should have helped, a gift of nondescript background noise, but it didn't. The muffling of the rain made me anxious. My brain wouldn't allow me to consider that the sound of it grated against my nerves because I hadn't seen Drew since the rain began on Saturday.

Around 2:00 a.m., I left the den, taking my quilt with me, and tiptoed to the backdoor. My plan was to stand on the back porch and listen to the rainstorm without the obstruction of walls.

Rain sounded different in the Smoky Mountains than it did in Chicago. The difference between a rainstorm in the city and a rainstorm in the mountains was the difference between hearing a song over the speaker of your cell phone versus listening to a live concert.

In the city, the sound was dull, rain hitting pavement, dumpsters, awnings, windows, and buildings. The sound was all treble with no bass.

In the old mountains, however, rain hit the surface of every leaf, every stone, every stream. It echoed, it surrounded, it felt layered and rich and comforting.

Paired with the smell of fresh, clean water, intermittent distant flashes of lightning, and the nearly constant gentle rolling of thunder—the soft kind that is felt in the chest and subtly shakes the ground—the storm was more than a sound. It was an experience that touched every one of my senses.

Standing on the porch, I closed my eyes, cleared my mind, and breathed in the storm.

And then I cried.

I didn't know why I was crying. Well, other than the obvious reasons. Really, the issue was that I didn't know why I was crying *now*.

I hadn't cried since the day I found out about my mother's prognosis. In the last month I'd come close a few times, but the tears hadn't come. I'd been able to hold them at bay and soldier on.

Maybe it was the rain making the world new and fresh; maybe it was the evening spent laughing with my brothers, enjoying them in a way I'd never done before; maybe it was the feeling of certainty that these next days would be full of *lasts*: the last time I'd laugh with my mother, the last time I'd see her smile, the last time I'd hear her voice.

Maybe it was everything.

"Ash?"

My back stiffened and I rolled my lips between my teeth at the sound of Drew saying my name. His voice sounded rumbly, sleepy, like he'd just woken up.

"Drew?"

"Yeah."

I didn't turn around. "What are you doing here?"

"I was asleep on the couch in the family room. I woke up when I heard you come out here. Are you crying?"

"No. I'm not crying." I shook my head, still giving him my back. "I am most definitely not crying. Nope. Not. Crying. I'm eye cleansing... with saltwater...made from my tear ducts." I sniffled, and I felt the corners of my mouth turn down. Try as I might I couldn't stiffen my chin or squeeze my eyes shut enough to stem the tears.

I knew Drew was still there, still behind me. But I didn't realize that he'd crossed to where I stood leaning against the wooden post of the porch until I felt his hands on my shoulders.

He didn't wait for me to assent to his comfort. He just grabbed me, turned me, pulled me to his wall of a chest, and encircled my body with his arms. One of his great paws was on my lower spine, the other on the back of my head, and his lips were at my temple.

Caring not one stitch about my pride, I held on.

I conveniently forgot all my previous objections against his offers of compassion. Instead, I immediately melted against him. I clung to his shirt and I buried my head in his chest. I pressed my body against his.

His embrace was a forceful promise of security, full of commanding comfort. In fact, it felt desperate. If a hug could be frantic, this hug was frantic. It felt as though he needed to hold me without accepting anything in return; he needed to demonstrate that he possessed enough strength for both of us; he needed to gather me close and carry my burdens.

Therefore, for a confusing, foggy stretch of time, I handed over my grief.

I was far away from my friends, from the life I loved and the family I had chosen in Chicago. I was surrounded by people I'd rejected, people who were essentially strangers, and now I was regretting pushing them away and missing out on years with my brothers. I wanted to apologize and mend those fences, but I'd been a mess of distracted anguish.

I was facing a life without my mother in it.

I leaned on Drew and just gave in, and it felt impossibly good. He was solid and warm. He was strong. He even smelled good, like the woods and rain and man. His T-shirt was worn cotton—soft and absorbent.

For a moment, I just let myself need someone. My hands gripped the fabric at his sides and I cried.

Drew's fingers threaded through my hair; his lips brushed a soft kiss against my temple and forehead.

"Ashley...Sugar...." He whispered, and his voice was so different from the usual gruffness, or the sardonic stoicism he employed when quoting Nietzsche. I was busy crying into his absorbent T-shirt and clinging to the fleeting relief of a temporarily shared burden. I had no attention to spare. I could dedicate nothing to deciphering the meaning behind the caressing quality of his tone and words.

"Tell me what you need," he said between raining soft kisses against my hair, temple, and cheek. "I'll do anything for you."

I heard him, but I didn't really process his words other than at the most basic level. He wanted to help me. That was the takeaway message.

Therefore, I wiped my nose on his shirt and said between tears, "I'm using your shirt as a tissue."

"That's fine." I felt his smile against my cheek. "It's yours if you want it."

"I'll wash it." I still needed to wash his other shirts. This would be shirt number three.

"Don't worry about it."

"I will worry. It's covered in snot, very unsanitary. You could get sick. I don't want you to get sick."

Drew chuckled. His hand on my back rubbed slow, soothing circles, and he gave me another squeeze.

"I'll let you wash my shirt if you tell me what I can do. Tell me what you need."

"I need...." I hiccupped. I'd cried so much that my breathing had dissolved into stop, starts, and hiccups.

"Anything, Ashley."

"I need...."

"Anything, it's yours."

"I need you to tell me a joke."

Drew stilled, his hand ceased moving on my back.

"A joke." He said the words deadpan.

"Yes. A joke. Make sure it's really funny." I could feel his heart beat against my cheek; instinctively, I snuggled closer as I said, "No pressure."

The sound of his heartbeat was eclipsed by his sudden laugh, deep and low and rumbly. I lifted my head from its comfy spot and glanced at him, his features just visible in the indigo night.

He was smiling and he was looking down at me and his eyes were completely captivating. They traced my face with reverence and, whether what I saw was real or imagined, his eyes told me that I was precious to him.

And then I kissed him.

I didn't know why I kissed him. Well, other than the obvious reasons. Really, the issue was that I didn't know why I was kissing him *now*.

CHAPTER FIFTEEN

"Any man who can drive safely while kissing a pretty girl is simply not giving the kiss the attention it deserves."

— ALBERT EINSTEIN

IF DREW WAS surprised by my lips suddenly against his, then he hid his surprise really, really well.

One of his hands gripped me around the waist, the other grabbed hold of my hair and he tugged, positioning my head as he liked. As though arranging me and opening me for his use…as though he'd been waiting for this…as though he'd planned and choreographed this kiss to guarantee perfection.

It was a thoroughly tuned, tactile tango. Where he led, I followed.

With no hesitation, he twirled us, backed me into and against the outside wall of the house. He gave me three sensual, carnal closed mouthed passes that made my stomach tighten and my chest expand with hot desperation.

Then he nipped at my bottom lip and tasted me.

Instinctively, I parted my mouth, my tongue darting out, seeking his. He gave it to me. He gave me his weight. He gave me the pressure of his fingers against the bare skin of my sides and stomach. He gave me a deep rumble in his chest that echoed in my head and sounded to my heart and body like *more*.

More of this...more of you. Give me more.

I was no longer sharing a burden. His entreaties had switched focus. His need to give had reversed and—with the same fervor he'd commanded my comfort earlier—he now demanded my unconditional surrender. My head was in the stars. Our bodies were heavenly instruments of careless need. Worries melted beneath us into nothing.

I think I whimpered, my hands under his shirt, touching the hard, hot expanse of his stomach. I think I whimpered because he felt as good as he looked, better than he looked. The thought of not touching him everywhere made me feel weak, and awakened an agonizing urgency within me.

It was a soul scorching, pride destroying, body claiming kiss. And he ended it.

Drew abruptly pulled away, walked away from me. I was left in the cosmos with no map, not knowing if a return trip to Earth were possible.

I lifted fingertips to my lips. I found them used and swollen, evidence of our frenetic kiss, and I released a short breath. My eyes searched the porch for him and discovered he was at the far end. His back was to me, and he was leaning on the railing, looking out into the night. It was so dark I doubted he could see much.

I'd never experienced a kiss before where recovery time was necessary for one or both parties. Needing a minute to collect myself, I closed my eyes and pressed my hand to my heart. My head fell back, connecting with the wall, and I tried to regulate my breathing. My heart would not cooperate. It beat like it knew better, like it understood what this kiss meant better than the rest of me, and it was both thrilled and frightened.

Gradually, like waking from a dream, I was once again aware of the rain and the rolling thunder and the lightning; the symphony that was a rainstorm in the old mountains.

"I've wanted to do that for a while." Drew's voice—the sound and the tone—startled me.

"You have?" I lifted my head from the wall and blinked at his inky silhouette, still some distance away. "For how long?"

"Since I saw you."

"Since you saw me?" My echo was a squeak.

"Yes." He admitted, stalking closer. His eyes glinted in the sparse light offered by a distant flash of lightning. They were focused with heated intensity on my mouth.

I sought to clarify his meaning. "Since you saw me tonight?"

"No. Since I first saw you. Since I first laid eyes on you and felt sorry for every beautiful thing that was made no longer resplendent— nullified by your being."

I didn't breathe for ten seconds. When I did, the air left my lungs in a whoosh, and with it departed my peace of mind.

"Fuck...." I said, because what I was feeling deserved a remarkably harsh expletive. "You really are a poet."

"Ash...."

I shook my head and closed my eyes because the memory of our damn hot perfect kiss, the vision of him standing in front of me, the whisper of his delectably distressing admission, became too much for my little heart to handle.

"No more talking," I begged. "I think your words aren't safe for me to hear."

They're weapons, I thought, *as sure as a martial artist's fists are weapons.* With enough use, practice, and honing of skill, words were the weapons of choice used by exceptional writers and poets. Minds can be changed, hearts can be lost and broken, souls can be surrendered given the right words.

Or the wrong ones.

"No more talking," he repeated, closer than I'd expected. His breath fell over my cheek and his hands slid around my waist, pressing my body to his. "No more talking." He said again, this time as a whisper against my neck.

"Drew...."

"Shh." His hand lifted and cupped my cheek, his thumb caressing my bottom lip.

I was mixed up and turned inside out. I didn't know what to say or do or how to move forward from this labyrinth of my own making.

So I blurted, "Can we forget this happened?" I didn't try to disguise the desperation in my voice. "Can't we call it a mistake?"

He was quiet for a long time, holding me in a full-body embrace, his hand caressing my cheek and then smoothing its way down my shoulder and arm. His fingers found mine, brought my wrist to his lips, and kissed it, his breath and beard tickling the sensitive skin.

Then he pressed my open palm to his chest.

At last, he said, "No, Sugar. You know I'm no good at pretending."

I released a shaky breath and gripped the front of his shirt. "I don't know what we're doing."

"Don't you?"

"I live in Chicago."

"I know."

"I have a life there."

"I know."

"Your life is here."

"Yes, Ash, I know." He bent and kissed my neck, made me shiver.

"When all this is over," I swallowed the last word, because *over* really meant *when Momma dies*, "I'm leaving. I'm leaving and I'm not coming back."

"Sugar, I know all this."

"I don't want either of us to get hurt," I pleaded, but I wasn't sure whether I was pleading with Drew or myself.

"Nothing you can do about that." He nipped my jaw then kissed it. "You underestimate how deeply you cut when your intentions carry no knives."

DREW WALKED ME back to the den, holding my hand as we navigated the dark, then he left me with a quick and impulsive kiss.

I watched his form depart, listened for the sound of him reclaiming his spot on the couch, and waited several minutes more. I don't know what I was listening for, but soon the only sound was my own breathing and heartbeat.

Finally, I ducked into the den and my cot. But my mother stopped me by calling out my name.

"Ash, is that you?"

I crossed to her bed and reached for her hand. Her eyes were still closed.

"Yes. It's me."

"What's wrong, baby? Can't you sleep?"

I opened my mouth to say that I was just using the bathroom, but I stopped. I didn't know how much time she had left, and I didn't want to spend any of it pacifying her or being polite just for politeness's sake.

"Momma, how did you meet Drew?"

Momma laughed lightly and gave my hand a feeble squeeze. "So... thoughts of Andrew are keeping you up?"

I swallowed uncomfortably. "Honestly, the rain woke me up. But I think thoughts of Andrew are going to keep me up."

She opened her eyes and peered at me. "You want to know about Andrew." It was a statement, not a question.

"Yes. I want to know. I'm not upset—at least, not anymore, but I was for a little bit—about you giving him your power of attorney. But why would you do that? How well do you know him? How did you meet him?"

"Well...let's see...." Momma slurred; she sounded drugged but not confused, yet not nearly as aware as she had seemed earlier in the evening.

"I'm sorry, am I pushing you? We don't have to talk about this."

"No, baby. It's fine." Another weak squeeze as we held hands. "Let's see...did you know Andrew is a poet?"

"Yes." I'd found that out several days ago, when he told me that fires leave behind Ash.

"I met him about three or four years ago. I'd started a poetry-reading group at the library. I think I told you about that when it started. Mostly it was me and Diane Sylvester and a few ladies from the senior center. Anyway, one day, in walks Andrew." She paused and I saw her mouth curve into a smile.

"I asked him if I could help him find something, thinking—of course—that he'd wandered into our little group on accident. He asked if we were the poetry group, and when I admitted that we were, he took a seat. Well, you should have seen Diane Sylvester's face; for that matter, you should have seen *my* face. I think we were both in a state of shock. Never mind those little old ladies from the senior center, except Mrs. Cooper. She was as pleased as salt on crackers. She's a cougar, not that there's anything wrong with that, but I think she made Andrew a little uncomfortable when she kept licking her lips at him."

I grinned at this image. "How old is Mrs. Cooper?"

"Eighty two, but she was seventy eight then, and—I apologize for being impolite—she's got lots of money."

In Tennessee, or maybe just in my little corner of it, it's considered impolite to say the word *money*. You can talk about gutting a deer and making venison sausages, you can talk about a bar fight, you can talk about your hemorrhoids and all the icky squicky details of childbirth— but if you say the word *money*, you must apologize for being impolite.

"So, what happened?"

"He didn't say much during the first meeting, but he was eyeballing me something fierce. I thought I might have offended him. But he came back a second time and read a few of his own works. After that, he asked if I wanted to grab some coffee, so we did."

"Did you ever think he was…interested in you?"

"Oh, Lord no! He's younger than Jethro!"

"But…."

"But nothing. I knew it wasn't like that. Andrew was lost, I could tell from his poetry, and he was looking for a home. He stirred my maternal instincts, not my womanly instincts. Besides, at the time he needed a woman like a cow needs a saddle. What he needed, and what I tried to provide him, was an unconditional ear and support."

"Why do you trust him so much? I mean, you signed over your medical decisions to him. He's the executor of your will."

"Because I know him. I know his history and his heart. He's...." she sucked in a breath and looked to be searching for the right words to continue. "Ash, he feels like a son to me. And I hope he knows that. I hope he sees me as the mother he never had, at least I hope I've filled that role for the years we've known each other."

"He didn't have a mother?"

She sighed, "Baby, that's not my story to tell. But I will tell you this: I trust Andrew Runous more than I trust you right now."

I flinched.

She sighed impatiently. "And that's not because I love you less. I love you to the stars and beyond, just like always. But you've got a sensitive heart, and your momma is dying, and your brain is all catawampus. I remember when my mother died. I made terrible decisions in the months that followed. I almost reconciled with your daddy. It was a mess."

I understood what she meant. Despite my initial reaction to her admission, I realized that I also trusted Drew more at this moment. He'd broken the kiss. He'd left me at the door to the den. I was thankful that he was there to deal with all the logistics and details so that my brothers and I could spend our time and energy on our mother.

"There is something else that's been nagging at me," I persisted. I didn't want to tire her, but she seemed especially lucid right now, so it seemed like a good time to ask. "Why didn't you ever tell me about how things had improved around here? The boys are doing so much better than I ever would've imagined. Why didn't you keep me up to date on all that? I know I should have asked more, but I thought...." I paused, searching my mind, then added, "I thought things were unchanged because you never told me otherwise. I thought they were still all rascals."

Momma was very quiet, and I could tell she was thinking; at last she shook her head, her eyes unfocused, and said, "I don't know. Your time here, growing up, it was hard in this house full of disorderly, unfeeling boys. Maybe I thought I was protecting you...they were so much like your father back then… but that doesn't make sense. I just don't know."

This answer surprised me, especially since she sounded lost. I couldn't think of anything to say.

Before I could form a response, she said, "Maybe I was living through you, maybe just a little bit. Maybe I envied the life you had, the one you made for yourself. Maybe I wanted to keep you all to myself. I don't know, baby. I didn't talk to them about you either; and you know, they never asked. Sometimes we behave in ways that make no sense, not even to ourselves. It's a madness; we all got it. And I'm not perfect. But I'm sorry. Will you forgive me?"

"Yes. Of course, yes." I wanted to hug her but knew that was impossible, so I settled for caressing her cheek.

"Now, Ash, I got a favor to ask of you." She shifted in her bed and her face grew sober, her eyes serious.

"Sure, Momma, anything."

"You're not going to like it. But I need you to listen to me, and I need you to trust me."

"You know I trust you."

"Ash, baby, I need you to call your father. I need to see him, but— more importantly—he needs to see all of you before I go."

I couldn't speak because I was certain I'd misheard her. She couldn't possibly be asking me to invite that man into this home. Not now. Not ever.

"Why, Momma? I just don't understand how you could…."

"Ash, you need to trust me on this. There are things you don't know."

I released a disbelieving snort. "Then tell me."

"No, baby, because then you'll go off and call him and tell him yourself. I know your daddy, and I know what I'm doing. I need to tell him face-to-face. He needs to see all of you, all of you together, united. He needs to see it so he knows he doesn't have any wiggle room— because all he needs is a little wiggle room in your head or Jethro's or Beau's. You all need to support each other. That's what he needs to see."

"What are you talking about? Wiggle room for what?"

"Ashley, Darrell knows I'm sick. He's waiting, biding his time, and then he's going to come after this place and everything with it—that means your trust funds too. He won't get it, not outright, but he'll try. And that'll be a nightmare for your brothers. You don't live here anymore, but this is their home. This place belongs to you all, but your daddy won't be happy about that. You think I want you all to deal with him during the funeral? We need to settle this now."

I stared at her, trying to determine what was at the root of this urgent request. Not everything she said was making sense to me because she was obviously hiding something.

Regardless, a reality that I'd been ignoring began to seep its way into my consciousness.

It hadn't occurred to me before now, likely because I was tangled and twisted in her terminal diagnosis, and I hadn't thought about what would come after, but—as far as I knew—my parents were still married. Everything that was in my mother's name also belonged to my father.

I let that truth sink into my bones.

Only Momma's name was on the deed to the house and the bank accounts; I knew that for certain. At least, that was the case when I was growing up.

My parents had been separated for two years before my grandmother died, and she'd left everything to my mother. But my father had never given my mother a divorce. She'd tried over the years and he'd resisted, threatened, and made her life hell. Now I understood why. As her husband, he stood to inherit everything.

"Oh, Momma…." I sighed, because I didn't know what to do.

I didn't want to see my father. I didn't want to call him. I didn't want to have the cloud of him hovering over her last days.

"Ash, listen to your momma. You need to call your daddy. I need to talk to him. He needs to see that you all stand united and that he's not going to be able to manipulate any of you."

I nodded, closed my eyes, and rubbed my forehead with my free hand. The thought of seeing my father made me sick to my stomach.

"Why now?" I whispered. "Why didn't you divorce him years ago? Why didn't you call him before now?"

"When Roscoe turned eighteen, I filed again. I didn't tell you about it because I didn't want you to worry. But we're two years into it, Ash, and we're still not close to a divorce. And you know why I waited until Roscoe came of age. You saw how it was; every time I tried to divorce your father it was a nightmare."

I nodded because I remembered. The last time my mother tried to divorce my father was when I was in high school. He didn't just harass my mother; he harassed all of us.

He picked up Roscoe from school then abandoned him in a field. Roscoe was ten.

He came to my high school and checked me out of class then took me to The Dragon Biker Bar. I spent the afternoon frightened out of my mind. My father had men pay him for a dance with me, which really just meant I was terrorized and manhandled for an hour before Jackson James and his police officer father showed up and took me home.

He went to the mill where Billy worked, showed up drunk, and nearly got Billy fired.

The list went on and on. I think Momma could have handled the harassment for herself, but she couldn't stomach watching us go through it.

"But what if he tries to…what if he tries to make medical decisions about your care? He's still your husband. Why invite him here when he can still hurt you?"

"He can't, baby. Even though we're not divorced, we're legally separated. The only one who can make decisions is Andrew. That was done months ago."

"Okay." I said, feeling close to tears again. I sucked it up, though. I didn't cry. "Okay, Momma. I'll call him."

"Thank you, Ash." My mother exhaled, her eyes closed, and her body seemed to relax as though a giant burden had been lifted.

I stood from her bedside and was just about to cross to my cot when she said, "I have something to tell you, Ash. It's really important."

I held her hand in both of mine and squeezed. "What is it, Momma?"

"I know you don't like needing people, but maybe—just this once —let yourself need someone. Maybe let yourself need Andrew. It would help him too, I think. He deserves to be needed by someone like you. Even if it's just for a short time...."

I waited for her to continue, but she didn't. Her hand had grown limp in mine, and I knew she was asleep.

I watched her sleep for a bit then went to my cot and laid on it. I didn't sleep much that night, for—again—obvious reasons. I tossed and turned and finally fell asleep some hours later.

When I woke up, Drew was gone.

CHAPTER SIXTEEN

"There is practically no activity that cannot be enhanced or replaced by knitting, if you really want to get obsessive about it."

— STEPHANIE PEARL-MCPHEE, AT KNIT'S END:
MEDITATIONS FOR WOMEN WHO KNIT TOO
MUCH

*I*F ANYONE HAD told me five weeks ago that I would be quoting Emily Dickenson in the woods with Drew, I would have told that person to invest in a good psychotherapist.

If anyone had told me just a week ago that I would be kissing Drew on the back porch of my momma's house as though his lips and body were my only source of nourishment, and I would be left with a lingering craving that could not be satiated, I would have told that person about the alien invasion happening in Poughkeepsie. I also would've mentioned that I was loyal to the kumquat trees. Because what else do you say to the severely insane?

Yet, there I was—consumed.

I love the fire most because of what it leaves behind....

Ash. It leaves behind ash.

I pressed the base of my palms against my eyes and gathered a deep breath. At present, I was upstairs in my room, trying to take a nap before my Tuesday night knitting group Skype call, and failing miserably. This would be the second time I'd been able to Skype in and attend my knitting group, and I'd been anxious all week about it, looking forward to it.

I was tired. I had the place, motive, and opportunity for a nap. But I couldn't sleep.

Earlier in the day, I'd called my father and left a message on his cell phone. I told him that Momma wanted to talk to him, and I hung up. Then I'd started spreading the word to my brothers that we were going to have a family meeting after my knitting group Skype call.

I could have been worrying about any number of things: my father's impending visit, breaking the news to my brothers, my mother's impending departure, how I was going to butcher all those roosters. But I wasn't.

I was thinking about Drew.

What was wrong with me?

How was it possible for me to be feeling this way—consumed—about Drew's kisses and words when I was already consumed with grief for my mother and the certainty of her death? It loomed in the distance like a deranged bully at the end of a schoolyard.

But kissing Drew had felt so good, and the idea of giving in....

I was quickly becoming addicted to the way my heart picked up and my belly twisted when I felt his eyes on me. I think I was a little in love with the way he said my name or called me Sugar like I was sweet and he just knew I'd taste delicious.

Frustrated and disappointed with my behavior, I kicked off my covers with a lot more force than was necessary and turned my face into my pillow. My muffled growl became a muffled scream, and I punched the mattress several times.

I glanced at the clock on the nightstand and saw that I had only fifteen minutes until I was supposed to call my friends on Skype. Giving up on the notion of a nap, I grabbed my laptop and knitting bag and made my way downstairs.

Cletus and Joe were in with Momma. Joe was on duty, which usually meant he'd stop in for a few minutes, maybe sit in the den for a bit and shoot the shit. Then he usually drove off to visit another patient. Tonight he decided to stick around. He said one of his other patients had died, so he had more wiggle room in his schedule.

At present Cletus and Joe were playing chess, which...I couldn't wrap my mind around. Regardless, they were supposed to come get me when she woke up. Momma had slept through most of the day, and when she did wake up, she didn't eat hardly anything.

I'd been keeping a log of her activities—when she slept, when she ate, how much she ate, how long she was up, her self-reported pain level, how much morphine she used. I hoped all the information would serve as an early warning sign—when the time came—that the end was near. I also knew the data gathering served as a placebo, soothed my need to control a situation over which I had absolutely no control.

Therefore, based on all the days that came before, today's sleeping and lack of food intake was a stark outlier.

I tried not to think too much about it as I sat on the couch—where Drew had slept the night before—and booted up my laptop. If I thought about it, I would go crazy.

"What are you doing?" Roscoe asked conversationally, flopping down on the sofa next to me.

"I'm signing on to Skype for my knit night."

"Why are you doing it out here? I thought the wireless worked everywhere in the house?"

"It does. But when I tried to do Skype from my bedroom, the video and audio kept cutting out. The signal is best down here."

Roscoe frowned. "Did you tell Drew?"

"No." I felt a little surge of awareness at the mention of Drew's name, like it was a secret, and hearing it spoken aloud was a thrill. I was truly ridiculous.

Swatting away the butterflies in my stomach, I opened Skype, made sure that it showed my avatar as available, then set the laptop on the coffee table and reached for my knitting.

"Why not?" Roscoe persisted. "I'm sure he'd fix it."

"I'm sure Drew has better things to do with his time. Besides, I'm just thankful it works at all. I don't mind doing the calls out here. Why?" I glanced at my brother. "Does it bother you? I did it here last week and no one seemed to care."

He shook his head. "Not at all. I really liked your friends, especially the blonde one. They were both hot, but Sandra scared me a little. Now, Elizabeth...she's the kind of health care provider I can get behind, if you know what I mean."

"Ugh." I rolled my eyes. "You're gross."

"I'm not gross. I'm at peace with my sexuality, and I'd like to give others a piece of it as well, spread a little peace around, get several pieces out there."

I stifled a giggle and smacked him on the arm. "Well, I'll be sure to tell Elizabeth's *husband* about your feelings."

"She's married?" He sounded forlorn.

"Yes. Here, if you stick around you can meet him. They're just about to call me."

"No thanks." He snorted, paused, then narrowed his eyes at me. "What's he like? Is he a doctor too? I bet they play doctor together."

"Ugh! Really, Roscoe? Really?"

"Seriously, what's he like?"

I inhaled a deep breath and held it, thought about how I would describe Nico to someone who'd never met him. It was difficult because I didn't know where to start.

Nico was a famous comedian. And he was hot. And sweet. And completely, totally, in love with Elizabeth.

"He's great," I finally said. "They have crazy schedules and hardly see each other. He learned how to crochet so that he could join our knitting group and spend more time with her."

"He learned how to crochet just to please a woman?"

I smacked Roscoe again. "Yes. He learned how to crochet—for a woman. And you're a dumbass."

"I would never do that," Roscoe said with a smirk. "Talk about losing your man card."

I grunted and sighed. My little brother would learn one day that falling madly in love with a woman and cherishing her was how a boy earned his man card.

The indicator on the screen announced that a call was coming through, so I clicked on the button to accept the call. An image of Elizabeth and Nico's penthouse materialized on the screen, and my heart was warmed by the sight. Sandra, Elizabeth, Janie, Fiona, Marie, and Nico were all sitting on the large sectional in the family room; a bay window in the background provided a stunning view of downtown.

It was Chicago. It was knit night. My friends were there. It looked like home.

"Ah! It's you!" Marie smiled a huge smile and tossed her blonde curls behind her back. "Look at your beautiful face. I've missed it." She blew me a kiss.

Marie always looked like she'd just stepped out of the pages of *Vogue*. Her ambition and her ferocious need for independence could make her come across as cool and calculating. Personally, I thought she was a badass.

"Hey, girl." I returned her smile and sighed, feeling content in a way that I'd missed since stepping on that plane to Tennessee. "Where is Kat?"

"She's getting beverages." Marie tipped her head in the direction of Elizabeth's kitchen, outside the frame.

"Who is that? Who is sitting next to you?" Elizabeth indicated to my right where Roscoe was sitting. "Is that Billy or Roscoe?"

"That's Roscoe, and he was just leaving."

Everyone in Chicago ignored me and waved at my brother, giving him friendly smiles and greetings.

"Hi, Roscoe. I'm Janie," She introduced herself with a short wave as she twisted her long, curly, red hair into a bun behind her head. "It's nice to meet you. You share a striking resemblance to your sister. But where she's exceptionally beautiful, you are exceptionally man beautiful, which means you would not look attractive dressed up as woman."

I knew Janie, so I knew she didn't mean anything by this *at all*. She frequently made observations out loud that most people merely thought...quietly...in their head...where those thoughts should be.

Roscoe sat up straighter and leaned forward, his voice infused with Roscoe-swagger. "Hey, nice to meet you."

"Down, boy." Sandra laughed and indicated Janie with her chin. "You don't want to mess around in the strawberry jam. Her husband is big and scary and makes people disappear on Fridays, or really any day of the week."

"He's not so bad." This statement came from Fiona, the most level-headed and also the oldest of our group, though only by a few years. She'd gone to school for engineering, but then left the world of work to become a stay at home mom.

"He's terrifying," Nico said, causing everyone to laugh. I could see he was crocheting; both he and Janie crochet while the rest of us knit.

"Hello, Nicoletta." I waved at him. We called him Nicoletta so he would feel like one of the girls. It didn't help, however. No one could ever mistake Nico for being one of the girls.

"Hi, Ashley." Nico returned my wave with a twinkly-eyed smile. "Marie is right, it's good to see your face. I miss your dairy farm analogies."

Before I could retort, Roscoe abruptly stood and darted out of the room. I frowned after his retreating form then shrugged, a bit perplexed by his sudden departure, but not curious enough to find out why he left so fast.

Just then, Kat's voice sounded over the speaker of my laptop. "Oh my goodness gracious, look who it is. Fancy Yarn McGee!"

I glanced at the screen and saw Kat standing at the edge of the frame, her hands holding two glasses of wine.

"What are you talking about?"

"That's my new name for you after raiding your yarn stash. Do you have any acrylic yarn in your stash? Anything synthetic? Or will only luxury fibers do?" Kat poked fun at me, obviously having dug through my yarn stash when she stopped by my apartment to water my plants. I didn't mind the teasing at all, but the behavior was very unusual for her. Typically, she was reserved and quiet. It was actually really nice to see her breaking out of her shell; it only took her four years.

"That's reverse yarn-snobbery, and I will not justify your questioning with an answer."

Kat laughed, took a swig of her red wine, and claimed the empty spot next to Marie. "Fair enough. Seriously though, I totally stole some of your yarn. And your life-size cutout of Charlie Hunnam says hi."

Before I could respond, I felt something hit me in the head, something unsubstantial. I turned and glanced behind the couch and saw a plastic cup on the floor. Lifting my eyes to the doorway of the kitchen, I found Beau and Roscoe standing there, out of the frame of my webcam.

I glanced at the cup then back at them, one of my eyebrows lifted.

They waved their arms frantically, indicating that I should join them in the kitchen, but said nothing aloud.

I turned back to the webcam, sighed, and announced, "Sorry, I'll be right back. Two of my hillbilly brothers want to play charades in the kitchen."

"Is it hillbilly charades?" Marie asked, her eyes on her knitting.

"What is hillbilly charades?" Janie perked up.

Sandra provided a definition that was only mildly offensive. "It's where the male players have to be drunk on moonshine and are only allowed to give hints by playing different tempos on a banjo."

"Or a jug. They can also give hints by playing on a jug," Fiona added.

"And the answer is always the movie, *Deliverance.*" This gem came from Nico.

"Ha, ha. Very funny." I rolled my eyes.

"Go right ahead," Elizabeth said, waving her hand in the air. "And while you're up, you might as well grab some red wine."

"We'll miss you while you're gone, Ashley." Nico grinned at me. He was really too adorable. Like, illegal levels of adorable. Someone should be held responsible for his adorableness in a court of law.

"Agree!" This came from Sandra. "Roses are red, violets are blue, rhyming is hard. Wine."

Laughing at her nonsense, I placed my knitting to the side and padded to the kitchen. My mission was two-fold: berate my brothers for throwing plastic cups at my head and find wine. I wasn't even sure we had wine. It suddenly occurred to me that I'd gone an entire month without red wine.

That was just not healthy.

As soon as I was within three steps of the entrance, Beau reached out and grabbed my wrist, pulling me into the kitchen.

"Ashley Austen Winston." His voice was a harsh whisper. "Do you know Nico Moretti? I demand you answer me now."

I assumed Beau meant Nico, Elizabeth's husband, because Nicoletta and Nico Moretti were in fact the same person.

I gave my brother a look that I hoped conveyed the extreme nature of my irritation. "Beauford Fitzgerald Winston, you do not make demands of me. Not ever. You apologize for this appalling behavior."

Roscoe darted forward, his eyes wide and accusatory. "Ashley Austen Winston! How could you not tell us?"

"It was none of your business, Roscoe Orwell Winston."

"You know Nico Moretti, Ashley Austen Winston. You *know* him. And he's hilarious." Roscoe threw his hands up.

"Do either of you know if we have any wine?"

"Wine...? Wine? You want to talk about wine right now, Ashley Austen?" Beau shook his head at me and huffed. "I feel like I can't trust you anymore."

"Beauford Fitzgerald Winston, you are being silly." Then, a thought occurred to me. My eyes narrowed as I surveyed them both. "Listen, if you can find me or go get me some red wine, I'll introduce you to Nico Moretti. Do we have a deal?"

They both nodded in unison. "Deal."

"Good." I spun on my heel and walked out to the family room, intent on getting back to knit night. I could hear the group's chatter coming from the small speakers of my laptop.

Just then, however, the front door opened revealing my brother Duane and my childhood friend / ex-boyfriend / now hottie police officer, Jackson James. Duane looked anxious and was pushing his fingers through his hair. Jackson was dressed in his police uniform, appearing much like he had a few weeks ago when I'd seen him briefly at the ranger cabin.

"No harm, no foul, Duane," Jackson was saying, and I faltered a step, glancing between the two of them.

Jackson's eyes lit up when he saw me. "Ashley!"

"Jackson." I blinked at him then looked to Duane for a clue regarding what was going on. Duane sighed and rolled his eyes.

Duane was not being helpful.

Police Officer Jackson stepped forward, a giant grin on his face, and reached for my hands. "It's good to see you, Ash." His grin faded into an earnest expression of concern. "How are you holding up?"

I blinked at him some more, frankly startled by the sight of him. He was Jackson, but he wasn't Jackson, and I hadn't thought about him in years.

"Uh, fine. I mean, things are fine. Well, you know, they're as fine as can be expected." I stuttered and my eyes flickered to the laptop perched on the coffee table. The group in Chicago could probably see and hear everything that was happening right now in my family room.

"I'm so sorry, about everything." Jackson said these words sincerely, gaining another step forward before reaching out and clasping my hands. His brown eyes held mine with such fixated concentration that I got the feeling he was apologizing for more than what was currently going on with my mother.

"Thank you for your concern, Jack. But Ashley's got her family to support her. And I don't think now is a good time. So...." Duane came up next to me, real close next to me, and crossed his arms, sticking his ginger beard in Jackson's handsome beardless face.

"Duane Faulkner, I am perfectly capable of speaking for myself." I nudged my brother's shoulder and tugged at my hands.

Jackson didn't release me straightaway, hesitating for about a half second before loosening his grip. He gave me his crooked grin, and his eyes were every brown shade of hopeful.

"Jackson." I gave him a reassuring smile. "What's your availability look like this week? I'd prefer not to leave the house, but I could make sandwiches. If Momma is up to it, I'm sure she'd enjoy a visit."

"Oh sure, I'd like to see her too. Let me give you my cell phone number." He reached into his pocket and pulled out a pen and paper.

I took advantage of the brief lull in conversation to glance at my computer screen and had to fight against an eye roll when I found my entire knitting group huddled in front of the webcam watching what was going on in my Tennessee family room with avid interest.

"I found the wine!" Beau came charging out of the kitchen grinning from ear to ear in triumph and holding a small bottle in front of him.

I sighed. "Beau, that's red wine vinegar. That's not red wine."

"It says red wine on it." He glanced between it and me. "What's the difference?"

"I told you so, dummy!" This shout came from Roscoe in the kitchen. "She isn't going to drink that. It's for salad dressing and marinating."

"We can't all go to college and drink fancy wine, Roscoe Orwell. Some of us *work* for a living!" Beau shouted back, then frowned at Jackson as he handed me a folded piece of paper. "What's this? What are you doing here, Jack? What's this paper?"

Beau and Duane stood on either side of me, red topped and bearded columns of suspicion and displeasure.

Duane snatched the paper from my fingers and handed it to Beau. I squeaked a shocked protest, but Duane cut me off. "Jackson, what is your middle name?" he demanded.

Jackson frowned at Duane and said, "Uh...John."

"Give me that," I said, reaching over Beau's broad chest to snatch the paper back.

"Well, Jackson John James, I don't appreciate you pulling me over tonight—for no reason—just so you could weasel yourself into this house."

"Duane Faulkner!" I scolded. "Quit being ugly—that is quite enough!" As I said this, the front door opened and in walked Jethro, Billy, and—of course—Drew.

I groaned and closed my eyes. Paired with my frustration was also a galvanizing restlessness, because Drew was here. He was in the room with me, breathing the same air. I took a deep breath and opened my eyes. As much as I wanted to keep them focused on my oldest brother, they instinctively searched and found Drew.

His face was devoid of expression, which meant he looked annoyed. His eyes flickered over my body once as though checking me for injury. It took all my power of sanity to extract my gaze from Drew and pay attention to my brothers.

"What's going on?" Jethro spoke first.

"Jackson is giving Ashley his phone number, that's what." Beau said this like Jackson was giving me a body to hide.

"And they're making plans to have sandwiches," Duane added, crossing his arms over his chest.

I groaned again, "Oh brother."

"Yes?" Jethro, Billy, Duane, and Beau all said in unison.

"Listen to me, you all need to back off and mind your manners. Jackson is an old friend. It is normal for two friends to engage in discourse!"

"Just as long as it isn't intercourse," Billy muttered under his breath.

I sucked in a sharp gasp. "William Shakespeare Winston!"

He gave me a scowl. "Don't look at me like that. We were all doing just fine before you showed up. Now that you're back, we suddenly have the attention of local law enforcement? We all know why Jackson John James is here, and it's not for sandwiches."

I heard some commotion coming from the speakers of my laptop and glanced at the screen.

Everyone in my knitting group was huddled together, obviously in front of the screen on their side. At some point, one of them must have made popcorn, because all seven of them were eating it, their eyes glued to the action going on in Tennessee.

All the bearded men in the room followed my gaze.

"Don't mind us!" Marie waved at the camera on her side—so, essentially, at my entire family room. "Keep going. This is more enter-taining than Nicoletta's Jell-O wrestling."

"I agree," Nico added, stuffing popcorn in his mouth.

"Wait a minute. Is that...?" Jethro tugged on my arm and with his other hand pointed toward my laptop. "Is that Nico Moretti? The comedian with that show on Comedy Central?"

"Hi," Nico said cheerily through a mouthful of popcorn. "Nice to meet you."

The room plunged into three seconds of silence as everyone in my family room stared at my computer screen and everyone on my computer screen smiled back.

I don't know how long this would have continued if Roscoe hadn't rushed out of the kitchen with a big toothy grin on his face, holding a bottle over his head and yelling, "Wine! I found the wine!"

CHAPTER SEVENTEEN

"We were not a hugging people. In terms of emotional comfort it was our belief that no amount of physical contact could match the healing powers of a well-made cocktail."

— DAVID SEDARIS, NAKED

*A*FTER INTRODUCTIONS WERE made, my plans for knit night were derailed, but in no way ruined.

All the seats in the family room were quickly taken, and I felt Drew's eyes follow me as I claimed my seat on the couch. Jackson sat on my right for about ten seconds before Billy told him to move. Then, Billy sat on my right.

This left Jackson with three choices: stand, sit on the floor, or leave.

He tapped me on the shoulder, told me to call him later, and left.

When Jackson shut the front door, I turned and found Drew looking me. His expression was still stoic, not quite irritated, but definitely withdrawn. Then, Drew also left—the room, not the house. He disappeared down the hall in the direction of the den, leaving me with my brothers and my friends in Chicago.

The rest of the hour passed in companionable conversation except at one point when Jethro shocked the butter off our biscuits by pulling out his own knitting work in progress. He was knitting himself a hat and using a gorgeous merino wool/alpaca blend, a homespun he must've picked up from a small shop or artisan spinner. It was brown and white four-ply worsted. I had to restrain my hands from yarn fondling.

My siblings and I all stared at him. He ignored us, instead asking Marie a question about her work as a freelance writer, and the conversation moved on.

Billy's comment earlier stuck with me, about how they'd all been doing fine before I showed up again. I knew we had some words unsaid between us. Of my brothers, he was the only one who appeared to be bitter about my leaving eight years ago. At some point, he and I were going to have to talk about it.

About two hours into the Skype call, the meet-up was wrapping up, so I stood to stretch and check in on Momma, leaving my brothers with my friends to say goodbye and feeling strangely fine about it. Although, when I reflected on it, it wasn't strange for me to feel fine about it.

The fact that my brothers and my friends got along so well would have been unthinkable to me a few months ago. But now that I actually knew them—or, at least, was starting to know them—it struck me as completely natural.

My chosen family in Chicago and my biological family in Tennessee were the same kinds of people. In fact, if I reflected on it, I'd actually surrounded myself with replacement brothers in the form of women who knit.

Fiona was Billy—logical and level headed, but hiding a sensitive side. Marie was Jethro—shrewd yet big hearted. Janie was Cletus—sweet and often oblivious. Sandra was Roscoe—a rascal. Elizabeth and Kat were the twins, with Elizabeth bolder like Beau and Kat shyer like Duane.

The personalities weren't a perfect fit, but they were pretty close.

This thought made me smile since I felt a bit like the monkey in the middle in both groups.

When I opened the door to the den, I found Drew sitting in his wooden chair writing in his leather notebook, Joe putting away the chessboard, and Cletus straightening up the room.

Momma didn't appear to be awake, but I approached the bed just to make sure. When I did, Drew glanced up and our gazes snagged. Unsure of proper etiquette, I gave him a brief smile and looked away before I could register a change in his expression. In the best of circumstances, I wouldn't know how to act around Drew after our kiss to end all kisses.

As it was, my Drew-distress was dialed back a bit since I was concerned that Momma was still asleep.

"Is she up?" I asked the room.

Joe came to stand next to me. "No. She's not. I saw your note about her not eating."

I nodded and looked her over. She was paler than usual, but that was probably because she needed to eat something. I'd washed her hair earlier in the day during the short time she was awake and had given her a bath with Marissa's help.

I turned to Joe. "Hey, would you mind sitting with her? Just for a half hour or so? We need to have a family meeting, and I don't want her to be alone."

"I can stay with her," Drew offered.

I turned my attention to him, my eyes resting on his face for more than the split seconds I'd rationed thus far. I allowed myself to experience a little burst of something—happiness? Desire? Wistfulness? I didn't know—when our gazes locked.

"No. You need to be there," I said.

His brow pulled low and he opened his mouth to question me, but I cut him off by saying, "I need you to be there, Drew. Please."

He watched me, his eyes inscrutable, but he nodded his unspoken assent. I studied him as he unfolded from the chair and tucked the notebook in one of the side pockets of his pants.

"Should I be there?" Cletus asked me this while balancing several dishes, two towels, a newspaper, and a toolbox.

"Yes, Cletus, you should be there."

"Okay, I'll be there." He nodded once then left the room.

"That boy...." Joe sighed.

Drew walked around my momma's bed and stood close to me; the backs of his fingers brushing against mine, causing a rush of heat up my arm and around my neck. I glanced from where our fingers touched up to his face and found him looking at me. There was a peacefulness, a stillness about him, and it sucked me in. The room fell away.

"Hey, Ash." His tone was quiet, gentle.

"Hey, Drew." I shifted a step closer. I couldn't help it.

"Did you have a good time tonight with your friends?"

"Yes. Thank you again for making that possible."

Drew's expression flattened as he said, "You need to stop thanking me."

"What if I don't want to stop?"

The hard angles of his face softened, and I witnessed something I couldn't identify flare in his eyes. But Joe's next statement pulled Drew and me from our heated gaze-exchange.

"That boy beat me in chess seven times."

Joe had taken a seat in my recliner, and he actually looked like he was pouting.

"Who, Cletus?" Drew asked, his tone disbelieving.

"Yep. Cletus. I'm part of a league organized by Mensa, and I've never been beaten seven times in a row before. He's a genius, I figure."

Drew and I glanced at each other. I imagine we wore similar expressions of wonder and confusion.

Cletus a genius. I couldn't fathom it.

My family never ceased to stun the butter off my biscuits.

I DIDN'T LIKE having to break the news to my brothers all at once. I'd thought about pulling them each aside and telling them separately, but then that felt wrong. Who would I tell first? What if I didn't get a chance to explain?

No. It was much better that they all be together and all hear exactly the same thing. They were gathered in the family room when Drew and I emerged from the hall. Drew continued walking when I stopped at the threshold to the room; he crossed to the couch, seemingly keeping his distance.

I was grateful that he didn't see any reason to advertise the fact that we'd kissed. But why would he? We'd kissed once. Well, technically, if you counted the jam session at the community center and that time in the hallway after the big, fireworks kiss, we'd kissed three times. And what did it really mean, anyway?

I might have been all mixed up about it, but he didn't seem to be much affected. I honestly didn't know what he felt about me or the kiss or what would come next, if anything did. He was so reserved at times and so intensely expressive at other times.

Besides, what I was about to say wasn't going to be easy or simple. I didn't need my six brothers questioning me about my relationship with Drew, especially since I had no answers about my relationship with Drew other than that I wanted to kiss him again, often, with feeling. I suspected he felt the same way—no, I knew he felt the same way—but beyond kissing I honestly had no idea.

"Is this about that dumbass Jack? I hate that guy." Beau sneered and took a long pull from his beer before adding, "Always douching things up."

Beau's insult succeeded in pulling me out of my own head. Drew came into focus and I realized that I'd been standing there staring at him for about a half minute. His eyebrows were arched in confused expectation, and he was looking at me like I might have lost my marbles in the hallway.

I cleared my throat and looked at the floor, half convinced I might find my marbles on the carpet.

"Why'd he pull you over, Duane?" This question came from Billy.

"He's an idiot. He said my tail light was out."

"Is your tail light out?"

"Yes. But he's still an idiot."

"Ash, please tell me you're not going to *have sandwiches* with him?" Beau gave me a look that clearly conveyed his disapproval of Jackson James.

My eyes flickered to Drew's and I noted that his eyebrows had descended; he was watching me with a narrowed glare.

I quickly looked away, ignoring Beau's question, and addressed my brothers. "I didn't call you all here to talk about Jackson. This is about Darrell Winston."

The room went quiet; I could tell I'd surprised them. Again, my eyes darted to Drew's. He was leaning against the arm of the couch, his arms crossed over his chest, a severe frown marring his features. This made him appear quite frightening and even more like a marauding Viking than usual.

Billy was the first to recover. "Has he contacted you? Have you seen him?"

"No. I'll tell you what's going on, but you all have to promise me that you'll listen and not interrupt until I'm finished."

A few grumbles sounded from various bearded sources, but in the end, they listened and didn't interrupt. I told them about my conversation with Momma the night before, and I told them I'd already called our father and left a message.

When I finished, I was again greeted with silence until Roscoe stood from his seat and began pacing.

"I don't like this," he said. Of the seven of us, Roscoe knew Darrell as a tormentor and not so much as a father-tormentor. I understood his initial reaction because I shared it.

"What does she need to tell him?" Duane asked, his face scrunched in confusion. "What could Momma possibly say?" Then, using his most cheerful voice, he said, "Hello, Darrell, you're an asshole. I hope you burn in hell."

"Maybe she'll murder him and save us the trouble." Jethro mumbled this from where he sat on the couch, his elbows on his knees, his eyes on the floor.

Billy stirred from where he'd been leaning against the fireplace.

"What I want to know is how does she plan to keep him from taking the house? Legally separated or not, they're still married."

"I think I can answer that," Drew said, staring forward, his jaw set. "I think I can answer both questions."

Drew's eyes sliced to mine and held my gaze. I thought I detected a hint of regret and longing before he addressed my brothers.

"When your mom signed over her power of attorney and made me the executor of the will, she also signed over all your trust funds to my control. I bought this house, everything in it, and the land from her, for one thousand dollars."

I'd always heard and used the term *silence filled the room*, but I don't think I'd ever experienced the sensation of silence actually filling a room until that moment. The silence filled the room until I thought the walls might buckle under the pressure of it.

Billy's mouth opened and closed, his mind obviously having difficulty grasping the situation. I imagined we all wore similar expressions.

Drew continued. "She also set up an S-corp with the two of us as co-owners. She transferred all her savings and investment accounts— the inheritance from your grandparents—into the company, then removed herself as a partner. The only account she's kept in her name is the checking account with the local bank in town where her paycheck is deposited from the library."

"Why…why would she do that?" Beau's words were choked, confused.

"She said at the time that she was afraid your father would somehow clean her out in the divorce. She wanted to put everything in my name, transfer all the assets, until the divorce was over."

"She must've known she was dying." Cletus' voice—steady and neutral—surprised me. Of my brothers, he seemed to be absorbing this news and seeing the situation with the most clarity. "If it was about the divorce, she would have asked one of us to help. She didn't want us to know she was sick. She didn't want us to be put in a bad position when she died."

Again, silence filled the room. It was the silence associated with seven brains working hard to understand the motivations of a dying woman.

Drew's eyes flickered to mine; he appeared to be bracing himself and his gaze was guarded like he expected me to be angry at this revelation.

But I wasn't angry. At first, I was astonished. Then, as the puzzle pieces came together, I felt relieved.

Because if any one of us—my brothers or me—had been placed in Drew's position, we would have been targeted by my father. He would have thrown everything in his arsenal of manipulation at us. I was not angry with Drew, but I certainly did not envy him. My father was not a good man.

I crossed to where he was still leaning against the arm of the couch. He stood as I approached, his arms falling to his sides, his expression cautious.

I stopped far enough from Drew to give him his space. "Have you met him before? Darrell?"

"Yes. Once." His gaze was watchful, like he didn't know what to expect from me, but he was bracing himself for the worst.

My eyes lowered to his chest and I watched it rise and fall several times before I spoke again. "I'm worried for you, Drew."

"Don't be."

I lifted my eyes to his, held them. "He'll make your life hell when he finds out."

He returned my sentiment with a small and rueful smile. "He'll try and he'll fail."

"Please let me know how I can help you."

Drew gave me a subtle shake of his head, his eyes growing both hard and heated. "I told you before, I don't need anything from you."

I flinched, rocked back on my feet, but Drew caught my hand and held me in place.

Just then, though I couldn't see him, I heard Billy's voice say, "I agree. I don't like being kept in the dark, but…man, Drew, you're in for a huge shit storm when Darrell arrives. All hell is fixin' to break loose. You got to let us know if we can help."

"Someone get that man a beer or a whiskey," Jethro said, and the room erupted in tension-breaking laughter.

"Or both!" Beau smacked Drew on the back and walked toward the kitchen, presumably to get the whiskey and beer.

The loud chatter of the Winston boys eclipsed the stunned rigidity. My brothers began discussing the full meaning behind all the planning my mother had done and Drew's part in it.

Meanwhile, in the midst of their conversation yet completely separate from it, Drew and I regarded each other. He still clasped my hand, staying any potential retreat.

At length he said quietly, "I mean it, Ash. I know your life isn't here. I know your place and your people are in Chicago."

I nodded, pressing my lips together in an *I-get-it* smile, because I understood him perfectly on this point. But when I tugged against his hold, he didn't release me.

"Drew."

"Yes?"

"Let me go."

He hesitated, his eyes moving over my face. "Not yet."

I scrunched my nose at him, not trying to hide my irritation, and huffed, "I thought you didn't *need* anything from me."

"Yeah...." His hand tightened before he released me. I heard him mumble, "But that doesn't mean I don't want something," just as Beau approached and handed us both a whiskey.

CHAPTER EIGHTEEN

"i like my body when it is with your body."

— E. E. CUMMINGS

 I HAD TO butcher the roosters.
Well, I didn't *have* to butcher the roosters, but someone had to, and I'd promised my mother that I'd do it.

I'd butchered plenty of animals before, when I was growing up. We used to keep goats, rabbits, chickens, and ducks. We didn't keep geese because they're partial to biting. Plus, they're nasty, ill-tempered bastards.

Three days had passed since I'd called Darrell Winston. We'd heard nothing from him, and everyone was on edge.

My time in Tennessee was growing short; the seasons were changing, and soon I would be back in my apartment, back to my job and my life. Even my brothers seemed to sense my impending departure.

Jethro asked for my address in the city. Roscoe and I consulted a calendar, trying to find a date in December when he could visit over the winter break. Cletus and the twins suggested a road trip to junk yards in Chicago, hopeful that they'd be able to discover a treasure trove of rusted classic cars that could be hauled back to Tennessee.

My mother was now sleeping most of the time, so visits from her friends at the library and the minister were usually brief, or we'd make an excuse. When she was awake, she was hazy and her speech was slow. I could feel her drifting away, disappearing. A growing part of me recognized that I had no control over the situation.

But another part, stubborn and willful, struggled against the slippery hours, wanting time to stand still.

So, instead of sitting inside all day and going crazy watching my momma breathe, I decided to let my brothers take a turn so I could butcher the roosters.

It was a solid plan. I had the cone all set up, and the knife; I was wearing my oldest jeans, a long-sleeved T-shirt with a tank top underneath, and work boots. I had on the same old, black apron I used to wear for the occasion as well as the fitted leather gloves.

Nevertheless, when the time came for me to do the deed, I couldn't. I just couldn't. I had that damn rooster upside down in the cone, disoriented and still, but I just couldn't do it.

I heaved a frustrated sigh, released the rooster, stood, and kicked a nearby bucket. Kicking the bucket felt really good, so I decided to punch a bundle of straw. That felt good too, so I kept doing it.

I don't know how long I spent raging against the straw—maybe a minute, maybe twenty. When I finally stopped I was red faced; my loose braid had come undone, and my hair was wild around my shoulders. My legs, arms, and stomach were sore from the workout.

Breathing hard, I ripped off the gloves and placed my hands on my hips, glaring at the straw. It looked just the same.

"Feel better?"

My head whipped around, searching for the origin of the voice, and found Drew standing at the edge of the chicken yard, his thumbs in his belt loops, his dark green T-shirt tucked into his dark green uniform pants, his cowboy hat on, and a stern expression on his face.

He would have melted my butter if I'd been in any mood to be butter...or to melt.

Who am I kidding? My butter melted as soon as I saw his hat.

I was irritated—with the roosters for crowing, with my momma for dying, with my father for being evil incarnate, and with Drew for melting my butter when I wasn't in the mood to be butter…or melt.

I eyeballed him, disliking that I noticed how exceptionally fine he looked, and I waited to catch my breath before I responded. "Yes, I do feel better now."

"What are you doing?"

"Well, you don't need Sherlock Holmes to solve that mystery." I reached around my back to untie my apron.

His eyes narrowed and his mouth flattened into a hard line. "Are you upset with me about something?"

"Yes."

"What?"

"The fact that you're breathing, I guess."

Over the last three days, Drew and I had spent plenty of time together. During all of that time, he'd quoted Nietzsche never, he'd recited poetry not at all, and he'd barely spoken. Even worse than that, he hadn't touched me—not once.

Meanwhile, there was a wild boar of need within me; one that he'd awakened with his quicksilver eyes, poetic words, velvet baritone, heroic deeds, and expertly choreographed kisses.

He'd left me to drown in want.

Drew shifted his weight, his head tilting to the side as he regarded me. Despite the shade and shadow provided by his hat, I could tell that he was fighting a smile.

"My breathing bothers you?"

"Sometimes." I removed the apron, ducked into the shed, and hung it on a nail where it lived.

If I'd said what was on my mind, I would have told him that his self-control bothered me.

Or maybe it wasn't self-control. Maybe he'd lost interest.

Or maybe there was something appallingly wrong with me. During this time of sorrow and stress, I wanted to lose myself, forget about my worries, and debate the merits of mustachioed eighteenth century philosophers, or relive our soul scorching, pride destroying, body claiming kiss.

Drew met me inside the shed and blocked the door with his body. "How are you doing today, Ash?"

"I'm just peachy, Drew. I've been trying to butcher a rooster for the last hour, and I can't bring myself to cut the damn cock. How're you?" I was hot and it was stuffy in the shed, so I pulled off my long-sleeved shirt and draped it over one of my shoulders; this left me in my tank top, jeans, and work boots.

He studied me, his eyes moving from the top of my head down to my stomach, likely taking in the sight of my wild hair, red cheeks, and sweatastic torso.

"You just browsing, or...?" I motioned to myself and lifted my eyebrows. I was hoping to convey impatience rather than the fact that his perusal was most definitely melting my butter.

"Are you feeling frustrated, Sugar?" He said these words softly, liltingly, like he was speaking intimately with someone, or like he was speaking to someone with whom he planned to be intimate. Drew reached behind him and pushed the door. It squeaked as it closed.

My eyes flickered to the door then back to him. He removed his hat and tossed it to the side, and that's when I saw intent in his eyes—clear as frosting on a cake—and I was momentarily stunned.

Before I could get a handle on the situation or process how to respond to it, he crossed to me in four steps, backing me up against the cabinet in the shed, and captured my mouth with his. My long-sleeved T-shirt fell to the floor. I barely noticed.

I'd like to say that I pushed him away. I'd like to say I didn't welcome his kisses and caresses. I'd like to say that I didn't greedily untuck his shirt and greedily touch every inch of his solid stomach, chest, and back, and greedily rub against him. I'd also like to say that I didn't greedily moan like a hussy when he reached one hand up my shirt, his fingers and mouth giving my breasts deliciously rough treatment.

I'd like to say all that; but if I did, I'd be a liar.

Because it happened.

His hands were hot and purposeful, and he used his body with delicious skill, rocking against me, causing me to gasp. His fingers deftly unbuttoned my jeans, slipped into my panties, parted me. I arched into him, clamoring to get closer, needing his touch and the friction of our shared embrace.

Flashes of him smiling, playing his guitar, quoting Emily Dickenson played through my mind; memories associated with *wanting*—wanting him, wanting this, wanting more. I wanted to be touched by him, possessed by him, claimed by him in a way that mirrored my desire and betrayed his need for me.

I opened my eyes and found him watching me, his silvery blue gaze piercing and savage. I saw his lack of self-control, the same feral madness that was overwhelming me.

Furthermore—and I know this will shock the hell out of people because it shocked the hell out of me—Drew brought me to the edge of euphoria and over its precarious precipice in less than sixty seconds. One minute I was fumbling to feel and taste him; then his mouth was on my breast and his hand was in my panties; then my head was thrown back and I was riding the rollercoaster, sky diving, and bungee jumping.

I was still so turned on, so hot for him, I couldn't muster enough common sense to be embarrassed. As the tremors subsided—leaving my legs weak and wobbly, my body spent and humming—Drew wrapped his hand around the back of my head and brought my face to his chest. He nuzzled my cheek, his hot breath fell over my ear, and he bit my neck. Then, he licked it.

I held on to him so I wouldn't fall on my ass. Speaking of my ass, Drew moved the lovely hand (that seconds ago had brought me to release) from the front of my panties to my bottom, and he squeezed me with a ragged sigh, like a moan escaping on an exhale.

"Fucking hell, I love your body," he growled. "You are perfect." He pulled me against him, alternately kissing and biting my jaw and collarbone.

My breathing hadn't yet normalized and my heart was still beating a thunderous pace in my chest, but my mind was clearing, and it couldn't believe what I'd just done, or rather, what we'd just done.

I exhaled roughly and blinked against the tears that were gathering in my eyes. Drew stilled, his mouth pressed against my shoulder. He must've sensed that I was crying or was about to cry, because he moved his hands to my upper arms and held me just far enough away to inspect my face.

"No, no, no...." he said in a rush, then he leaned forward and placed gentle kisses on my eyes. "No, don't cry. Please don't cry."

"I'm a bad person," I said, though it wasn't precisely what I meant. If my brain had been functioning properly, I would have said something like, *What in tarnation is wrong with me that I can't stop thinking about you when my mother is dying and my evil father is about to show up and make all of us even more miserable, and you're going to bear the brunt of his awfulness, and yet never far from my perpetual melancholy is the hope that you'll find some way to take me in your arms, read me your poetry, rile me up with Nietzsche quotes, engage me in a battle of wits, and make me feel good.*

"No, Ash. You're not a bad person."

"I am. I'm a horndog. I just got off in the shed at three o'clock on a Friday like a farm hussy, or a…a tool shed hussy."

He chuckled and wrapped me in his arms, brought me against his delightful chest.

"No, Sugar. You are not; you aren't any of those things. You are loveliness personified; you are grace and fascination. I think of you and I stop breathing. I worry that any movement will steal the image of you from my mind's eye. But the memory is a pale, hollow specter to luminous reality. Because when I see you, when I touch you-"

"Oh my God, you have got to stop talking!" I grabbed his face with both my hands and brought his mouth to mine. If I hadn't, I might have spontaneously exploded.

When I was sure he wouldn't extract himself and continue torturing me with his prose, I wrapped my arms around his neck and stood on my tiptoes, relaxing into the delectable sensations caused by another perfect kiss.

Oxygen became a concern, and I was getting worked up again, so I pulled away, lowering my forehead to his shoulder and breathing heavy.

"I like how you shut me up." Drew was also breathing heavily. He tried to run his fingers through my hair but failed. It was just too tangled from my fight with the straw pile.

"I like shutting you up."

My admission made him laugh and he kissed my forehead and cheek. We stood together embracing in the shed for several short, quiet moments until our breathing evened and our hearts slowed.

I gnawed on my bottom lip, pulling it between my teeth, my mind occupied by the fact that I was standing in my momma's shed with a man that I craved, trusted, but didn't really know anything about. And he'd just brought me to orgasm in sixty seconds.

If there was ever a man I should get to know better, this man was him.

THE WALK BACK to the house wasn't weird, and that was what was weird about it...if that makes sense. Also weird, we took the long way —the really, really long way.

Drew put his arm around my shoulders and I wrapped mine around his waist. I stole his cowboy hat and plunked it on my head. It was too big, so I pushed it back and let it rest at a precarious angle.

"I found a joke for you."

I glanced up at him. "Really? What is it?"

"Have you heard my Nietzsche joke?"

"Uh, no."

"Well, there isn't one."

I waited for a beat, confused. Then, I got it all at once and I rolled my eyes. "That's a terrible joke."

"Okay, how about this one." He cleared his throat and tried to flatten his smile. "What did God say at Nietzsche's funeral?"

"What?"

"Nietzsche is dead."

This one made me laugh. I closed my eyes and shook my head, allowing Drew to guide our steps. "That one is hilarious. Good job."

We walked a ways in companionable silence, and I allowed myself to enjoy the comfort of his arm on my shoulders, being tucked into his side like I fit there; like a space had been made just for me. The late afternoon sun was at our back, and the first real autumn chill danced over my skin, making my shoulders shiver.

"Are you cold?" he asked, looking down at me.

"No. Not really. It feels good."

Drew pulled his hat from my head and released my waist, instead holding my hand and tugging me toward a felled tree in the midst of wildflowers. Most of the blooms were gone as summer was giving way to cooler weather, but their stems came to our knees like tall grass.

"Come, sit." He instructed, forgoing the tree trunk in favor of sitting on the ground amongst the flowers.

I plopped down next to him, and we sat in companionable silence for a while, absorbing the general splendor of the field. It was untouched, unlike the area around the house. My brothers and their hobbies and messiness had cluttered the acre or so nearby the house, but the rest of the fifteen acres were woods, fields, and wilderness.

The trees in Green Valley were still green, but the trees on the mountains were already changing color. Red, orange, and yellow-carpeted misty mountains reached to the blue sky. With the coronation of vivid fall colors, the mountains announced the change in seasons.

I felt Drew's gaze on me, so I turned to face him, my expression open and questioning. But he didn't say anything. Instead, he just stared.

"What are you looking at?"

"You."

"Yes. Obviously you're looking at me, but why? Do I have food in my teeth? Lettuce in my hair?"

"Nope."

"So, you're just, what? Just looking at me?"

"Yes."

I wrinkled my nose and wagged a finger at him. "There is something wrong with you…in the head. You're odd."

"Ash, there is nothing odd about me looking at you."

"Keep your eyeballs to yourself."

His mouth pulled to the side as he openly admired my face, and then he recited, "'There is an innocence in admiration: it occurs in one who has not yet realized that they might one day be admired.'" He repeated this oft quoted Nietzsche-ism liltingly, almost coyly.

I rolled my eyes. If ever a Nietzsche quote had been misused, this was the time.

"*Puh*-lease. If you haven't figured out by now that ninety-nine percent of females in eastern Tennessee and western North Carolina admire you coming and going, then you're an idiot. And I know you're not an idiot."

"You misunderstand." His stony face cracked with a smile. "I don't care about ninety-nine percent of females, Ash. I was referring to just one."

I watched him, studied him, inspected him; and Drew watched me right back. My stomach twisted, and my chest was heavy with a growing disquiet.

I was feeling more than I should.

Drew, holding my gaze, tugged on my hand and lowered himself to the earth and me with him. He then spent a few seconds positioning us so that I was tucked into his side, his arm around me, my cheek on his chest.

I lay still for a full minute, staring forward with wide eyes, confused as to what was going on.

"Relax," he said. "You're all stiff."

I lifted my head and looked at him, searching his face for clues; it gave me no hints. If anything, his expression made me more muddled. This was primarily because his eyes had gone all soft and were caressing my face. Furthermore, he'd threaded his fingers into my hair and was rubbing it with his fingertips like it was silk and he was enjoying the texture.

"What's going on?" I blurted, my face and voice betraying a hint of panic, I'm sure. "What are we doing?"

"Lying here." The side of his mouth hitched.

"But why? What did I miss?"

"I don't think you miss much."

"But I missed something. I definitely missed something...." I looked up and down the length of him. "I missed something big."

His hand was still in my hair, his fingers moving in and out of the thick curtain and softly brushing my curls to one side then the other. My body began to relax, because what he was doing felt good.

"Drew...." I sighed his name, but when I heard the sound of it— what I sounded like saying it, like it was an invitation—I shook myself and refocused. "We're laying in a field of wildflowers."

"What do you have against wildflowers?"

"Nothing, except...we don't even really know each other."

"I know you."

I *tsked.* "Well, I don't know you."

"What do you want to know?" He asked this softly, his cherishing eyes trailing a path from my forehead to my neck, shoulders, arms, stomach, then back up in an equivalent unhurried study.

I paused at that, because the answer to that question was *so much.* There was *so much* I wanted to know.

My mouth opened and closed and I blinked at him. I officially had a blinking problem. "I...I...I guess I'd like to know how you met my mom, how you met my family, where you come from." I knew Momma's point of view, but I was curious about Drew's perspective. I also wanted to know how his sister knew my father.

He nodded, but didn't stop playing with my hair or giving me his distracting, reverential looks. "My sister committed suicide after your father pretended to marry her when he was already married to your mother."

My mouth?

The one that was already open?

Yeah, that one.

It dropped.

My eyes also blinked in rapid succession—big surprise!—and I shook my head, managing to say only, "Oh my God."

I couldn't believe that he just…said it. He said it like he was telling me about his first grade science project. I felt like a bomb had gone off. My ears were ringing.

But he continued like he hadn't just said something completely life altering. "My sister basically raised me after my mother died; she died shortly after I was born. My sister, Christine, was fifteen years older, and she had a lot of mental health issues." Drew shrugged, his eyes shifting to a passing cloud. "She was manic depressive."

"Oh my God. Drew…." I placed my hand on his cheek and turned his face back to mine. "I'm so, so sorry. I'm so sorry."

I couldn't help myself; I shimmied up his body and gave him a quick kiss.

He swallowed, and his features hardened as if he'd willed them to. Yet, when he spoke, his tone was gentle, verging on indulgent. "You don't need to apologize. You didn't do anything wrong."

"My father is a bastard."

"Yeah." Drew nodded. "So is my father. Your dad and mine have a lot in common."

I gave him a sad frown. "Is your dad a polygamist?"

"No. But he's a US senator, and he seduces other men's fiancées."

The first part I remembered Roscoe telling me weeks ago.

"Other men's fiancées?"

"Yep. Like mine for example. But, to be fair, she wanted to be seduced."

Again, it was like a bomb had gone off. My breath left me on a whoosh and we stared at each other.

Well…isn't that like shit on a shoe at a wedding.

I glanced at his lips then kissed him again. This time I made sure that the kiss conveyed how much I'd been thinking about him—and his kisses—over the last several days.

He responded immediately and we kissed for several minutes. When things started to escalate, he gently pushed me away, holding my face in his hands.

Drew gazed into my eyes as though searching them—or me—for the answer to life's great questions. I met his stare straight on, held it, dared him to find one trace of pity or reluctance or regret.

I felt none of it.

Instead, I felt fierce loyalty and pride—in him for all he'd accomplished despite his family, and pride in my family for taking him in as one of their own.

I also might have been feeling desire. In fact, I *was* feeling desire. I'm not going to lie.

Whatever he found in me must've satisfied his implicit concerns, because Drew's expression lost some of its severity and he sighed. "Ash."

"Yes?"

"I wish we could...." He said this in a rush then stopped, licked his lips, and affixed his eyes to the sky. I sensed that he was holding himself back from speaking his mind. He seemed to be literally biting his tongue. Yes, literally. His tongue was between his teeth and he was biting it.

At length, looking pensive, Drew cleared his throat before starting again. "I looked up your father when I was in college, then I found out where he married your momma, and I discovered that she still lived here. I was curious about her. So when a game warden position opened up, I used the job interview as an opportunity to meet her."

I propped my head up with one hand and laid the other on his chest, peering down at him. "And how'd that go?"

He smiled. "She was something else." Then he frowned again. "In a lot of ways, she reminds me of Christine: soft hearted and sensitive, but also with a talent for sass."

I chuckled and rested my chin on his chest. "She does have a talent for sass."

"Sass has a genetic component. It's passed down from mother to daughter."

I rolled my eyes, "Whatever, Nietzsche." Then I recounted one of my least favorite Nietzsche quotes, "'There are no facts, only interpretations.'"

Drew reached his hand into my hair and began combing his fingers through it as he'd done a few moments ago, and I had an out-of-body experience.

I honestly didn't know how I'd arrived at this place, this time, this moment. I was a person I didn't recognize, but I had a faint sense of knowing from a long time ago. I was someone from my past when trust was freely given, and my overly idealistic mind jumped to romanticized conclusions even when faced with realistic expectations, good judgment, and logic.

I was lying in a field of wildflowers...*wildflowers*. I was half on top of fictionally handsome Drew. His hand was in my hair. We'd just been kissing. I trusted him because he'd proven himself, through his actions, to be trustworthy. And I was giving no thought to real life, sorrow, or the ramifications of willfully surrendering to this mountain of a man.

I had to shake myself out of my trance, because Drew was speaking again, and I wanted to hear.

"...At the library, so I came by the next week again. This time I brought some of my own poetry and, I don't know why I did it, but I showed it to her. She read it, made some suggestions, then gave me a book of poetry by e. e. cummings."

"Ah, I love e. e. cummings." I sighed when I said this, because I really loved e. e. cummings. Whenever I needed a shot of romance or a dose of raw galvanized euphoria, I'd read e. e. cummings. He jump-started my heart. He made me feel like I held a light within myself that could scorch and smolder and rage like an inferno—or that showed me I at least had the potential to burn. I just needed someone who knew how to light the match.

Drew smiled at me then kissed my nose.

This should have struck me as strange, these careless intimate touches, but it didn't. They didn't. He didn't.

Obviously, I was insane.

And because I was insane, I snuggled closer to him and asked, "Roscoe said you beat the crap out of Jethro one time."

Drew nodded as he picked up my hand and laced his fingers through mine, studying my fingertips.

"Yeah. It was after I accepted the job. I'd been here for about two months. Your mother had me over for dinner a few times. Jethro knew who I was, had met me more than once...." He was quiet for a long time as he investigated my fingers, tested how we fit together, compared the sizes of our palms.

I was mesmerized by this little dance of our hands and lost track of what we were discussing. When Drew continued, it took me a few seconds to remember the topic. "I think he did it because it was the only way he knew how to get attention."

"What? Who?"

He placed my hand over his heart then gave me a quizzical grin. "Jethro. My bike. I think he stole my bike in order to get my attention."

"Ah, and you beat him up?"

"I didn't know it was a call for attention at the time. I just thought he was an asshole stealing my bike."

I couldn't help but laugh at this. Poor Jethro. He'd had a hard time of it, being the oldest. He knew our father the best out of all of us, and being Darrell Winston's firstborn wasn't an enviable position.

"But then you became friends."

"Yep. We did. Good friends."

"Like brothers?"

Drew looked at me for a beat then glanced away as though pondering this concept. "I hope so, but I wouldn't know. I don't have any brothers."

"What about other family? Aunts? Uncles? Cousins?"

"My mom was an only child. And my father's family...they're all high society, rich oil people in Houston. They don't much understand me, and I don't care to understand them."

"What do you mean? They must be proud of you. You're a friggin PhD from Baylor for hootenanny's sake."

His smile was warm, but it barely met his eyes. "I mean, to them, my sister was an embarrassment because she was mentally ill. When she died, they milked it so that my father would win his election. Then, when he and my fiancée started carrying on, they wanted me to publically endorse their relationship, because my father was slipping in the polls."

As he spoke his eyes hardened; obviously, the memory was distant but the feelings were fresh.

"My sister Christine was an embarrassment because she'd been born differently and needed help. My father marries my fiancée, and I'm a disappointment because I won't publically endorse their marriage. The hypocrisy of society, what is considered appropriate behavior, is completely baffling to me."

I twisted my mouth to the side and contemplated the man that was Drew. He recited the details of his broken past with a detachment that was heartbreaking because it didn't sound at all forced. And he'd just thrown it all out there, all his baggage filled with dirty laundry. He didn't ask me to wash it, or pick it up, or like it, or smell it.

He simply said, *Here. Look at this shitty mess. This is me.*

But he wasn't a mess. His family was a mess. Drew was beautiful and poetic and raw and real.

I thought about reciprocating. I thought about telling him about my father, how he'd been drifting in and out of our lives, conning us all. About how he used to hit Momma, how she put up with it. I thought about telling him the story of the day she finally threw him out, when she came home and found twelve-year-old Billy black and blue, and called the cops. Roscoe was two at the time.

Instead, I was quiet, like a coward. I wasn't ready to open up my baggage and share my dirty laundry.

"What are you thinking about?"

Drew's softly spoken question pulled me from my thoughts. He was watching me closely, and I briefly wondered if I'd verbalized any of my internal musings. We were face to face now, one of my legs was thrown over his stomach, chest to chest, and I was leaning over him on my elbow.

I shrugged and gathered a deep breath. "I guess I was thinking that you're pretty brave, just throwing everything out there about yourself, about your family and your past."

"I don't have anything to hide."

"Really?"

"Really."

"Then what were you fixin' to say earlier? You started to say something: *I wish we could....*"

Drew's eyes seemed to burn brighter—intense and hot—at my mention of his unfinished statement.

At length he shook his head subtly and said, "I don't want to say things you're not ready to hear."

"Can you give me a hint?"

His mouth hooked to the side, but his eyes were melancholy. "No, Sugar. I can't. Please don't ask, because I can't think of anything more difficult than saying no to you."

Of course this made me smile and feel warm from my chest to my toes. "Why do you suddenly like me so much, Drew?"

Drew touched his nose to mine and gifted me with a soft kiss before responding. "There's nothing sudden about it."

CHAPTER NINETEEN

"Don't cry because it's over; smile because it happened."

— DR. SEUSS

 ILL YOU MAKE pie?"

"Pie?"

"Yeah, pie. I think I could get Momma to eat your pie. She hasn't been eating much."

We'd resumed our earlier position; Drew's arm was on my shoulders, mine around his torso. This time we were taking the direct path back to the house.

We hadn't stayed long in our field of flowers because I felt anxious about getting back to check on Momma, and it was time to get dinner started.

"What kind of pie? Does she have a preference?"

"You've never made my momma pie before?" For some reason this surprised me. Drew made fantastic pie. It was pie that should be shared.

"No. I guess I haven't. But she made me her lemon meringue pie a few times. I guess if I'd had to choose between any of my pies and hers, I would have picked hers." He scratched the back of his neck then his beard. "Maybe I'll try to make her lemon meringue."

"Hey, that would be great." I smiled up at him. "I think she'd really like that."

"Well, don't you two look cozy?" Beau called from a few feet away. Neither of us had noticed his approach, and we stumbled to a stop.

My brother smiled, glancing between Drew and me. "Mind if I join you?"

Without waiting for a response, Beau slipped his arm around my waist and encouraged me to do likewise with him. He then propelled the three of us toward the house, walking as a unit.

"I need to clean out the barn; it's getting too messy to pull the cars in." Beau spoke over my head at Drew then shook his head. "By the way, it's nice to see you two getting along so well. I was a little worried at first after I heard about the titty-twister episode. Real big of you, Drew, to let all that go."

"Hey! He was the one who woke me up at six in the morning."

"Settle your mettle, woman. I'm just saying it's nice to see you guys behaving like brother and sister is all."

I felt Drew stiffen beside me, his hand on my shoulder flexed. I stole a glance at him and found his handsome face marred with a pensive frown. We walked several more paces in strained silence before Drew cleared his throat and slowed our steps.

"Beau," Drew said, and his tone brought the three of us to a stop. "It's not what you think."

My eyes widened and I faced Drew, gave him my very best *what-the-hell-are-you-doing* face. He ignored me.

Beau gave both of us a perplexed grin and stepped away, holding his hands up. "No, Drew. Man, I wasn't thinking that *at all*. I would never think that. Like I said, brother and sister."

"Beau, it's not like that." Drew said this slowly, his arm on my shoulders tightening.

"Oh God," I said on a quick exhale then closed my eyes.

"Drew, man, I know."

"No. Beau, listen to me. I have feelings for your sister that are not brotherly." He paused, his hand dropped to my waist, and he pressed me against his side.

My blood pressure spiked. I couldn't open my eyes. The silence was just too awkward, too awful. Furthermore, I didn't understand why he'd done it. He could have just walked along saying nothing, agreeing to nothing, contradicting nothing.

"Wait...wait, wait, wait...." I heard Beau huff. "Are you saying that you and Ash, that you two are...."

"Yes," Drew said. "That's right. And I respect you and Ashley too much to mislead you."

Beau huffed again, and I opened one of my eyes to peek at my brother. Beau was looking at me with incredulous worry.

"Ash...." He took a step closer to me, his tone solemn. "I like Drew and all, he's done a lot for us, but are you sure about this? No offense, Drew." He shot a look at Drew then back at me. "What do you have to say?"

I glanced at Drew, found him watching me with his quicksilver eyes, his expression open, unguarded, and trusting. I couldn't help but smile at him.

"Yes," I said to Drew then faced my brother. "Yes, Beau. The answer is yes. Yes, I have no sisterly feelings for Drew. Yes, we're getting along just fine, better than fine, *way* better than fine. But thank you." I stepped away from Drew and reached for my brother's shoulders, standing on my tiptoes to give his cheek a kiss. "Thank you for caring what I think."

He smiled down at me like I was crazy. "Ashley, of course I care what you think. You're my sister. If you're not happy, then I'll make sure...." His eyes slid over to Drew's. "I'll make sure no one is happy."

MOMMA HADN'T WOKEN up since I'd left to go butcher the roosters, which meant she also hadn't eaten anything.

We still hadn't heard from my father.

Drew went to work on the pie as soon as we arrived home, but I couldn't sit still. My neck itched and I felt like I had bees behind my eyes all through dinner. The food, Jethro's meatloaf, which was usually exceptionally tasty, was like sawdust in my mouth.

I insisted on doing the dishes, mostly because I needed to be moving around, I needed to be doing something. I finished in record time then set my mind to reorganizing the spice drawer.

When Joe, the night nurse, arrived, I followed him into the den. Cletus was there, sitting on my cot in his pajamas and reading what appeared to be a scientific journal.

Drew was also present. He was reading to Momma from the book *The Neverending Story*. I managed to give him a small smile, and the smile he tossed back did a good bit to both increase and settle my nerves.

"She still hasn't eaten?" Joe asked this to the room, his voice quiet and concerned.

"No, she hasn't," I said, and my eyes met Joe's. "Is it time for a tube?" I already knew the answer to this question.

Before Joe could respond, Drew said, "She doesn't want that. It's in her living will. She said she doesn't want a feeding tube."

My gaze darted to his. His eyes held an apology, but the set of his jaw told me it wasn't negotiable.

"On Monday she was laughing and joking around." Cletus said this from the cot. "Why is she so quiet? It's only been five days."

"Maybe she's just tired," I said, but it sounded completely lame.

I looked her over. A small sheen of sweat glistened on her forehead and upper lip. I laid my hand from temple to temple to check her temperature. She was cool.

"She doesn't have a temperature," Joe said. I could feel his eyes on me.

I nodded then addressed my next words to Cletus. "What do you think you're doing? You're in my spot."

Cletus shook his head. "Nah. This is my spot tonight. You've been hogging it, and I want it."

"Cletus...."

"Don't look at me that way, baby sister. I'll tell you what, if you can lift me up and carry me to my bed, then you can have this one. As it is, I'm tired and ready to sleep." As though to punctuate his words he yawned and waved us toward the door. "Now get out of here. I already beat Joe at chess sixty times this week."

"It was twelve times."

"Yeah, might as well have been sixty." He yawned again. "Go on, get."

Joe chuckled as he left. Drew stood, placed his book on the wooden chair, and crossed to me. I wasn't watching him. I was focused on and thinking about the perspiration covering my mother's upper lip. It didn't make any sense. The room was cool, but not cold. She felt cool, not clammy. I didn't get it.

Drew fit his hand in mine and tugged on it, leading me out of the room. Once the door closed behind us, he pulled me down the hall, to the stairs, and up to my room. I followed him, still thinking about Momma's lip and forehead, thumbing through my brain and all the possible causes for her sudden sleepiness and lack of interest in food.

I wondered if I should wake her up to eat the pie. I was pretty sure she'd be interested in pie.

"Hey...where you going?" Jethro called after us, rousing me from my thoughts.

"I'm taking Ashley to bed," Drew responded without turning to look at my brother or stopping our ascent up the stairs.

"Oh." I saw Jethro nod, his gaze watching us. Abruptly his eyes narrowed and he planted his hands on his hips, but he said nothing else.

Drew led me into my room and closed the door behind us. I was tired. I was also distracted. So when Drew turned and kissed me—a soft, lingering closed-mouth kiss that made me forget what I'd been thinking about and where I was—my hands twisted around his neck and I kissed him back, pressing my body to his.

We did this for a while. He kissed me. I kissed him back. He seemed to be holding himself on a tight leash, because he was controlling the intensity level by withdrawing every so often and placing feathery kisses on my neck and collarbone. His hands stroked and massaged my back, yet never felt anything but frustratingly comforting.

However, when the back of my knees hit the bed and I fell backward, and he climbed onto it and loomed above me, the room—and everything else—came into focus.

"Wait a minute, wait a minute…." I pressed my hands to his chest as he hovered over me, bending to bite my neck. "What are we doing?"

"Kissing, he whispered in my ear then licked my earlobe.

I shivered, swallowed, and squeezed my eyes shut. "I don't think we should be doing this."

"Why?" He continued to kiss, lick, bite—repeat.

"Because I…." I breathed out a ragged sigh. "Because I'm worried about Momma."

He stopped his sweet ministrations and lifted his head, his eyes moving over my face. He seemed to be considering me as well as what I'd just said.

After several long moments, he lay on his side next to me and threaded his fingers through the long locks.

"I know, Sugar. I was just trying to distract you."

I turned on my side and faced him. "You were doing a good job."

His lips twisted to the side and he watched me, his hands moving in my hair, then he surprised me by saying, "I'd like to sleep here with you tonight."

I opened my mouth, but didn't know how to respond because I wasn't sure what he was asking.

Reading my mind, he added, "Just sleep. I just want to sleep."

"Oh." I nodded my understanding, thinking about *just sleeping* next to Drew and finding that I quite liked the idea. The thought of hugging someone all night long was really appealing, especially if that person was Drew. It would be like having a big, strong, Viking man-pillow.

I realized he was still waiting for my answer, so I leaned forward and brushed a kiss against his mouth. "Yes. That would be nice. Thank you."

His eyes narrowed as I drew away. "You need to stop thanking me."

"I can't help it." I kissed him again then whispered against his mouth, "I was raised with manners."

♥ ♥ ♥

I AWOKE ABRUPTLY for no reason in particular and was startled by the surrounding darkness. It took me about ten seconds to figure out that I was in my room—not in the den—and that Drew was next to me, fast asleep.

He was warm and solid, and our limbs were knotted in perfect chaos. His arms were around my torso. My arms were around his neck. His head was on my breast. One of his legs was between mine, and our calves were hooked around each other.

It felt divine.

So I relaxed into the feeling for several minutes before searching for the clock on the nightstand; I found it, and next to it was Drew's leather notebook. I looked at the brown binding, studied the Norse symbols on the front, and found myself wondering what was inside. I'd witnessed him writing in the book from time to time and somehow doubted it contained field notes.

Shaking myself, because what Drew wrote in the notebook was really none of my business, I glanced at the clock. It was just before 4:30 a.m. and, despite my current epic levels of snuggly comfort, I felt like I had a stone in the pit of my stomach and a bug in my ear.

I was gripped by a desire to get up.

Despite the carefulness with which I tried to extract myself from Drew, I woke him.

"Ashley," he started awake, saying my name before he'd left his dream state, his arms tightening around me.

"Shh...Drew," I whispered. "I need to get up."

He peered up at me as though confused by the sight of my face. "Ashley?"

"Yes."

"What are you doing here?"

"Drew, you're in my bed. We fell asleep."

"Oh." His hand slid down my body—from waist to thigh—as though checking to see if I were real.

His confusion made me wonder what he'd been dreaming about if he'd said my name upon waking but was surprised to see me there.

"Why'd you wake me up?" He asked my chest.

I wrinkled my nose at him. "I didn't mean to. I was trying to get up without disturbing you; it was an accident."

"Oh…" Again, he said this to my chest. His hand caressed its way up my body until it rested on my ribs just below my breast. "This is a really nice way to wake up." This time he spoke mostly to himself, but his eyes didn't budge from my boobs.

Growing warm around my neck, I tamped down the desire rising within me and tried to sit up. "Drew, I need to pee. Remove your arms before my bladder explodes."

He reluctantly released me, falling back onto the bed with a heavy flop as I stood. "On second thought, we shouldn't do this again," he muttered.

I reached for my robe and shrugged it on. "Why not?"

"Because…reasons," he growled.

I pressed my lips together to keep from smiling, my eyes moving over his bare chest and stomach, illuminated only by the faint glow of the moon and starlight streaming in through my window. He was right, of course. Waking up tangled together wearing very few clothes—it wasn't a good idea. Not if I was planning to walk away when all this was over and return to my life in Chicago.

Maybe that's why I'd woken up so suddenly with a hard feeling in my belly. Maybe my brain and my stomach were in cahoots, trying to warn me against my heart.

The thought made me sad and flustered, so I quickly left the room without another word and took two steps toward the bathroom, but then stopped. I stood motionless in the upstairs hallway until the count of ten, because a sense of foreboding was nagging at me.

Impulsively, I changed courses and descended the stairs, walked down the hallway to the den, and pushed open the door.

It was quiet except for the sound of Cletus's gentle snoring and the beeping of Momma's machines. Of course, I knew the name of the machines and what their beeps meant from my schooling, training, and years as a floor nurse; but now, attached to and monitoring my mother, they became just beeping machines.

I inspected the room for some sign or source of my disquiet, and I realized that Momma was awake.

I crossed to her, smoothed the hair back from her forehead with one hand, and reached for her fingers with the other.

"Momma," I whispered. "Are you okay? What can I get for you?"

Her eyes were wide, but she struggled to swallow. I released her for a quick minute and opened the cooler by her bed where I kept her ice chips. I filled a cup and brought it to her lips. She accepted a few gratefully, closing her eyes and sighing.

I felt a stab of guilt that I'd been upstairs snuggling up with Drew, and she had been down here thirsty and awake. I vowed that I would sleep only on the cot from now on.

"I'm so sorry, Momma. I should have been down here."

She shook her head, her voice barely above a whisper. "No, baby. I just woke up. Don't do that."

"Don't do what?"

"I know that look." She paused and inhaled. I could tell that she did this with effort; she then said, "You're feeling guilt about things you can't control. Never feel guilt for things beyond your influence."

I gave her a brave smile as I smoothed her hair. "All right. I won't do that anymore if you promise to eat a slice of pie. Drew made your lemon meringue."

Her eyes closed as though she couldn't keep them open, but her mouth curved slightly at my words. "That sounds great, baby. It's a deal. You go get me a piece."

I set the ice chips down on the table and turned to leave, but then stopped when I heard her say, "Ash, wait."

I walked back to her. "What's up? Do you want something else with it?"

"No, baby. I just wanted to tell you I love you."

"Oh." I nodded, gave her a little smile, leaned forward, and kissed her forehead. "I love you too, Momma, to the stars and beyond."

She gave me her little smile again, her eyes still closed. "Just like always."

I squeezed her hand and whispered, "Okay, I'll be right back with the pie." Then I turned to the door and made my way to the kitchen.

When I opened the fridge, I found that only two pieces of pie remained. That irritated me. First of all, I hadn't had a piece of pie yet, and the pie was my idea. Secondly, those charlatans I called brothers knew that the pie was meant for Momma.

I scooped a slice out and placed it on a plate, then decided to hide the rest of the pie in the back of the fridge so she could have a second piece later.

Pleased with my efforts to conceal the last slice, I grabbed a fork and the pie, walked back to the den, and crossed to her bed.

"Momma, I have your pie," I whispered. "I haven't tried it yet, so I don't know if it's as good as yours, but it sure is pretty."

She didn't move.

I watched her for a minute, wondering if I should wake her, then noticed that the machines weren't beeping.

I didn't come to the realization all at once.

Rather, I stared at the flat line on the small monitor for several seconds...maybe even a minute before I recognized what it meant. When I did, the world went silent.

There is a stillness that accompanies the death of a loved one. Everything becomes quieter, but it's not just sound that is dimmed. Movement, action, perception, emotion—everything is distant and removed.

Maybe the stillness was because I'd been so busy leading up to this moment. After waking up from the shock of her diagnosis and facing reality, I'd thrown all of myself into her care and the care of my family.

But now—reality being the flat line on the monitor—she was gone.

The subjects and tasks that had filled my waking hours for more than a month went with her. The pie in my hand was meaningless, and the world felt like a strange and foreign place.

I was at the bottom of a lake. I was drifting. I felt like I could hold my breath for years. And I was beyond the reach of all the things that mattered before, but suddenly seem so trivial in the face of death.

CHAPTER TWENTY

*"You know what charm is: a way of getting the answer yes without
having asked any clear question."*

— ALBERT CAMUS, THE FALL

E ALL DID a lot of staring that day.

The point that struck me as most interesting about
our collective staring was the objects at which people stared.

Jethro stared out the window. Billy stared at the fireplace. Cletus
stared at the front door. Beau stared at the kitchen table. Duane stared
at the refrigerator. Roscoe stared at Momma's sewing desk.

I sat in my recliner and stared at the spot where the hospital bed
had been.

I kept looking for and trying to assign symbolism to everything: the
den's emptiness and bigness; a sudden rainstorm that started right after
they took her away; the book *The Neverending Story* that Drew had
been reading to her the night before.

Drew kept us all moving.

He made us breakfast and told us to eat. He made us sandwiches
and told us to eat. He made pheasant soup with biscuits and told us to

eat. He saw to it that everyone showered and dressed. He turned on the TV in the living room and streamed all the *Pink Panther* movies, one right after the other.

After dinner, we were all in the kitchen helping with the dishes, and I had the thought, *Someone should go check on Momma.*

And that's when I started to cry.

Jethro was nearest. He wrapped one of his big arms around my shoulders and pulled me to his chest. I cried on his flannel shirt as he shushed me and held me close. My mind was a jumbled mess, so I didn't protest—or even think to protest—when I was picked up off my feet and carried out of the kitchen to the family room.

I didn't notice that it was Drew who carried me out of the kitchen until sometime later when he said, "Sugar, you are not allowed to wash this shirt."

I peered up at him, surprised to find myself in the living room, on his lap, his arms around me, his hand in my hair.

"Why?" I said, two hot, fat tears rolling down my face.

"Because you haven't given me back any of the others, and I'm running out of T-shirts."

I considered his words then laughed and buried my face in his neck. "Quit being stupid. You'll get them back."

"When will I get them back? Do you want me to walk around the mountains shirtless?"

This was a comment that might have elicited a completely different reaction twenty-four hours ago; but as it was, Drew was providing me with humor and comfort, and that was what I needed. I didn't need anything beyond that.

"Have you called your friends yet today?" he asked, surprising me.

I gathered a deep breath, held it in my lungs, and responded on an exhale. "No."

"You should. It'll help. They likely miss you." He set his chin on my head and—as though the thought had just occurred to him—added softly to himself, "You'll be leaving soon...."

I sat motionless and let those words wash over me. He was right of course. I would be leaving soon, most likely once the funeral was over. It shouldn't have felt like a shock, but it did.

I was yanked out of these thoughts when the front doorknob rattled followed by a sharp, insistent knock.

Drew craned his head around toward the kitchen; when none of my brothers appeared, he set me down on the couch. "Just a sec," he said. "Let me see who this is."

I grabbed a throw pillow and hugged it to my chest. I noticed that a box of tissue had magically appeared on the coffee table, so I snagged a few and wiped my eyes, feeling the futility of the action. These were only the first tears.

"Who the hell are you? And where is my wife?"

I froze in terror. Like a lightning bolt splitting a tree, the man's words and aggressive tone sliced through the fog of my grief like nothing else could.

"Darrell," Drew said in a laconic drawl. He blocked the door with his body and added, "Bethany died this morning. You're too late."

"Get out of my way. This is my house."

I jumped from the sofa and ran to the kitchen. Knowing my father, strength in numbers was necessary.

"Guys, he's here," I loud whispered to the room. My face must've showed my panic because they all stiffened for a half second then were spurred into action. My brothers moved like the devil himself had arrived, and the only way to keep him out was to stand him down at the door.

I waited a half minute, inhaling and exhaling until I felt my courage buoy, and then I followed them out. The sound of rising voices and tempers made me flinch, and I saw that Roscoe was standing in the doorway. The rest of them were outside in the front yard.

I walked up to Roscoe and placed my hand on his back. He glanced down at me, his face strained, his jaw set; but his eyes softened when they met mine, and he wrapped an arm around my shoulders, tucking me close to his side. We watched the scene unfold from the house.

Darrell Winston was some distance from the porch, maybe five feet, and Jethro and Billy were standing in front of him. Jethro had his arms crossed, but Billy had taken an aggressive stance, his fists balled, and his feet braced apart like he was ready to throw a punch.

"Son, this is my house." Darrell was speaking to Jethro, and his tone was entirely reasonable. "Why you going to keep a man from his house?"

"Darrell...."

"I'm your daddy. You will address me as such."

Jethro's Adam's apple moved as he took a hard swallow, and his eyes were heavy-lidded with aggravation. "I'm trying to explain things to you. Momma died this morning. You're not welcome at the funeral, and you're not welcome here. This ain't your house."

"Son, this is the house I made my family in with your momma. This house belongs to me and all you kids; we need to come together and support each other."

Billy rolled his eyes. I got the sense he was purposefully trying to bait him. "You're delusional," he said. "We haven't ever been your kids. You're a sperm donor, and your services haven't been needed for a long time."

Surprisingly, my father didn't take the bait. "Where's your sister? Where's my baby girl?"

"I don't think it's right you calling her that," Cletus said, rubbing his chin thoughtfully. "She hates you and she's like, twenty-six. It just feels wrong."

"Ashley." My father called my name, obviously not yet noticing that I was watching the whole ugly scene. Again, I froze. His voice was demanding, and so many terrible childhood memories burst to the surface. "Girl, you come down here."

"We told you to leave, old man. This place ain't yours. It wasn't Momma's neither when she died. She sold it." Beau said this standing on the stairs of the porch just in front of me with Duane at his shoulder.

"Sold it?" Darrell shot an angry glance at Beau, and I felt the moment that he realized I was there, the second his eyes settled on mine. "Ashley, girl, look at you." He placed a hand over his chest like the sight of me made his heart hurt. "You're beautiful."

I stared at him from my place next to Roscoe, drawing from my little brother's strength.

"Your daddy needs to speak to you, Baby."

"Don't you speak to her." Drew stepped forward, though he'd been quiet up to this point.

My father ignored him, kept his voice calm. A beseeching smile— such a pretty smile—tempered his features as he said, "Come here, baby girl. I can see that you've been crying. I know your momma loved you best. Come to your daddy so I can make it better."

I saw so much of myself in him, in his gently spoken words, his eyes and smile, how he moved, how he sounded when he was trying to appear sincere. It made my stomach turn.

"Jethro, you make him leave, or I'm going to arrest him." Drew's threat was quietly spoken, but it felt like a gunshot in the thick, tense dwindling light.

"How are you going to manage that?" Darrell turned his smile on Drew, but now it was more like a smirk. "This is my house, son. This is my family."

"This is not your family, and don't call me son." Drew's words were eerily stoic and emotionless.

"Darrell," Cletus drawled, sounding oddly at ease. I thought for a moment that Cletus was going to put his hand on my father's shoulder, but instead he gestured toward Drew. "This here is a federal officer, and you're on his land. You see, he purchased this house some time ago. Now, according to Tennessee law, even if he weren't an officer, he could shoot you dead right now—if he felt threatened."

"That's right," Beau put in, "and we'd all be witnesses."

"That's right," Duane echoed his twin. "That's seven witnesses."

I saw a brief shadow of confusion and apprehension fall over my father's handsome features. He glared at Cletus—he never liked Cletus —then his eyes cut to Drew's.

"Those are lies. Bethany couldn't have sold this house, not without me knowing." His attention moved back to me as though I were the family litmus test of truth. He didn't seem to like what he saw, because his eyes grew large then narrowed. He lifted a finger and pointed at Drew but his eyes never left mine. "Is this your man?"

"Darrell Winston, get off my property. This is the last time I'm telling you." Drew stepped forward and Jethro flanked him. I didn't want Drew to touch him. He was an awful, evil man, and I didn't want Drew to have any contact with him.

I walked out from Roscoe's hold and stood in the center of the porch, crossing my arms over my chest. "Yes, Darrell. That's my man. And he just told you to get off his property. There is nothing for you here. All the money is gone. The house belongs to Drew. Momma left you a checking account with exactly sixty-three dollars in it. That's enough money for you to buy a tank of gas, a six-pack of beer, and get out of town."

"Ashley, did your momma give you my house?" My father was shouting now, and his smile was gone. Even in the stark twilight, I could see his face growing red.

"No." I shook my head. "No, she didn't. She left us nothing." *Nothing except peace of mind, love, memories, laughter, wisdom...and Drew.*

My father backed up as Drew, Cletus, and Jethro strolled forward, yet his gaze was affixed to me. "This ain't over. You think just 'cause I'm leaving this is over, but it ain't. This house is mine. That money is mine. You are all mine. You belong to me. What's yours is mine. You're my blood."

"You ain't shit." Billy spat.

"Shut your mouth, William." My father was even with the door to his car now; he turned a snarl on Billy, his blue eyes flashing mean and wicked at his son who might as well have been his physical clone. "I've beat you once, and I'll beat you again."

Billy surprised us all by laughing. "You think I couldn't have fought back, old man? I was twelve, but I knew where the rat poison was kept. I let you beat me. It was the only way to get you out of our lives. You hit Momma, but she would've taken it forever. You hit one of her babies, she became a momma bear."

I was gratified to realize that I wasn't the only one staring at Billy with shock and wonder. It seemed none of my brothers had known that Billy was the architect of our freedom, and at twelve years old.

My father made a movement like he was getting ready to charge at Billy, but Jethro and Cletus blocked his path and pushed him back to his car.

"It's time to go," Jethro said, pointing at our father.

"Yes. It's time for you to go," Cletus said, then he pointed at the wheels of Darrell's car and added, "But it might also be time for you to invest in a new set of tires. At least get them rotated for the safety of other vehicles on the road."

Darrell scowled at his third son then he aimed his anger at me. "This ain't over. I'll be back."

He slammed the door to his black Mustang and peeled out of our gravel driveway. We all watched the car until it left the property and pulled onto Moth Run Road. Then we waited until it was out of sight. Even then, we all stood in our places for several long seconds.

Cletus was the first to move. He walked to Drew and clapped him on the shoulder. "Welcome to the family, Andrew. You two will make beautiful children."

CHAPTER TWENTY-ONE

"Indifference and neglect often do much more damage than outright dislike."

— J.K. ROWLING, HARRY POTTER AND THE
ORDER OF THE PHOENIX

I WAS UP in my room laying down when Drew found me.

"There you are." He crossed to the bed, sat on the edge of it, and pulled me into a big bear hug. Then, he cussed. He cussed and he cussed, and he did this for a long time. He also mentioned my father's name more than a few times.

Darrell Winston had left approximately two hours ago. I was the first one in the house, and I made a beeline for my room. I lay on my bed and stared at the ceiling. I needed some quiet time with my thoughts. I wasn't hiding so much as trying to get my head on straight.

But I was also hiding. I didn't want to face my brothers after claiming Drew as my man. Heck, I didn't want to face Drew either.

I thought about Momma and the upcoming funeral.

Over the past forty days, I think I grieved for her every hour. In a way, I grieved for her before she died. And now that she was gone, I grieved for her still. Part of me wondered, however, if the grief would have been sharper, more debilitating, if I hadn't been given the month to say goodbye.

I thought about her sickness and wondered if I could have done anything differently. Then I remembered one of the last things she'd said to me: not to feel guilty about things that were beyond my control. These words made feel better, steadier.

And then I thought about Chicago.

I thought about my life there, my friends, my job, my apartment, my books, my things. My job allowed three months' leave of absence to take care of an ailing family member, but they only allowed five days for funerals and bereavement. It was quite likely that I would be back in Chicago in one week's time or less.

This thought gave me pause. I was excited to see my friends. I missed them terribly. I missed the city. I also missed my apartment and my job, but to a much lesser extent.

This last month and a half happened. My mother's sickness and death happened. The bonding and rekindling of my relationships with most of my brothers happened, the notable exception being Billy, who still seemed to hold me at arm's length.

Also, Drew happened…and that's where my brain stalled. Because I didn't know what to think about Drew. I didn't know how to feel about him or what I was allowed to feel about him.

He'd told me more than once that he didn't need anything from me. He'd said that my life was in Chicago. What did that mean for us?

Furthermore, was there an 'us'?

Or was all this just a good man trying to help his friend's family through a difficult time?

Now, sitting on my bed, angry with my father on my family's behalf, I felt absolutely no clarity on the issue. Drew holding me close made it especially hard to imagine a future without him in it.

My hands went to his hair and I stroked it back from his face, encouraging him to lean away so I could look at him.

My words were meant to sooth his waspish temper. "Hey, it's over, yeah? He's gone. He doesn't know it yet, but there's nothing he can do to hurt us. You and Momma made sure of that."

Drew studied me; his eyes felt more vivid to me than before, hot steel and silver. "Ashley, let me take you home with me, just for the next few days until the funeral is over and the will is read and Darrell sees that there's nothing for him here."

His offer caught me off guard; I stared at him and he stared back. A little voice in my head wanted to say, *You're confusing me, Drew. You can stop taking care of me now. She's gone. And I'm going to be okay.*

I decided I didn't know what to say or think about the two of us. Maybe there wasn't anything to say. Maybe we would get through the funeral, he'd wish me well, I would board a plane back to Chicago, and that would be that.

This thought left me numb, so I opted for honest politeness. "Thank you, Drew. That's a really nice offer. But I'm afraid I can't accept."

He winced at my words, blinking twice. His expression changed as he studied my face. "What's going on, Ash?"

I disentangled myself from his arms and stood; I walked to my dresser and faced him. "I don't want to leave my brothers alone, not now."

Drew's eyes narrowed as he watched me. "Darrell's fixated on you. You can't take a step outside this house, Ash; it's not safe. He might charge in here."

"I know, I know—it's just, I left them before. When I went to college, I left them." Billy had taken a beating for all of us. There was no way I was going to leave my brothers now.

"No, Sugar. You lived your life." Drew stood from the bed and walked to me. He was reaching out for me, but he stopped when I crossed my arms.

Drew took a step back, frowning, but continued to press his point. "You didn't abandon your brothers then, and you're not doing it now. Just…come with me."

"I did. I did abandon them." I thought over the last six weeks or so and how Billy was perpetually irritated by my presence. "I can't leave them now."

"Your daddy's focus will be on this place because he doesn't understand yet. No one in town knows where I live. He can't get to you up on the mountain. Plus, I think your brothers need this. They need a battle to fight. You come with me."

"Drew...."

The door to my room opened. Jethro and Billy walked in, glancing from Drew to me then around my room.

Billy frowned at my suitcase, open and messy on my floor. "You getting ready to go?"

I surmised they were talking about Drew's offer to take me to his house. I glared at Drew for a quick second to show my displeasure that he'd talked to my brothers about this before talking to me, and then I placed my hands on my hips and addressed Billy directly.

"No, I am not ready to go. I'm not going anywhere. And I do not enjoy being discussed while I am not present." Then, not hiding my disappointment and frustration that he'd gone behind my back, to Drew I said, "You should have talked to me about this first."

"Ashley Austen Winston, this wasn't Drew's idea. This was my idea. You cannot be here. You need to leave." Billy's quarrelsome tone was a surprise, and I found his eyes boring into me with stark exasperation.

After my initial astonishment wore off, a surge of heated irritation swelled, leaving me seeing red. "William Shakespeare, you quit being ugly. You've been throwing snarky remarks in my direction since I arrived. I know you don't like me much, and I'm sorry that I left you all eight years ago, but I'm here now. And that's got to count for something."

Billy looked like he was ready to pitch a fit, but Jethro stepped between us, blocking our view of each other, and spoke to me in his most reasonable voice.

"Now, rest your feathers, Ashley. You know that's not true. Billy loves you same as the rest of us. Honey, let Drew take you to his house. He explained everything, and I know he's not your man. He'll keep you safe from Darrell."

I blinked at that, again taken by surprise, and opened my mouth to protest, but Jethro *shushed* me and pulled me into an embrace. "Listen, it's just for a bit, maybe just one night. But I think we all would sleep better knowing you were out of our father's reach."

"I'm safe here," I argued. "How much safer can I get? I'm surrounded by my six hillbilly brothers."

He breathed a laugh and laid his cheek on the top of my head. "Ash, I honestly don't know what Darrell is going to do next. He could break in here with a gun; he could try to set the place on fire. He's crazy. What I do know is that Drew is a federal law enforcement officer and his daddy is a US senator. He can arrest Darrell on sight if he has to. Besides, he lives on top of the mountain at Bandit Lake. Navigating those roads is like trying to pee in a thimble while drunk and blindfolded. No one knows exactly where Drew lives except me and maybe Roscoe."

"But...."

"But nothing, hon." Jethro pulled away but his hands rested on my shoulders, his light brown eyes penetrating, almost hostile. "Please, Ash. Please go with Drew. Please let him take you home and keep you safe."

I blinked and glanced to the side. My eyes were scratchy from crying. My voice was nasally when I spoke, and I knew my frustration was bleeding through. "I'm not helpless, Jethro. I've been taking care of Momma for the last month. I made sure she was bathed and comfortable, and that she'd eaten. I live by myself in Chicago. I put myself through college."

"Honey, Ash, no one is questioning the fact that, out of all of us, you are the most capable of living in the real world and making good decisions. But Darrell Winston is not one to be reasoned with." Jethro released a pained breath, his eyes were glassy. His fingers flexed on my shoulders and he shook me a little when he spoke, his voice unsteady. "Honey, you are precious to us. You are precious to me. We just lost Momma. You are my baby sister, and I can't-"

"Okay, okay." I cut him off because he was working himself into a tiff. The last thing I wanted was to argue with my brothers. If they wanted me to go with Drew, if it gave them peace of mind, then I would go with Drew.

Jethro exhaled, closed his eyes in relief, and he gave me a big hug. "Thank you."

My eyes locked with Drew's, whose gaze was inscrutable; his mouth was a flat line. I couldn't guess what he was thinking for all the world.

"It's fine," I sniffled, not liking that I'd been emotionally black-mailed into leaving. When Jethro finally took his hands from my shoulders, I spoke to all three of them, holding my index finger in front of me like a sword. "But let the record show that I've agreed to this only under duress."

"So noted," Billy snapped. "But honestly, Ash? If you hadn't agreed, I was prepared to tie you up and have Roscoe drop you off on Drew's doorstep. You're more stubborn than Momma sometimes."

Something in me snapped at his harsh tone. I was tired of this distance between us. I was tired of earning his censure. I needed to own up to my mistakes, and I needed him to understand that I was sorry.

So I reached for his hand and held it. "Billy, will you forgive me? Will you please forgive me? I'm fighting to stay now because I'm trying to learn from my mistakes. I don't want to leave you all like I did before. I feel like I abandoned you."

I watched his throat work without swallowing. At length he said, "Don't be stupid."

I ignored him and apologized again because I had to, because he needed to hear it. "Billy, I'm so sorry I left."

Billy's eyes moved between mine, and I could see a raw wire of emotion in his blue eyes. I'd struck a nerve.

"Ashley Austen Winston," he said, his voice rough and unsteady, "it was never about you leaving. You had to go. I get that. We all knew that. Never regret needing to better yourself."

I nodded, tears springing to my eyes; I thought he was finished and I was grateful for his words.

Therefore, he surprised me when he continued, "It was the staying gone that pissed me off. I can handle your irritation and hard looks. Hell, I can even handle your disappointment, your anger, your sarcasm, and your screaming like a banshee about nothing much that matters. What I can't abide is your apathy. Apathy between family members makes the blood they share turn to water."

NEITHER OF US spoke during the ride up the mountain. Lost to my thoughts, I was caught in a net of my own making.

Drew grabbed my suitcase from the bed of his truck before I had a chance to reach it. I thought about reminding him that the giant bag had wheels but decided against it. He looked restless like he wanted to carry something heavy.

I'd packed everything, even the vibrator and condoms from Sandra, as I didn't know when or if I would get a chance to go back to the house before returning to Chicago. Also, God forbid one of my brothers found the vibrator and/or condoms in my room. The roof would blow off the house.

Life was happening too fast. Momma had died at 4:33 in the morning; now it was 10:30 at night, and everything had changed.

He unlocked the front door and opened it, motioning for me to walk in first. I did.

The last time I'd been at Drew's place was several weeks ago when I'd called him an ass for calling me sexy. I couldn't help but smile at the memory because I was so mad at him I could hardly see straight. Now Momma was gone and I missed her. Drew and I would also be indefinitely separated in just a few days.

But that wasn't quite true. I was thinking of coming home to Tennessee for Christmas. Maybe we'd see each other then....

For some reason, the idea of seeing Drew in passing during family holidays made me feel worse than not seeing him at all.

Drew led me down the hall, past the bathroom where I'd dulled his razor, to a large bedroom. The walls were painted a pale green. A double bed anchored the center of one wall; the comforter looked to be an old quilt made with white and yellow hexagons of fabric hand-stitched neatly together in the honeybee design. A side table was next to the bed and a wooden bench was at the foot of it.

Much like the library I'd woken up in during my first visit, one entire wall was windows, but two of the glass panels were also doors leading out to a large porch or balcony. I couldn't see much of the porch now, but in the daytime, I would have to explore it.

"You'll sleep here." Drew carried my suitcase to the wooden bench and added, "You can use the bathroom you used before. If you're hungry, help yourself to anything."

I nodded, thinking that the bed looked sublimely comfortable. It had that cushy appearance, like the mattress was that super swanky orthopedic memory foam and the pillows were feather.

He lingered at the bench, glancing around the space as though inspecting it.

"You should get some sleep," he said, not looking at me as he moved toward the door.

Just then, an owl hooted.

I shivered and murmured, "Hootiedoom."

Drew stopped in his tracks, his eyes moving to mine. "What?"

I gave myself a little shake. "Sorry, I said hootiedoom."

His brow furrowed, but his mouth curved just slightly. "What is hootiedoom?"

"It's when you experience a sense of dread right after an owl hoots."

Drew stared at me for a beat then smiled. "I've never heard of hootiedoom. Maybe I should add it to my field notes."

I was grateful for the break in tension, and I managed a small smile. "You have a PhD, and you've never heard of hootiedoom? What kind of graduate school was this 'Baylor University'?" I used air quotes for emphasis.

"Obviously not a very good one."

"Obviously. Then I'm guessing you never heard of Snipe-shivers?"

He pressed his lips together and faced me, his feet braced apart like he was planning to stay awhile. "No. I've never heard of Snipe-shivers."

"Oh, bless your heart." I'd said it before I knew I was going to say it. Obviously, some part of me craved bantering with Drew, engaging in a battle of wits and thinking about something other than death and funerals, and crazy dangerous family members, and leaving in a few short days for Chicago.

His mouth dropped open and his eyes became wide saucers under arched eyebrows. "I can't believe you just *bless your heart*-ed me."

"What?" I shrugged, hoping my forced expression of obliviousness was halfway convincing, "What's wrong with saying *bless your heart?*"

"Ashley, I grew up in Texas. Ladies all over the south use *bless your heart* for one reason and one reason only."

I shrugged. "I don't know what you're talking about. I have only good intentions for your heart."

The air in the room shifted as soon as the words left my mouth, my last statement echoing between us, and I realized their double meaning way too late.

"Do you?" He said this simply, the smile waning from his lips.

Drew broke eye contact first, took a step back, and lowered his eyes to the floor. "I'll let you get some sleep."

Unthinkingly, I stayed his retreat by grabbing his arm just above his elbow. "Wait, Drew."

His eyes sliced to mine and a grim smile seemed to curve his mouth both up and down. He covered my hand with his. "The funeral will be on Wednesday. I imagine you'll want to get your flight booked as soon as possible. I have a satellite connection up here for the wireless."

I sighed, my heart feeling like dead weight in my chest, so I likely sounded overwhelmed when I said, "I honestly don't know what I want."

"Ashley...." Drew stepped forward and cupped my face with his big paw. I immediately wrapped my hands around his wrist to keep him there. His eyes became lost while studying my face. The fact that he was staring at me didn't feel weird because I was staring at him. I had a mounting urge to memorize every detail of his features, just in case—after this week—I never saw him again.

His expression sobered, like his eyes were once again focusing, and he said, "Ash, you just lost your momma, and I just lost a really good friend. Now you know I don't think of you as a sister..." His eyebrows lifted as he said this, his voice dipped with Texas charm, and it made me laugh even though I felt close to crying.

"Yes. And you know I don't think of you as a brother." I sniffled, proud of myself for not succumbing to tears.

"Good." He kissed my nose, his thumb tracing my cheek, and then he held me away and looked into my eyes. "So let me be the friend you need to help you get through these next few days. Stay here, with me. I've told you before, I've got no expectations of you. I'm not asking anything from you. You have your life in Chicago; I know that. There's no pressure here."

I nodded, feeling a twinge of both disappointment and relief—but mostly disappointment, which made me feel wholly disoriented—when he reminded me that ours was a relationship with no expectations.

Despite my confusion on the subject, I wanted what he was offering. If we could focus on comforting each other, then I was going to make the most out of the next few days. I was going to take as much comfort from Drew as he was willing to offer. And I was going to try to be the friend he needed in return, even if he didn't actually need anything from me.

"Okay," I said, shuffling a half step forward. "If that's the case, then I want you to sleep with me—just sleep—like we did last night. Because I could really use a Viking man-pillow right now."

"Viking man-pillow?" His lips pressed together again and his beard twitched.

I nodded, gazing into his silvery eyes, my hands slipping from his wrist to wrap around his waist. I wanted to commit his closeness and comfort to memory. I wanted to live the next few days like we could spend forever on top of this mountain. I wanted him to teach me how to just be.

CHAPTER TWENTY-TWO

"From which stars have we fallen to meet each other here?"

— FRIEDRICH NIETZSCHE

*W*E VISITED WITH the minister to talk about the service, and I cried.

We went to the funeral home to confirm the details, and I cried.

We stopped by the cemetery to check out the burial plot, and I cried and cried.

Several of Momma's friends called Jethro while we were out and about, wanting to know about the wake, the funeral, the reception after the funeral. Jethro told me that casseroles had started to arrive *en masse*, and he asked if I thought a new deep freezer would be a good idea.

This made me cry.

Other things that made me cry: washing Drew's T-shirts while doing my laundry; knitting; reading books; eating pie; playing chess with Cletus when he and Roscoe came over to Drew's house to bring me Momma's jewelry, her antique books, and all the letters she'd kept from me over the years; learning that the twins had finally butchered the roosters; hugging any of my brothers; making plans to visit over Christmas; and booking my return flight to Chicago.

I was set to leave Thursday afternoon, the day after the funeral, in two days' time. I'd called my boss, let her know I'd be back to work Monday morning, and would have the death certificate faxed to the hospital's human resources department. All my laundry was done. My bag was all packed.

Things that didn't make me cry: laying and snuggling with Drew in bed; listening to the rain; drinking coffee with Drew before he left for work and arguing with him about the negative influence of the German composer Wagner on Nietzsche's philosophies; Skyping with my friends; walking in the woods; making dinner with Drew for my brothers when they came up the mountain to visit; listening to Drew read novels out loud after dinner while I knit (of note, for some reason, knitting without his vocal accompaniment made me cry); then, discussing the merits of fiction versus non-fiction until 1:00 a.m.; Drew teasing me; falling asleep in Drew's arms; kissing Drew; holding Drew's hand; looking at Drew; being with Drew.

I tried not to dwell on how much I loved being with Drew, because if I did, I cried.

"I'm glad we cancelled the wake," Jethro said; his eyes narrowed on the road. We were on our way back from the funeral home in town, and I could tell he was concentrating. The drive to Drew's wasn't simple; missing one turnoff could mean wasting an hour trying to find the way back. "It gives Darrell one less opportunity to spread his shit around."

I nodded because I had to agree.

Since the confrontation on Saturday night, Darrell had been to the police station, the town hall, The Dragon biker bar, Momma's church, Billy's work, the ranger station where Jethro's office was, and the Winston Bros. Auto Shop. He'd also been back to the house several times, so I'd been told, but left before the police arrived each time.

Darrell wasn't the only reason we'd decided to cancel the wake. We didn't want an open casket. As well, we were planning a reception after the funeral. There was no reason to have both a wake and a reception other than to give people additional time to make awkward conversation.

I could feel Jethro's eyes on me, so I looked at him. His attention was split between me and the road.

"Ash, can I ask you something?"

"Shoot."

"What's going on with you and Drew?"

I held my brother's gaze for a beat, then inhaled slowly, closed my eyes, and let the back of my head hit the headrest.

"Jethro...I honestly don't know."

"But something is going on...more than just friends?"

I shrugged, still not looking at him. "What did he say? I mean on Saturday after I stood on the porch and told Darrell that Drew was my man. What did Drew say to you all downstairs while I was in my room?"

Jethro cleared his throat before he spoke. "He just said that he didn't have sisterly feelings for you, but that he'd been trying to help you deal over the last month or so, trying to give you a sympathetic ear, comfort. He wanted to be what you needed."

I nodded and swallowed; my mouth tasted like salt and disappointment.

Jethro continued. "He also said that he didn't have any expectations because he knows you belong in Chicago. He was real insistent that he wasn't trying to keep you in Tennessee. He said he wanted you to be happy. He said he wanted all of us to be happy."

"And you all didn't press him for more information?" I peered at Jethro, but his eyes were glued to the winding mountain road.

"We did, but Beau backed him up. He told us to stop badgering Drew and just ask you directly."

"Hmm...." I watched the road ahead as a quick series of switchbacks had me holding on to the door. The trees were changing color, and some would argue that the old mountains were at their most resplendent in the fall. They were every shade of vibrant orange, yellow, and red. A few stubborn greens remained.

I briefly wondered if Drew had written any poetry about it, the beauty of the leaves changing. I felt confident that he'd do justice to the phenomenon.

"So...Ash? Are you okay with Drew? I trust him not to take advantage, but I'd like to hear it from you."

I sighed. "Yes, I'm okay with Drew. He's not...he's not taking advantage." If anyone was taking advantage, it was me.

"Are you two going to keep talking after you leave?"

I didn't answer immediately because I hadn't talked to Drew about it. As much as I wanted to keep in touch with him, I also didn't want anything about our interactions to change. The thought of keeping in touch filled me with dread, because that meant talking on the phone or via email, not in person. It would be utter torment; we wouldn't be able to kiss and touch and tease and argue.

It would be like watching the leaves change or listening to the rain in the Smoky Mountains via web cam. Sure, it's pretty, but it's a hollow experience. It only makes you sad because you're not there to live it. I wanted to live Drew.

"I don't know," I finally said. "I haven't decided."

It was Jethro's turn to say, "Hmm...."

We drove several more miles in silence, he with his thoughts, me with mine.

Then he blurted, "Today is Tuesday!" He might as well have screamed "Fire!"

I gasped and grabbed my chest, startled by the volume of his declaration. "Bejeezus, Jethro! You scared the tar out of me. What's the matter with you?"

He shifted in his seat and said quietly, "I just forgot that today is Tuesday."

"Well you don't have to shout about it. You're not going to make Tuesday any more of a Tuesday by hollering about it."

He nodded, staring out the windshield, but I noticed he wore a suggestion of a smile. It was his *I've got a secret* smile.

I stared at him, trying to reach into his mind and read the reason behind his badly hidden grin. Obviously, it didn't work.

"What are you hiding, Jethro Whitman Winston?"

We pulled into Drew's short, gravel drive, Jethro still smiling. "No reason. I just like Tuesdays."

He put his truck in park then jumped out, light on his feet, and opened my door for me. Now I knew something was amiss.

"What is wrong with you?" I said this as he reached for my hand and pulled me out of my seat.

"Nothing is wrong." He kicked the door shut with his foot and gripped me by the shoulders, pushing me toward the porch.

"I am capable of walking in a straight line, you know. I'm not drunk."

"Not yet," he mumbled.

"What did you—?"

Just then, the screen door opened and Janie, my dear friend and member of my knitting group, stumbled out of Drew's house.

Upon seeing us, her face brightened with a ginormous grin and she shouted over her shoulder, "She's here!"

I stared at her and literally took a step back, quite frankly dumbfounded by the image of Janie standing on Drew's porch dressed in sensible gray pants, a red long-sleeved fitted knit shirt, and four inch crimson stilettos. Even though she was naturally Amazonian height, she enjoyed walking around on girly stilts.

Jethro's steps slowed as he caught sight of her, and I heard him say under his breath, "Butter my biscuits, now that's a woman."

I ignored him because everyone—male and female—reacted this way when faced with Janie for the first time. Janie was boobs and butt paired with a tiny waist and long legs. But my dear friend was completely oblivious to the effect her physique had on men; rather, she assumed men stared at her dumbfounded because she had a tendency to spout trivial information at random.

I still couldn't believe my eyes that she was there, in the flesh; a towering, red-haired sight for sore eyes.

She rushed forward and hugged me, her cheek pressed to mine. "We just arrived. This place is amazing! The view is spectacular," she gushed, and I knew it was only the beginning of a typical Janie observation. She stepped back, releasing me, and gazed around at the autumn color, which was at its peak. "Now that the chlorophyll is receding, the glucose is trapped, thus turning the leaves different colors. The ultraviolet light and diminishing temperatures are, of course, to blame. Kind of like how people become paler in the winter, it's important to get enough vitamin D."

She turned to Jethro, whose mouth was agape. "Hi, I'm Janie. You're Jethro, the oldest. Did you finish your hat? Can I see your yarn?"

♥ ♥ ♥

"I COULDN'T FIND my way back up here if my entire yarn stash were at risk. How many turns did we take? Fifty? One hundred?" Elizabeth said this from her seat by the hearth.

Drew had started a fire because the weather had turned rainy and cold rather abruptly. As well, the temperature at the top of the mountains was always a good five to ten degrees cooler than it was in the valley.

"More like fourteen," Drew answered, handing both Marie and Elizabeth a glass of wine.

I followed him with my eyes, looking up from my knitting just long enough to watch his easy stride and lissome movements as he crossed to the fireplace and added another log. He was grace in motion, and he'd arranged for my friends to surprise me by coming to Tennessee.

I had no idea they wanted to come for the funeral. During the Skype conversations since Momma's passing, they hadn't said a word about it, and I hadn't asked. They all had their own lives and troubles.

But Drew had stepped in and contacted Sandra. Sandra contacted Janie. Janie asked her husband Quinn for the use of his private plane so that everyone could fly down together.

The men were in the kitchen and spilling out on the back porch, drinking beer and talking about who knows what, while the ladies were in the library knitting.

The house handled an impressive amount of people with ease. All my brothers were present, plus Drew and me. All the knitting group was accounted for, which meant six ladies and Nico. Plus, Fiona, Janie, and Sandra had also brought along their spouses.

Greg—Fiona's husband—was currently in the kitchen making everyone laugh. He was a petroleum engineer and was gone most of the year for work; I was truly touched that he and Fiona had opted to come down, especially when their time together was so fleeting and precious.

"This place probably doesn't even show up on aerial photos," Fiona said thoughtfully. Her chair was next to the wall of windows, and she was gazing into the red, yellow, and orange wilderness. "It would make a great safe house."

"Everyone is going to know where you live now." Sandra pointed this out to Drew, and he gave her a smirk over his shoulder. She continued, "I'm going to take pictures and post it on Google Earth. You'll have people knocking on your door trying to sell you cookies by next week. You can thank me later."

"I'll thank you now for *not* doing that."

"Come on, Charlie," Sandra implored, and she narrowed her eyes at him for effect. "Don't you like cookies?"

"The name is Drew, and I like cookies just fine."

A burst of laughter from the kitchen invaded our cozy respite, and I noticed Fiona shaking her head as her husband Greg's voice rose above the others.

"…I didn't care if it had bullet holes—the car was free. Are you telling me you'd turn down a free car just because it had bullet holes?"

Quinn's tone was incredulous when he responded, "Please don't tell me you drive your kids around in that car."

"Uh, yeah. Of course I do." Greg responded like Quinn had asked a ridiculous question, "That's their inheritance, Quinn. I'm leaving my kids that holey car and my collection of antifungal cream when I die. No need to be jealous, but feel free to take notes."

Kat chuckled as their voices faded; she turned to Fiona and said, "Greg is the funniest guy I've ever met. He should talk to Nico about becoming a comedian."

271

Fiona snorted. "Um, no. I can't imagine what would come out of his mouth in front of an audience."

I saw that Drew cracked a smile, one that he was trying to hide.

I narrowed my eyes at him. "What? Why are you smiling?"

"Because your friend Kat is right, and so is Fiona. No offense, Fiona, but your husband isn't right in the head. The stuff he says is hilarious, but it might not be ready for prime time."

Fiona nodded once to Drew. "Exactly. That's exactly right. Drew is a smart man."

Drew stood, glancing around at us as he said, "If anyone needs anything, feel free to help yourself. There's more food in the kitchen..." his gaze swung to Marie, "...and wine."

"What?" Her eyes widened and she looked from side to side. "Why are you looking at me?"

He didn't say anything, just gave her a good-natured suspicious glare. Before he left, he held my eyes and gifted me a small smile, then left the room to join the men on the porch. We heard a wave of chatter as the glass door off the kitchen opened then closed with his departure.

And that's when everyone—but me—stopped knitting and shifted forward in their seats and leveled me with expectant stares.

Sensing their eyes, I sunk lower into the couch and said, "The fire is nice, isn't it? So cozy...."

"Cut the poo, Ashley. What's going on with you and the mountain man? When did this happen? How did this happen? Tell us everything. Leave out nothing. We want details! Also, I love that he wears suspenders. He totally pulls it off. I'm now buying Alex suspenders." Sandra always did have a lovely way of cutting to the chase.

Marie raised her hand. "I second the motion about suspenders."

"Third," Elizabeth said.

"So passed," Sandra announced.

I huffed hair from my forehead and set my knitting down, closing my eyes. "I have no idea. All I know is...he's been awesome. He's like...he's...gah."

"He's 'gah'? Uh oh." Fiona said this, and I could hear the tempered amusement in her voice.

"No." I opened just one eye, meeting her gaze. "No, there is no *uh oh*. There can't be an *uh oh*."

"Why, pray tell, can't there be an *uh oh*?" Marie lifted her eyebrows, her eyes narrowed.

"Because he doesn't...because I don't...." I opened my other eye and struggled to put into words all the reasons Drew and I had no future; I settled on, "Because we just can't...we just can't *uh oh*."

"Why not?" Kat pressed. "He clearly cares about you, and you care about him, and your family seems to like him—not that it should make a difference what your family thinks—so why not go for it? I mean, no one is perfect. And if you have feelings for him, you should act on them instead of pushing them aside and waiting too long. If you wait too long it'll be too late, and he'll start dating someone else, like a business analyst on the seventeenth floor." At the end of her little tirade, it was clear that Kat was talking to herself.

We all stared at her, waiting for her to realize that she'd just inadvertently spilled a figurative can of beans.

"Uh...what?" Marie asked.

Kat sighed, finishing her wine with three gulps, her face shading a color to match; she continued in a quiet voice. "I just meant, don't push him away if you care about him."

Fiona cleared her throat, drawing our attention to her, and gave a little shake of her head. This meant that we should leave Kat alone and not press the issue.

Sandra, as usual, was the one to pick up the dropped ball. "Well, back to delicious Drew. I can understand why you're hesitating. He's a game warden in Tennessee. It's not like he could get a job in Chicago."

"He could, just not as a game warden," Janie volunteered. "He's got a PhD in biology and wildlife management from Baylor. He could easily get a job in Chicago."

I shook my head. "No. No—I would never ask him to move to Chicago. He doesn't belong there. He belongs here, in the woods and wilderness. He would wither and die in a big city. He needs wide open spaces and wild animals and breathtaking views and the quiet of the mountains. It wouldn't be right; I would never ask that."

"But what if he wanted to be near you?" Elizabeth squinted at me. "Nico left New York; he moved his TV show to Chicago to be with me."

"That was different." I was still shaking my head. "Nico moved from a big city to another big city and got the bonus of being closer to his own family. Doesn't he have a sister in Chicago? And the rest of his family is nearby in Iowa?"

"Most of them, yes. That's true."

Sandra interjected. "But please tell me you two have done the deed."

My mouth fell open in stunned indignation. "Sandra Fielding Greene, I know you did not just say that to me."

"I did just say that. You two are having eye-sex every time you're in the same room together. If you haven't taken a roll in the hay yet, then you need to before you come back to Chicago with us. Tap that keg, Ashley. Tap it!"

"Fiona? Help me out here?" I looked to Fiona to be the voice of reason and found her watching me with a measured expression.

"Ashley," she started, stopped, sighed, and began again. "Ashley, it's clear to me that you are leaving Tennessee with a broken heart." Her mouth tugged to the side and her eyes were sympathetic. "Your mother just passed away. You have to give yourself some time to grieve. Your path leads back to Chicago, at least for a little while. And Drew's path is here in Tennessee. Whether those paths meet or cross again is entirely up to the two of you. Don't let Sandra push you into an intersection before you're ready."

Sandra *tsked*. "Oh, you and your traffic analogies. Twerk and jerk, that's what I always say." Sandra smacked her thigh for emphasis.

"Ugh, Sandra. Can we have one conversation without you making twerking references?" Marie shook her head. "I am so over twerking."

Fiona held my eyes and we shared a smile. Her advice gave me a measure of peace, but my selfish heart wanted everything now. It wanted Chicago and knit nights. It wanted my brothers. It wanted the old mountains and the fall colors, the winter snowfall, the spring blooms, and the summer fields of wildflowers.

My heart wanted my momma back.

And my heart wanted Drew.

Sandra's crass response pulled Fiona and me out of our moment. "You know you love it. And besides, if you're twerking right, you should be under and he should be over."

"What is twerking anyway?" Fiona asked the room. "I saw someone on Ellen talking about it."

"You don't have enough junk," I said. "Go eat more pie."

"My junk's in the front—the stomach," Elizabeth said. "Is there a way to twerk with your belly?"

"No. That's berking." Sandra said this right as Kat was taking a sip of water, which promptly shot out of her mouth.

"Damn it, Sandra!" She wiped her chin.

"You're lucky it wasn't wine." Sandra shook her head at Kat and *tsked*. "When will you ever learn, don't drink when I'm talking."

"Berking?" Janie asked. "Like the artist Bjork?"

"Completely different. Berking is belly twerking," Marie explained.

"That's not berking," I said flatly. "That's jelly rolling."

The room erupted in laughter, and I couldn't help giggling at my own joke.

"Oh my stars! I have missed you," Sandra said, standing to give me a hug, pressing her cheek against mine. "I'm so glad we have you back."

MY BROTHERS AS well as my ladies and their husbands departed after midnight. Jethro led the caravan back to town where they were all staying in a quaint old inn until after the funeral.

Drew and I tidied up the house, bagging the remaining bottles for the recycle bin and wiping down counters. There wasn't much to straighten, as Elizabeth and Janie had gone through the living area before departing and gathered all the empties. Fiona and Greg had washed and put away the dishes, and my brothers carted the trash away in the bed of Jethro's truck.

As I was walking past the sliding door to the porch, I caught my reflection. I was smiling. It felt good to smile, and I was grateful for the distraction of my friends on the night before the funeral.

Drew caught up with me and kissed me on the cheek. "Go get ready for bed."

I acquiesced and shuffled down the hallway to the bathroom, stretching my arms over my head as I went.

After I was all washed up and minty fresh, I changed into my pajamas and turned down the covers of the bed. A bright star out the window caught my attention, so I turned off the lights and opened the balcony door, stepping out to the porch.

It was still cold, but the rain had cleared. There was no moon. The stars were pinholes of brilliance against a black sky, vivid and bright. A sudden thought struck me: stars felt like a distant idea or concept in the city sky. They were dim and faraway.

But here, I felt as though I might be able to touch them if I lifted my hand, reached out, and wished hard enough.

"'From which stars have we fallen to meet each other here?'" Drew quoted from behind me, and I turned to see him leaning against the doorway. He was still dressed in his black pants, white button-down shirt, and suspenders. But his boots were off.

I smiled at him over my shoulder then turned back to the sky. "Who said that?"

"Your old friend Nietzsche, as a matter of fact."

I huffed a disbelieving laugh. "Are you sure? That sounds far too romantic for Nietzsche. It sounds more like Shakespeare or Byron."

"In the context of the original text, the quote isn't romantic. But I think Nietzsche was a romantic soul, in a way." Drew's voice was deep and thoughtful.

"How so? Was he very fond of cows?"

I heard Drew gather a breath before responding, a smile in his voice. "No, not precisely. He did say that women and men love differently, and I think there's a lot of truth in his philosophy on the matter."

"Let me guess, when a woman declares her love, she does so with sweet grass and clover. Cows love clover."

"You're never going to forgive me for the cow comment, are you?"

"Nope." I shook my head.

We quietly watched the stars, and I thought about how I might be able to steal this moment and keep it, take it out and relive it when I needed Drew, when I missed him. Because I was going to miss him.

Drew broke the silence by saying, "I think Nietzsche would have appreciated the irony of his end-of-life situation."

"What do you mean?"

"During his last years, he was completely reliant on the kindness and morality of his mother; then, after her death, his sister. In his professional life, he insisted that, at best, women were cows and that morality was an arbitrary construct of society. But it seems to me that women and morality showed him the truth in the end."

I smirked at this, mostly because I was surprised by his words, but also because the thought was sadistically satisfying. This touch of sadism irked me about myself.

Humans are at their worst when they're in the role of spectator. We eagerly watch as others receive comeuppance, yet we reject simple truths about ourselves even when the truths are gently administered.

I pushed these strange philosophical meanderings to the side, likely a sign that I'd been spending too much time in Drew's company, and asked him for clarification on his earlier statement. "Specifically what truth was he shown in the end?"

"Well, to a dying man, intellectualism, pride, and philosophy have as much use as sand." Drew felt closer, though I didn't hear or see him move; his voice dropped in volume and tenor when he added, "Our will is only as strong as our body; the desire for what we need will always trump ideals."

I shivered.

He continued, but he sounded distracted, like he was talking mostly to himself. The meditative, low timbre of his voice was hypnotic and paralyzing, and it made my heart beat faster.

"That's always the way of things, isn't it? In the end, our vision is clearest." I felt the heat of him at my back just before he brushed his knuckles from my shoulder to my wrist in a whisper light caress. "Without being impugned by ideals—of image, perception, ambition, good intentions, even honor—we gain the knowledge of what really matters, knowledge that would have saved us from...."

I could hear the hesitation in his voice, so I prompted, "Saved us from what?"

"From wasting time."

CHAPTER TWENTY-THREE

"For after all, the best thing one can do when it is raining is let it rain."

— HENRY WADSWORTH LONGFELLOW

THOUGHT I knew what I wanted. I thought I wanted to scorch and smolder and burn. I was so wrong.

My desire for Drew wasn't a fire. It was a rainstorm. More precisely, it was a rainstorm in the wilderness of the Great Smoky Mountains.

When desire is a flame, it ignites—bright and hot. It's exciting and sexy and physical. Fire is a danger to which we are drawn; we like to play with it to see if we can escape unsinged. You can see it, but you can never touch it. You can never get too close. It's about wanting. That's the fun, the allure, of fire.

But standing on that porch with Drew at my back—not touching me, not speaking—nothing about my desire for him felt fun, and it didn't feel sexy or exciting either.

Yes, I burned. Yes, the desire was physical, but it was so much more than a craving.

It hurt like a thirst.

"Drew, I don't...." I whispered, and I surprised myself because my voice wavered then cracked. I cried. I bowed my head and leaned on the railing of the porch. I wanted to say, *I don't want to waste any more time*, but my throat wouldn't work because I was drowning.

He must've heard the tears in my voice because his arms surrounded me at once, turning me so that I was against his chest.

"I'm sorry," he said, then he kept saying it. "I'm sorry, Ash. I'm so sorry."

I shook my head and pushed against him so that I could seek his mouth and quench this painful thirst. He released me immediately. His arms fell away as he stepped back to give me space I didn't want. He pulled a hand through his hair and looked miserable and dejected.

I couldn't yet speak, but I didn't want him to misinterpret my actions. I launched myself at him, my arms coming around his neck, my lips covering his—moving, working, pursuing, chasing—until he comprehended my intent.

He was stunned at first. I could tell because, though he was kissing me back, his hands lingered in a hovering touch on my hips, cursory and tentative.

Then his hands were on my body. His touch echoed, surrounded, felt layered and rich, comforting. He sought to soothe me, but I would have none of his softness. I wanted the storm. I needed a downpour.

I tugged off his suspenders and he helped me by working them over his shoulders. I pushed him, walking him backwards through the door, into the room, all the while frantically pulling at his clothes, untucking his shirt, unbuttoning his pants, unzipping him, reaching for him.

"Ash," he breathed, lifting his head and catching my wrist.

"I need you." I pulled my wrist from his grip and whipped off my shirt, pushed down my sleep pants and underwear and captured his mouth, launching another assault. "I need you. Please, I need you."

Drew was the rain. I needed his touch on every inch of my body, on every surface. I needed him to cover me, saturate, flood and fill.

My words and nakedness seemed to ignite a torrent within him because he grabbed me. His hands searching, moving, pursuing, and chasing.

My fingers were greedy for his skin, and I touched him. I needed the granite smoothness of his torso, back, and chest. I needed the solid curves of his bottom and thighs. I needed the silky hardness of his length. And when I gripped him he gasped in my mouth, shuddering, his fingers flexing and digging as though to anchor me to him, sink claws into my flesh to halt any escape.

He turned me and I fell, my back hitting the bed, and I watched him as he stripped off the remainder of his clothes, but I couldn't stop touching him. My hands frenetic as they sought to steal caresses.

He was naked when he joined me, and I had no time to delight in the sight of him because the thirst was building. It burned low in my belly and wrapped around my heart like a fist. I couldn't breathe because I was drowning in my own desire and need.

He kissed me while I grabbed him, stroked him, held his body in my hands, and tried to memorize every sensation. His mouth moved to my breast, and his tongue, hot and wet and covetous, sampled me, savoring.

He kissed a path to my stomach, his hands everywhere, and I knew his intent as he inched lower.

"No, no—stay with me." I reached for his hands, his arms, whatever I could grab. "Stay up here. I need you. I need you."

With Drew, it wasn't about the pleasure of the act. It was about being *with* him, becoming with him. I needed his heart next to mine, his mouth on my mouth.

"Ash," he came to me, hearing my name on his lips was torture. "Sugar, I have no condoms. I don't, I haven't-" I saw his throat work as he swallowed.

"I do." I nodded frantically. "I have them. I have condoms—in lots of different sizes."

He stared down at me, his eyes searching my face. "You have condoms?"

"Yes." I kissed his stunned mouth. "Don't—just don't ask." I pushed on his chest, jumped up from the bed, and flew to my bag, digging to the bottom of it. My hand found the vibrator first and I pushed it to the side. Then I found the packages of condoms, grabbed a handful, and returned to the bed.

I was already tearing into a package with my teeth when I returned to him, extracting the sheath and reaching for his shaft. His hands came up to help but I smacked them away, rolling the condom down the length of him, his perfect head, the straight silky shaft, yet almost despairing when I fully realized his largeness and length.

But then a miracle happened. Because it fit. It fit perfectly. Bless Sandra and her magnum sized condoms.

And hell, he was beautiful.

People may claim that talk of condoms or safe sex makes the act less spontaneous and erotic. Those people are wrong. Protection only ruins the mood when one partner isn't as committed to safety as the other is. Looking at Drew, laying on his back, hard and prepped and ready for me; his eyes echoing the intensity of my need, ready to fill me up and quench this crippling desire—there was nothing more erotic.

He reached for me and I straddled him before he had a chance to turn me. Drew sat up, grabbing my hips as I reached for his length. I brought him to my apex, lowered myself, and threw my head back as he filled me.

I gasped and he muttered a curse. His mouth found my breast, licking and sucking and biting; his fingers dug into my hips, then my ribs, then my bottom, wild and needy. I stilled, adjusting to the invasion that I'd initiated, then sunk lower, taking the entire length.

He cursed again, exhaling the words like he couldn't grasp what was happening, and his mind fought for sanity in the face of insane desire. I lifted myself, then lowered, then rocked, my hands on his shoulders, our bodies rubbing together in a mutual caress.

Drew was the constant gentle rolling thunder, the soft kind that is felt in the chest and subtly shakes the ground.

Our breathing quickened. Despite the chilliness of the night, our bodies were hot and slick, my movements fumbling, rapacious, and clumsy.

I recognized the moment his mind finally comprehended and accepted what we were doing, felt it the second he took the reins. He overtook my maladroit lead, assuming control and setting the rhythm. His hands were guiding instead of searching, and he moved me how he liked, how he knew would bring me the most pleasure and the most contact. He knew what I needed, how I needed him.

He taught me that you don't dance in the fire; you dance in the rain.

I willingly surrendered. Where he led, I followed. Where he pushed, I ceded. The rain became torrential, a rising tide, a claiming swell, a violent thing.

"Ashley, look at me," he growled.

I gave him my eyes and we clashed, silver against blue. The sounds I made were silent to my ears, but I couldn't hold them within as I surrendered to this galvanized euphoria. My release came like a flash, a strobe, and it stayed, claiming me again and again. It blinded me to everything but him and his climax, the ecstasy he found in me and my body.

Drew was the lightning, harsh and painful and wonderful. Overwhelming bursts of piercing brightness, frightening and beautiful in his intensity.

I'd thought of him as grace in motion, but I was wrong.

Drew was poetry in motion. Like his words, his lovemaking was a weapon.

The rain, like the flame, is dangerous. But you don't realize its power until it's too late.

THE SECOND TIME we made love was just before sunrise.

I'd fallen into a deep sleep, naked and wrapped in his limbs.

He woke me with tender kisses on my neck, his skillful fingers between my legs. I turned to him, my arms open, and pulled him to me.

The pace and rhythm were slower, measured, and set entirely by Drew. It reminded me again of a tango, artfully choreographed like he'd been planning the steps. The kisses and touches were gentle, worshipful, prolonged. It was a spring rain, bringing life to new blossoms.

My release was intense but sweet and sustaining, like honey. And I drifted back to sleep, feeling satiated in the moment.

I awoke with a start some time later.

I was alone. I was naked. I was warm. And where Drew had slept was also warm, a clue that he'd just recently left the bed.

I sat up, automatically bringing the sheet with me, and glanced around the room. Red and purple maples tapped against the window, the sun was bright, but not terribly high in the sky. The sleep fog receded, and reality—both good and bad and confusing—didn't come crashing down.

Rather, reality arrived via swift, wonky UFO. My life was served to me on a bizarre platter that I didn't recognize. My mother was gone; today was her funeral. Drew and I had made love together twice last night; tomorrow I would say goodbye to my brothers and fly back to Chicago.

Tomorrow I would leave Drew.

The door to my room was closed; even so, I heard voices on the other side coming from someplace in the house. I dressed quickly in my hastily discarded clothes from the night before and walked to the door.

My hand hovered over the handle, but I didn't touch it. Instead, I stared at the wall and let the weight of my decisions settle on my shoulders. I nearly lost my breath.

I didn't know what I was doing. Drew had left me again with no map. But that was my fault, because I was a big girl and knew how to work a GPS. I shouldn't have relied on him to be my compass.

Gathering my courage and my resolve to plot my own course, I opened the door and, having never found myself in this kind of situation before, I walked as naturally as possible down the hall.

The voices grew louder as I approached the kitchen, and I recognized them at once. My brothers were here—all six of them.

I peeked around the corner and my suspicions proved true. All six of my brothers were there, plus Drew, plus Alex and Sandra.

Alex saw me first. He was about to wave, but I shook my head frantically and withdrew further into the hallway. I didn't know how to do this. I didn't know how to walk in there and act natural.

Drew had a history of announcing things before discussing them with me, like how he'd told Beau that his feelings for me were not sisterly. Therefore, I worried that he would immediately tell the room that we'd consummated our relationship. Also, I worried that he *wouldn't* tell the whole room that we'd consummated our relationship.

What if he was having regrets? What if our night together didn't mean to him what it meant to me?

And, by the way, since I was thinking on the matter, what did our night together mean to me? What was my opinion?

The vital point being, I was freaked out and flustered and over-wrought and emotional, and wished my GPS wasn't on the fritz.

I heard footsteps approach so I turned and prepared to flee into the bathroom, but a hand caught my arm and turned me around.

"Ashley, what's wrong? Are you okay?" Upon seeing Alex, I breathed a huge sigh of relief. He was the most benign of all potential males currently inhabiting the house.

I pressed my finger to my lips and motioned for him to follow, pulling him into the library and shutting the door.

I should admit that Alex was striking in that he looked like a dangerous, sexy hooligan; tall with a swimmer's build, dark blue eyes that were sometimes violet, jet black hair, and a ragged scar that ran from his chin to his neck. He was also five years younger than me and almost eight years younger than his wife, my good friend Sandra.

Oh, and his voice melted butter. Seriously.

"Hey...." His eyes narrowed on me. "Is everything okay? Other than the obvious."

Oh, and he often lacked customary social skills like appropriate displays of sympathy and/or empathy.

I nodded, releasing a breath. "Yeah, I guess so...when did you all get here?"

"Just a few minutes ago. I stayed with your brothers last night at the house. You now have free access to that streaming video website you like. Also, the NSA's black ops fund has made a contribution to National Cervical Cancer Coalition in the name of your mother."

Oh, and he was a genius.

My eyebrows lifted, "Alex. Don't do that. That's stealing."

"Which part?"

"All of it."

"Fine." He frowned, looking annoyed. "Why are we hiding in here?"

"We're not hiding. I just—I'm just not ready to face everyone."

His frown flattened as he studied me. "Why?"

I ignored his question. This could go on all day. "Why is everyone here? I thought the plan was to meet at the house."

He shrugged, stuffing his hands in his pockets. "Something about your crazy dad. He came by last night. I don't think your brother wants him to follow the funeral procession. By the way, do you want me to ruin his credit score? I could erase him from the central databases."

"No. He ruined his own credit score years ago, and there's a high possibility he's wanted for some crime some place. Best to leave him in the central databases. So, uh," I glanced over Alex's shoulder, "Is Drew out there?"

"Yeah." Alex looked thoughtful for a moment. "Do you think he'll take me fishing? I've never been fishing."

I squinted at him and his randomness. "Fishing?"

"Yeah. Maybe Sandra and I could come back with you when you visit. Drew is good people, and he seems like he'd be really good at fishing. We couldn't fish today, obviously; we don't have time. He mentioned about you coming back with us today. It'll be nice to have you back. You're better at chess than Nico."

My body froze like I'd been doused with ice water, but my eyes immediately cut back to Alex. "What?"

"You know, Quinn's plane. We all flew down together. You're coming back with us."

I stared into Alex's violet eyes for a beat, hoping that I'd misunderstood him. "To Chicago?"

He narrowed his gaze on me. "Yes…to Chicago. Where else would we be going?"

"Today?"

He nodded, stuffing his hands in his pockets. "That's right. Drew and Quinn arranged it all."

I exhaled and felt like my heart left my body with the breath. "Drew did? Drew arranged it?"

Alex *tsked.* "Yeah. Like I said, it was Drew's idea."

I glared at Alex, but I didn't really see him.

It was Drew's idea. Drew wanted me to leave today. I was leaving for Chicago today, and it was Drew's idea.

The door to the library opened and I sucked in a startled breath. Luckily, it was just Jethro.

"Ash, there you are. How're you doing? We brought food, and Drew put on some coffee." Jethro crossed to me and gave me a quick hug. "Hey, Alex."

Alex gave Jethro a little wave. "Hi, Jethro."

"You need to go get ready," Jethro said to me, and he pushed me out the door, down the hall, and into the bathroom. "You'll ride with me for the funeral. We need to leave in the next half hour because you know it takes forty-five minutes to get into town from here. Reverend Seymour is expecting us, and I left my suit at the church."

Then he abruptly closed the door, leaving me alone with my mixed-up, broken-hearted thoughts as company.

CHAPTER TWENTY-FOUR

"We are afraid to care too much for fear that the other person does not care at all."

— ELEANOR ROOSEVELT

I HURRIED THROUGH my shower. This was because I needed to see and talk to Drew, and I needed to do it as soon as possible or else I was going to lose my mind.

When I was drying off, Sandra knocked on the door then handed me my underthings and a black dress. I dried my hair, dressed quickly, applied minimal makeup—no mascara—and rushed to the kitchen only to find that Drew was taking a shower in the other bathroom.

Sandra pushed a cup of coffee into my hands and two Danish pastries wrapped in a napkin. "Eat this. Drink this."

I nodded, glancing past her toward the hallway and Drew's door. I was struck by the realization that I'd never seen his bedroom. We'd only ever slept in my room, the guest room.

I handed the pastry and coffee back to Sandra, not looking at her as I walked past and said, "Hold this for me a sec, would you?"

"Uh, yeah. Sure. But you have five minutes," she called after me.

I gave her a thumbs-up. When I arrived at Drew's door, I hesitated in front of it—caught between wanting to barge in and knowing that knocking was the right choice.

Eventually I knocked. He didn't respond.

"Drew?" I asked, not liking that my voice was higher pitched than I'd intended. I cleared my throat. "Drew, can I talk to you?"

I listened to him walking around, a drawer opening and closing. "Yeah, give me a minute."

More walking. More drawers opening and closing.

Then I heard him coming closer to the door. I placed my hands on my hips then crossed my arms over my chest. I couldn't figure out what to do with my limbs.

He opened the door about four inches, just enough for me to see his eyes, that he was shirtless, and that he wore a towel around his waist.

"Drew, can I—can we talk for a minute?"

His eyes darted over my shoulder, then back to my face. He didn't respond, but he looked troubled.

I felt a little stab of pain in my chest and a rising heat over my neck. I released a slow breath, trying to reason my way through this and not jump to conclusions that were unflattering to us both. But it was hard not to. Jumping to unflattering conclusions was in my genetic makeup.

"Drew…." I licked my lips, swallowed. "I really need to talk to you."

His eyes moved between mine, then he stepped away from the entrance and opened the door wider so I could enter. He glanced around his room like he was searching for something.

"Drew, I…."

I didn't know where to start. A sudden and uncomfortable distance had grown between us; it had happened sometime after he'd made love to me this morning. I wanted to talk about last night. I wanted to ask why he'd arranged for me to leave today. I wanted to ask him if I was the only one who was feeling like I'd been caught in a rainstorm naked.

"What is it?" He stood apart from me, his back stiff and straight like he was bracing himself. His usually vibrant eyes were cool, guarded.

"Did you arrange with Quinn for me to leave today?"

"Yes."

I stared at him, hoping he would continue with some explanation. When he didn't, I blinked several times (because blinking was my default when I was confused and flustered).

I didn't know what else to say.

Perhaps if I'd been in my right mind; perhaps if it weren't the morning of my mother's funeral; perhaps if every single one of my previous experiences with physical intimacy hadn't ended with me being discarded, I might have asked him for an explanation.

But I didn't.

I didn't have the energy.

I pressed my lips together, nodded slowly, and pretended. "I see. Well, thanks. That makes things a lot easier. I guess I should pack."

"Sandra already did that," he said, his face and his tone expressionless.

"What?"

"Sandra, she already packed your stuff." Drew tightened the towel around his waist.

I nodded again and removed my eyes from him, not wanting to see him. Instead, I glanced around his room, not really noticing much. The bed was bigger than mine. His leather notebook was on his bedside table. He had no pictures anywhere.

I inhaled a steadying breath, turned, and walked to the door, mumbling, "Jethro is probably going to give me the stink eye if I make him late."

I was out the door, down the hall, and outside the house before I started to cry. I wasn't watching where I was going, and I nearly collided with Sandra. She was still holding my coffee and pastry.

♥ ♥ ♥

MOMMA'S FUNERAL WAS an exercise of going through the motions for the sake of going through the motions. I've never been a fan of funerals for more than the obvious reasons. Of the emotions, mourning in particular feels like something that should be sacred and intensely private.

The entire town showed up at the church. My brothers and I sat in the front pew, and I couldn't help but feel like I was on display.

Regardless, other than having to share my grief with a few hundred people, it was a lovely service.

I didn't cry until Mrs. Beverton, the choir director, sang the second verse of "Amazing Grace." I feel like it's compulsory to play "Amazing Grace" during a Christian funeral. It's the only way to make sure everyone leaves sobbing like a baby.

Billy put his arm around me and held me close; my other brothers and Drew were the pallbearers. Drew stood out from the rest as the tallest, and he was the only blond one in the bunch. All I saw was the back of his head as they carried the casket to the hearse. All I felt was empty.

Billy and I were swarmed on our way out and spent as much time as we could listening to people recount stories of my mother's kindness. Eventually we had to break from the crowd and drive to the cemetery in order to make it in time for the burial.

Upon arriving, we were ushered to a tent set up next to the burial site. Billy and I took the last two chairs in the front row next to Jethro and Cletus. Drew and my younger three brothers were in the second row behind us, but Drew was on the far side, four seats from where I was seated.

I told myself I didn't care, and I think I believed it, mostly because I was burying my mother. Drew, me, us—it didn't really matter. I was having one of those *nothing matters because we're all going to die anyway* moments.

I watched with some fascination as they lowered Momma's casket into the ground after a few prayers.

Reverend Seymour then expected us all to place a handful of dirt on top. I refrained.

When it was over, I glanced over my shoulder and saw my friends and their husbands standing at the back of the tent, all in black dresses and suits. Drew was talking to Quinn and Fiona. The three of them seemed to be in deep conversation. My attention moved over the rest of the group, and I caught Marie waving and blowing me a little kiss. I gave her a grateful smile.

I also noticed that two of Momma's hospice nurses were present, Marissa and Joe. They were standing together, holding hands, and both gave me gentle smiles as our eyes met. I suddenly realized that neither Roscoe nor Billy had ever been in the running for Marissa's affections, and I wondered how I could have been so blind to what was happing around me over the last six weeks.

What else had I missed? What else had I not seen?

As the crowd departed for the reception, several of Momma's friends from the library started blowing bubbles over the gravesite.

"Naomi Winters is a wiccan, I think." Billy leaned close and whispered this information in my ear.

"What do bubbles have to do with being a wiccan?"

He shrugged and shook his head. "I honestly don't know, but if it bothers you…"

"No. It's fine."

Billy and I stayed behind from the crowd, let the cars clear out, and watched the ladies blow their bubbles. I glanced at his usually serious face and found his mouth curved upwards in a half smile.

Unprompted, he said, "Do you remember when we were kids and we had that bubble machine?"

I nodded, immediately recalling the memory. "You and Cletus put it up in a tree and told me the bubbles were fairies."

He grinned, his eyes losing focus. "You were so cute. I think you actually believed in fairies and unicorns and all that stuff."

"I used to." I nodded, remembering fleetingly how it felt to believe in magic.

"I think when you left, you took that with you," Billy said unexpectedly.

I glanced at him again, searching his face. I didn't want to tell him that when I left, I'd buried that part of myself, much like we'd just buried our mother.

"You're a good woman, Ash. You deserve happiness, unicorns, rainbows, and bubble fairies. Don't settle for less."

I swallowed and smiled at my brother; when I managed to respond, my voice was rough and uneven, "Thanks, Billy. You too."

Of the seven kids, he was definitely the toughest. But I suspected he also felt things the most deeply.

♥ ♥ ♥

THE RECEPTION WAS held at the library, and that's when Darrell showed up.

Really, we were lucky. He could have crashed the service, making the entire day unpleasant. For him, it was quite thoughtful to wait until the end of the day's events to make a scene and attempt a kidnapping.

Unluckily for Billy and me, we were his targets.

Billy pulled into the library parking lot, which was so full we had to park on the grass. I was just getting out of the car, straightening my dress before walking in with Billy when I felt a hand grab my wrist and yank me off my feet. I would have fallen except my father wrapped his arm around my waist, half lifting me.

I gasped then screamed. He slapped me hard across the face twice, and my cheek hurt like a bee sting radiating outwards, down my jaw, around my eye.

"Shut your mouth, girl. You do not scream at your daddy." He shook me roughly, tossed me against the car, then grabbed me again.

In my peripheral vision, I saw Billy run around the car and charge my father. Unfortunately, my father wasn't alone. Two very large bikers reached Billy before Billy could reach me. One punched him in the gut and the other hit him over the head with a metal pipe of some sort. He crumpled, falling face first into the grass. He didn't have a chance.

Fear for my brother spurred me into action. I struggled in my father's grip and managed to stomp his foot and elbow him in the ribs.

His hold loosened just enough for me to head-butt him; the impact of my crown hitting his nose gave a satisfying crunch. I hoped I broke his nose, because my head hurt like a futher mucker.

He released me at once, his hands coming up to his face. I screamed long and loud as I debated what to do next.

Should I run to Billy? No. The bikers were between me and my brother. That effort would be futile.

Should I look for a weapon? No. I was on the edge of a library parking lot, not in a ninja locker room.

Should I try to make a break for the library? Yes. Because Darrell was the only one between me and the building, and Darrell was busy cussing and screaming about his nose.

Just for good measure, I kicked him in the shin with my pointy black flats as I ran past. I was aiming for his balls, but chickened out at the last minute.

I heard the bikers shout behind me, but I didn't spare a glance to see if they were in pursuit. I sprinted around a large bush and began to cross the throughway separating the parking lot from the library when I was nearly run over by a car.

The car swerved to keep from hitting me, and it missed by itches. It was a police cruiser, and sitting inside was Jackson James. He was staring at me like I'd beamed down from space.

I ran to the driver's side door and nearly tackled him when he opened it.

"Jackson, I need your help, I need your help."

"Ashley, slow down, slow down. What happened to your face?"

"Forget about my face, you need to come with me." I tugged on his sleeve, trying to get him to move to where Darrell and his biker buddies were doing God knows what to my brother.

Jackson dug in his heels and placed gentle hands on my shoulders. "Calm down, I know you just came from the funeral and you got to be real upset, but you shouldn't just run in front of cars—"

I growled, "To hell with this!" and reached for his sidearm.

That's right, I took his gun.

That must've shocked the poo out of him because I was already around the hood of his car and beyond the bush when I heard him shout, "Ashley Winston! Did you just take my gun?!"

I had no idea if he followed.

I jogged back to where Billy's car was parked and found the two bikers loading my brother into his trunk; my daddy was leaning against the side of the car holding his nose, his head tipped back.

I flicked off the safety and pointed the gun at the bikers. "Do not touch him," I said with steel in my voice.

The bikers, who looked like any of the other bikers I'd ever seen growing up—old, dirty, sweaty, unshaven but without a beard, big belly, covered in leather—stilled, their widened eyes moving between me and the gun I held.

At the sound of my voice, my father glanced up. Peripherally I saw him hold one hand out to me, palm up, as though beseeching me.

"Now, Ashley, baby girl, you need to give me that gun."

The bikers hadn't moved from where they stood on either side of the trunk, Billy's incapacitated form half in, half out of the car. They were staring at me and seemed to be sizing me up.

My father moved like he was going to take a step in my direction. On instinct, I lowered the gun to the tallest biker's knee, aimed, and fired.

He fell to the ground, clutching his thigh. I'd aimed too high.

At the very least, I hoped the gunshot would get someone's attention. We were in the parking lot of a library, for hootenanny's sake! Shouldn't someone have come around by now? Didn't people read books? And where was everyone from the burial site? The parking lot was basically filled with cars. Wasn't anyone done checking out his books and heading to the parking lot by now?

"Holy shit!" The shorter of the bikers exclaimed. To shut him up, I lifted the gun and pointed it at him.

"You will step away from my brother or I will make you a eunuch."

He nodded, his hands held up in surrender. "Sure thing, sweetie."

"Don't call me sweetie!"

"Fine, fine. Just let me get my brother here and we'll get out of your way." The shorter biker shuffled to his fallen compatriot, who was cussing and hollering on the ground.

I watched them both with narrowed eyes, looking for any sudden movements.

"What the hell is going on?" I heard Jackson's exclamation paired with the pounding of his footsteps on the pavement. Obviously, he hadn't come after me until he heard the gunshot. He was maybe the worst police officer in the history of ever.

I didn't take my eyes off the bikers. "Jackson, you remember my father, Darrell? Well, he and his friends just jumped Billy and me, and as you can see, they've loaded Billy into the trunk of his car, and I think they were trying to make off with both of us."

My father's ability to speak smoothly was inhibited by his broken nose. "Now, that's not true. I came by to pay my respects, and Billy, he…."

"Billy knocked himself out and landed in the trunk?" Jackson asked, his voice laced with sarcasm. Jackson might have been a terribly derelict police officer, but he did know my family history. He used the radio on his shoulder to call for backup, and I could feel his eyes on me. I found it curious that he hadn't yet tried to take the gun out of my hands.

When he finished calling in the situation on his radio, he took a pair of handcuffs from his belt and said, "Cover me," as he walked by.

He then walked straight to my father and began reading him his rights. The shorter biker was next, then the taller one. Of the three, Darrell complained the loudest and barked something about police brutality.

Jackson was slapping cuffs on the man I'd shot when I heard the sounds of people approaching by foot. My eyes flickered to the side and I did a double take, almost dropping the gun. Relief flowed through me quick and warm.

Jethro was at the front and broke into a run when he saw me. Drew, Quinn, and Duane were close behind.

"Ashley, what's going on? What are you doing?" Jethro slowed as he neared, his eyes bouncing around the scene like a Ping-Pong ball.

Quinn withdrew a gun from the back of his suit pants, nodded to me, and announced his presence to Jackson.

Drew, however, walked straight to me—never slowing, holding my eyes the entire time—and slipped his hand over mine, fluidly taking the weapon from my grip. He flicked the safety on with his thumb and wrapped an arm around my waist.

"Are you okay?" His free hand moved over my body as though searching for injury.

I nodded, looking up at him. "Yeah…I'm okay."

He placed one hand on my chin and turned my face, his eyes shooting fire, his jaw clenching as he looked at my cheek and eye. "You're going to have a black eye."

I blinked at him and realized he was probably correct. My right eye must have been very swollen, because I was already having trouble seeing out of it.

"We heard a gunshot," Quinn explained. "Who fired? Who was shot?"

Jackson spoke before I could. "I fired. I shot this one," he pointed to the biker with the toe of his boot. "I handed the gun off to Ashley to provide cover so I could get the three of them sorted."

"Which one of them hurt you?" Drew asked through gritted teeth.

I studied him through my one good eye. "Does it matter?"

"It matters to me."

My next words echoed what I'd been thinking all day and emerged from my mouth before I knew I was going to say them. "Why? I'm not your problem anymore."

Drew flinched, his hand falling from my face, and he leaned back as though I'd pushed him away.

"What's wrong with Billy?" Duane was at the trunk of the car, leaning over his brother.

I stepped away from Drew and immediately missed the brief oasis of comfort he'd offered, comfort which I stupidly took even though he never needed or expected anything from me in return. I crossed to Billy to see what could be done for him before the ambulance arrived.

Jackson walked to Drew; in my peripheral vision, I saw him hold his hand out as he said, "You can give me my gun back now."

"Hey," Duane was standing next to me. "What happened to you?"

"I got hurt." My fingers were on the back of Billy's head, probing for signs of bleeding; I responded without turning. "But, don't worry, I'll recover."

CHAPTER TWENTY-FIVE

"I have learned that to be with those I like is enough."

— WALT WHITMAN

*T*IME HEALS ALL wounds. Time is of the essence. Time is short. Time is on my side.

Lies. All lies.

Time is the enemy. Time was playing for the other team. Timed stretched like an endless desert. The only thing time does is stagger along like a drunk sailor and give you wrinkles. And syphilis.

Summer begot fall, fall begot winter, and winter begot seven thousand feet of snow in Chicago—give or take six thousand, nine hundred, and ninety feet. And it was only the last week of November.

Luckily for me, it was my turn to host knit night, and I had the next day off work. This meant that once I arrived home, I didn't have to venture out into the howling wind and driving snow for thirty-six hours. I could get dressed in my thermal PJs and get drunk.

But I wouldn't get drunk. I didn't like how I felt when I got drunk, how I lost control when I imbibed beyond reason. I'd done it once since returning from Tennessee and had to be physically restrained from drunk-dialing Drew.

It hadn't been pretty. While I was intoxicated, I spilled the entire story; my friends provided seven shoulders to cry upon.

Sandra, Nico, and Fiona were huge Drew advocates at first. They didn't exactly pressure me, but they did take every opportunity to subtly hint that I should contact him and be honest about my feelings.

I couldn't. I kept picturing his face, gently letting me down. When I played the scene in my head, I was that poor girl Jennifer I'd heard the women murmuring about at the jam session, all gussied up in my yellow dress and wielding a banana cake to a man who could probably out-bake anyone he knew. He would tell me how beautiful I was—pretty face, nice piece of ass, trashy accent—but that he didn't need anything from me.

He'd been honest from the start about not needing me. I couldn't fault him for that.

Once the three of them realized that the only thing accomplished by their subtle hints was my silence and a growing rift between us, they stopped pushing.

Now we—my knitting group and I—collectively called him Dr. Ruinous. Note the addition of the 'i'. Sandra thought of the nickname. I think it was her peace offering, a way to show me that she was on my side.

Still, I rarely discussed him. Instead, I marinated quietly in my hurt feelings. When my friends brought up my unusual silence during our knit nights, I attributed it to the lingering grief caused by my mother's sickness and death, which was true to a great extent.

I missed her every day, and I didn't know how to mourn openly and loudly.

Therefore, I escaped in books, but I avoided reading romance novels. I didn't need to read any happily-ever-afters. Instead, I settled into the contentment of just being with the people I liked.

When I arrived home from work Tuesday night, Kat was already there. She'd never returned the key to my apartment, and I'd never asked for it back.

"Hey!" she called from the kitchen. "I hope you don't mind, I stopped off and picked up wonton soup and eggrolls for the gang. I'm using your one pot to keep it warm."

I couldn't help my smirk. "I have more than one pot."

"No, you don't. You literally have one pot. By the way, I grabbed your mail. It's on the coffee table. You got a package."

"A package, eh?" I was intrigued; my momma used to send me packages with some frequency before her death. I had no second source of packages other than Amazon Prime.

I stripped off my winter gear—boots, hat, gloves, scarf, second scarf, outer jacket, inner jacket, a third scarf, sweater—and strolled over to the coffee table, leaving my wool socks on. The package was really a large, padded envelope; it had no return address and the postmark indicated that it had been sent from Franklin, North Carolina.

I didn't know anyone in North Carolina. At least, I didn't remember knowing anyone in Franklin, North Carolina.

I gathered a deep breath and set to opening the package, but was interrupted by the external intercom. Tucking the envelope under my arm, I jogged to the speaker and pressed the button.

"Who is it?"

"Let us in! We're freezing our tits off." Sandra's voice was distorted and clouded in static.

"Okay, let me hit the buzzer," I replied. I pressed the button and added, "I'll leave the door unlocked so you can come on in when you get up here."

I walked into the kitchen to check out the soup. Kat must've gone to General Tso's. They put baby bok choy in their wonton soup and use both shrimp and pork.

"Mmm, that smells good."

"I know you like General Tso's soup." She gave me a shy smile—most of Kat's smiles were shy—and pulled out a bottle of plum wine. "And I picked this up."

"Oh, nice. I'll open it." I placed the unopened package on the kitchen counter and searched for the bottle opener.

Kat and I had been talking recently about sharing an apartment to save on rent. After Christmas, we planned to finalize the details. Originally, I'd wanted to go to Tennessee for the holiday, but as the date approached, I was seriously considering staying in town and picking up extra shifts, which was typically very lucrative. Plus, I didn't particularly like the idea of being in my mother's house without her in it. As well, the Dr. Ruinous issue was an ever present dung beetle in my pie.

However, I really missed my brothers. The thought of spending Christmas without them felt unacceptable. I wondered if I could talk them into meeting me halfway between Chicago and Green Valley, or maybe just an hour or two from the homestead.

I heard the door swing open followed by Elizabeth's shout, "It's us: Janie, Sandra, Nico, and me."

"Quinn and Alex might be by later," Janie announced.

"It is colder than Satan's balls out there!" Sandra's voice bellowed from the hallway. Kat and I shared a smile and I rolled my eyes.

"Well, come in then, and take off your clothes," I called back.

"I can't. Nicoletta is with us."

"Don't let me stop you." Nico's teasing tone made me laugh.

"It's not you, Nico." I heard Janie's voice respond from beyond the kitchen. "It's Alex and Quinn. The last time they dropped by knit night unexpectedly and we were having a panty dance party, it took me twenty six days of constant physical intimacy before he started to relax again."

Nico chuckled. "Because it was a coed party?"

"Honestly, no. I don't think he was jealous...." Janie walked into the kitchen, pausing to give Kat then me a hug.

"What was it then?" I asked her, curious.

Janie pressed her lips together, her eyes growing wide as she stared at me for a long moment. Abruptly, she leaned forward and whispered in my ear, "I think it turned him on."

I barked a laugh and covered my mouth. "Oh, my God. By all means, we should all keep our clothes on."

Sandra burst into the room, still removing layers of clothing. "Yeah, it's not a good idea. Alex couldn't keep his hands off me for months after. It's like I was Alex-catnip."

I couldn't help but smile at Sandra. Where Janie whispered intimate information, Sandra just put it all out there. It struck me that they were a perfect yin and yang. Janie was overly verbose about trivial information and made strangers uncomfortable with her random factoids, whereas Sandra was unsurpassed in social settings; she knew exactly what to say and when to say it—when she set her mind to it.

With her friends, Sandra was the queen of personal TMI, whereas Janie never spoke of personal issues unless pushed or prodded.

"What smells good?" Nico hovered in the doorway to the kitchen, eyes twinkly, eyebrow raised, boyish grin in place.

It took me months to get used to Nico, maybe even a year. I definitely had a little—and very benign—crush on him. In fact, I was pretty certain we all did. Never mind the fact that he was a celebrity, he had dangerously unnatural levels of charisma. It was like having a crush on a nebula or a painting; you just wanted to look at him.

Over time, however, the sensation and feelings became similar to the girl-crushes I had on the rest of the knitting ladies. I admired him, enjoyed his company, and wished him happiness in all things.

"Kat picked up wonton soup and egg rolls for dinner," I explained.

"Hey, thanks, Kat!" The group echoed this grateful sentiment, and Kat ducked her head, her cheeks turning pink. Since she and I had started spending more time together, I'd noticed that she did not accept praise or compliments very well. I would have to start saturating her with comments about how awesome she was.

"It's no big deal." She waved away their gratitude.

"Hey, Ashley, what's this?" Sandra strolled into the already crowded kitchen and picked up the package I'd left on the counter.

I pulled several wine glasses from the cabinet. "Oh, I don't know. It just came."

"Can I open it?" She asked. "You know how I love to open other people's mail—so annoying that it's a felony."

I shrugged. "Sure."

She began ripping into the package while I filled the goblets with plum wine.

"I need some advice," Janie announced. She was leaning against the kitchen table, her arms folded, her pretty face marred by a pensive frown.

"What's up, buttercup?" Elizabeth squeezed into the kitchen and grabbed the bowls from the counter to set the table.

"I don't know what to get Quinn for Christmas."

"You—in a bow." Nico said this deadpan. "Maybe forget the bow."

"No—I mean, I have it narrowed down to two things. I need help deciding between the two."

"What are they?" Sandra asked as she pulled a rectangular bundle wrapped in newspaper from the envelope. "Why don't you make him something?"

"Well, I already crocheted him that hat and scarf. So, that's done."

"And it's black and very dark gray, so you know he'll love it." Elizabeth said this with some sarcasm. We had a running joke that Quinn was actually Batman.

Janie nodded, both because she agreed and because she got the joke. "But the other two things are a little complicated. I can either fly his parents out for Christmas, or I think I can get his sister to come."

"But not both." Kat stated this, her voice warm with sympathy and understanding.

Janie sighed. "His parents would be fine with seeing his sister, but I think Shelly wouldn't come if his parents were there. She still has…issues."

I listened to the conversation with interest because it mirrored my situation. I wanted to see my brothers for Christmas, but I didn't want to face Drew. Whether I liked it or not, my brothers considered him a part of the family. Actually, he *was* a part of the family—especially after all he'd done for us, for my mother, for me.

Hearing Janie struggle with the situation made me realize how selfish I'd been about the whole thing. I didn't want my brothers to choose between us. I wasn't that person. My momma raised me to be better. I would just have to find a way to need nothing from Drew like he needed nothing from me.

I cleared my throat, prepared to tell Janie that she should invite both of them—Quinn's sister Shelly and his parents—but then Sandra gasped.

I was mid pour, so I gave her a cursory glance. "What is it?"

"Oh!" Elizabeth's startled exclamation came next.

At this, I set the bottle down and crossed to where Sandra held the contents of the envelope, but Elizabeth was blocking my view.

"What is it?" I asked again, insinuating myself between them so I could see what the fuss was about.

Then I saw it.

"Oh…." I exhaled, my eyes moving over the object in Sandra's hands.

It was Drew's leather notebook; the one he carried around in his pocket, always seemed to be writing in, and was never without. I immediately recognized the Norse symbols on the front. But it was singed; the cover was burnt as were several of the pages. The edges were black and brittle, but—other than the scarred cover—it was mostly intact.

Sandra held it out to me, her eyes wide. "Drew sent this to you?"

I shook my head, not taking the notebook. "I—I don't know."

I couldn't believe my eyes. I wanted to be irritated or ambivalent, but I wasn't.

Elizabeth put her hands on her hips. "Is he okay? Why is this burnt?" Picking up the envelope and giving it a closer inspection, she added, "The postmark is from Franklin, North Carolina. Did he move there?"

I shrugged, lifting my hands palms up, my eyes glued to the notebook. "I don't know. I have no idea. I haven't talked to him since Momma's funeral."

The last words I'd said to him were *I'm not your problem anymore.*

I couldn't get over Drew until I started disliking him. I wasn't going to be able to forgive and forget. This wasn't going to be one of those relationships where we could be friends. He'd cut too deep with his good intentions, not to mention our brief interludes of perfect physical chemistry.

Anger was essential because otherwise I was just tremendously sad. Bitterness and anger provided harvestable energy, something on which to focus, something through which to work. Sadness simply left me adrift.

But now, dread gripped my chest as I studied the book; my stomach coiled into a knot at the sight of the charred cover. This book had been in a fire.

I rubbed my fingers over my chest because my heart felt like it was going to jump out of my ribs. Without accepting the notebook, I rushed out of the kitchen and ran to my cell phone. I hesitated for a minute then decided to call Jethro just in case Drew was alive and well and I was overreacting.

His phone went straight to voicemail. I called twice more. Both times it went straight to voicemail.

Then I called Drew. His went straight to voicemail.

Then I called Billy. He picked up on the third ring.

"Hey, Ash. What's up?" I knew he was still at work because I could hear the telltale sounds of saws in the background.

"Billy! I tried calling Jethro and Drew. Neither of them picked up. Are they…is everything okay?"

"Uh, yeah, as far as I know. They're in North Carolina on that Appalachian trek for two weeks. Jethro will be back Friday. They turn off their phones because there's no service where they are, but they have the satellite phone with them for emergencies. It's probably off to save battery life."

North Carolina.

"They're together?"

"Yep. Why?"

"When is the last time you spoke to either of them?'

"Uh, this morning. Hey, are you still coming for Christmas? Jethro said not to count you in this year."

I breathed a huge sigh of relief, the tension in my chest easing.

"Yes." I nodded, even though he couldn't see me. "Yes, of course I'm coming for Christmas. I said I'd be there. I'll be there."

For Billy, his response sounded almost chipper. "Oh. Good. Cletus is making moonshine eggnog."

"Ugh, that sounds gross." I laughed, my head hitting the wall as I closed my eyes. My brain was still coming down from its skyscraper of worry.

"Listen, I'll talk to you later. I have to get back to work. Did you want me to tell Jethro something?"

"No. It's nothing. They get back Friday?"

"Jethro gets back Friday, yes."

We said our goodbyes, and I glanced at the phone screen after hanging up, absorbing the information Billy had just related. I became aware of a presence at my elbow and glanced to my right. Everyone was hovering around me. Their expressions tense.

"So? Everything okay?" Elizabeth asked.

"Yes. Jethro and Dr. Ruin...*Drew*...are doing some trek in North Carolina. Their phones are off. Billy just talked to Jethro this morning."

"The envelope was sent before yesterday." Elizabeth held it up like it was evidence. "Whatever fire burned the book happened before yesterday, so Jethro and Drew must be fine."

"If either were injured, Billy would know."

Sandra held the notebook out to me. "Ashley, I think he must've sent this to you for a reason."

I glanced at the burnt book then met her green eyes, wide with earnest concern. I gathered a deep breath before responding.

"I don't...." I shook my head. "I don't know how to feel about that."

"Why don't you start by looking at it?" She held it out to me.

I didn't take it. The deep breath I'd taken felt insufficient, so I crossed to the couch and sat down.

Field notes. That's what Drew said was in the book.

Sandra followed and sat on the coffee table facing me. She took my right hand in one of hers and placed the book in it.

"He sent this to you. You don't have to read it, but it belongs to you now. You have to take it."

I nodded, holding but not looking at the book. I wasn't ready to speak, not yet; I didn't know my own thoughts. Sandra seemed to sense this because she stood abruptly and walked back to the kitchen.

"Where are Marie and Fiona?" I heard Elizabeth ask, and the subject was officially changed. My friends left me alone with Drew's burnt notebook.

I listened to their discussion from the other room, the sounds they made gathering around my table to eat. I loved their noises, their laughter. It felt like home, comfort, contentment, safety.

My emotions were a stampede of conflict as I looked at the notebook in my hands. I brushed my fingers over the brittle, charred leather.

It was covered in ash.

CHAPTER TWENTY-SIX

"If you read someone else's diary, you get what you deserve."

— DAVID SEDARIS

*I*T WAS 6:14 A.M. and I was awake.

In fact, I hadn't gone to sleep.

After my knitting group left, I paced the apartment, cleaning, straightening, turning the TV on, turning the TV off, trying to read *The Brothers Karamazov* and failing, though to be fair, I was only reading *The Brothers Karamazov* because I'm a bit of a masochist.

I tried to go to sleep, but I couldn't.

The notebook rested on the desk in my bedroom. It looked angry. Its presence felt like a rabid raccoon perched at the edge of the wilderness, ready to lunge forward and attack me until I succumbed to madness.

I realized in the wee morning hours that ignoring the notebook was futile.

Therefore, around 2:30 a.m., I surrendered to madness and opened it to a random page near the front. On the page was a poem.

For Ashley—

I expect man,
You are woman
Resplendent
Resilient
Refined
I turn
Before you see
The way
You affect me

It was lovely, simple, and sad. The next one I recognized, and it made me sigh, thinking back to the day I'd first heard it.

For Ashley—
Fire burns blue and hot.
Its fair light blinds me not.
Smell of smoke is satisfying, tastes nourishing to my tongue.
I think fire ageless, never old, and yet no longer young.
Morning coals are cool; daylight leaves me blind.
I love the fire most because of what it leaves behind

Then, I read another one, then another. Soon, an hour had passed and I was still reading. Some of the passages were poems; some were letters. I skipped over the ones that weren't addressed to me and was astonished to find that toward the center of the book all the poems and letters started with my name.

Ashley Austen Winston,
You don't know how deeply you cut when your intentions carry no knives.

Ash,
When you cried, I learned what helplessness tastes like. Because all I could do was swallow.

Ash,
I want to give you a book so I can watch you read it. Your lips

move. I watch them as I watch you. I want you to speak to me. I want
your lips to move for me.
   - Drew

For Ashley—
   You are my Sugar
   Sweet to taste, sweet to see
   Cravings last until
   Your body surrounds, comforts, and ignites
   Your skin velvet, your hair silk
   Your tongue honey

Ash,
   Your sheets, still a white pile on the table, know that envy keeps me
from washing them. You left an impression, deep creases where you lay
your head, where they cradled your body. It was only three days, but
they memorized your scent, they carry it even in their stillness.
   Were they too gentle? Was their touch too light? Do you remember
how it felt when they held you? Or did you never commit it to memory?
   Was I too gentle? Was my touch too light? Do you remember how it
felt when I held you? Or did you never commit it to memory?
   - Drew

Ashley,
   I caught a bear today in the new trap. We're taking it a hundred
miles north. That's a hundred miles closer to where you are. I've
decided units and measurements of distance are bullshit. With you
there are only two distances that matter:
   Here.
   Not here.
   You are not here.
   - Drew

. . .

Dear Ashley,

I've been reading your e. e. cummings. I hear your voice in my head when I read his words, and it's a peculiar kind of torture. I can't seem to stop doing it. I love your voice, even when it's a peculiar kind of torture. I miss you in a way that causes words to fail me. They are as inadequate and empty as I am.

I wonder, did you like your body when you were with my body? Do you carry my heart with you (in your heart)? He speaks of carving out places, but I didn't feel like I was given a choice. I removed nothing. I made no room for you.

Yet you arrived. I saw you. You spoke. That was it. I gave up nothing, but I lost everything.

- Drew

Sugar,

Tonight the silence sounds like a scream. If you were here, we could chase it away with our whispers.

- Drew

Ash,

I walked to our field today.
It was cold and the flowers are gone.
All color is absent.
Did you take them away when you left?
Why would you do that?
- Drew

For Ashley—
Your indifference feels like the end
Of a life without meaning

A life without being
Must eventually stop
Else the being
Loses its life

For Ashley—
If I told you I love you now
How many seconds would it take
How long would you allow
All that I am to break
I turn away
Before you can see
How badly I need you to stay
With me

And so I passed the next several hours sitting at my desk poring over Drew's field notes, reading them over and over. At first I tried to keep an emotional distance from the words, from his thoughts, from the depth of emotions he'd hidden so masterfully during our time together.

He might not have been good at playing make-believe, pretending, or lying, but he was damn good at hiding.

I cried a few times, smudging the skin under my eyes with soot from my fingers. The chair grew uncomfortable; I ignored the pain, strangely feeling like it was deserved.

In the end my soul was moved. There really was no other way to describe it. Reading Drew's thoughts was like being catapulted into the heavens against my will. He loved me, or so he'd written. He needed me, but he'd never said it. Never out loud.

I reflected on our time together, seeing things more clearly through this new lens of enlightenment, and—though he never said the words — realized that he'd shown me in a million different ways. With every look, embrace, and desperate need to shoulder my burdens, he was telling me that he loved me.

I flipped back to some of my favorites, the ones that made me feel like I might faint with overwhelming swoony joy. But as I re-read the passages, a balloon of doubt subtly worked its way into my consciousness, and tied to it were so many questions.

Why had he hidden himself from me? Why push me away? Why not fight for me? He wasn't a coward. He was the bravest man I knew. And why send it to me now? With no explanation, no letter, no nothing. And why in tarnation did it look like he'd tried to burn it?

Restlessness seized me. I needed to talk to him. I needed to see him, but I knew that wasn't possible. Seeing his words in black and white, ink on a page, written in his hand, made them feel real to me; maybe more real than if he'd said them out loud.

Spurred by this thought, I grabbed a pen and a piece of paper and began to write him a letter.

My Drew,

I love you. I love you desperately. I don't have your way with words. If I could, I would write you poetry. Instead, you'll have to settle for my haphazard thoughts and explanations for my behavior.

I am so sorry that I've been blind, that I didn't understand the extent of your feelings. I didn't see you clearly, and that's my fault.

When we were together, when we met, I admit that I was in a fog. I was blind to everything but my own grief and mourning my mother before her death. During those six weeks, I was focused on making every moment with her count. She was my mother and I loved her, I do love her, and I couldn't see beyond my own heartache and sorrow.

That's not an excuse. It's the truth.

Regardless, I feel like I'm one of those stupid, enviable romance novel heroines. The ones that have been hit with a vanilla ninny stick, devoid of personality and blind to the gift before them. I was doomed to wander in ignorance until the last thirty pages of the book.

Part of me is actively rooting against my own happy ending because the fictional hero deserves better than a girl who is blind to his love and devotion.

But this isn't a novel. I suck at interior design. I don't always use the tissue seat covers when they're available in public restrooms (sometimes I'm in a rush or I'm feeling lazy); but I always wash my hands.

I wake up with morning breath and frequently make poor fashion choices. I read too much, I eat too many cookies, and I have a yarn problem (meaning, I own more yarn than I could possibly knit into finished objects; there is NO WAY I'll use it all before I die, yet I'm still buying more yarn. I probably need an intervention). I also own only one pot.

I feel it's important that you know these things about me because I am flawed.

I jump to unflattering conclusions. I'm a little judgy (something I'm working on). I'm a coward and I don't tell people how I feel unless I'm pushed beyond my doubts. I hate how I look because I look like my father.

And I understand that you are not an alpha billionaire plagued by ennui. It annoys me that you leave your socks all over your house. I do not think dirty socks are going to help in a zombie apocalypse. Also, what is with the ketamine under the sink in the bathroom? It's creepy.

I also find it irritating when you tell me what to do or talk to my brothers without first talking to me—like arranging to have me fly back on the day of the funeral, that really pissed me off. You take too much on yourself. Why do you do that? Why do you insist on carrying the burden for everyone else? Don't you understand that I need you to need me? How can I give if you won't take?

Also, you might not be good at playing make-believe, but you are a master of avoidance. Work on that.

I wonder if you stayed silent for so long because you feared my rejection? Or maybe you feared I would grow to resent you if you'd asked me to stay in Tennessee? Regardless, I understand that you are also imperfect. I understand that you are brave, but that you are human and not immune to fear.

I understand that you feel things deeply, maybe so deeply the feelings become paralyzing.

I understand that about you and I still love you desperately. I love you beyond reason. I want to be with you right now. I want to live you.

Love, Ash

I didn't give myself time to think about what I'd written.

I folded it, placed it in an envelope, affixed a stamp, wrote out his address—surprising myself when I knew it by heart—and jogged downstairs to mail it. I fitted it through the mail slot and watched it flutter away until it landed on a pile of other letters.

I stared at the mail slot for several minutes. I wondered if any of the other letters were love letters.

Slowly, I made my way back to my apartment. When I reached the second landing, I allowed myself to think about the letter. The thoughts within were sporadic and likely poorly organized, but all the words were true, and I that's what mattered most. Honesty.

It was only when I'd made it back inside my place and shut the door that it occurred to me that Drew might not write back. Maybe Drew had sent the notebook because he'd moved on. Maybe it was his way of releasing me, letting me go.

I thought about that for a minute then rejected it. If Drew sent me the book, it was because he wanted me to read it. He wanted me to know his feelings. He wanted me to respond. Maybe he'd waited the two months because he wanted to give me more time to mourn my mother. Time to heal. Time to see.

I nodded at this train of thought; in fact, I jumped on this train of thought like a love-train-hopping hobo. My steps were lighter as I walked to my room. I picked up Drew's notebook on the way to my bed and placed it on my bedside table.

I gazed sleepily at the burnt leather binding as I drifted off, images of Drew, me, and our future as love-train-hopping hobos filling my dreams.

CHAPTER TWENTY-SEVEN

"Men trust by risking rejection. Women trust by waiting."

— CAROLYN MCCULLEY

I DIDN'T START to panic until the end of the third week in December.

Drew didn't write me back. After a week, I wrote him another letter. This one went through several drafts and was a proper love letter. I scoured novels for good examples, and even browsed a selection of famous love letters on the Internet. I wanted it to be an amazing love letter.

I then resolved to write him a letter every day, and I did so for two weeks, each carefully crafted. I waxed on for pages about his goodness of heart, his strength, his eyes, his bottom—he had an exceptional bottom—his hands, his smile, how smart he was, his voice, his poet-prowess.

During this time, I avoided my friends' phone calls and made excuses to skip knit night. I didn't want to talk about the journal, not yet—not until I could report on my happily ever after.

At the end of those two weeks, receiving nothing in return, I called him.

His phone went to voicemail.

I decided I would wait and call him twelve hours later so I didn't seem like a desperate stalker. His phone went to voicemail again.

It was at this point that I panicked. The panic didn't last long, however. It quickly gave way to intense, angst-filled depression. I couldn't find anger because I was buried under wallowing and self-pity; that's just south of ridiculous and a little west of pull-yourself-together.

I was a pathetic, heartbroken train-hopping hobo.

In the past, I would call Momma during these times. I would call her up and she would give me advice; she was my soft place to land. But she was gone. I missed her terribly, and not just because my soft place was gone, but because I missed *her*.

I thought about talking to Sandra about it, but chances were she'd turn into a psychotherapist.

I thought about talking to Kat about it, but she seemed to be going through some kind of family drama and was away in Boston.

Everyone else was busy with the holidays, I reasoned. Really, it was just an excuse. If I'd called, they would have answered, they would have listened, they would have helped. I didn't call because I didn't want to. I wanted to hurt, as crazy as that sounds. I wanted to mourn privately—for Momma, for Drew, for myself—before I had to talk about my stupidity with someone else.

Christmas now loomed as an inescapable doom. Since air travel was so spotty around the holidays, I planned to drive from Chicago to Tennessee over two days. Jethro didn't want me to go by myself—even though I'd explained that I was perfectly capable—so he and Beau decided to take a road trip up to fetch me. They'd rented a car for the way up. We were going to take my truck for the trip back to Tennessee.

I think Jethro suspected I might back out of a Tennessee Christmas if I was left to my own devices. I honestly didn't know what I would have done if left to my own devices. Probably curl up in a ball with cookie dough, fruitcake, and wine.

As it was, I had little choice but to spend two weeks in Tennessee with my adorable, loveable, tremendously fantastic hillbilly brothers. Thoughts of drowning myself in a punch bowl full of moonshine eggnog got me through the requisite motions of packing.

They were due to arrive at 4:00 p.m. We would spend one night in the city to give them a chance to rest, then start on the journey to Tennessee the next day.

Presently, I was sitting on the couch watching Dr. Phil, drinking wine and eating fruitcake and cookie dough when my phone rang. I glanced at the caller ID, prepared to let it go to voicemail. I'd been avoiding Sandra and Fiona's calls for the last week in particular. They were worried about me, I could tell. I just wasn't ready to face them and their sympathy.

To my surprise, it was a Tennessee number that I didn't recognize. My heart skipped a beat and I stiffened, gripping the phone tighter. I cleared my throat, swallowed, and brought the cell to my ear.

"Hello?"

"You have been avoiding my calls." Sandra's stern voice cut through the line.

I sighed. "I haven't…I've just been…busy."

"That's a lie. I can tell when you're lying."

"What number are you calling from? It's a Tennessee number."

"Alex hacked the line and got me a Tennessee number. I suspected you wouldn't pick up if you thought it was me."

I sighed again, rolling my eyes. "Can't you just let me wallow?"

"No, hon." This was Fiona, apparently also on the line. "We can't let you wallow. That's not how we roll. You know better than that."

"Plus," I heard Janie's voice, "we don't know what you're wallowing about."

"Last time we saw you was three weeks ago. You'd just received that burned journal." Elizabeth, it seemed, was also on the call. "You never told us whether you read it, and we have no idea what's in it. Feel free to keep the details to yourself, but something happened; don't try to deny it."

Marie was the last to speak. "Now let us in. We're downstairs and we have wine."

I glanced at the bottle on my coffee table and the half-empty glass next to it.

"Isn't it a little early to drink wine?" I asked.

"Don't give me a line about wine," Sandra's voice was still stern. "I know you're up there right now and feeling just fine. As you can see, I'm so upset I made up a rhyme."

"She's really upset," Marie chimed in. "Best to let us in before things get ugly."

I groaned, closing my eyes, and rubbing my forehead. "Fine. Fine —bring up your wine."

I hung up the phone and crossed to the door, opening it and waiting for them to arrive. They made a big commotion climbing up the stairs, and I heard the tail end of their plans right before they reached my landing.

"…Let her do the talking. She looks trustworthy." Marie said this, but to whom, I do not know.

Then Fiona said, "Thanks. Always nice to know I look trustworthy."

Sandra snorted and said, "Little do they know…."

Then they were at my door.

I stood there and regarded them. They all gazed back at me with sympathy—wretched, wretched sympathy. Sighing for a third time, I turned from the door and called over my shoulder, "Come in, and bring your wine."

Disrobing commenced—winter attire—and then I was assaulted from behind by a group hug.

Fiona, the trustworthy-looking one, spoke first. "Ashley, darling, we're not leaving until you tell us what happened and why you've been avoiding us for nearly a month."

"It's only been three weeks," I said in lame protest.

Just then, the buzzer to my building's outer door went off. I glanced at the wall clock. It was only 10:20 a.m. I had another six hours of wallowing planned before my brothers were set to arrive.

"Who is that?" Janie asked as the group hug dissolved. "Are you expecting anyone?"

I shrugged. "My brothers aren't supposed to be here until four," I said, and I shuffled to the door and pressed the button.

"Who is it?" I said into the intercom, and in the background, I heard Sandra say, "Her brothers are coming? Did anyone know about this?"

"It's Jethro and Beau. We're outside."

I stared at the speaker for a long second then buzzed them in. I'd been saved by the buzzer and my brothers' randomly excellent timing. I unlocked and opened the door a crack so they could walk right in.

"Sorry to cut this short, but—as you heard—Jethro and Beau are here to take me to Tennessee."

Fiona put her hands on her hips and shook her head. "Nope. As soon as they see you they'll want to join the intervention."

I glanced at myself, noticed I had fruitcake crumbs on my sweatpants. Absentmindedly, I brushed my hand up and down to dust myself off. "What are you talking about?"

"Ashley, you look like you haven't brushed your hair in days." Elizabeth said this as a concerned friend, with no condemnation in her tone.

"And you have dark smudges on your cheeks." Marie pointed to her own cheeks and jaw to show me where.

I touched my face and my fingers came away with soot stains. It was from Drew's book. I'd been reading it off and on.

Jethro and Beau walked in and filled the arched entry to the living room. They were glancing around my apartment, obviously absorbing the lack of décor and lack of general splendor.

"Hey, ladies." Beau waved to my friends.

They all exchanged greetings for a minute or two. I felt like I was watching the beginnings of a very bizarre nature program on PBS.

"Nice place." Beau said this like he meant it.

I gave him a flat smile and shrugged. "Thanks."

Jethro turned his gaze to me, and I watched as his eyes swept up and down, narrowing on the return pass.

"Ashley Austen Winston, you look like a lard bucket full of armpits."

"Right?" Sandra said, her hand coming up in a swooping motion then falling flat against her thigh with a smack.

I gave him a flat smile and shrugged. "Thanks."

My oldest brother put his hands on his hips, his gaze piercing and irritated. "Care to tell me what the hell is going on?"

"What do you mean?"

His eyes darted between my friends, who surprisingly remained silent.

At length, apparently making up his mind that he could speak freely, he asked, "Is it Momma? Are you having a hard time with... with everything?"

I nodded. "Yeah. That's a big part of it."

He watched me for a long minute, his expression softening, then he shocked the bejeebus out of me by asking, "Did you get my package?"

All of the ladies in the room gasped, and I felt their eyes shift to me. I stared at Jethro, I stared at the words he'd just said, my mind going quiet then loud then quiet again.

When I spoke, it was barely above a whisper. "What did you say?"

He shifted on his feet, his eyes darting to Beau, the ladies, then back to me. "The journal. Did you get it? Did you read it?"

"Did you..." I blinked like a hummingbird flaps its wings, falling off the non-blinking wagon spectacularly and with style. "Jethro Whitman Winston, did you send that journal to me?"

Jethro frowned at me. "Of course I did. Didn't you get my note?"

"Note? Note?" Still blinking in rhythm to my confusion, I shook my head, glancing at Sandra, "No! What note?"

She held her hands up. "I didn't see a note either."

"Go get the journal. I'll show you."

I didn't need to be told twice. I jogged into my room, grabbed the journal from my desk, and sprinted back to the living room.

Beau had crossed the room and picked up my fruitcake. He took a bite, leaned close to Janie, and confessed, "I'm starving."

She gave him a pleasant smile. "I'm not surprised. Based on your height and weight, you likely consume over three thousand calories a day, assuming you engage in moderate exercise."

I ignored them and handed the book to Jethro.

Jethro fanned open the book and a slip of paper fell out. It had been tucked in the very back where the pages were blank. He retrieved it from the floor and handed it to me. "There's my note."

I opened it up, gave him one last look, then read the words on the paper.

Dear Ash,

I saved this from a campfire for you. Drew tossed it in when he thought I was asleep, then he walked away. I pulled it out because I suspected I knew what it was. Sorry the edges are burnt. I fished it out as soon as I could.

When you were here, while Momma was dying, he wrote in it every day. I saw him at work. When you left, he carried it everywhere he went.

I read the first two pages, and I knew you needed to see this because Drew is a good man and you're a good woman. You both deserve to be happy.

I know you got a life in Chicago and it's a good one. I like your friends and I think you should keep them. But I also saw how sad you were when you left, and I think only half of that was because of Momma.

Also, not that we get a say in things, but I'm sure I speak for all of us when I say it sure would be nice having you closer by.

Love, your brother,

Jethro

I placed my fingertips to my lips when I got to the part *he carried it everywhere he went.*

My chin began to wobble when I read *I like your friends and I think you should keep them.*

The first tear fell at *I think only half of that was because of Momma.*

And I was a blubbery mess when Jethro confessed *it sure would be nice having you closer by.*

325

Jethro walked to me and gave me a hug. It occurred to me that I'd cried more since August than I had in my entire life. I'd also received more hugs from my brothers than I had in my entire life.

"I didn't know it was you. I didn't know." I cried into his sweater, gripping the front of his jacket.

"Well, who else could it have been?"

"I thought it was Drew." I confessed on an epically big, ridiculous, movie-worthy, embarrassing sob. Jethro's revelation changed everything. I was never meant to see the notebook. He never wanted to share those feelings with me. He wanted to burn it. He'd walked away—from me, from the possibility of us—and I'd stupidly sent him my heart in the mail.

"So it was you?" Fiona asked, seeking to clarify for the group. "You sent her the journal?"

Jethro nodded. "Yep. I thought I was helping."

"What's in it?" Elizabeth asked. "What is so terrible that it's thrown you into this kind of depression?"

I hiccupped, sniffled, and tried to explain through my tears that it wasn't terrible. I tried to explain that the book meant the world to me. Then I tried to explain why I was in my deep, deep funk.

"I stayed up all night reading it. It was…it was just…it moved my soul. So I wrote him a letter and I mailed it. And then I mailed him a letter every day for the last two weeks, and he never responded. He never responded!"

Jethro opened his mouth to speak, but I interrupted him, my voice oscillating between rough and high-pitched hysteria. "So I called him and he didn't answer. I wrote him fifteen love letters and he ignored them all and he won't even answer the phone when I call!"

Several of my friends *tsked*, throwing me compassionate and sympathetic gazes. Janie wrapped her arms around me from behind.

"What a bastard," Sandra breathed. "He really is Dr. Ruinous. We hates him."

Jethro held up his hands as though trying to calm a riot before it became violent. "Now, wait. You don't know the whole story. Stop jumping to conclusions."

"What excuse could he possibly have?" Marie asked. "Is he injured? Is he trapped under a heavy object? Has he fallen without the ability to get up?"

Then Beau shocked the bejeebus out of me by saying, "No. He's on the Appalachian Trail and doesn't have cell reception."

I stared at Beau, I stared at the words he'd just said, my mind going quiet then loud then quiet again.

When I spoke, it was barely above a whisper. "What did you say?"

"I said he's been on the Appalachian Trail for the last six weeks. Jethro came back weeks ago, but Drew hasn't been home in six weeks. I imagine his mail is collecting in a pile just inside his door. That's where your letters are. Also, he's got no cell reception." Beau announced this casually while scooping his finger into the cookie dough, digging out a large chunk, and eating it.

Then, glancing at me and my friends' stunned faces like we were aliens, he reached forward and picked up my wine. "And he gets back tomorrow. So, don't worry. He'll get your letters then. Mind if I drink this?"

CHAPTER TWENTY-EIGHT

Bran thought about it. "Can a man still be brave if he's afraid?"
"That is the only time a man can be brave," his father told him.

— GEORGE R.R. MARTIN, A GAME OF THRONES

I WAS STRUCK with an intense feeling of déjà vu.

I was sitting on Quinn's plane. We were all loaded up—the knitting gals and I, plus my brothers, plus Quinn—on our way to a distant place, banding together to help each other, off on another adventure.

We'd done this before.

But this time it was quite different, because this time, everyone on board was trying to help me.

After Jethro and Beau had dropped their information weapons of mass destruction all over my life, my knitting group and I held a quick conference. It went something like this:

Fiona: "How are you feeling about Drew reading your letters when he gets home tomorrow?"

Me: "Not good. Not good at all. I want them back."

Marie: "Why?"

Me: "He didn't send me the notebook."

Sandra: "Do you think his feelings for you have changed?"

Me: "He obviously never wanted me to see it. Heck, he wanted to get rid of it so badly he tried to destroy it. I honestly don't know what his feelings are, but I wrote those letters thinking that he'd sent me that book. I want the letters back."

Fiona to Sandra: "Not that you asked, but I agree with Ashley. She wrote the letters under false assumptions. If she wants the letters back, I think we should do everything in our power to get them back."

Elizabeth: "What's the plan?"

Janie: "I'll call Quinn; we'll use the plane. We can probably fly out sometime today."

Me: "Don't do that. I can drive through the night."

Janie: "No. Unacceptable."

Fiona: "I agree with Janie. If we have to put up with a grumpy Quinn all year, then we should be able to use his plane for emergencies."

Elizabeth: "Agreed. Let's move!"

Jethro and Beau had been strangely silent during the whole rigma-role. While the knitting group sprang into action, they went out and grabbed Italian beef sandwiches for everyone. We all ate lunch with vigorous appetites, drank three bottles of wine, and planned our strategy in the comfort of Command Central (aka my kitchen).

And so it was that I found myself buckled up and preparing to land in Knoxville, Tennessee. My heart was in my throat, and I couldn't keep my hands still enough to knit on the plane. They kept shaking. Therefore, I gave up and balled them into fists in my lap for the remainder of the flight.

Our plan was straightforward. Jethro would drive me up the mountain. I would retrieve the key from its hiding place on the back porch. I would then go inside, retrieve my letters, and leave. Jethro would drive me home. Then we would all do shots of moonshine eggnog to celebrate.

Well, me and my friends would do shots. Looking at Quinn, Jethro, and Beau's faces, I doubted they would be celebrating with us.

Quinn had secured a takeoff time out of Knoxville for just after midnight. Therefore, all the ladies—plus Quinn—would be able to make it back to Chicago by 2:30 a.m.

Before we left, Fiona insisted that I take a shower and wash my hair. Then she supervised me getting dressed and putting on makeup— just like Billy had done all those months ago. The similarities between the two of them warmed my heart.

This time, however, I wouldn't be facing a bear. I would be stealing in and out of Drew's house undetected then celebrating Christmas with my family like the past three weeks never happened.

"Betty arranged for a car to meet us at the airport," Quinn said, referring to his secretary as the plane taxied from the runway. He was sitting next to Janie across from me.

I found his blue icicle eyes somewhat disconcerting, so I simply nodded and spoke to his chin. "Thank you. Thank you for your help."

I imagined he thought I was pretty ridiculous. Janie had explained the situation to him during the trip to Knoxville in the way that only Janie was capable of doing—like a police report, just the facts.

Quinn runs his own global security firm, and is perpetually taciturn. I often wonder what he thinks of his wife's crazy friends.

He probably thinks we're crazy.

"Don't mention it." His gentle tone surprised me.

I glanced up and found him watching me with a piercing, narrowed glare. This was his baseline disquieting stare—in other words, the norm for Quinn.

He further caught me off guard when he leaned forward, his elbows on his knees, a frown on his face, and said, "I know I just provide the mode of travel for these trips, and this is none of my business, but I think you should give Drew and yourself a little more credit."

I blinked my confusion at him. "What do you mean?"

"Drew is a good guy, a smart guy. Like any smart, good guy, when presented with a remarkable woman, he's going to do the right thing by her, the honorable thing, even if that means giving you up. That's what he did; he gave you up because he thought it was the right thing to do.

But if you tell him you want him, he'll move heaven and earth to make that happen."

I stared at him for a beat then leaned forward and asked quietly, "Why didn't you give up Janie? There was a time when you thought you were putting her in danger, why didn't you give her up? Do the right thing?"

His eyes narrowed further, but a hint of a smile moved over his lips. "Because, unlike Drew, I wasn't a good guy."

♥ ♥ ♥

QUINN'S WORDS ECHOED in my head the entire drive up the mountain.

If Drew was one thing and one thing only, he was a good guy. He was *the best* guy. He was loyal to a fault. He was self-sacrificing. He was the epitome of the strong, sacrificing, silent type.

In a lot of ways he reminded me of my mother, honorable to the point of madness. But he wasn't a martyr. He was sneaky about his honor, held it close, was secretive about it.

It drove me crazy and it pissed me off. Maybe if he'd been a little more selfish, we wouldn't be in this mess. Then again, if he were a little more selfish, he wouldn't be Drew.

At the same time, he'd tried to burn the notebook. He'd tossed it in the fire and walked away. He knew I was coming home for Christmas. Obviously, he'd had no intention of telling me how he felt. Or maybe his feelings had changed.

My emotions might have been a tangled skein of yarn, but every-thing was going according to plan; we were even running ahead of schedule. The ladies were back at the homestead, likely causing a ruckus.

My heart hammered in my chest when I recognized how close we were to Drew's house, though the scenery looked different because the trees were wintry bare. I sat a bit straighter, my hands clenching and unclenching in my lap. Finally, Jethro pulled into the short driveway and stopped the truck.

He put it in neutral and set the emergency brake.

"Ash."

I swallowed, nodded. I didn't look at Jethro because I was too busy greedily memorizing every detail I could about Drew's house.

"Ash, go get the letters so we can get back home. I'm starving." Jethro sounded irritated.

I glanced at him. "I'm sorry I dragged you into my drama. I promise, Jethro, this is not like me. I never have drama. I'm usually completely drama-free."

Jethro placed his hand on my knee and squeezed, his kind eyes moving between mine. "It's okay. We've all been through a lot. Momma's death; Darrell being crazy. I'm glad he's locked up, and it looks like the charges will stick. But this year has been rough."

I covered his hand with mine. "Thanks for being such a great big brother."

He gave me a small grin. "You know I'll always do what's best for you, right?"

I nodded, returning his smile.

"Okay, go do this thing. Go on, get going." He lifted his chin toward the house.

I took a deep breath and exited the cab of the truck. It was cold outside, and there was a thin layer of snow on the ground; nothing like Chicago, but just enough for winter to make its presence known. I rubbed my hands together and jogged around the side of the house to the porch where I found the large ceramic pot next to the guest bedroom door where Drew hid a spare key.

It was then that I heard the sound of wheels on the gravel driveway.

My body was motionless with astonishment. I shook myself and forced my feet to move. As quietly and as sneakily as I could, I tiptoed to the side of the house and peeked around the corner just in time to see my brother Jethro leaving.

That's right.

Jethro abandoned me, in the Smoky Mountains, on Drew's porch, in the winter.

Instinctively, I jogged to the front of the house and down the porch steps to the drive. I was about to call out my brother's name but stopped myself. He wouldn't come back even if he heard me. I couldn't believe it. For several seconds I stared stupidly where his truck had just been, my mouth wide open.

Meanwhile, another completely unexpected thing happened. I heard the front door to Drew's house open and footsteps behind me, the unmistakable sound of boots on a wooden porch.

My heart stopped. Time—the hussy—stopped. Everything stopped. And then he said, "Ash?"

I closed my eyes. The sound of Drew's voice saying my name, so uncertain, so hopeful, so confused—he was my summer rainstorm. He did things to me, bizarre things that I was incapable of describing. My feelings eclipsed my ability to think.

I inhaled a steadying breath, opened my eyes, and recognized what I was feeling. I was feeling fear. It was like facing down the bear on the side of that hill. I needed to woman-up and stop playing dead. This was my life and I needed to live it.

My throat worked and I finally managed to swallow as I lifted my eyes to Drew.

He stood just outside the door. He had a towel in his hands. He was wearing jeans slung low on his waist because he was without his SAVAGE belt. His shirt was a dark green thermal. His beard was ridiculous, bushy, untrimmed, unkempt…like a marauding Viking. And his eyes moved over me as though he couldn't believe I was there. I think he half expected me to be someone else when I faced him.

My heart gave a giant lurch and my stomach tumbled into oblivion. I had to stuff my hands in my pockets to keep from grabbing my chest.

He was so handsome…so epically swoony. I wanted to stare at him all day while he read me field notes. But more than that, I wanted to be with him. Just be.

I swallowed again and cleared my throat. "Hi, Drew."

His eyes flared when I spoke, settled on mine, and his expression transformed from confused to guarded.

"What are you doing here?" He glanced behind me, obviously looking for my means of transportation.

I thought about that question and how best to answer it, which version of the truth to tell.

For some reason, my momma's words from months ago chose that moment to echo in my head: *Fear don't count if you really want something.*

She was right. She was so right. And besides, being completely honest couldn't be any more dangerous than flashing a four hundred pound bear Mardi Gras style.

Gathering every ounce of my courage, I took a step forward, then two, then three. My voice was shakier than I would have liked when I said, "I sent you some letters while you were gone. Did you get them?"

His eyes narrowed on me, a new shadow of confusion falling over his features, and he responded haltingly. "I don't know. I haven't gone through the mail yet."

I nodded, pressing my lips together, and mounted the steps. "There should be about fifteen of them. I came by to...." I stopped, feeling a little out of breath for no reason. I waited until I reached the final step before continuing.

"I came by to get them before you had a chance to open them."

We were now face to face, just three feet between us.

His brow pulled low at my confession even as his eyes—heated, intense—moved over my face. The hunger in his gaze was a raw, tangible thing. I almost took a step back under the weight of it, and I wondered if he'd always looked at me this way. Had he been as obvious before? Had I been so completely blind?

"Why?" His voice was rough and the single word sounded like a demand.

"Because," I stopped again, overwhelmed under the intensity of his gaze. Unthinkingly, I took a step forward.

Drew flinched at the movement, his hands on the towel gripping it with tight fists. In that moment he reminded me of a wounded animal and my chest felt like it might crack from the force of my admiration and love for him.

I remembered his words from the notebook, and I realized that my suspicions had been right. He lived his life in an unfathomable labyrinth, paralyzed by the depth of his feelings. Poetry was his outlet, his pressure valve; he held close, a carefully guarded secret.

"Because Jethro sent me your notebook." I said on a rush. He didn't appear to understand my meaning immediately, so I used his disorientation to explain the entire story.

"Jethro saved your notebook from the fire and he sent it to me. I thought you sent it, so I read it."

Understanding dawned in his eyes and he straightened, stiffened, and I recognized his panic because it mirrored my own from just minutes ago. Urgency fueled my words. I needed to tell him everything before he had a chance to process this betrayal of trust. "He thought he was doing a good thing. When I read it, I…I…words cannot describe what I felt. I immediately wrote you a letter telling you how I felt, how I feel, how I love you."

I swallowed the last word because my own fear had finally caught up with me. I squeezed my eyes shut and shook my head. I couldn't look at him and continue speaking, so I didn't look at him.

"I love you, Drew. I love you. I love you so much. I don't know how to say it any other way. I sent you fifteen letters over the last three weeks. They're love letters, and they're the best I could do. And when you didn't send me anything back, I tried to call you, but you didn't answer. Then Jethro told me that he'd sent the notebook. He told me that you wanted to burn it. And I panicked. I thought…."

I had to press my lips together because my chin wobbled and I absolutely refused to cry.

"I thought your feelings must have changed…that you didn't want me anymore…that those beautiful poems and letters…that you didn't want me. So I came here to get my letters back before you could see them." I ended by covering my face with my hands. My neck was burning, and I knew my cheeks and chest were a bright crimson.

Drew didn't respond; he was quiet for so long I thought he might have walked away. But then I heard his boots scuff against the wood of the porch and I felt the heat of his body as he approached. His fingers gently surrounded my wrists and he pulled my hands from my face.

"Ash, open your eyes." His tone was infinitely gentle.

And it scared me, because this was always how my nightmare started. He would let me down with infinite gentleness.

"I can't." I dropped my head so he wouldn't see my face.

"Why not?"

"Because I'm afraid."

"Of what?"

"Of you letting me down gently."

Drew released my wrists and his hands covered my cheeks, warming them. He tilted my chin upward, and I felt his lips brush over mine with an infinitely gentle kiss.

He whispered, "Sugar, open your eyes."

I opened my eyes. I peered up at him, into his quicksilver gaze. I saw desire, I saw relief, I saw admiration, and I saw love.

Before I could speak, he said, "I'm not going to let you down, and I'm not ever going to let you go."

CHAPTER TWENTY-NINE

"There is always some madness in love. But there is also always some reason in madness."

— FRIEDRICH NIETZSCHE

*H*E ENCIRCLED MY waist with one arm and lifted me off my feet, his mouth capturing mine for a kiss that started as a tender, yielding exploration and quickly escalated to code red situation. My arms wrapped around his neck, holding him tighter, instinctively clamoring to get closer.

His big shoulder hit the doorframe as he tried to navigate his way into the house, jarring our teeth together, my top lip a casualty in our rush to reacquaint ourselves. It also had the effect of jarring me back into the present moment and why I was here.

"Are you okay?" He asked, but his eyes were on my mouth even as he pulled the door shut with his free hand.

I nodded. "Yeah, but-"

He cut me off, his lips moving against mine again, as though he planned to devour me with sensuality and his perfectly choreographed tongue tango. It was sinful, invading, and conquering, like I imagined a marauding Viking might kiss in order to establish his dominance.

Despite the delectableness of his mouth, hands, chest, sides, back, bottom, thighs, arms, features, and—let's face it—unruly beard, I couldn't let things progress before clarifying what was happening.

This wasn't some neurotic need to define everything; at least, I didn't think so. I just didn't ever want to fall into the pit of wine, cookie dough, and fruitcake sweatpants ever again. Nor did I want Drew's precious heart to be put in jeopardy.

I placed my hands on his shoulders and leaned my head back; the rest of me was pressed tightly to his front.

"Wait, wait—first we need to talk." I shouted this because I have no idea. Really. I have no idea why I shouted it. Just know that I did.

He stilled somewhat, his hold loosening a tad, but he didn't let me go. Instead, he gently set me down and pushed off my jacket, biting then licking my neck.

"Talk," he commanded.

I shivered, exhaled a sudden breath. "I can't talk, not while you're melting my butter."

This gave him pause. Drew's mouth ceased its assault, and he lifted his face from my shoulder, his eyes bright with palpable desire, but also amusement.

"Melt your butter?"

I nodded and tried to step away but failed; his hands gripped my waist like he was afraid I'd run away or disappear.

"That's right. Put me in a pan and turn me on. Melt my butter." I was breathing heavily, mostly because—even though he'd stopped kissing me—he was still melting my butter.

I could feel myself growing increasingly apathetic about discussing anything except whether he'd remedied his condom dearth.

On that note I blurted, "I don't have any condoms with me."

His eyebrows jumped and he blurted, "Well, are you clean?"

I nodded.

"I'm clean. Are you on the pill?"

I nodded.

"Okay. Next subject."

The blurting continued. "Why did you push me away after our night together?"

His eyebrows jumped higher, but he didn't answer; not right away. Instead, he glared at me—not with malice but with heat—and his grip on my body tightened.

At last he said, "Ash, I wasn't trying to push you away, but I didn't want to hold you back. Bethany told me about you many times. Granted, she called you Ash and let me think you were a man, but she was so proud. She told me about how you fought your whole life to leave this place, how it was all you talked about growing up."

This was true. It was all I ever wanted as a child. But it wasn't about leaving Tennessee. Tennessee was beautiful; its beauty was why I believed in magic as a child.

I wanted to escape my father's awfulness and my brothers' pedestrian antics. I wanted to be educated by the world, see it, and find my place in it.

"It was never about Tennessee, Drew. It was about escaping an unhappy situation and finding something else for myself other than a house full of perpetual adolescents. I was so blind, Drew. I was so blind to how you felt. You kept saying you didn't need me, and I believed you. I thought you found nothing in me, nothing that you'd ever need."

He shook his head before I finished speaking, his hands moving to my face, pushing my hair back from my temples. "No. No, Ashley. You weren't blind. You were just incapable of seeing anything but your heartache. I watched you every day for six weeks as you took care of your mother. You could only see her during that time. She needed you. Your brothers needed you. And that's how it was supposed to be. You were here for her and your family; I understood that. I didn't want you to feel any pressure from me. I had no expectations that you would feel for me what I felt for you. I wanted to be a comfort, not a burden."

I watched him through narrowed eyes. When he finished, I (again) blurted, "Well, start putting some pressure on me. Start needing me. Start having excessively high expectations."

His mouth tugged to the side like he was trying to suppress a smile, and his hands threaded through my hair then stroked down my back, eventually coming to rest on the base of my spine. "Okay. I will."

I wasn't finished. "Like, tell me to stay."

"Stay. Stay with me."

"And, not just for Christmas-"

"Ash, I want you to move here."

"Yes." I nodded, feeling the matter was settled, and I'd work out the logistics later because I knew in my heart that this was where I wanted to be. I didn't want to see Drew. I didn't want to talk to Drew.

I wanted to live Drew.

Besides, I was a nurse. Nurses were needed everywhere.

"And another thing...." I grabbed the front of his shirt. "Stop making decisions for me and having discussions about me behind my back. You should have talked to me before sending me away on Quinn's plane."

His mouth flattened, and the trace of humor in expression transformed into mild frustration. "That was for your own good. Darrell had been making a fuss all over town about how his children had stolen from him. Your name was the one he'd shouted the loudest. We needed to get you out of town."

"Or, I could have stayed here with you."

He licked his lips, the frustration easing. "I didn't know that was an option."

"Well you would have known if you'd talked to me about it."

Drew's eyes narrowed and he seemed to be inspecting me.

I took the opportunity to twist my arms around his neck and press my front to his. "Just think, you could have spent the last ten weeks melting my butter."

His hands moved to my bottom and he squeezed me through my jeans. "Your point is a good one."

This made me smile big and wide and maybe a little smugly. Drew shook his head at my smug smile then proceeded to kiss it off my face as he walked me backward to his bedroom.

We navigated the hallway without incident and soon my scarf was off, and my shoes, and my sweater, and I was pressing myself against his hot hands as they grabbed and caressed and massaged my bottom, stomach, back, and breasts.

I opened my eyes as he knelt over me, my hands reaching for the front of his pants, reaching for him. The light was on in his room and —despite all the really wonderful and necessary euphoria accompanying Drew's skillful fingers—my attention snagged on a photo above his dresser.

"Is that...?" I stared, blinked, then frowned at the picture.

He kissed my jaw as I tried to focus, unbuttoning my jeans, making me feel like heaven.

But the picture was so surprising, I had to ask. "Drew, is that me?"

Drew stiffened; his hands on my body stilled. Seconds passed while I stared at the picture while Drew knelt motionless above me, his face again buried in my neck.

I released a huff, pushing him away so I could see his eyes, but also gripping his arms so he couldn't go too far.

"Drew...." I made sure my voice was soft and calm as our eyes met; he gazed at me with wary watchfulness. "On your dresser, is that picture of me?"

He didn't respond. But after a beat, he tried to extract himself from my hold. I wouldn't let him go; my grip tightened. When he felt the force of my fingers, his mouth tugged to the side.

"Ash, I'm not leaving you. I'm just getting the pictures."

"Pictures?"

"Yeah. Pictures."

I released him and he gave me a quick kiss before sauntering over to his dresser and grabbing three picture frames. He returned, sat on the edge of the bed, and patted the space next to him.

I scooched closer to him, tucked my hair behind my ears, and peered at the pictures on his lap. I was right. The first picture was of me. It was of me and Momma in Hawaii. I'd taken her there three years ago on vacation. We both looked happy and tan.

"Bethany gave these to me."

"When?"

"When she figured out that I was in love with you."

My heart flip-flopped in my chest and I looked at him. He was watching me, his features open but hesitant. I didn't like the hesitance, so I leaned forward and kissed him, needing to remove the uncertainty from his expression.

A thought occurred to me, so I broke the kiss and rested my forehead against his, my hand on his jaw and neck to keep him close. "Drew, that day I left, when I knocked on your door and I heard the drawers open and shut, were you hiding these?"

"Yes."

I *tsked*. "Oh, Drew...." I kissed him. "Is this part of *the not wanting to hold me back* thing?"

He threaded the fingers of one hand through my hair and tugged until our eyes met. "Ashley, I need you. I need you like lungs need air. But I need your happiness, not your obligation."

"Well, this explains why you like Nietzsche, bless your heart...."

Drew's gaze immediately turned into a glare, the hesitation giving way to reluctant amusement. "Did you just *bless your heart* me —again?"

"Bless your sexy, sexy Viking heart," I said, my eyes moving back to the pictures.

He rubbed his jaw, handing me the frames. "If you're going to insult me, then I'm going to go get those letters."

My body stiffened and a jolt of anxiety shot down my spine, radiating outward to my nerve endings. I'd already forgotten about the letters. I was about to tell him to stop, and beg him to give them back to me. The thought of watching Drew reading my words and declarations of love was thrilling, but mostly terrifying.

And yet....

He was studying me, his mouth twisted to the side, his eyes still narrowed.

I cleared my throat then swallowed, inhaled slowly, and said, "Yeah. You should. You should read them. You should know what's in my heart, because if you think having pictures of me on your dresser is going to freak me out, then you are in for a big surprise. 'Cause those letters…those will freak you out."

Drew rolled his lips between his teeth, fighting a smile. Abruptly he leaned forward and kissed me, his mouth moving against mine, demanding entrance, tasting me like I was cake with frosting and he'd decided to lick first then take a bite.

Just as abruptly, to my infinite frustration, he pulled away. Drew was halfway down the hall when I realized that he really was going to get the letters. I braced myself even as a small, nervous laugh passed my lips.

"Fear don't count if you really want something…." I muttered under my breath, Momma's words again calming my thundering heart, and I glanced at the pictures on my lap.

I set the one from Hawaii to the side. The next picture was of me graduating from nursing school. I was in my cap and gown, and I was holding my diploma. Momma had been so proud, and I'd desperately wanted to make her proud.

The last picture was of me when I was eighteen, a few days before I'd left for college. I was surrounded by all my brothers. We were standing at the edge of the woods against a backdrop of spring flowers. The scene was beautiful. We were laughing. I remembered the moment; I think Beau had just done something crazy.

I stared at that one the longest. I was surprised by what I saw. Eighteen-year-old Ashley was a beautiful young woman, a smart girl, a girl with hopes and dreams who maybe still believed in fairies and unicorns —not much, just a very little bit. Yes, I looked like my father, but so what? Looking like Darrell didn't make me Darrell any more than Cletus's banjo playing made Cletus like Darrell.

It would be a shame if Cletus didn't love music. It would be a shame if Roscoe weren't charming. It would be a shame if Billy weren't so smart.

This Ashley also loved her brothers despite their torment, and I could see on their faces that they loved her too.

When I thought about myself at that age, all I remembered was wanting to leave, wanting to escape, wanting to be different. But now I didn't want to be different. I wanted to be her. But I wanted to be more, just like a building wants to be more than its foundation. Being more didn't mean I needed to abolish who I'd been.

And being with Drew wouldn't be a step back; it would be coming home.

♥ ♥ ♥

"Do you want another pancake?"

I tossed this question over my shoulder without looking up from the skillet. I wasn't used to Drew's fancy pots and pans or his fancy gas stove. Therefore, I was watching the pancakes like I'd watch a hawk. I was a pancake falconer.

"No, thank you," Drew responded from someplace near my shoulder just before his hands lifted the hem of my nightshirt. It was another of his T-shirts. At some point, I would have to wash it.

Drew caressed a path from my thighs to my hips to my lower back then stomach. His hands were hot. I shivered, instinctively arching, pressing my bottom against his front.

When I spoke next, I sounded a little winded to my ears. "Shouldn't we call the boys and get your car back?"

Roscoe, it seemed, had dropped Drew off just hours before I arrived. Drew's truck was at the Winston Bros. Auto Shop and, despite having been there for six weeks, hadn't yet received its tune up. Imagine that.

As well, my brothers weren't answering their phones when we called. Neither were any of my friends. I had no idea whether they'd already left for Chicago, but I guessed that they had. We were stuck. Cut off from the world. We had no way of coming down the mountain. It was glorious.

Drew's fingers slipped lower, dipping into the waist of my panties. I gasped. He didn't respond to my question. Instead, he reached around me with his other hand and turned off the stove.

Drew melted my butter.

He melted it standing, sitting, crouching, leaning, reading, smiling, hugging, laughing, frowning, writing, changing a light bulb, milking a cow—basically, if it was a verb and he was doing it, my butter was melting.

I rediscovered this fact over the thirty-six hours after our big talk, while we were stuck in his house on the top of the mountain, not that he milked any cows. Yet.

I also rediscovered that he was a man of his word. When he'd told me on the porch that he wasn't going to let me go, he'd meant those words quite literally. I don't think he'd gone five minutes without grabbing, fondling, cuddling, kissing—basically, if it was a verb that involved touching, he was doing it.

I was still holding the spatula when, after several minutes of his clever attentions, I lost my mind. I lost it standing in front of his combination range and oven. Unthinkingly, as I came apart in his hands, I reached behind my head to grab on to him and nearly fly-swatted his face with the spatula. He deftly ducked my inadvertent attack, and I felt his chest rumble with a laugh.

My head fell back against his shoulder and I loitered in this position as I tried to normalize my breathing. He removed his fingers from my panties and rubbed his big palms from my thighs to my waist and back again in a soothing, sensual ellipse.

"You can do that anytime," I said on a faltering exhale, staring at his ceiling.

"I will." Drew paired this evocative, growly declaration with an earlobe bite.

I'd never looked at his ceiling before. It was covered in decorative copper tiles, at least they looked like copper. In that post-orgasm mind-randomness, I found myself fixating on the ceiling.

"Drew, can I ask you a weird question?"

He nodded, turned his lips to my temple, and gave me a kiss.

"How did you manage to buy this house? Or, I guess, how did it come into your possession? Aren't all these places deeded such that you have to sell to the US government?"

His hands ceased their rhythmic assault and I felt him smile against my cheek. "This place belonged to my mother. It's been in her family for generations. My sister lived here for a time, but it was pretty well neglected when I took it off my father's hands."

I nodded, still looking at the ceiling. Many of the tiles were beginning to oxidize from orange to turquoise; the effect was stunning.

"And it's yours now?"

He nodded. "Yes. It's mine now."

I smiled. I liked that this was his mother's house and now he was living in it, that he'd restored it. I took a deep breath, straightened from his shoulder, and turned to face him.

I was about to tell him about how much I liked the ceiling when I was interrupted by the blaring of a horn being honked loud and long from the vicinity of the driveway. We both stiffened, listening for additional sounds. The horn honked again and we were spurred into action.

I jogged down the hall looking for my pants and pulling them and my boots on in a rush. Drew, sadly for me, shrugged into a long-sleeved shirt, but he didn't make any attempt to change out of his flannel pajama bottoms or put on shoes. He then tossed me one of his sweaters. When it was over my head, he looped his arm around my waist and pressed me against him for a quick kiss.

"I love you," he said.

"I love you, too," I said.

We both smiled at the certainty in each other and headed for the door.

The sight that greeted us was unexpected but in no way unwelcome.

A parade of cars was pulling into the short driveway. I recognized Drew's truck, which Beau had driven up the mountain. Roscoe, Sandra, and Alex were stepping out of the passenger side, Alex from the front seat, and Sandra from the back of the cab along with Roscoe.

Then came Jethro's truck loaded up with the rest of the Winston boys.

Then came a police cruiser.

Drew glanced at me and wasn't quite frowning. Rather, it was a glare of mild irritation because we both guessed that Jackson James was driving the cruiser.

The crowd unloaded themselves and started toward the steps, chitchatting with each other like today was Sunday and they'd just left church.

Jethro reached us first. He was carrying what looked like a cake container and he wore a shit-eating grin. "Well, hello, you two. My, aren't you a sight for sore eyes."

"Jethro." Drew nodded at my brother once. "What's going on?"

"It's Christmas Eve. We thought we'd bring the party up here. Also, Ashley forgot her clothes at the house, so we brought those too." Jethro patted Drew on the shoulder and walked into the house like he'd been invited.

Roscoe came in next. He was carrying my suitcase and looking pleased as punch. "I'll just go put this in your bedroom. You know, the one you two share."

Beau and Duane followed, their arms full of food, Beau shaking his head as he mounted the steps. "I swear, Drew. You need to get rid of Jackson James; let him know Ash is your woman. He didn't say it when he pulled us over for speeding on the way up, but I'm pretty sure he's expecting to share *sandwiches* with Ash here sometime soon."

Duane nodded his agreement. "I hate that guy, always pulling me over."

"Were you speeding?" I asked.

"Hell, yeah." Duane paired this with a wink and a grin.

Cletus and Alex were deep in conversation as they approached the porch; I saw that Cletus was clutching his chessboard, and Alex was holding several boxes.

"Oh, hey Ash...Drew." Alex nodded to us like it was perfectly natural for him to be there. I loved that. I loved that he felt that way.

Cletus stopped just long enough to give Drew an intense stare. "So...now can I welcome you into the family?"

Drew nodded. "Yep. Now you can welcome me into the family."

"Okay. Welcome to the family."

Then Cletus and Alex disappeared inside.

Sandra came next, carrying a large punch bowl full of white fluid.

"It's moonshine eggnog," she explained, huffing a little under the strain of the heavy bowl. "It's not actually all that bad. Quinn didn't like it, but then he doesn't like anything except his wife."

"Where is everyone? Did they fly back?" I asked, moving to help her.

"No, no—I got it. Everyone flew back that night after Jethro told us what he'd done. To be honest, it was a relief." Sandra walked quickly inside, calling over her shoulder, "It saved us from having to plan something similar."

Billy climbed the stairs with leisurely steps, holding bags full of wrapped presents. His expression was cool yet untroubled. When he reached Drew and me, he stopped. He glanced at me then he moved his eyes to Drew and said, "I expect you to treat her right. I expect you to make her believe in magic again—fairies, rainbows, all that shit. We understand each other?"

Drew nodded, reaching out his hand to my second brother. "Yes, sir. We understand each other."

Billy glanced at Drew's hand, placed one of the bags on the porch, then accepted it for a brief, firm shake. He then glanced over his shoulder as he picked up the bag and added, "Ashley, will you get rid of that guy, please?"

As Billy walked inside, Drew and I turned our attention to Jackson James. He was hovering in the driveway, standing just in front of his car. When he saw me looking at him, he gave me a little wave.

I gathered a deep breath and returned his wave with a polite smile, saying to Drew, "Do you think you can handle that crowd in there?"

"I think so...for a little while, at least."

"I'm going to go find out what he wants," I said, tilting my head in Jackson's direction.

Drew nodded, his eyes tranquil and bright. "You do that."

He leaned down and gave me a soft kiss, then walked inside to deal with our crazy family.

I eyed Jackson for a beat before I walked leisurely down the steps to meet him on the driveway.

"Hey, Jackson."

"Hi, Ashley. I hope you don't mind me following Duane for a

stretch. When he said you were in town, I thought…well, I need to talk to you about what happened with Darrell, when you took the gun."

I crossed my arms over my chest, hugging myself against the cold. "Did I take the gun? I don't remember that. I remember you handing me the gun." This was the story I'd told the police on the day of the attempted kidnapping.

Jackson smiled. "Yeah. Well, thanks. And I'm sorry I went to park my car rather than come help you. I didn't know what you were doing. I should have followed you."

I shrugged, walking to the hood of his car and leaning against it. It was still warm. "It's over now. Nothing can be done about the past."

Jackson turned so that we were still facing each other, the house behind him. A troubled frown cast a shadow over his handsome features; he studied me for a beat before adding, "Well, your daddy and his buddies pled guilty, no contest. They're doing three to five in Bledsoe County. So, at least you won't be seeing him for a while."

"That's a relief."

"Ashley," he said suddenly, taking a half step forward, "I'm really sorry about your momma. She was a very kind woman…a good woman."

"Thanks, Jackson. I appreciate that." My eyes drifted over his shoulder, detecting movement from the house. Beau and Duane were standing in the window facing the driveway. Their arms were crossed. Their faces wore similarly stern expressions. They were looking at us.

Jackson, noticing the direction of my gaze, twisted to look over his shoulder. Both my brothers took this opportunity to use the index and middle fingers of their right hand to point to their faces, then turn the fingers back on Jackson in the universal symbol for *I'm watching you.*

They did this in unison.

I rolled my eyes. "Just ignore them."

Jackson looked back at me and grinned. "Nah. It's fine. They don't like me much since Darlene Simmons and I went on a date."

"When was this?" I remembered Darlene from high school. She was two years younger than us—same grade as Duane and Beau—and every guy's cheerleader fantasy.

"Oh...." Jackson squinted, bent down, and picked up a rock from the driveway. "I guess about three years ago."

I barked a laugh. "Looks like they need to get over it."

He nodded, his warm brown eyes searching my face, a hesitant smile on his lips. A brief silence fell between us as he looked at me and I allowed him to look.

At last—seemingly shaking himself—he said, "Ashley, I didn't want to be bugging you while you were going through everything with your momma, but I did want a chance to speak with you for just a few minutes." He halted, hesitated, his eyes sweeping over my face.

"Sure." I shrugged.

"The thing is," he started, stopped, glanced at the rock in his hands, "I wanted to apologize, for the way I treated you after high school. I wasn't nice, and I wasn't fair, and you deserved better."

The words were nice and they made me realize that I needed to hear them. I also realized that it's never too late to apologize, but some apologies come too late.

"Don't worry about it, Jackson. I appreciate the apology, but that was all a long time ago."

He nodded, looking up at me again. "Yeah, but I've wanted to tell you for a long time."

I pressed my lips together and gave him a smile, which he returned. We stood quietly looking at each other for another beat before he said, "So...you and Drew Runous, huh?"

My smile grew. "Yeah. Me and Drew."

His eyes narrowed. "Is it serious?"

I nodded, my smile morphing into a giant grin. "Yep. In fact, I'm pretty sure it's a chronic condition."

OUR FIRST CHRISTMAS together was a happy one because it was spent with our family surrounded by people who loved us.

Although, I could have done without Sandra leading the twins in a rendition of "She'll Be Coming Down the Mountain When She Comes"—note the verbiage change.

As well, Momma's bits of wisdom whispered in my head from time to time. *Happiness and rheumatism keep getting bigger if you tell people about them.* She was right. Sharing happiness with my family made it feel bigger.

With the whispered words came a big *ah-ha* moment. I realized that those seemingly random sayings, the ones I didn't understand at the time, were her way of telling me everything I might need to know. They were how she tried to answer all the questions I wouldn't be able to ask after she was gone. I was so thankful.

They gave me comfort. They gave me peace. And they made me feel like she was still here somehow, guiding me along my clumsy path.

Drew and I still had issues to discuss and details to work out. I still needed to go back to Chicago, give notice, find a job in Tennessee, and go through the motions of uprooting my life so that we could be together. So we could live each other every day.

It was a hassle. I didn't want to leave him, but life is hard. Change takes time. And change that is lasting takes planning and care.

On the day before I was set to fly back to Chicago—since I didn't have my truck, I wasn't going to drive—I found Drew in our wild-flower field. He was sitting on the cold ground surrounded by dead stalks and stems.

He appeared to be staring at the mountain above our valley, eyes squinting, elbows resting on his knees. His cowboy hat was in his hands, and his fingers held it lightly, like he trusted the hat to stay put without having to support its weight.

I was bundled in a blanket from the house. It was the old quilt that covered my bed, and it reminded me of my mother. She and my grand-mother had worked on it just before my grandmother died. My momma had finished the quilt on her own.

"Hey, care for company?"

Drew glanced over his shoulder, a welcoming—albeit almost imperceptible—smile warming his features. "Always, if it's you."

I crossed to where he sat. The snow had melted then refrozen, leaving ice on the ground. It crunched under my boots with each step.

We stayed like that—him sitting, me standing—for a few minutes. The world was cold. The wind smelled like ice. The trees had lost all their leaves. The top of the mountain was covered in snow.

"Poetry isn't for civilized society." Drew said this suddenly, breaking the moment, but then saying no more.

I decided to prompt him when I sensed he would not continue without a push. "How so? I've read plenty of safe-for-work poetry."

"I'm not talking about greeting cards and sentimentality, not the stuff that gently warms your heart or makes you feel nostalgic." He lifted his eyes to mine, his expression stark and sober. "I'm talking about the kind that burns you, leaves scars, the kind that you regret reading because you can't forget it. It's a wild, feral thing. It has claws and it bites."

I studied him as he said this, how his eyes flamed with ferocity. I wondered if the same could be said about him. He was a bit of a wild, feral thing. I didn't doubt that he would leave a scar. I'd been given a sneak peek into what it would be like if he decided one day that I wasn't his cup of sweet tea.

I closed the remaining distance separating us and took a seat next to him; lifting the quilt so it wouldn't get wet and not particularly caring whether the frost covering the ground made my pants damp.

Drew glanced at me, his gaze quickly taking a survey of my face. "You look like you want to say something."

"I wondered...." I hesitated because my thoughts weren't fully formed. Rather than keep him waiting, I spoke what I felt. "I wondered, when I first arrived, why Momma put so much trust in you. But I think it was because she'd read your poetry. Reading it is knowing you. Poetry is the representation of feelings as words. It reveals a person's heart."

He studied me, his silvery eyes flashing as they moved between mine. "I'm glad you know my heart, because you are my heart."

I smiled. I couldn't help it. I smiled so hard it hurt my face and I thought I might sprain something.

He didn't seem to mind. His eyes grew soft, distracted as they moved from mine to my lips. "You ruin me with your smiles."

I frowned, shaking my head at him.

"What? What did I say?"

"You've got to get the poetry under control, otherwise I'll drag you into my room and we'll never leave, I'll never find a job, we'll become sexy hobos."

I was gratified to see a massive grin spread over his features, lighting his eyes. He lifted a single eyebrow, his voice dipping low with Texas charm. "Really? Then allow me to say...."

I cut him off by covering his mouth with my hand. "Yes, really. I'll become a sex addict and need counseling, maybe start going to sex addict anonymous meetings." I removed my hand and pulled it through my hair, adding as an afterthought, "Which aren't at all that anonymous in Green Valley, Tennessee, because everybody knows everybody."

"I'm not thinking about every body. I'm thinking about your body."

I nudged his shoulder with mine, enjoying the way a smile changed his face. His eyes became the color of a luminous sky, his mouth and teeth framed by his bushy beard.

Without intending to, I blurted, "I love you."

"I love you, too." He said without hesitation.

My heart skipped in my chest; it was a happy heart skip. "Really? Are you sure? You know, I have trouble believing anything that's not written down. Maybe you should write a book about it."

"About it?"

"About how much you love me."

"I already did that." He squinted at me, and I could tell he was trying to fight a smile.

"I know." I couldn't help my grin. "Write another one. And after that one is done, write another...then another."

"How long am I expected to write books on this subject?"

"For as long as you love me."

"Then I guess I'll be writing about it for the rest of my life."

EPILOGUE

"Out of the quarrel with others we make rhetoric; out of the quarrel with ourselves we make poetry."

— W.B. YEATS

"*I* THINK ALEX and Sandra are coming for Christmas," Ashley says to me from the other end of the couch. "It was nice visiting them in Chicago over Halloween, taking the kids out with Fiona, but I think he likes your fishing excursions."

I nod, listening. Sandra and Alex are our family, and I want them to stay in Tennessee. I have told Alex this. Through Ashley's chosen family, I have found the benefits of society. They are vast, and these relationships are priceless.

"Also, I'd like for you to admit that I made an excellent point about the flaws in Linas Vepstas passage of time theory. I'm not saying I believe in predestination, but as my momma would say, *predestination makes everything part of the plan.*"

"It is an issue of quantum mechanics, Ashley, a universe of probability. Determinism of any sort is impossible."

"Yes, but you assume time travel is impossible. Even Einstein never conceded as much. You and I are meant to be, and you've acknowledged that point. Therefore, you must admit that factors beyond our control, or perhaps our ability to comprehend, may have a hand in determining our path."

"I admit nothing."

"Typical...." She makes a little sound, and it makes me smile. "What are you writing?"

"Field notes."

"If those are field notes then I'm a one-eyed Cocker Spaniel with halitosis."

This makes me laugh, but I don't stop writing. I think I've never laughed in my life as I have since knowing Ashley. She brings a spark to all things, lights every empty place.

"Read it to me," she says, nudging me with her toes.

I look down, away from where my notebook rests on the side table. Her toes are painted pink, and they sparkle, and they are on my lap. She wiggles them like she's waving at me with her feet.

"Please," she says.

My eyes travel the length of her and enjoy her form. The shade and shape of her legs, heightened by shadows cast from the single light source. She's reclining on the couch, eReader propped on her stomach.

Desires war. As such, I can only watch her in stillness.

I need her.

When I write, speaking is an obstacle. I struggle to abdicate thoughts that are shadows of my feelings and passions. Giving words to these feral impulses never does them justice because they are not my will; their course leads to no action, and expressing them is an exercise in unceasing frustration. But withholding them from the page is a path to insanity.

I once tried to burn the words, thinking passage through fire would release me. I was wrong. I mourned the loss, and rejoiced when I found the book had been saved.

"Drew, will you read it to me?" Her eyes remind me of the ocean.

I shake my head. "Not yet."

Her smile widens. She peers at me as though she knows me. She does. She knows me.

"We've been together, what? Almost a year now? And I can count on one hand the number of times you've read your poetry to me out loud. Besides, you're giving me that look."

"What look?"

"Like I'm cake, so I know it's a good one." Her eyebrows move up and down.

I continue to smile, but I say nothing.

Words are clumsy things. Raw, wild, hunger, need, desperation, fascination do not adequately define how I long for her complete capitulation. I want her to weep. I want to quietly tear her apart and lovingly watch her bleed. I crave knowing that I can inspire one tenth of the torment she inspires in me. How can I speak such things out loud?

I need her.

Her surrender, mine to possess and exploit. This ambition remains intangible because, though I feel it, I do not wish it. I communicate this greed only through poetry, and poetry serves as an imperfect allegory.

Ashley huffs. Her eyes narrow. I know the workings of her mind; she is contemplating trickery. She sets her eReader to the floor and comes to me on her knees, her arms around my neck, her breasts pressing against my shoulder. I lament the invention of clothes.

"Drew, if you won't read to me, maybe you'll sing for me?" Her lips are close to mine and I need to taste her.

I shake my head, keeping my words soft so as not to betray the ferocity of my need. "No, Sugar. Not tonight."

"Are you going to the jam session with me tomorrow? Cletus is back in town, and I'm bringing coleslaw for the twins."

"Yes. We should go." I'm coming out of the tunnel and speaking, communicating is less cumbersome.

"And you will sing for me then?"

"Yes, if you'll sing with me."

"It's a deal." She seals it with a kiss and I don't let her go. I take her sweet mouth until I feel her grow restless. I close my book and turn away from it. I remove the veil of her clothes and I settle for being the implement by which she loses control.

I would never hurt her, not through action, deed, or word. I long to soothe her, pet her, hold her fears, burden her sorrows, be the instrument of her ecstasy. I am her safe place and she is mine.

I need her.

Being the method of her madness fuels me. I watch her pant, feeling her uncontainable hot breath spill against my skin, and it is like water to the thick weeds that tangle and choke my ignoble instincts.

I should not always like to write poetry. I should like to live it.

But if I could pick and choose the poems I live, I would not always be joy, nor would I want inert contentment. Sorrow and struggle bring gravity to the soul and to the mind, a gravity that cannot be achieved through mere happiness. We are most awake to the world and to our own longings and desires when we suffer.

Ashley stretches, arching her back, and the lithe movement demonstrates how powerless my body is to the promise of her body, and with it, the promise of pleasure, of vulnerability, of communal closeness. Her hands are above her head, and her obsidian hair tangles with pale arms. I hold her wrists.

If sorrow as a force is gravity, and mere happiness is inertia, then love and being in love is momentum. A force built upon actions of the past, moving us.

We move.

I see her. She is beneath me. Her body is slick, yielding softness, sweetness replete. I want to worship, yet need to possess. I suffer because she is forever anticipation, even when I hold her, fill her, taste her, dominate her, consume her.

I need her.

~The End~

Subscribe to Penny's awesome newsletter for exclusive stories, sneak peeks, and pictures of cats knitting hats. Subscribe here:
http://pennyreid.ninja/newsletter/

ABOUT THE AUTHOR

Penny Reid is the *New York Times*, *Wall Street Journal*, and *USA Today* Bestselling Author of the Winston Brothers, Knitting in the City, Rugby, Dear Professor, and Hypothesis series. She used to spend her days writing federal grant proposals as a biomedical researcher, but now she just writes books. She's also a full time mom to three diminutive adults, wife, daughter, knitter, crocheter, sewer, general crafter, and thought ninja.

Come find me -
Mailing List: http://pennyreid.ninja/newsletter/
Goodreads: http://www.goodreads.com/ReidRomance
Email: pennreid@gmail.com ...hey, you! Email me ;-)

OTHER BOOKS BY PENNY REID

Knitting in the City Series

(Contemporary Romantic Comedy)

Neanderthal Seeks Human: A Smart Romance (#1)

Neanderthal Marries Human: A Smarter Romance (#1.5)

Friends without Benefits: An Unrequited Romance (#2)

Love Hacked: A Reluctant Romance (#3)

Beauty and the Mustache: A Philosophical Romance (#4)

Ninja at First Sight (#4.75)

Happily Ever Ninja: A Married Romance (#5)

Dating-ish: A Humanoid Romance (#6)

Marriage of Inconvenience: (#7)

Neanderthal Seeks Extra Yarns (#8)

Knitting in the City Coloring Book (#9)

Winston Brothers Series

(Contemporary Romantic Comedy, spinoff of *Beauty and the Mustache*)

Beauty and the Mustache (#0.5)

Truth or Beard (#1)

Grin and Beard It (#2)

Beard Science (#3)

Beard in Mind (#4)

Dr. Strange Beard (#5)

Beard with Me (#5.5, coming 2019)

Beard Necessities (#6, coming 2019)

Hypothesis Series

(New Adult Romantic Comedy)

Elements of Chemistry: ATTRACTION, HEAT, and CAPTURE (#1)

Laws of Physics: MOTION, SPACE, and TIME (#2)

Irish Players (Rugby) Series – by L.H. Cosway and Penny Reid

(Contemporary Sports Romance)

The Hooker and the Hermit (#1)

The Pixie and the Player (#2)

The Cad and the Co-ed (#3)

The Varlet and the Voyeur (#4)

Dear Professor Series

(New Adult Romantic Comedy)

Kissing Tolstoy (#1)

Kissing Galileo (#2)

Ideal Man Series

(Contemporary Romance Series of Jane Austen Re-Tellings)

Pride and Dad Jokes (#1, coming 2020)

Man Buns and Sensibility (#2, TBD)

Sense and Manscaping (#3, TBD)

Persuasion and Man Hands (#4, TBD)

Mantuary Abbey (#5, TBD)

Mancave Park (#6, TBD)

Emmanuel (#7, TBD)

CPSIA information can be obtained
at www.ICGtesting.com
Printed in the USA
LVHW041628120120
643360LV00005B/730/P